KINGDOM OF CINDERS

THE KINGDOM TALES BOOK THREE

DEBORAH GRACE WHITE

LUMINANT PUBLICATIONS

KINGDOM OF CINDERS: A RETELLING OF CINDERELLA

By Deborah Grace White

Kingdom of Cinders:
A Retelling of Cinderella
The Kingdom Tales Book Three

Copyright © 2021 by Deborah Grace White

First edition (v1.0) published in 2021
by Luminant Publications

All rights reserved. Without limiting the rights under copyright reserved above, no part of this publication may be reproduced, distributed, transmitted, stored in, or introduced into a database or retrieval system, in any form, or by any means, without the prior written permission of both the copyright owner and the above publisher of this book.

The characters and events portrayed in this book are fictitious. Any similarity to real persons, living or dead, is coincidental and not intended by the author.

ISBN: 978-1-922636-03-4

Luminant Publications
PO Box 201
Burnside, South Australia 5066

http://www.deborahgracewhite.com

Cover Design by Karri Klawiter
Map illustration by Rebecca E. Paavo

*For all of us who spend our days on seemingly endless housework...
we are royals of our own kingdoms*

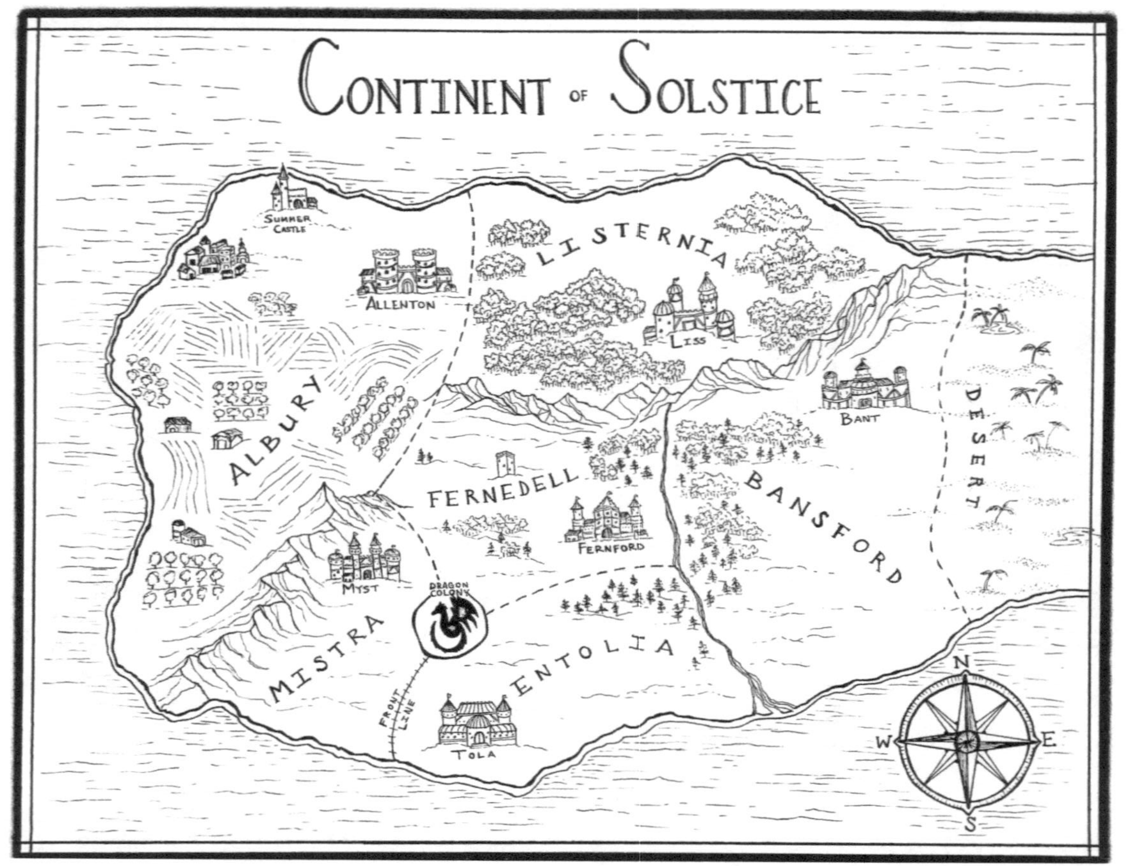

Continent of Solstice
SUMMER CASTLE
LISTERNIA
ALLENTON
LISS
BANT
DESERT
ALBURY
FERNEDELL
BANSFORD
FERNFORD
MYST
DRAGON COLONY
MISTRA
ENTOLIA
FRONT LINE
TOLA
N
E
S
W

PROLOGUE

Penny

Penny turned, suddenly overwhelmed by the sensation of being watched. She wanted to whip around, but found she could only move slowly, her head leading her body in a gradual, controlled swivel. In turning, she took in her surroundings, realizing all at once that she had no idea where she was or how she had gotten there. She didn't think she was in the kingdom of Bansford anymore.

Wherever she was, the overwhelming impression of the place was one of many bright colors. The blue of the sky was so strong it was startling, and the stately evergreen trees crowned hills greener than anything she'd ever seen. There was a lake, darker in color than the sky, but no less eye-catching, disappearing into a cave at the bottom of a solitary mountain.

Then Penny completed her turn, and forgot all about her surroundings. The creature before her was as tall as three men, with bearded ridges running along its temples. Triangular spikes trailed down its back, all the way along the tail that curved around its taloned back feet.

She recognized it at once, of course. Who could mistake a dragon for anything else? But it wasn't how she'd imagined the creatures.

"I've never seen a dragon before," she said blankly. "You're so purple."

She flushed as the words came out, feeling like an utter fool. But it was true. The dragon's scales were such a bright purple, Penny squinted in the sunlight glinting off them.

The dragon's orb-like eyes were unreadable, but its mouth curved slightly in what might have been a smile.

"Greetings, Enchantress." The musical voice identified the dragon as a female, but Penny was no longer interested in learning more of the creature. The dragon's words pierced her with terror, and she stumbled backward with an audible gasp, desperate to get away.

"Penelope!"

Penny emerged from sleep with the ghost of her gasp still on her lips. The feeling elicited by the dragon's words—not unlike the sensation of being doused in freezing water—still lingered. For a moment she sat huddled on her bed, arms around her knees, shivering. What had the strange vision meant? Why had it felt so impossibly real, so unlike a normal dream?

"Penelope?" Her father's voice once again came through the door. "Are you awake, child? It will be time to leave shortly."

Penny unfolded herself so quickly she almost tumbled out of bed. "Coming, Father!" she called, as she wrapped a woolen shawl around her and slid her feet into slippers. "Just a moment!"

She hurried to the door of her room, but paused with her hand on the handle, trying to compose herself. She told herself firmly that it was foolish to feel either guilty or afraid. There was no way her father could possibly know she'd just been dreaming about a dragon, or that the dragon had called her—no, she wouldn't even think it.

Putting on a bright smile, she pulled the door open to reveal a tall, dark-haired man. He didn't bear much resemblance to her own face that she saw reflected in her mirror every day, except perhaps for the perpetual hint of wistfulness around his mouth. The expression was misleading in her practical father, she knew.

"Sorry, Father, I overslept," she said. She took in her father's impeccable attire, and straightened. How *could* she have overslept on this all-important morning? It wasn't like her. "You look positively resplendent, Father," she said, beaming up at him.

He returned the smile. "Thank you, child," he said, in his calm, steady voice. "I trust I will be able to return the compliment by the time we leave for the wedding."

Penny chuckled, glancing down at her disheveled appearance. "I'll be ready in no time," she reassured her father.

"Indeed you will," came a grim voice, and the manor's most formidable maid bustled past Penny's father.

"Just a moment," her father said, as Penny made to shut the door. "I have a gift for you, Penny. Something to mark the occasion."

Penny raised an eyebrow. "Shouldn't I be giving you a gift?" But she was bouncing on the balls of her feet, peering around for the present. She didn't often receive gifts, and she couldn't imagine what it might be.

Her father nodded to someone Penny couldn't see, and a grinning manservant hurried into sight, his arms full of a writhing bundle of fur.

Penny gasped. "A dog? Father, really?"

Her father nodded, smiling slightly. "I know I said we didn't need one, but apparently there's a rat problem in the barn." He gave her a speaking look. "He'll have to earn his keep, Penny."

"He's a boy, is he?" Penny asked, running her hand over the puppy's ears as he tried eagerly to lick her face from the servant's arms.

Her father nodded. "He's an alaunt."

"An alaunt?" Penny repeated. "I'll call him...Al, then." She smiled secretly, scratching the squirming dog's belly. A flash of rebellion went through her. "Yes," she muttered, "Al."

"You'll have to get acquainted later," said her father sternly, as she made to take the dog from the servant. "We have somewhere to be, remember?"

Penny nodded, watching regretfully as the puppy was borne away. With a grimace, she gave in to the impatient clucking of the maid and disappeared back into the room.

When she met her father at the manor's door about half an hour later, she was attired in her best gown—a simple but becoming dress of dusky pink—and her golden hair fell about her shoulders in decently tidy curls.

"I'm not late, am I?" she asked, a hint of anxiety in her voice as she took in the look in her father's eyes.

He shook his head, handing her into the waiting carriage. "No. I was just—you look more like your mother with every year that passes, Penny."

"Do I?" Penny asked, her tone slightly stilted.

She arranged herself on the seat, trying not to crinkle her gown. As always, she yearned to ask more about her mother. Her father seemed deep in reminiscence, the wistful tilt to his mouth accentuated by the posture. His demeanor suggested he would be more receptive than normal to her questions. But she didn't ask. Surely the morning of his wedding to a second wife was a strange time to wax nostalgic about his first wife.

Silence fell as the carriage moved forward, and Penny gazed out the window. The road was bordered on both sides by her father's vineyards, but she wasn't really seeing the familiar rows of neat plants. She was lost in thoughts about her mother. Nine years had softened her grief, so it was no longer sharp and biting. But those years had also eroded the memories. So much of it was hazy, like looking through dirty glass. She strained her memory, trying to recall her mother's image.

Soft, golden curls draped over a four-year-old Penny's shoulder, and a gentle hand slid under her leg. She stopped crying, looking up into her mother's face.

"What's this now, my little Pen?"

She sniffed theatrically. "I fell over."

"So I see." Her mother inspected the bleeding knee.

She glanced around the yard, and Penny copied her. There was no one in sight. A look of great concentration came over Mama's familiar face. She held out her other hand, palm down, so that it hovered over the injury. Penny felt a tingle begin in the knee, barely noticeable at first alongside the stinging graze, but growing stronger. Just as it was crossing from discomfort to pain, it stopped abruptly. She looked down at the smooth skin, still stained with blood, but no longer injured.

"How do you do it, Mama?" she asked, looking up in awe.

Her mother chuckled. "The same way you breathe, Pen. It's my magic, it's just part of me. I don't know how to explain it."

"Will I have magic?" Penny asked eagerly.

Her mother ran gentle fingers through Penny's hair, pulling out the tangles. "I don't know, darling. Enchanters and enchantresses don't necessarily pass their magic to their children. Sometimes they do, sometimes they don't. No one can predict it."

"I hope I do," breathed Penny.

Her mother looked troubled. "I don't know what to hope," she whispered. Her face became uncharacteristically sharp. "Remember that you mustn't talk about it, Pen. You mustn't tell anyone I used it, or talk to anyone else about wishing you had it."

Penny nodded solemnly. "I know, Mama. If I have it, I'll hide it forever, like you."

. . .

The carriage went over a jolt in the road, and Penny was pulled from her thoughts. She cast a nervous glance at her father, illogically afraid that he would guess what she'd been remembering. She hadn't even realized she was still holding that incident in her memory. But now that she'd recalled it, the image was vivid. At the time, she hadn't known what to make of the look that crossed her mother's face when Penny said she would hide her magic forever. Now, looking back, she would describe it as anguish.

Inevitably, her thoughts turned to her dream, and the title the purple dragon had given her. A chill went down her spine. It had felt so real. Was that really how the beasts looked, up close? Or was her imagination simply painting an image based on what she'd heard? She'd told the vision the truth when she said she'd never seen a dragon before. As far as she knew, not a single one had so much as flown across the sky in Bansford since the kingdom had outlawed magic fourteen years before. They were offended by the ban, or so people whispered to one another. No one spoke too loudly about it. It was frowned upon to appear to care what the magical creatures thought of Bansford's laws.

"You're glad, aren't you, Penny?"

Her father's abrupt question pulled her from her abstraction.

"What was that, Father?"

"You're glad I'm marrying Sapphira? That she and the girls are coming to live with us?"

Penny looked at him in surprise. Why ask her this now, when it was surely too late for her opinion to make any difference?

"Of course I'm glad for you, Father," she said carefully. "Aren't...aren't you glad?"

"I wouldn't be marrying her if I didn't wish to," he said, in his calm, steady way.

Penny was silent, unsure how to respond.

"Do you like them?" her father tried again. Then he added, before she could speak, "For yourself, I mean, not for me."

"Well, I...I don't really know them," said Penny honestly. "It's not very long since they moved here from Entolia, and I don't know much about—"

"Sapphira comes from a good family, back in Entolia," interjected her father, quickly. "I checked."

Penny took a moment to answer, feeling increasingly uncomfortable. "I didn't mean I don't know about their family tree, Father. I meant I don't know them. I've only met them a couple of times." She saw that her father was looking solemn, and she hurried on, "But I have no reason *not* to like them."

Her father's expression softened a little as his eyes passed over her face. "And you will look to like, won't you, my Penny? You always do."

"Of course I will," she said, smiling back at him. "They're going to be our family." She heard the wistful note to her own voice, and for a moment she was distracted in hoping. It would be nice to feel like a real family again, in a way she hadn't since her mother died.

Her companion nodded slowly, and Penny wondered if she dared ask the questions burning in her mind. Her father, while never unkind, wasn't precisely warm. And although he was generally a patient man, there were certain topics on which he was quick to repel any curiosity.

"It's not quite like I expected," Penny said, gathering her courage. "When you said you planned to marry again, I thought it would be a little more..." She trailed off.

Her father raised an eyebrow. "A little more what? Romantic?"

Penny shot him a sheepish look. "Well, yes. You speak of it

almost like a business deal, Father. Perhaps it's impertinent of me to ask, but...do you love Sapphira?"

Something almost like a flush moved up her father's neck. "Love needn't always be about romance, Penelope."

"Is this how you felt before you married Mother?" Penny pressed.

Her father looked out the carriage window, and his eyes once again took on a far away look. "No," he said at last. "Your mother was a rare and special person. And I was a much younger man, then. It was a different matter." He glanced at his daughter. "I didn't have the same motivations for marrying then that I have now."

"And what motivations are those?" asked Penny.

He gave her a searching look. "Well, I don't want to be alone, for one thing."

Penny felt her mouth fall open. She'd never heard her father express anything akin to loneliness. "But you're not alone, Father," she protested. "You have me."

His smile was a little sad. "For now. But you will grow up, marry, have your own life."

"Father, I'm fourteen," Penny said flatly, and he chuckled.

"I'm not saying it's imminent. But one day you'll have your own home, your own life, as well you should. I wouldn't want anything different. But you can't understand, young as you are, what it means to face the prospect of growing old alone."

Penny was silent, thinking this over. Her father looked more human, more vulnerable, than she could remember seeing him in years. Her heart ached to think of him concealing this secret fear of loneliness, but at the same time it was hard to believe it. He always projected such steady confidence.

"I am also thinking of you," he continued calmly, and her eyes jerked up to his.

"Of me?"

"You should have a mother, Penelope. And you will benefit from having sisters as well, I think."

"Father, I'm quite content as I am," Penny started, but he cut her off.

"For now, perhaps. But you will be a woman soon. And you are so like your—well, you need a woman's guidance as you become a woman yourself. That's something I can't give you."

Penny was openly staring now. She was sure he had been going to say that she was like her mother, but she couldn't imagine why that would make it more important for her to have a stepmother. She was still debating with herself whether to challenge her father on his half-finished thought when the carriage slowed. They had arrived, and the opportunity for private speech was over. With a stepmother and two stepsisters joining their family, who knew when there would be the chance for another?

Penny's thoughts were in a whirl as she was led to her seat, in the front, next to Sapphira's two daughters. They exchanged awkward greetings, none of them knowing how to walk the line of the near-strangers they were, and the sisters they were about to become.

"I'm Sophia," said the youngest of the two, who Penny knew was her own age. "Just in case you—"

"I remember," Penny assured her, trying to smile naturally. She turned to the older sister. "And Olivia."

Olivia nodded, her expression a little strained as she looked Penny over. At sixteen, Olivia looked less a girl, like the other two, and more a woman. She was unusually tall, Penny noted, and her hair was an indeterminate color between brown and gray. There was nothing unpleasant in her face, but nothing striking, either. Sophia, on the other hand, looked more like her mother. Perfectly straight nose, incredibly thick hair of a rich brown, and large brown eyes. She still had the roundness of youth, and lacked the stately elegance of Penny's soon-to-be stepmother. But she would surely get there.

Penny felt out of place beside the pair, knowing her fair hair and green eyes marked her as clearly not related to them. But remembering her promise to her father, she tried to notice only positive things, like how Sophia gestured invitingly for her to sit down, or how the shared experience of losing a parent might help them all bond.

The ceremony passed uneventfully. It was a simple affair, suitable—or so Penny's father had told her—for a couple past the prime of life. For all that, the bride looked beautiful, almost regal, Penny thought. And the groom looked his usual calm and collected self, albeit more immaculately dressed. The dinner served afterward for the few guests was extravagant, however. The food was lavish, and the wine, from her father's own vineyards, was plentiful. It had been a particularly good harvest the previous year.

Penny felt herself unwind slightly on the ride home to the manor house. The newly married couple occupied their own carriage, and the three girls rode in a separate one, along with a couple of servants who were to join the household as well.

"Is that the house?" Olivia asked, as they emerged at last from the final vineyard and pulled into the carriageway.

Penny nodded. "This is home."

Olivia raised an eyebrow. "My father's house was bigger."

A defensive retort rose to Penny's lips. But when she frowned at Olivia, she swallowed the words. The older girl clearly didn't realize Penny was watching her, and she swiped surreptitiously at her eyes. Looking beyond her own emotions, Penny realized there wasn't just pride behind Olivia's unflattering comment, but grief. She knew that Olivia and Sophia's loss was more recent than hers, and was determined not to take offense at comparisons between their father and hers. She remembered her own mother too little to make many of her own such comparisons.

"It looks nice," said Sophia softly, and for a moment Olivia looked torn, like she was regretting her critical comment. But she said nothing, and Penny wondered if she'd imagined the earlier glimpse of softness.

When the carriage came to a stop, Penny, who was closest to the door, made to alight. A compulsive movement from Olivia caused her to hesitate. She and her father had never bothered much with formalities, but did politeness require her to let the others go first, or some such thing?

As she hesitated, Olivia pushed past her, skirts rustling. Somehow, in the kerfuffle, Penny's dress was trodden on, and she heard a ripping sound. Olivia didn't pause, continuing out the door of the carriage. Sophia hesitated for the briefest moment, her gaze passing between Penny, bent low in dismay as she examined the damage to her best gown, and Olivia, already nearing the door of the manor. There was an odd look on Sophia's face, but before Penny could say a word, Sophia had alighted from the carriage and hurried after her sister.

Penny remained in place for a moment, a feeling of great unease stealing over her. She didn't understand the interaction that had just happened, and she didn't like the feeling that she was playing a game where she was the only one who didn't know the rules. For a fleeting moment she wished she could retreat back to her familiar old life, the one where she had no mother and no sisters, and lock herself away there.

Her hand remained clenched on the fabric of her gown, but the door of the carriage swung smartly shut, closing her into a silent cocoon. Penny gasped, unclenching her hand. She knew no one had touched the door. A cold rush passed over her. She needed to get control of herself. It had been years since she'd used it without meaning to, without even realizing she was doing it.

Trembling slightly, she pushed the door back open and climbed down from the carriage. Her father was waiting at the door of the manor with his new wife, and the other two girls were behind them. When Penny caught up, they started to walk inside. Just before she crossed the threshold, Sapphira turned back.

"Penelope," she said, no particular emotion in her voice, "do you realize we were all waiting for you? What took so long?"

Penny blinked, taken aback. She glanced at the other girls. Sophia was looking away, apparently uncomfortable. Olivia, on the other hand, was watching tensely. Penny suddenly realized Olivia must be wondering if Penny would tell her new stepmother that Olivia had ripped her gown, and that was what had delayed her. But Penny had no desire to carry tales about the other girl. That was no way to build a friendship.

"I—I'm sorry," she stammered, seeing that her stepmother was still waiting for her answer.

"Oh, there's no need to apologize, my dear," said Sapphira calmly. "No one is perfect, and there's no shame in needing improvement, you know." She inclined her head graciously. "I wish to help you, not criticize you. Punctuality is important, however. And consequences help us learn. As you were the last to join us, it will be appropriate for you to assist in bringing in the baggage. It will help you remember to be quicker next time."

With a serene smile, she turned and walked into the manor, the other two girls hurrying after her without a backward glance. Penny saw her father pause just inside the door. She was sure he'd heard what had passed, and for a moment she thought he'd turn around and say something, tell his new wife that wasn't how things were run in their family. But after a moment he seemed to stiffen his shoulders, and he walked on.

As if Sapphira's words had been a signal, the servants who had come with the new family members put down the baggage they were carrying, leaving it right in the dusty carriageway and walking into the house as well.

Bewildered, and flushing with embarrassment, Penny turned to the manor's familiar servants, who were also bringing in the bags. All of them looked as taken aback as she felt. Her eyes passed to one servant in particular, a grizzled man who'd been with the family since before she was born. He was frowning after Sapphira, a crease between his bushy brows, but he seemed to feel Penny's gaze. His eyes flicked to hers, and he gave her a reassuring smile.

"Never mind the baggage, Pen," he said cheerfully. "We've got it. The new mistress is still learning her way around."

"Thanks Harry," said Penny, trying to smile at him. "But I think perhaps I'd better start out on the right foot with my new stepmother."

"I think so, too," muttered Harry, but he made no further attempt to convince her. Shouldering a large bag, Penny made her way into the house. Discomfort swirled through her stomach, edging almost toward fear. But she pushed it down, telling herself firmly that she would look to like, as she'd promised her father.

Her new family would learn the way she and her father did things, and she would learn their ways as well. She would try—truly try—to be helpful and patient with her stepmother. It was just going to take some time.

FOUR YEARS LATER...

CHAPTER ONE

Penny

"Penelope!"

Penny felt herself stiffen involuntarily at the sound of the calm voice, drifting out of the house into the manor's little kitchen garden. Breathing slowly, she forced herself to relax before she answered.

"Coming, Stepmother."

She pushed herself to her feet, brushing dirt from her hands as she surveyed her work. The carrots would be ready soon, if she was any judge. And somehow she seemed to have become a judge of these things over the last two years.

"You stay out here, Al," she said sternly to the dog gamboling around her feet. "There'll be trouble if you track mud into her sitting room." Al flattened his ears, looking reproachful. When Penny took a step toward the house, he followed.

"Al," she said, exasperated. "We'll both be in trouble if you follow me inside." She looked around for assistance, and saw with relief that Harry was crossing the yard, headed for the barn with a sack of feed over his shoulder.

"Harry!" she called, and he stopped, looking around inquiringly. "Can you take Al for a minute? He's trying to follow me inside again."

"Oh aye," said Harry cheerfully. "Here, you ol' mutt!" He gave a lilting whistle, and the dog bounded over to him, tail wagging furiously.

"No need to look so happy about it," Penny scolded Al. "Whose dog are you, anyway?"

Harry, leaning down now to run one of Al's ears through his hand, grinned at her. The old man certainly had a way with her dog.

Smiling in spite of herself, Penny hurried into the house, pausing only to exchange her garden boots for slippers as she entered through a side door. Her stepmother was in the sitting room, reclined on a settee with not a hair out of place. She cast an eye over Penny's gown, lingering on the dirt smudged down its front.

"I see I was right, Penelope dear, to give that new gown to Sophia rather than you. I hoped its loss would be a helpful reminder to you to keep your attire clean, but I understand that not everyone learns these lessons quickly. There's no shame in being slower than other people."

Penny clenched her hands at her sides, willing herself to keep her temper. She wasn't fourteen anymore. She understood her stepmother's games perfectly now, but she was no more interested in playing them than she had been four years ago.

Sophia, who was wearing the dress in question, shifted uncomfortably on her chair. Did it burn her a little, that soft fabric? Knowing the gown had been purchased specifically for Penny by her father, and never intended for Sophia? But her father knew nothing of the dress's final destination, and Penny had no intention of telling him. She knew it wouldn't help, and the last thing she wanted to do was add to his troubles.

"You called for me, Stepmother?" Penny asked, with as much patience as she could muster.

"Yes, I want to speak to all three of you," said Sapphira. "Get Olivia, won't you, Penelope?"

Swallowing her irritation at the thought of the half-weeded bed of vegetables, Penny moved past her stepmother and stepsister. If Olivia wasn't with the others, she was probably sulking in her room. She seemed to have taken their reversal in fortunes hardest. But Penny had only just left the sitting room when her oldest stepsister loomed into view.

"No need to fetch me, Penny," said Olivia, in an imperfect imitation of her mother's stately tones. "I was already coming." She paused, looking Penny over with her usual calculating expression. "I heard the whole thing. I knew that dress must have been for you." Suddenly her expression faltered. "Don't you want to fight for it, if it's yours?"

Penny shrugged. "It's only a dress."

"No," Olivia made an impatient noise in her throat, "it's not only a dress, is it?" For a moment her eyes searched Penny's. "If my father was still here to give me a gift, I wouldn't discard it so lightly. Stepfather almost did himself in going out to that traveling market. He wouldn't have done that for a step-daughter."

"I'm sure he would want to be considered your father as much as mine," said Penny, a little stiffly. She knew she should have more sympathy, but after four years, her patience had worn a little thin with Olivia's comparisons between her own deceased—and apparently wonderful—father, and Penny's father.

Olivia raised an eyebrow. "Just like Mama would want to be considered your mother as much as Sophia's?"

"I notice she didn't give *you* the dress," snapped Penny, goaded. But she regretted it instantly, partly because of the flash of pain that crossed Olivia's face, but mainly because of the expression of triumph that followed it.

"Honestly, Penny." Olivia's moment of honesty had passed. She adopted a lofty tone, her voice now raised for all to hear as she pushed past Penny into the sitting room. "Don't try to pull me into your resentment about not getting a new dress. I don't care about some gown."

Penny glared after her stepsister. Anger prodded at her forced calm, but she didn't have the energy to engage with it. It had already been a long morning, and she was tired, and worried about her father, and what would become of them all.

"Complaining about such things is childish, Penelope," scolded Sapphira, as soon as Penny reentered the sitting room. As always, she looked disapproving rather than angry, like she was simply disappointed that her endless attempts to help Penny learn life's lessons weren't yielding the results she expected. "You know money is in short supply since your father fell ill. These last two years have been difficult for all of us, and none of us can afford to be pining after luxuries."

"Yes, Stepmother," said Penny dully. She knew there was no point in saying that she didn't care about the dress. Someone would just twist her words, make it sound like she was scorning her father's gift, or something like that. She remembered with a flash of bitterness how she'd once thought that her new family would learn her ways, and she'd learn theirs. Well, one of those things had happened.

"Now, girls," said Sapphira. "I'm afraid it isn't good news."

"The vineyard?" Penny asked, petty resentments forgotten. The look on her stepmother's face was grave, and Penny had feared something like this.

Sapphira nodded. "The return on the last harvest was even lower than our conservative estimate. The vineyard will have to be sold."

Penny rocked back on her heels, surprised by the tears trying to get free. She didn't often cry, but the blow felt unexpectedly personal. All her life, she'd lived on the vineyards. It had been her kingdom as well as her family's livelihood. She couldn't remember a time when she hadn't run free, playing between the rows, reading in hidden nooks where no one would interrupt her, sneaking a few grapes when they finally began to ripen each year.

"But that's the last one," said Sophia hollowly.

Another pang went through Penny. Her father had always been a vintner. And now he wouldn't be. What would he do now? Icy hands seemed to crawl up her insides at the question. She knew the answer. The only reason the vineyards had to be sold were that her father wasn't well enough to manage them anymore. He wasn't changing livelihoods. He would cease to be a vintner because he would cease to be anything before much longer. They all knew it, although none of them said it.

Sapphira nodded in response to Sophia's comment. "We are fortunate that the same buyer is interested, and that he has no need of the house. We can continue to live here, and we will keep the land attached to the manor, at least for the time being."

Olivia looked sulky again, and Sophia subdued. Penny found she couldn't manage a word, not even a nod. She was still wrestling with emotions which she knew her stepmother wouldn't approve of her expressing.

"We will, of course, need to practice even more economies," said Sapphira, neither voice nor expression betraying any emotion. "And the first of these is that Joseph has been dismissed."

Penny's eyes flew to her stepmother's. She wasn't surprised—she'd known he would be next to go. But he'd been with the family since Penny was a small child.

"But surely we still have the rest of the stock to deliver?"

Penny protested. "Shouldn't we keep him on until it's all sold? He's our last able-bodied man, except perhaps for Harry." She frowned. "And he's really too old to be—"

"That's what I wish to speak to you all about," interrupted Sapphira placidly. "I said we need to practice economies, and paying Joseph to do work we can do ourselves is not what I consider economy."

Penny's heart sank. She knew what was coming. She'd learned years ago what "we" meant. She didn't even care about the work. It was the dance she hated. She would infinitely prefer her stepmother to just tell her to do the deliveries.

"What seems like a hardship is often an opportunity," Sapphira continued. "I have been considering which of you would most benefit from the opportunity to—"

"I'll do it," said Penny dully. She found all at once that she just couldn't bear it. She didn't even want to know what veiled competition her stepmother had been going to create in an attempt to justify the decision she'd already made. "I know how to drive the cart."

"For which I hope you will thank me," interjected Sapphira calmly.

Penny was silent for a moment, mastering herself.

"Yes, Stepmother."

It was indeed thanks to Sapphira that she'd learned to drive. Naturally her exuberance in springing first into the carriage one day had demonstrated not only an impolite failure to allow others to go first, but a lack of appreciation for the hard work of the carriage driver. It was pure coincidence, of course, that Penny's behavior had shown how much she would benefit from learning what was really involved in driving a vehicle right when a dancing master had been hired to teach the girls to dance.

If her stepmother had just been honest, and told Penny that

she was being excluded from the lessons as an economy, and not because she desperately needed Joseph to teach her to drive that very week, Penny wouldn't even have minded missing out.

Or at least, not very much.

"Harry can probably come with me," Penny continued, "to help unload the barrels."

"Harry can't be spared from the manor," said Sapphira firmly. "You must find a way to manage. It is a wonderful opportunity to practice resourcefulness."

"Yes, Stepmother."

"The first delivery you will need to do is expected next Saturday evening, at the castle."

"Yes, Stepmother," Penny repeated.

But Olivia's attention had been caught. "To the castle? Next Saturday evening? But it's the night of Prince Bentleigh's betrothal ball to the Listernian princess!" She shot Penny a suspicious look, as if she'd been plotting to trick them all and be the one who got to go to the castle.

"You're welcome to do it, Olivia," said Penny, barely refraining from rolling her eyes. "I have no interest in going to the castle."

She grimaced internally at the understatement. The castle was the last place she wanted to be. The way the other girls gushed over the royal family made her feel ill sometimes. She knew she couldn't really blame them. If *their* very existence had been turned into a crime by that same royal family, they might be as disinclined as she was to giggle over how handsome Crown Prince Rian was.

"Are you going back on your word, Penelope?" Sapphira asked sharply.

"No," said Penny, frustrated. "I just meant that if Olivia *wants* to do it—"

"You won't be attending the ball, you realize," Sapphira cut in sternly, as though Penny was the one exclaiming about going to the betrothal ball. "You'll be attending at the servants' entrance only, to deliver the wine. You won't see the guests, or enter the ballroom."

"I understand," said Penny. "I don't wish to go to the ball, Stepmother, honestly."

Sapphira raised an eyebrow as if she doubted it, but she said no more. Olivia also made no further complaints. Penny knew her stepsister wasn't stupid. She must have realized that for anyone with social ambitions, delivering goods to the ball in the guise of a servant was even worse than not attending it at all.

Fortunately, Penny had no social ambitions whatsoever.

"Well then, that's decided," said Sapphira briskly. "Penelope, I'm told we need produce from the markets, but cook can't be spared right now. She has a list for you."

Penny sighed. Her half-finished task in the kitchen garden was niggling at her mind, demanding to be completed. But she knew better than to argue. Her stepmother would just remind her that the reason she had been appointed to go to the market was because she'd shown herself to be too easily manipulated by a traveling merchant. Sapphira assured Penny that the man had gotten far too high a price from her for the trinket Penny had bought for her father's birthday present.

Never mind that it had been Penny's own pocket money, or that Sophia had paid even more for a music box that was for herself rather than a gift, and had broken within a week. Not that Penny had told anyone that. She hadn't been willing to get Sophia in trouble just for the sake of lessening her own punishment.

Never mind that the incident had been three years ago, when money hadn't been tight. Penny had been decreed to need more practice haggling with salesmen, and Penny was accordingly the one who trudged to the market three times a week.

She'd never even bothered pointing out the absurdity of entrusting the family's food money to the person who supposedly needed the most improvement in bargaining. They all knew perfectly well that it was only another excuse to give her an additional job. And, whatever her stepmother's motivations, it was certainly true that Penny had become a shrewd bargainer thanks to all the practice.

She knew that the earlier she got to the market, the better her options would be, so she decided to go straight to the kitchens for the list. To her surprise, Sophia followed her from the sitting room.

"Penny," she said awkwardly, once they were alone, "about the dress. I know it was intended for you, and if you want it..."

She trailed off, and Penny tried to conceal her impatience.

"Keep the dress, Sophia," she said. "I don't need a new gown. Where would I wear it? To the castle on Saturday?" Her voice was heavy with sarcasm, and she tried to keep her eyes from the garment itself. It was a lovely gown, and deep blue was a very becoming color on her, Penny knew. She was surprised, actually, that her father knew it enough to select a dress in that color. Or perhaps it was a happy coincidence. Not that it mattered, since the dress was now Sophia's.

Sophia mumbled something, and started back toward the sitting room. Penny felt a pang of sadness as she watched her stepsister retreating. She had so hoped to be friends with the other girl. She still hoped it. But somehow they had never fully banished the awkwardness of trying to merge from strangers to family, not even in four years.

"Sophia," she said, and the other girl turned. "I wasn't complaining about it before, to Olivia."

Sophia rolled her eyes. "I know you weren't, Penny. I know Olivia, remember?" She hesitated. "She still misses our father, you know, and our life back in Entolia. He was...well, he was a good father. To us both." Sophia colored, stammering into silence.

Penny bit her lip. She understood what her stepsister meant, but she had no idea how to respond. It hadn't exactly escaped her notice that Sapphira favored her younger daughter over her older. And from Olivia's veiled disparagement of Penny's father, it seemed that she'd held her own father in high esteem. Penny sometimes suspected that the parent Olivia had lost was the only one who'd shown her much kindness.

Eventually she settled on giving Sophia a sympathetic nod. With a shy smile, the other girl hurried back to the other room.

Penny made her way to the kitchens, her steps as heavy as her heart. She wanted to appreciate Sophia's gesture in offering to give her the dress, but it felt empty. Sophia had known perfectly well that Penny would say no. And she'd waited until her mother couldn't overhear, which meant she wasn't willing even to make the gesture if it risked Sapphira's displeasure.

Collecting the list from the family's cook, Penny waved away the woman's apologies. Cook looked harassed as she bent over the fire. Penny couldn't help feeling wistful as she remembered the days when the cook had two assistants. Now she had no one. Well, except for when Sapphira discovered a burning need for Penny to learn to do something particular in the kitchen. Penny actually quite enjoyed those times.

With the list tucked into her pocket, Penny left the kitchen. But her steps didn't take her to the front door. They took her up the stairs, into a now familiar room. She hadn't spent much time in her father's room before his illness, but she had spent many hours over the past two years sitting beside his bed, reading to him, or just watching through those dreadful nights when his lungs were affected, and she wasn't sure he'd see the dawn.

"Father?" she asked softly, peeking in at the door. A maid was sitting beside the bed, and at the sight of Penny she rose, edging out and leaving the two of them alone.

"Penny." She could hear her father's smile in his voice. "Come in." She moved quietly to the bed, and was surprised to find him lying down, rather than sitting up and reading as she'd expected. Seeing her concern, he gave her a wan smile. "I feel particularly poorly today, I'm afraid. But I'll come around again."

Penny searched his face, wondering if he believed his words. She wondered, also, if he knew about the loss of the final vineyard. If not, she wouldn't tell him. She couldn't bear to bring him lower than he already was. His tall frame was no longer powerful. He looked hollowed out, from the bags under his eyes to the wasted arms. A rush of grief overwhelmed Penny, and she blinked back tears at the thought of all her father had lost. All she had lost.

"If Mother was here, you'd get better." The words, no more than a whisper, slipped out without her permission.

Her father's eyes sharpened, and his head whipped around nervously.

"We're alone," Penny assured him.

He relaxed slightly, but he still looked agitated. "You shouldn't say such things, Penny. You know you shouldn't."

She remained silent, mutinous. His eyes were on her face again, and his expression suddenly softened.

"It's not true, you know," he said. "She could only heal injuries, not illnesses."

"Really?" Penny sat up straighter. Her father had always refused to talk about her mother's magic.

He nodded. "She wasn't the most powerful healer in Bant, not by a long shot. She couldn't heal life-threatening injuries, or anything like that. But her magic was still powerful enough that she kept it quiet, even before the ban."

"But why?" Penny pressed. "Why keep it quiet when it hadn't been outlawed?"

Her father gave her a twisted smile. "To avoid having half the countryside badgering her to heal their hurts," he said. "She still did it, all the time. But in secret wherever possible." His eyes took on a far off look, increasing the wistfulness of his mouth. "It's why she was able to stay, when so many others had to flee. She wasn't widely known as an...well, you know. She was probably the only one left in the city. In the kingdom, for all I know."

Penny knew that wasn't true—the recent series of arrests demonstrated that she herself was far from the only one still hiding in Bansford. But she didn't think her father knew of the arrests, and she wasn't going to worry him with the information.

"And now she's dead," she said instead, speaking dully.

Her father suddenly seized her hand, his grip unexpectedly tight. "You don't have it, do you Penny? It hasn't developed since I asked you? You're eighteen now, you'd be considered fully responsible...There hasn't been any sign, has there?"

Penny stared into his eyes, a myriad emotions swirling within her. Memory washed over her in an irresistible tide. For a moment she was five years old again, standing by her mother's grave.

Penny wondered why she wasn't crying anymore, how she could have run out of tears. She felt hollow, like an empty jar that could never be filled again. Someone had given her a flower, and she knew she was supposed to lay it down on the freshly turned earth. But she was clutching it in her fist, unable to let it go, horrified at approaching the place where she knew her mother's body was lying.

She fought within herself, clenching and unclenching her hand slightly, torn between the desire to add her flower to the others already there, and the irresistible urge to retreat from the grave, to get as far away as possible.

And then, without her meaning to do it, without even knowing how it happened, she felt her mind reaching down toward her hand, not through her body, but outside of it. She lifted the flower from her own fist and sent it spinning through the air, to land, furling and unfurling with unnatural speed, on top of the mound.

"Penny?"

Her father's gentle voice made her whip around. She wasn't sure if it was guilt or fear that was filling her, only that it was potent. So much so that, for the moment at least, it was overwhelming even the grief that had held her in its grip since Mama's death. Her father took one look at her white, terrified face, and knelt down beside her.

"Penny," he said again, his voice choked with emotion as he took her hand. "I need to ask you a question. It's important."

Penny had nodded, her heart in her throat.

"You know Mama's..." he'd glanced around, making sure none of the other mourners had lingered, "Mama's special gift?"

Penny nodded again.

"Do you have...have you ever felt anything like..." He trailed off helplessly. "Do you understand what I'm asking, Penny?"

Again, she nodded, her eyes wider than ever.

"And?"

Penny swallowed, her mouth unnaturally dry. She read her father's eyes, and she could see that he too was feeling something other than grief. He too was afraid, more afraid than she'd ever seen him in her life.

"No, Father," she whispered. "I don't have magic like Mama."

The relief that washed over his face was unmistakable. There was no anguish—he wasn't torn like her mother had been, unsure what to hope for. He pulled her into a rare hug, his whole demeanor relaxing.

"Thank goodness for that," he murmured into her ear. And Penny's

tears still didn't come, even as her heart was breaking at the first lie she'd ever told.

"Penny?" Her father's anxious voice brought her back to the present, back to a new deathbed, a new parent leaving her. She might be almost nineteen now, but she felt as alone as that five year old girl had done.

"No, Father," she said softly. "There hasn't been any sign."

That long ago lie had been her first, but certainly not her last.

CHAPTER TWO

Penny

As on that previous occasion, Penny's father relaxed, lying back across his pillow with evident relief.

"You'll be all right, then," he muttered, as if to himself. "Sapphira will take care of you."

Unable to help herself, Penny shifted slightly. Her father's eyes darted to hers again. He was unusually agitated today.

"She is taking care of things, isn't she?"

"Yes," said Penny, with a clear conscience. Her stepmother was taking care of *things*. If they'd been talking about people...

"She manages extremely well with limited resources," Penny added. "I'm sure we wouldn't have kept things running half as long if it wasn't for her. And she never complains about having less than we used to."

It was all true. Her stepmother didn't tolerate extravagance, in herself any more than in the rest of the family, or in the household expenses. She had capably and calmly steered them along a delicate balance of continuing to run the vineyards for as long as possible without falling irretrievably into debt. Thinking about how lost she would have been in managing the business without her stepmother made Penny feel childish and ungrateful for the disclaimer she couldn't help adding in her head. *If only she'd be kind as well as capable.*

"Poor Sapphira," sighed Penny's father. "It's not quite what she expected when she married me." He glanced over at his daughter. "I know you sometimes find her approach difficult, Penny. But you must listen to her, you know. When I married her, I asked her particularly to guide you, to show you how to become a respectable young lady. She's only doing what I asked her to do."

Penny stared at him. "You never told me this," she said. "Is that...is that why you married her?" For some reason, a slight chill passed over her at the thought.

"Only one of the reasons," her father said, although he didn't quite meet her eye.

She frowned, unsatisfied with this answer. "And do you feel she's doing a good job of molding me?" she asked, unable to keep a hard edge from her voice.

Her father grunted as he shifted slightly on the bed. "I'm no judge of these things, Penny."

"You're my father!" Penny protested. "What better judge than you when it comes to my upbringing?"

"You know what I mean," her father said wearily. "I don't know how to teach you what a lady needs to know." Penny started to protest again, but he cut her off, seizing her hand, that feverish light back in his eyes. "You need to be careful, Penny! Most didn't know, but there were some who knew what your mother was. You don't know who might be watching, waiting for some sign. You need to learn what you can from Sapphira, learn how to blend in."

Penny couldn't quite repress a shiver. Her father's strange manner unnerved her quite as much as his words. She pressed his hand.

"Don't worry about me, Father," she said reassuringly. "I'm all right. You just worry about getting healthy."

He released her, a dull look in his eyes as he laid his head down. "You're so like her," he said, half to himself. "And not just in looks. She never had enough thought for her own safety, either." There was a long pause. "I still miss her, you know," he whispered. His eyes found hers, and his face softened. "You're a good girl, Penny. You always have been."

Penny felt her eyes filling with tears again, but she held them back. She mustn't let him see her cry. She stood, leaning down to kiss his forehead and somehow managing to muster a smile.

"I'll be back soon," she promised.

It was with a heavy heart that she made her way through the yard. She was so distracted, she failed to even notice Al's antics until a sharp bark brought her out of her stupor.

"Sorry, Al," she murmured, reaching down to stroke his head. "I was in another world. Are you ready to go? We need to visit the market again."

Al bounded around her, barking his pleasure at the prospect of an outing.

"Unless you'd rather stay with your best friend, Harry," said Penny reproachfully. Al wagged his tail unrepentantly, his tongue hanging out as he trotted beside her, and she couldn't help laughing.

"You know he can tell how you're feeling, don't you?"

Penny turned at the sound of Harry's voice, tilting her head questioningly to the side.

"He could sense your tension earlier, that's why he didn't want to be left behind. He only tries to follow you inside when he thinks you might be in danger."

Penny raised an eyebrow. "He abandoned me to 'danger' pretty quickly when you whistled for him."

Harry chuckled. "Ah, we have an understanding though, don't we, boy?"

Al waved his tail more frantically still, and Penny rolled her eyes, still smiling. "Shameless," she told the dog.

"Not off to market again, are you?" Harry asked, frowning at her. "Shall I come?"

Penny shook her head. "No, I'm sure you have plenty to do. And I'll be easier in my mind if I know you're nearby to the manor. Father seemed agitated when I spoke to him."

Harry turned sad eyes toward the house, nodding slowly. "All the same," he said, his concerned gaze returning to her, "I don't like you going to market all alone. It's not seemly, a young girl like you."

Penny laughed. "I'm not as young as you think I am, Harry. And I won't be alone. I'll have Al with me." She could see he was still unconvinced, so she added more seriously, "I don't take it lightly, Harry. You know I wouldn't go if I couldn't bring Al."

Harry nodded reluctantly, and Penny hurried off before he could say more. At a soft call, Al bounded after her, keeping close to her side.

The manor wasn't far out of Bant, the capital city of Bansford. Ordinarily Penny enjoyed the walk, but she was still too troubled from her conversation with her father to appreciate the pleasantly warm morning. Plus the knowledge that the familiar vineyards on either side of the road now belonged to strangers made their beauty bittersweet.

She passed through the city gates after only half an hour's walk. Her pace slowed as she traversed the cobbled streets, climbing the gentle hill upon which Bant was built. The castle, of course, sat at the very top of the slope. She scowled up at it. It was natural, she supposed, that the royals placed themselves above everyone else, but the physical reminder always brought her resentment to the fore.

Her preferred market was in a seedy part of the city, and she knew a much more genteel one could be found further up the hill. But that market was situated almost in the castle's shadow. No matter how unknown she was, how secret her magic might be, going anywhere near the castle still felt like walking past the lair of her enemies. She realized it wasn't as though the king himself haggled for his own produce, but she still felt more comfortable frequenting a market closer to the city wall.

Al didn't frisk around once they reached the city. He was well-trained, for all his playful ways, and he always stuck very close to Penny's side when strangers were nearby.

The market was bustling, full of animated faces and shouting voices. Penny slipped through the crowd, scanning the stalls for the choicest produce. The chaos was familiar, from the middle aged cooks haggling with gusto, to the distracted house-wives trying to order eggs while their children wove uncon-trolled through the legs of other shoppers, pursued by exasperated shouts that mingled with their laughter. Penny's dress was finer than most of the clothes she saw, but thanks to the dirt still spread down its front, she didn't stand out too much. At least, no more than a girl of eighteen braving the markets alone always stood out. Not many households sent their young girls into the city unaccompanied, especially not in this part of town.

But Penny was used to being an anomaly. She ignored alike the calculating looks of greedy-eyed men and the concerned clucking of older women. She paused on the way to her favorite produce stand, considering a farmer selling eggs. Their own chickens hadn't been laying well lately, on top of everything else. Cook hadn't mentioned eggs, but perhaps she hadn't yet been aware that Penny had found only three eggs in the hutch that morning.

"All alone, my dear?"

The wheedling note to the stranger's voice made Penny's skin crawl, but she didn't even bother to turn.

"No, actually, I'm not," she said shortly.

The words had barely left her mouth when Al began to growl. He was pressed so close to her that his side was touching her skirts, his warmth seeping through to her leg. Penny glanced down at him absently and saw that his hackles were raised.

Sighing, she looked back up at the eggs. "No, I'd better not buy any," she muttered to herself. "In case there isn't enough for everything else on the list."

Her decision made, she turned, slightly surprised to find the stranger still hovering close by.

"Tell your dog to stand down," he said, his eyes fixed warily on Al, who was still growling quietly at him.

Penny ignored him. "Good dog," she said instead to Al, reaching down to scratch between his ears. He gave a perfunctory wag of his tail, but his eyes didn't leave the stranger.

The man stepped forward. Immediately, Al's growl increased in volume, and he bared his teeth.

"I don't think my dog likes you very much," said Penny amicably.

The man hesitated for a moment, then seemed to decide it wasn't worth it. "I was just being friendly," he muttered, as he loped off into the crowd.

"Good boy, Al," said Penny again, pushing through the throng toward the produce section. Al, restored to his usual good humor, wagged his tail in self-satisfied acceptance of her praise as he stuck to her side. How he managed it in the chaos of the market she didn't know, but he'd never failed her yet.

"Ah, young Penelope! I have such a bargain for you today!" The jovial voice made Penny smile, even as she shook her head.

"Nice try, you old rogue, but as I've told you, we've no use for persimmons. I don't care how exotic they are."

"But my dear, you can't go past a deal like this! Half the price they were last week!"

Penny snorted. "That just means you tried to cheat me even worse last week."

The merchant, a rotund man in his early middle age, made a noise of horrified protest. "Cheat you? Would I ever—"

"Any day of the week, if you thought you could get away with it," Penny cut him off. "But I'm only here for a few bits and pieces today. Do you have any parsnips left?"

They entered into some friendly haggling, and Penny's burlap sack was soon half full. Al, uninterested in their conversation, was watching the crowd with his attentive gaze, still pressed against Penny's leg.

The hush was what made Penny look around. The market was such a noisy place that the sudden drop in volume could hardly fail to catch everyone's attention. The merchant broke off mid-sentence to look for the source of the change, and Penny followed his gaze.

She stilled as she caught sight of a tall, strong figure. The man's tawny hair looked like it wanted to curl riotously, but was being rigidly restrained by a rather severe style. His eyes, brown and serious, scanned the crowd as attentively as Al's. His clothes were exceptionally fine, although he wore no embellishments of any kind upon them. His boots were the tallest Penny had ever seen. She would have expected them to be more polished, though. They were dusty and worn, suggesting a morning filled with activity, rather than the indolent life she imagined he led.

He seemed to have been hovering a few stalls down, but as Penny turned, he began to move, striding confidently through the now quiet market and nodding a little stiffly to the market goers as he passed. Penny didn't need either the pair of guards following a few steps behind the young man, or the whispered exclamations that preceded them through the crowd to recognize the new arrival. She'd never been quite this close to him before, but like most of the inhabitants of Bant and its surrounds, she knew Crown Prince Rian by sight.

A rush of fear passed through her—what was the prince doing in this market, on the other side of town from his castle? But she pushed the fear instantly down, refusing to give it power. The royal family wanted people like her to be afraid, to flee before the might of the crown. But she'd done nothing to be ashamed of. And neither had her mother. The prince might not know that an untrained enchantress stood secretly in front of him, might not know that she was in danger with every breath she took. But Penny stood straight nevertheless, taking satisfaction in her small act of defiance as she refused to flinch before him.

People bowed clumsily as the prince passed them, and Penny supposed she would have to do the same, although it would lessen her rebellious gesture. She hadn't expected to attract his notice, so she was surprised and a little discomposed when his eyes slid straight to her as he approached. She had the sudden inexplicable feeling that he'd been watching her from where he stood nearby, but she shook off the thought. It was vanity to think the prince had noticed her in a crowd of so many.

Her own discomposure irked her, however, reminding her of the terrible abuse of the crown's power that led her to feel fear when she saw the prince, although she'd done nothing wrong.

Instead of lowering her eyes, like those around her, she held his gaze unblinkingly. She thought his eyes would skate over her and right past, but they didn't. He actually slowed his pace, and for a horrible moment she thought he was going to stop and speak to her. Her courage failed, and she found her defiance didn't extend so far as to seek any kind of confrontation. Lowering her eyes at last, she bobbed into an awkward curtsy, forgetting everything she'd learned in her long-ago etiquette lessons, before money had been too tight for such things.

The prince was almost before her now, and his pace was still alarmingly slow. With her eyes lowered, Penny had a good view of Al, and she saw to her irritation that the dog was regarding the passing trio with bright-eyed interest. There was no sign of the suspicion the dog's instincts should have raised when confronted with one of the authors of Penny's worst troubles.

The prince passed by, muttering following in his wake. For a long minute, Penny kept her eyes lowered, waiting for her heart to slow. She was therefore looking right at Al when the dog whipped his head around, and let out a low whine. Penny knew the sound—he was asking for permission for something, although she had no idea what. Following his gaze, she drew in a sharp breath as she saw the focus of his attention. Another dog, bigger in frame than Al, but emaciated, with tufts of fur missing all over its poor body, was cowering underneath an abandoned stall nearby.

A red-faced man, apparently having lost interest in the spectacle of the passing prince, was berating the dog, a crude walking stick in his raised hand. The way the animal shied away from the stick told Penny that it was used to rough treatment. As she watched, Al gave another whine, and the man lost his temper at last, beating the dog around the haunches with the stick.

Abandoning her sack of vegetables, Penny hurried toward the pair, Al at her heels.

"Stop it!" she cried. "That's no way to treat a dog."

"Stay out of it, girl," growled the man. "I'll deal with the stray how I want. It's no business of yours."

"Watch me make it my business," said Penny furiously. Perhaps it was the encounter with the prince, but the sight of the man beating the dog into submission just because he was stronger seemed to have ignited all the resentment that had been smoldering in her since the encounter with her stepmother that morning. She felt ready to do battle, and wasn't in the least intimidated by the man's size or angry words.

"Watch it, wench," he hissed, abandoning the dog and stepping closer to her. He had a stale smell about him.

Al growled, and the man's eyes passed derisively to the dog.

"You think you scare me, mutt? I know how to deal with your kind."

Penny felt her hand curl into a fist, and for a moment it took all her attention to prevent herself from lashing out. The desire to use her magic, to shut this man's cruel mouth with the smallest taste of what she could do, was overwhelming. But she must master it. She would be as bad as he was if she subdued him by using a power she had and he didn't, just to prove herself stronger than him.

Al gave a warning bark, but the man's eyes were no longer on the dog. They'd slid past Penny to something behind her, and she saw them widen. She half-turned her head, and an unpleasant jolt shot through her stomach at the sight of the prince and his guards, frozen in place several stalls down from where she'd left her bag. Apparently he hadn't moved as far along the market as she'd thought. Either that or the commotion caused by the confrontation between her and the dog's tormentor had brought the royal back. The prince's expression was nothing like the serious mask he'd worn a few minutes ago. He looked angry, almost outraged.

Penny whipped her gaze back to the man who'd been abusing the stray. She could hardly believe she'd let herself get so caught up in the confrontation that she'd forgotten the most compelling reason for not using her magic. It made her blood run cold to imagine what would have happened if she'd lost control of herself at that moment, after so many years of caution.

The man seemed to also realize that the situation called for caution. Mumbling something Penny couldn't hear, he cast the cowering mongrel a half-glance then strode away, disappearing into the crowd. The dog emerged warily from its shelter, then hurried away in a different direction. Penny watched it until it disappeared, then looked down at Al.

"Time to go, old boy," she said quietly.

The crowd was muttering excitedly, everyone's attention still focused on the rare sight of the prince, not on the commonplace event of an altercation involving two market goers and a stray dog. The angry look was gone from the prince's face now that the confrontation was over. He was speaking quietly with a merchant Penny didn't recognize, still standing some way along from her usual stall. Nevertheless, she could have sworn she felt those serious eyes on her as she hurried back to retrieve her bag. Brushing off the scolding of the merchant, who apparently didn't think the well-being of a mongrel was worth Penny risking her safety, she paid him and hurried away from the market.

It was probably only in her imagination that the prince's gaze followed her all the way out of sight. But one thing was fact. Instead of keeping her head down in her first true encounter with a member of the royal family, she had attracted a dangerous amount of attention to herself.

As alarming as the incident had been at the time, after a few days, it faded from Penny's mind. She would be very surprised to learn that Prince Rian even remembered it, and Penny had plenty to occupy her at the manor without worrying over an encounter that was unlikely ever to be repeated.

The largest of her worries was her father. She had returned

from the markets to find him sleeping, and he had been conscious for an alarmingly small part of each day since then. She knew the end must be close, but she couldn't bring herself to face it, not until it was absolutely necessary.

The whole household seemed to be living in a hushed state now, although that may have been the significantly decreased number of its members. Only Sapphira showed no change in demeanor. She was her usual calm, practical, unemotional self.

Helping Harry to haul a sack of grain into the kitchen on Saturday afternoon, Penny was surprised to find Sophia hovering there, speaking with the cook. It was rare to see either of her stepsisters in the kitchen.

"Penny," said Sophia, the usual hint of awkwardness in her voice. "I left something for you in your bedroom." She gave the kitchen at large a vague nod of farewell, then hurried from the room.

The cook stared after her. "What's she left for you? It's not a dead mouse or some such, is it?"

Penny was bemused herself, but she laughed at the suggestion. "Sophia doesn't do nasty things like that," she reassured the cook. "At least," she amended, "not when her mother isn't even watching."

"You realize that's about backward, don't you?" Harry said dryly.

Penny sighed, but didn't answer. What was there to say?

"Why didn't she just tell you what it was, then?" the cook persisted.

Penny shrugged. "Sophia's not good at speaking directly," she said. "It's best to let her communicate in her own way, or she wouldn't communicate at all."

Whatever it was, the surprise would have to wait, because there were several more sacks to be moved. Penny followed

Harry back to the barn, chatting cheerfully with him as Al chased birds he had no hope of catching.

They were on their fourth trip to the kitchen when a pale faced maid—the manor's last—hurried in.

"Miss Penny," she whispered, her voice barely audible, "you're wanted in the sitting room."

Penny felt the sack drop from her nerveless hands. Silence had fallen over the kitchen, and she knew they all understood. She turned beseeching eyes on Harry. His face was ashen, but he gave her a reassuring nod.

"Come on, Pen. We'll go together."

Penny knew her stepmother wouldn't approve of Harry's inclusion, but she didn't argue. The two of them walked silently to the sitting room, where Sapphira, Olivia, and Sophia were all waiting. The tears running down Sophia's face told their own story. Olivia was pale but dry-eyed.

"I'm afraid your father has passed on," said Sapphira, even now showing no obvious emotion.

She said more, but Penny didn't hear it. There was a buzzing in her ears, and the floor seemed to slide under her feet. She was aware of Harry's hand on her elbow, bracing her. It seemed to be the only solid spot in the room. She felt in a trance as she followed her stepmother up the stairs, and into her father's room. She didn't even feel like she was saying goodbye. He wasn't there. He was already gone.

The next few hours were a blur, everything made foggy by the press of inexpressible emotion that overwhelmed all of Penny's senses. She was aware that Sophia sat with her for a space of time, not speaking, just present. She had a vague sense of not being entirely alone in the enormous well of loneliness opening beneath her feet. It was comforting, or it would be if she had the capacity to feel such things.

She didn't emerge from the merciful haze until the sun had

sunk low in the sky. She was sitting unmoving, almost unfeeling, at the scrubbed wooden table where the family ate their meals. An untouched plate of food was before her, placed there some time ago by the cook. For the last few hours, Penny had felt submerged, as though her head was just below water. It was her stepmother's calm voice that brought her abruptly back to the surface.

"You'd better go and change, Penelope."

Penny looked up, uncomprehending. "Change?" Her thoughts struggled to catch up. Was her stepmother telling her to change into mourning clothes already? Surely that didn't matter, not yet.

"You won't wish to go to the castle in those clothes," said Sapphira, with a touch of impatience. "We may be selling our last vineyard, but we still have a name to uphold."

Penny looked slowly down at her gown. It was an old, worn one she'd donned to help Harry in the barn, and it was still dusty, despite the hours that had passed since she'd helped him carry the sacks inside.

"The...the castle?" she repeated blankly.

"You are to take the delivery of the wine," said Sapphira, definitely impatient now. "If you don't leave soon, it will be late, and we can't have that. Not when there's a gala happening."

Penny stared at her. "You want me to take the wine to the castle? Now?"

"You were the one who offered to do it," said Sapphira, raising her eyebrows.

"That was a week ago," Penny said, anger surging into the void that had been cushioning her. She fanned it desperately, knowing that without it, and without the numbness it had driven away, she would be crushed by the grief. "Surely you don't still expect me to do it now."

"Today and always I expect you to keep your word," said Sapphira calmly.

"My father just died." Penny found herself on her feet. She was breathing hard, her limbs trembling. The salt cellar on the table rattled, apparently of its own accord, but Sapphira didn't seem to notice.

"And my husband just died," she said. "I am not unfeeling, Penelope." Her voice was devoid of any feeling Penny could detect. "But life must go on. You and I have both learned this long before our current loss."

Tears trembled on the end of Penny's lashes, but she refused to let them fall. This woman had no right to refer to the loss of Penny's mother, as if she somehow understood that grief, as if she felt it. How dare she even refer to Penny's father's death as a shared loss? She felt nothing, knew nothing. Cared about no one.

"I don't want to go to the castle," she said, through gritted teeth.

"I daresay you don't," said her stepmother, still calm. "And I don't blame you for that. I'm not asking you to want to do it. I'm just telling you that you must do it."

For a moment Penny teetered, on the point of resisting, defying, standing her ground for once. But under her stepmother's unyielding gaze she deflated, curling in on herself. She didn't have the fight in her. At the best of times she was hampered from exerting herself as she knew she was capable of doing. In this moment, doubly so. Simply existing was the limit of what she could manage.

"I'll change," she said dully.

She walked past her stepmother without another word, and climbed the stairs to her room. The sight of her own, familiar bed almost undid her. She wanted nothing more than to fling herself on it and let the tears come at last. But she couldn't afford to fall apart now, not if she had to drive to the castle alone and somehow unload a cartful of heavy wine barrels within the next hour.

Something on the bed caught her eye, and she stepped toward it. She blinked several times before she could make sense of the folded blue fabric. There was a note on top of it, and she picked it up slowly.

I know you meant it as a joke, but you should wear this to the castle tonight. It's yours, after all. And you should look your best, even if you're not attending the ball.

Penny stared at Sophia's handwriting for a long, frozen moment. Then, without warning, the tears came, pouring down her cheeks in torrents. The kind gesture undid her in a way Sapphira's coldness could never have done. This was what Sophia had been talking about earlier in the day. Penny had forgotten all about it. And she'd been so sure Sophia's offer to give her the gown hadn't been sincere.

The storm was brief but intense, and when it had passed, Penny found that the release had helped. She washed her face, dressed her hair, and slipped on the gown. It fit her beautifully —she and Sophia were similar in size, if not in looks.

Galvanized, she swept down the stairs, a spark of defiance once again burning inside her. It was too late to defy her stepmother this time—that moment had passed. But she was sick of being trampled on, sick of being afraid.

Without a word to anyone, Penny harnessed their sole

remaining horse to the cart, which was already loaded with barrels. She knew her attire was unsuited to her activity—a practical detail that would never have occurred to Sophia—but she didn't care. Against every instinct she possessed, she was going to the castle, and Sophia was right. She should look her best. At a soft whistle from her, Al leaped nimbly up into the cart and nestled himself beside her, ready for the drive.

CHAPTER THREE

Rian

"Any idea what this is about, Ri? I was supposed to meet Zayla before the ball, but at this rate there won't be time."

Rian looked into his brother's impatient face, pulling his own thoughts back from somewhere far away.

"I don't know any more than you do, Ben. A servant just told me that Father wanted to speak to us both immediately."

"*Immediately* passed half an hour ago," muttered Bentleigh.

Rian couldn't help chuckling. "I dare you to say that to his face when he arrives." Bentleigh looked rueful, but Rian was suddenly hit with another gloomy reminder of what that night's celebration really meant. "I suppose you *could* get away with it now," he said, a little wistfully. "You're leaving tomorrow afternoon, aren't you? I guess you can afford to burn bridges."

Bentleigh rolled his eyes and elbowed his brother in the ribs. "No one's burning any bridges, Rian. I won't be gone long."

Rian sent him a look. "You know what I mean, Ben. Maybe you won't be gone long this time, but you'll be moving to Listernia permanently soon enough."

Bentleigh's eyes searched his brother's face, his expression growing more serious. "I might be living in Listernia once I'm married, but I'll always be your brother, Rian. You can always count on me. You know that, don't you?"

Rian met his brother's eyes with a heavy heart. "Neither of us knows what to expect, Ben," he said seriously. "Can you really be sure friendship between the two kingdoms will continue? Mother and Father will never be comfortable with the Listernian crown's encouragement of magic. The relationship has been a struggle ever since our ban, and that was with you here, holding everything together with your bare hands. Now we're losing you."

I'm losing you, he added in his head. The impending loss of his closest friend and ally was weighing on him more heavily with every passing day. Bentleigh had always been able to get away with expressing opinions Rian often shared, but couldn't say aloud. Who would argue that cause now?

Bentleigh grimaced, making no attempt to deny his brother's words. "I know it's not going to be easy on you, Ri, and for that I'm sorry." He gave Rian a hard look. "But it's not like I could really solve things if I was here. You know what needs to change. You know the ban on magic is the problem."

Rian looked away, unable to meet his brother's eyes. They'd had this conversation so many times.

"You're the crown prince, Ri," Bentleigh insisted. "Can you really tell me you agree with a total ban on magic because of the risk of a few rotten apples? Listernia's just emerged from a king-dom-wide curse, and even they have never considered going that far!"

Still Rian said nothing.

"At least tell me you'd be willing to consider lifting the ban, if you wore the crown," said Bentleigh, exasperated.

Rian whipped his head back around. "Consider it?" He glanced around, making sure the throne room really was empty, and lowered his voice. "If I was king, I'd lift it tomorrow."

Bentleigh's mouth fell slightly open, and for a moment he seemed too stunned to speak. "You've never admitted that before," he said at last.

Rian shrugged. "What's the point? I'm not the king, and I won't be for a long time. Until that day, my loyalty is to our current king, and my duty is to enforce his decrees as faithfully as if they were my own. That's what it means to be his heir."

Again, Bentleigh was silent for a long moment. "Did you know," he said, a hint of dryness behind his conversational tone, "Zayla calls her father 'Father' rather than 'our current king'?"

Rian rolled his eyes. "I call Father 'Father'."

"Aloud, sure," said Bentleigh. "Because it would sound strange not to. But in your head?"

Rian sighed, not bothering to respond. He understood what Ben meant, and there was no getting around the truth that King Rhinehart was king first, and father second. The cost of a crown, presumably. Rian supposed he would have no choice but to be the same with his own children one day.

The thought did nothing to cheer him.

"Ri, it goes both ways," Bentleigh argued. "As his heir, as his *son*, you have influence, too. Can't you at least *try* to convince him that the law needs to change? How much deeper will the fractures across the kingdom be by the time you're king? It might be too late to heal them."

Rian threw his brother a look. "You've been trying to convince him for as long as I can remember, Ben. How successful has that been?"

It was Bentleigh's turn to sigh. "I still hold to it that you have more influence," he insisted. "You're his heir, and these things mean something to him."

"If you say so," said Rian vaguely.

"You certainly always seem to be better informed than I ever was," said Bentleigh, with meaning. "So enough of this nonsense about having no more idea than I do what this is about. You must at least have a guess. Don't pretend it's not ominous that we've been summoned here of all places."

Rian glanced around at the long throne room. "It is ominous," he agreed. "But I don't think you have anything to worry about."

Bentleigh frowned, his words slightly anxious. "So you don't think it's about the betrothal ball? They're not going to change their minds, are they?"

"What?" Rian's eyes flew to his brother's, startled. "Of course not! That would be an offense no one would expect Listernia to swallow. Don't worry, Ben, your betrothal is secure now they've owned it publicly. I promise."

Bentleigh raised a suspicious eyebrow. "Promise is a big word." When Rian didn't respond, he pushed on. "So if I shouldn't be worried, does that mean you should be?"

Rian shrugged. "I can't see how worrying will help anything."

A frown once again creased Bentleigh's forehead. "What's in the wind, Ri? Why do I get the sense that you're not looking forward to our betrothal ball tonight?"

"Of course I am," said Rian quickly. "It will be great."

"Ri." Bentleigh threw him an unimpressed look.

Rian sighed, trying not to think about how much he was going to miss this when his brother had left Bant—having someone around who knew him well enough not to let him get away with polite lies.

"I'm delighted about the betrothal," he said honestly. "But the ball, less so."

"Why?" Bentleigh asked, frowning more deeply. "Is it because of whatever Father is about to drop on us?"

Rian laughed in spite of himself. "I'm telling the truth, Ben, I honestly don't know what he's about to *drop on us*, as you put it. I'm just guessing it's to do with, you know...my betrothal."

Bentleigh stared. "Your betrothal?"

"My lack of one," Rian hurried to clarify.

"Ah. I see." Bentleigh looked him over thoughtfully. "My marriage is your cue to hurry up, is it?"

"Something like that," acknowledged Rian.

"What's that got to do with the ball, though?" Bentleigh pressed. "Don't tell me they're going to force you to choose on the spot, out of the attendees or something?"

Rian's laugh was more genuine this time. "Hardly. They'd be too worried I'd marry a Listernian, like you."

Bentleigh chuckled. "True. Plus," he added, "I somehow doubt they actually intend to let you choose."

Rian grunted in acknowledgment. "Of course they're not going to let me choose."

"The law is on your side this time," Ben reminded him. "You have the right to choose, same as I had."

Rian didn't respond. He hadn't told his brother about his promise to their parents not to invoke that right in exchange for them dropping their opposition to Bentleigh's chosen bride. And he didn't intend ever to do so.

After all, it hadn't been a difficult promise to make. He knew that, somewhat ironically, given Bentleigh and Azalea had been betrothed since childhood, Bentleigh was particularly fierce about the issue of choosing one's own bride. But Rian had never been overly distressed by the idea of his parents making the choice. His situation was different from Ben's. As the future ruler, he couldn't reasonably expect to just follow his heart, without thought for wider consequences. He'd never imagined being able to choose his own wife, and he knew from his parents' example that a marriage didn't need to be a love match to be adequately harmonious and effective.

Rian had made it to the age of twenty-three without his heart getting entangled. Perhaps he was well-suited to a more political marriage.

So why did his mind fly instantly to the pale-haired girl from the market? Bentleigh was still silent, letting Rian pursue his own thoughts in peace, and for a moment Rian was lost in the memory. He experienced once again the concern he'd felt at the realization that the girl—so young, so frail, and so undeniably pretty—was in that seedy market all alone. The concern that had turned to genuine fear when she'd confronted that angry man.

But she'd surprised him. Her behavior had belied her fragile appearance. Something about her demeanor had suggested not vulnerability, but strength held firmly at bay. It made no sense— the presence of the dog at her side might provide protection from opportunistic predators, but it didn't truly give her security against a determined attacker. Yet he didn't know how else to describe the sense he'd had from her. It was the same restraint that he exercised constantly, the restraint that kept him from being a tyrant who exerted his will on others every minute of every day simply because he could, because the crown on his head gave him the power.

That girl certainly had no crown to give her power. She had looked out of place in the rough market, but she was clearly no member of the nobility. She wouldn't be at the ball tonight, that much he could count on.

And he was back to the ball. His thoughts turned gloomy again as he remembered his mother's words.

We have a few candidates in mind, and most of them will be at Bentleigh's betrothal ball. We will begin our process then.

Rian let out a heavy sigh. He could almost feel the little

freedom he had slipping away from him. He wasn't at all surprised that his father wanted to give him a lecture on the matter prior to the ball. But he had no idea why Ben needed to be present.

At that moment, a door leading into an antechamber opened, and King Rhinehart entered the throne room at last.

"Rian, Bentleigh, good," he said, striding toward them.

Rian had barely greeted his father when Queen Eliza also sailed into the room, behind her husband. The brothers exchanged a look. Both parents together? Even more ominous. Rian's heart beat a little more quickly. Had they already chosen someone? Were they going to skip even the pretense of letting him consider his options? Surely they didn't want to announce anything tonight. It would steal attention from Ben and Azalea's betrothal.

"Bentleigh," said King Rhinehart solemnly, "we do not wish to distract from tonight's celebration, but something has arisen which I wish you to be aware of."

Rian realized he wasn't breathing, and took a deep pull of air.

"There has been an arrest today, which may create some reaction. It will likely be discussed amongst the attendees tonight."

Rian let out his breath, then felt immediately guilty for the sense of relief. An arrest was nothing to celebrate even in his opinion, and he knew Ben felt much more strongly. The incident was sure to dampen the festivities for his brother.

"An enchanter?" Rian asked, frowning slightly at his father.

"Not exactly," said King Rhinehart, without any obvious emotion. "The man who was arrested doesn't seem to be an enchanter. He was arrested for concealing his son's magic."

Rian's eyes flew to Ben's, then back to his parents. "How old is the boy?"

"Twelve," said the king.

"Twelve," repeated Rian, half to himself. "So he was born after the ban was in place."

"Precisely," said King Rhinehart crisply. "There has been ample time for his parents to comply with the law, but they have remained in Bansford, attempting to hide his situation. And there is, of course, reason to suppose that they knew even before his birth that he was at risk of the condition."

Rian nodded vaguely. He knew what his father meant. There had been no dragons in Bansford for a long time—they no longer so much as flew over the kingdom. So there was no way that enough magic had been shed on the land for any humans with the aptitude to imbibe it in recent years. Enchanters born in Bansford in the last fifteen years must have been born with the magic in their blood, which meant that if not a parent, most likely a grandparent had been an enchanter or enchantress.

"What will happen to the child?" Ben asked sharply.

"Nothing sinister," said Queen Eliza reprovingly. "He will be relocated outside Bansford, along with those of his family who wish to accompany him."

Rian heard Bentleigh make a small noise in the back of his throat at the word 'relocated', and he knew what his brother was thinking. He agreed that his parents should acknowledge the sanction for what it was, but they could never be brought to use the word exile.

"Of course he will not be harmed," said the king coldly. "He is under age. If he was eighteen it would be a different matter. But we do not punish children for something they cannot control."

"Yet you punish adults for something they can't control," muttered Ben. But Rian cut him off. It would help no one for an argument to erupt mere hours before Bentleigh's betrothal ball.

"And the father?" he asked, half of him not wanting to hear the answer.

"He has been placed in the dungeons," said King Rhinehart curtly. "He will spend a day in the stocks, then atone for his crime with labor."

"For how long?" demanded Ben hotly. "You're uprooting a child—a whole family—and separating them from their father in the same stroke? He was most likely their only breadwinner!"

"He attacked members of the royal guard, Bentleigh," said the king, a note of anger creeping into his voice. "Such conduct cannot go without consequence."

"Something tells me he was defending rather than attacking," Ben started, but again Rian cut him off.

"Enough, Ben," he said, exasperated. He'd never get the full story out of his father if Bentleigh kept drawing the king into argument instead. "Why do you expect the matter to be so talked of tonight, Father? Just because the arrest involves a child this time?"

The king's gaze moved to his oldest son, the tiniest measure of approval visible in response to the shrewd question.

"No, it is because of the identity of the individuals in question. They were trusted retainers of one of our noble families. The family themselves are being investigated, to discover if they were aware of—perhaps even played a part in—the deception."

Rian stilled, alarm coursing through him. A nobleman's household implicated in an incident of magic? His father wasn't wrong that the matter was going to be the subject of considerable gossip.

"How was the boy discovered?" he asked slowly. He had been expecting his father to say the boy had been younger, less able to control his actions. But if the child had hid his ability for twelve years, what had caused him to be unmasked now?

"Dreyton received information that there was an enchanter hidden in the household," said the king, a little too casually.

Rian frowned at the mention of the city's chief guard, who personally oversaw the enforcement of the ban on magic. "Someone within the household reported it?" he pressed.

The king's gaze was cold. "That cannot be confirmed, as the report was anonymous."

Rian's frown grew. "The same as the last half dozen arrests," he said. "Is it the same person each time? And if so, how do they identify these hidden enchanters who've gone unnoticed for so long? Are they sneaking around looking for signs of magic?"

"Who knows?" said the king, his tone discouraging further discussion. "If that is the case, the person is doing our kingdom a great service. I have been appalled by the number of magic-users still hiding within our borders. The recent spate of arrests has shown me that we need to increase our vigilance."

Bentleigh's brow was stormy well before the end of this exchange, but at a speaking look from Rian, he held his peace. Rian could only be glad. The king dismissed his sons, and Ben wasted no time in taking his leave of Rian as well.

"I'm going to go warn Zayla," he said shortly. "She's not going to like it, and she'll need to let out her first reaction before the ball, while no one else is around."

He strode off down the corridor, his steps agitated. Rian moved more slowly toward his own suite, ready to change his clothes for the evening's festivities. He was troubled by what he heard, but he felt none of the urgency that sent Bentleigh scurrying to warn his betrothed. The problems were nothing new. He did feel uneasy, however, about this supposed anonymous source of the information leading to all the recent arrests. Rian had the feeling that his father knew more about it than he was willing to say, and that was never a comfortable position.

CHAPTER FOUR

Penny

The sun had just set by the time Penny reached the city gate. The guards chuckled at the peculiar picture she presented, perched on top of a rough cart in an elegant gown with a dog curled beside her. Penny ignored them, directing her vehicle straight up the cobbled high street, toward the castle she had always so carefully avoided.

It wasn't hard to find the tradesmen's entrance. A steady stream of fancy carriages were moving along the wide semi-circle of road that went past the castle's front door. Well-dressed nobles were alighting, joining the throng of brightly clad figures passing through the castle's wide open doors.

But another, smaller convoy trundled slowly past a humbler entrance, these vehicles loaded with goods rather than passengers. Penny joined the trail, her mood darkening at the sound of the music that drifted through the castle's doors. This was a night for mourning, not celebration.

It seemed to take an age for her cart to reach the front of the line. Flushing with embarrassment, Penny explained to the incredulous steward that she had no one to help unload the goods. With a scandalized look at her out of place attire, the steward sent a servant scurrying back into the castle, presumably to fetch some able bodied assistants. He then directed her to pull her cart to one side of the small side courtyard, to allow the rest of the vehicles to continue past.

The gala had clearly begun, so Penny could only assume that her delivery was overflow, in case the wine already being served ran out before the end of the night. She was therefore unsurprised to be kept waiting for some time before assistance was available. Shivering slightly, she wrapped her cloak around her shoulders, half-regretting her pointless act of defiance in wearing the lovely gown. It wasn't suited for sitting in an open cart.

When someone finally came to unload the barrels, Penny descended from the cart, leaving Al to threaten off anyone who might be tempted by the unmanned equipage. Still shivering a little, she approached the servants now hefting barrels onto their muscled shoulders. It felt ridiculous, watching idly while the men heaved the heavy load inside. If she had free rein, she could shift all the barrels into the castle in a fraction of the time, without breaking a sweat. Without even lifting a finger.

But she didn't have free rein. Swallowing her frustration, she set her sight on the nearest servant.

"Shall I...?"

"Bless you, lass, no," said the man, casting her a look of astonishment. "You shouldn't be out here all alone. Sure you're not at the wrong entrance?"

"Very sure, thank you," said Penny dryly. "I'm not a guest, I'm from the vintner's."

The steward glanced over, his attention caught. Penny saw him peer at the brand on the barrel bobbing past him on the shoulder of one of the servants, then his head whipped toward her.

"I know the one." He frowned, looking again at her attire.

"You don't look like a delivery hand. You're not...surely you're not the vintner's daughter?"

Penny hesitated, but there was no reason to conceal who she was. Eyes burning, she nodded.

The steward clucked his tongue. "I heard the business had fallen on hard times, but to send his own daughter to the city alone at this hour..."

A rush of heat passed over Penny, and she opened her mouth to defend her father. But the words wouldn't come. She couldn't bring herself to say that he hadn't been the one to send her. That he knew nothing of where she was. That he knew nothing of anything, because he was lying still and silent on the great bed in the room upstairs.

To her horror, she felt tears leak out of her eyes, rolling without permission down her cheeks. She tried to wipe them surreptitiously away, but both the steward and the servant who had addressed her were still staring at her, and there was no way they could miss her sudden distress.

The steward clucked his tongue again, and before she knew it, Penny was being bustled across the doorway into a building she'd sworn to herself never to enter. She heard Al's uneasy whine as she passed from his sight, but there was no resisting the gentle but inexorable pressure of the servant's ushering hand.

"You oughtn't to be out in the night by yourself," he frowned, "freezing to death in that thin bit of a gown."

"Really, I'm fine," gasped Penny, pulling herself together and wiping furiously at her cheeks. "You're very kind, but I don't wish to linger. I'll just take the payment and be off home again."

"All in good time, child," said the steward sternly. "I'll have someone fetched to see you home. Things are in a bit of a bustle at the moment, with the young prince's betrothal ball and all, but I'm sure someone can be spared. Meantime you go and sit with old Mrs. Lane. She's retired from the housekeeping staff now, so she won't be busy, but she'll be glad of your company while you wait, and will give you a hot cup of tea as well."

"Please," said Penny, a little desperately. "There's no need. I'll be perfectly safe driving home. I have my dog with me, and—"

"No arguments now," cut in the steward, "I don't have time for them."

That much was clearly true. Already Penny could see things falling apart behind the steward, now that he was no longer directing operations at the delivery entrance. He shot out some directions that evidently seemed clear to him, but left her no wiser as to how to find this Mrs. Lane. Her best clue was his vague wave as he sent her off down the corridor.

Penny walked in the direction indicated, hoping someone would appear along the way to give her better instructions. She didn't want to sit with a stranger before being allowed to drive home, but at the same time, she was touched. She hadn't expected such kindness from anyone in the castle.

In spite of her various overwhelming emotions, she couldn't help looking around her with great interest. Her fear at being inside the den of the magic-hating royals was momentarily eclipsed by her inevitable curiosity at seeing the inside of the castle.

It was a hive of activity. People bustled past, everyone too busy to spare her more than a second glance. But just as she rounded the corner, wondering anxiously which way to go from there, pattering feet approached from the direction she'd just come.

"If you please," said a voice breathlessly, and she turned to see a boy who looked no more than eleven or twelve, ducking his head in a respectful salute. "You're going the wrong way."

"Am I?" she said, grimacing apologetically. "I'm afraid I'm a little lost."

He nodded. "I'll help you," he said, with an eagerness that she couldn't help but find endearing. He must have witnessed her interaction with the steward, and taken pity on her obvious confusion. "This way."

She had followed him down several corridors before it occurred to her to wonder, uneasily, whether some mistake had been made. As bewildered as she'd been by the steward's directions, she'd definitely gotten the impression that the proposed sanctuary wasn't far. The servant boy seemed to be leading her to the other side of the castle.

"Here you go," he said brightly, pulling up in front of a door. The sounds of merriment had increased as they crossed the castle, so the ballroom must be nearby. But the door indicated was small and plain, and Penny was reassured. It looked like it could belong to a retired servant of high enough standing within the castle to be given her own rooms.

"Shortcut," the boy added, with a cheeky wink. And with one last nod of encouragement, he took off at a trot, disappearing back to whatever task she'd interrupted. Penny blinked after him. That had been a shortcut? She hated to think how long it would've taken to get there by the longer route.

She gazed at the door, wondering if she should just go back to her cart, and try to slip away unnoticed. But she doubted she'd be able to find her way back alone, and she wasn't altogether averse to postponing returning to her unfeeling stepmother. She raised her fist and knocked, but there was no answer. After a moment, she pushed on the door, and it swung open. The room beyond was small and, from what she could see, empty. There were only a few low candles burning.

"Hello?" she called quietly. "Mrs. Lane?"

There was no answer, and Penny stepped into the room. It didn't seem like a retired servant's quarters. It didn't seem like a living space at all. She was just thinking that the boy must have been confused, when a footman swept into the room through another door, and stopped short at sight of her.

"Forgive me," he said, with a bow, "but you shouldn't be in here."

"I'm sorry," Penny gasped. "I—"

"Allow me to assist you," he said courteously, as he ushered her toward a third door. "Right this way."

More bewildered than ever, Penny allowed herself to be chivvied through the doorway, realizing a moment too late that the sudden blaze of light and sound could mean only one thing.

Sure enough, the room into which she had so unceremoniously emerged was, without doubt, the ballroom. The boy hadn't heard her conversation with the steward at all. He must have mistaken her for a guest, bless his heart, and thought she had wandered into the servants' wing by mistake. And in the low light of what she now realized was an anteroom, the footman had repeated the mistake. He must have assumed that she'd wandered in there from the ballroom, not from the corridor beyond.

For a moment, Penny was unable to move, frozen to the spot in horror. Not only was she in the heart of the enemy's domain, but she had—most humiliatingly—weaseled her way into a ball for which she had no invitation, and for which she was woefully underdressed. Only an eleven year old serving boy could mistake her new dress for a ball gown.

But once the first thrill of shock passed, Penny couldn't help looking around her in fascination. Her saving grace was that the anteroom was not a main entrance to the ballroom, and she hadn't emerged into the center of the action. She found herself standing behind a row of pillars that ran along one long wall. Another row mirrored them on the other side of the ballroom, although that row bordered a wall of windows and glass doors rather than doors into the rest of the castle.

From her sheltered position, Penny observed the revelers. The betrothal ball was in full swing, and the space seemed filled with swirling skirts in every color imaginable. The flash of wistfulness surprised her—she'd been honest when she said she had no desire to attend the ball. Yet she couldn't help but be mesmerized by the movement of the dance, and to imagine the release of allowing herself to be swept along into it. She tried to remember the dancing lessons her father had paid for, back before his second marriage. But it was years ago, now. She wouldn't be confident in her steps anymore.

"And what are you doing, hiding back here?"

The jovial voice made Penny jump in sudden fear, but no one was in sight. The speaker, whoever she was, must be a couple pillars down, and she didn't seem to be speaking to Penny.

"It's not my betrothal ball, Your Highness, so I can get away with melting into the background."

Understanding washed over Penny, and she stiffened at the realization of who she was eavesdropping on. The female voice must belong to Princess Azalea of Listernia, the one about to marry Bansford's younger prince. But who was she speaking to? Whose was the serious voice, that still somehow managed to convey a touch of humor?

"No 'Your Highnesses' between future family, please," said the princess, sounding pained. "And you forget that you're speaking to a fellow heir to a throne. I highly doubt that any crown prince has ever had the luxury of melting into the background."

"Too true," said the man heavily, although still with that unexpected hidden laugh in his voice.

Penny stilled, fear and shock washing over her. Unable to help herself, she shifted slightly, so that the tawny head of Crown Prince Rian came into view. He was two pillars away from

Penny, and his back was mercifully turned to her. She couldn't see the princess at all.

His voice didn't match the impression she'd formed of him when she saw him in the markets. He sounded much less stiff than he looked, but of course she was hearing him among his equals, not his subjugated populace.

The thought sent a fresh wave of bitterness over her. What business did the prince have to be cheerful, when his family had exiled people like her for daring to possess a skill they didn't have? How dare he sound endearingly humorous as he bantered with his brother's Listernian bride, while his own people were denied the freedoms her kingdom extended without question?

The overheard conversation went on, but Penny couldn't take it in anymore. The temporary distraction of her surroundings could no longer keep her thoughts from her pain. Her fascination was quickly souring into something else. She looked with new eyes at the revelry around her, and a bitterness, more fierce than anything she'd ever felt, rose within her. It was corrosive, and it seemed to burn her from the inside out.

Figures swirled before her eyes, and coquettish laughter rang across the crowded space as privileged maidens flirted with the lords they hoped to win. One girl flashed past, quite close to Penny's hiding place, her jewelry blinking in the light of the hundreds of candles. Her attire would yield enough income to buy a vineyard. Following the dancer's progress, Penny's eyes fell on a long table positively groaning under the weight of a feast the likes of which Penny had never seen, not even at the height of her father's success.

She saw the younger prince, Prince Bentleigh, cross the room, two goblets in his hand, toward the place where his betrothed stood speaking with his brother. He didn't see Penny, of course. What was she to a prince? Nothing more than a shadow, a nameless face in a sea of subjects, whose job was simply to follow the rules.

The bitterness clawed at Penny's insides, demanding release. She tried to hold it in, to deny it, but it only made it worse. Just like her magic, she thought bitterly, that had only ever grown stronger and more dangerous the more she had tried to contain it.

Magic that made her a criminal, merely for existing. Magic that had taken her mother from her. Magic that made her hide herself from her father, never able to truly let him in, even to the hour of his death.

Her resentment had reached a crescendo now, and she felt an anger so powerful it was almost hatred. The intensity of the feeling scared her. She didn't recognize the angry, bitter woman who seemed to be inhabiting her mind. But still, she couldn't master the emotions.

She realized it wasn't logical, realized the trio of royals before her knew nothing of the bereavement she'd suffered that very day. But it didn't lessen her resentment. She couldn't forgive them all for dancing, gorging themselves on fancy food, drinking her family's wine by the barrel while her father lay dead on his bed back at the manor.

Even worse, it was because of them that she was alone, orphaned now. Her mother had died because of their selfish, evil decree. And in that moment Penny was convinced that had her mother survived, her father never would have weakened, never would have fallen ill. They had taken everything from her, and there they stood, feasting and laughing like the world was theirs.

It happened almost without her conscious will. She half raised a hand—that was all. One simple movement was enough to lift an enormous decorative urn—large enough that she could comfortably have hidden inside it—several inches into the air.

And she knew that one more tiny gesture would send it hurtling, faster than anything she could throw with her hand, so that it slammed straight into the two princes and the princess.

In that moment Penny hardly cared what would happen to her next. She only knew that if she didn't release some of the tension building inside her, she would explode. The younger prince gave a delighted laugh in response to something his princess said, and Penny's anger rose inside her, unreasoning and destructive.

She drew her hand back, ready to thrust it forward, and was almost thrown off balance when someone seized it firmly.

"Easy now, child."

The voice was unexpectedly gentle. Penny whipped around, staring wildly into the eyes of a tall woman with beautiful, delicately formed features. Her dark hair was piled elegantly on top of her head, and she was dressed with all the opulence of a noblewoman.

"Let—let go," Penny stammered, her heart thundering in her ears.

The woman didn't obey. Her eyes had slid past Penny's face, and following her gaze, Penny saw with horror that the urn was still floating improbably, suspended inches above the ground. The moment of madness had passed. Penny was already regretting her angry impulse, and not just because of her terror over being caught. Hardly daring to breathe, she flicked her free hand gently, and the urn lowered itself slowly to the floor. In spite of her best efforts, it rattled slightly as it landed. To Penny's dismay, the tawny head of Prince Rian turned sharply at the sound. His profile was revealed for a moment as he gazed suspiciously at the now-still urn.

Strong cheekbones, straight nose, surprisingly heavy brows for his pale coloring. A well-formed face, in spite of the thoughtful frown now marring it. Even in the midst of everything going on, Penny had to admit, to her own irritation, that Olivia and Sophia were right. The crown prince *was* very handsome, little as he deserved to be.

Then he started to turn further, perhaps looking for the source of the noise. Before she even had time to react, Penny felt herself whisked fully behind the nearest pillar by the woman who still grasped her hand.

"Quiet, now," said the stranger.

She held Penny firmly for a prolonged moment, then peeked back around the pillar. Relaxing, she released Penny and stepped back. Penny stumbled away herself, but her back connected with the pillar, and she made no attempt to run. All she seemed capable of was to stare at her captor with wide eyes while her breath came in heaving pants.

"That was quite a trick," the woman said calmly, her gaze flicking back to the urn. "But it won't do anyone any good to throw vases at royalty, you know."

"I—I didn't—I wasn't," Penny stammered incoherently, and the woman came to her rescue.

"In my experience," she said, her voice again surprising Penny with its gentleness, "when people want to hurt others, it's because they have been hurt themselves."

Penny felt her eyes filling once again with those inconvenient tears. "I don't want to hurt anyone," she whispered. "Not really."

The woman regarded her silently for a moment. "What's your name, child?" she asked. When Penny didn't answer, she smiled. "Will it help if I go first? I am Lady Amaranthe."

Penny swallowed. "My name is Penelope," she said.

"Well then, Penelope, how do you come to be here?" Lady Amaranthe's eyes moved down Penny's form, then back up. "I think you are not a guest at tonight's ball, am I right?"

Penny nodded miserably. "That's right, My Lady. I was

making a delivery, and I was led here by accident. I never planned to..." She trailed off.

Lady Amaranthe raised an eyebrow. "Please, call me Amaranthe. Let's have no titles between kin."

"Kin?" Startled, Penny stared into Lady Amaranthe's eyes. "What do you mean?"

The older woman raised an eyebrow. "Surely you can tell that we are of a kind? How do you think I noticed you, hidden all the way across the room? My dear, your power was so flagrant, it pulled me like a moth to flame." She frowned at Penny's astonishment. "Can you really not sense it?"

Penny's thoughts were swirling erratically, but she tried to focus her senses on the woman before her. Her eyes glazed over, and she realized all at once that she *could* feel something, something intangible but powerful, weaving through the air between them. It was familiar, although she couldn't remember the last time she'd felt it. Not since...

"You feel like my mother," she whispered, before she could stop herself.

Lady Amaranthe laughed, the sound light and musical, and Penny felt her spirits lift slightly, in spite of everything.

"I'm sorry," she said quickly. "I didn't mean to imply that you're old enough to be my mother, just that..." She trailed off. Lady Amaranthe, whom she judged was fifteen years older than her at the most, didn't look offended.

"So it's your mother who has magic, then?" she asked.

Both caution and sorrow made Penny drop her gaze to the polished floor beneath her feet, returning an evasive answer. "My mother died a long time ago."

Lady Amaranthe's expression softened. "I'm sorry," she said, and she sounded sincere. She looked thoughtfully around the room. "I think you'd better leave now, Penelope, as unobtrusively as possible. But I would like to speak further. Where do you live?"

Penny hesitated, and Lady Amaranthe smiled indulgently at her wary expression.

"Don't look so worried. I'm not going to expose you. You have no more to fear from me than I have from you. Only another enchantress could sense your magic, you know."

Penny was so astonished by the noblewoman's casual use of the forbidden title, that she blurted out her directions without thinking about it.

"I'll find you," Lady Amaranthe said, the words a promise. "Now you'd best go."

Still dazed, Penny nodded, taking a step toward the ante-room. But at that moment, the voice of the nearby princess, raised with emotion, caught her ears.

"Well, I think it's outrageous. Arresting a child simply for being born with magic?"

Lady Amaranthe and Penny both froze. Penny felt a rush of horror. There had been another magic-related arrest? She hardly remembered hearing of any in her childhood, and now they seemed to happen every other week. And had the princess said this one was a child? She felt her hand curl into a fist.

Prince Rian's voice, although quieter than the princess's, was still audible now that the two listeners had stopped their own conversation.

"The child wasn't actually arrested, you realize. It's his father who's being punished."

"You don't think forcing the poor boy out of his home, away from everything he knows, is a punishment?" the princess objected dryly. Penny's heart warmed to her. She'd known that other kingdoms weren't so harsh on magic, but she hadn't expected any royal to champion the enchanters' cause.

"I didn't say that," said Prince Rian, more quietly still. "Just that the unfortunate child isn't the one in the dungeons."

"He's only unfortunate because of how he's being treated," said Princess Azalea, still sounding fierce. "Being born with magic isn't a misfortune."

"Zayla, Rian isn't the enemy." The low voice of Prince Bentleigh broke in. "He knows half your family has magic. It wasn't his decision to punish that boy's father any more than it was his decision to ban magic."

"Forget the ball," the princess muttered, clearly not listening to her betrothed. "We should sneak that poor man out of the dungeons while everyone's distracted. Then he can flee with his family." Her voice brightened. "They can come and live in Listernia."

Penny could hear the exasperation in Prince Bentleigh's voice as he responded. "Zayla, you know I would do anything for you and all that, but I would prefer to leave Bansford because of our marriage, not because I was thrown from the kingdom for crimes against the crown."

Penny could tell Princess Azalea was grinning as easily as if she could see her. "I'm surprised I'm even allowed in, to be honest, with so much magic in my history."

"Well, we can send you to the dungeons if you'd prefer," said her betrothed amicably. "I might finally win my parents' favor."

Prince Rian reentered the conversation, his head turning toward his brother so that Penny again saw his profile. "More likely you'd be in there with her," he said, that ill-fitting laugh lurking once again in his serious voice. "I know your dark secret. Azalea told me you went to the dragons for help to break her curse, and if our parents ever—"

The rest of his speech was lost in the sharp gasp that seemed to slip out of Lady Amaranthe's mouth before she could stop herself.

Prince Rian, who evidently had inconveniently good hearing, whipped his head around, stepping to one side to get a clear view around the pillar. His eyes latched on Lady Amaranthe, and Penny saw the flash of alarm that crossed his face at the proximity of the eavesdroppers. But then he schooled his expression to the same controlled and serious front he'd presented in the market.

He moved away from his brother and the princess, but he'd only taken one step toward them when his gaze slid to Penny, apparently noticing her presence for the first time. He froze midstep, his eyes widening in what she could have sworn was recognition. But the idea that he remembered her from their fleeting encounter at the market seemed so absurd that Penny thought she must be mistaken.

"Go, Penelope." Lady Amaranthe's sharp whisper brought Penny out of her stupor. With one last glance at the prince, who was still staring at her in open shock, she turned and stumbled toward the door to the anteroom.

"Wait!"

She heard him hail her, but she didn't pause. Hastening through the door, she ran across the dim room beyond and hurtled out into the corridor. Pushing her way through the astonished servants, she raced in what she hoped was the right direction.

By some miracle, she reached the servants' wing without getting lost. Hurtling without explanation past the steward, who stared at her in amazement, she ran to her cart. Al barked a relieved greeting as she clambered up into it. Forgetting all about the payment for the wine, she turned the horse's head toward home, thinking of nothing but putting distance between herself and those clear brown eyes.

CHAPTER FIVE

Rian

Momentarily losing track of his purpose, Rian started after the girl. He took two steps before he realized he was running, and pulled himself up short. Running in a ballroom was one of the many things princes didn't do. The girl had reached a side door by now, and was slipping through it.

"Wait!" Rian called, without thinking. But she was already through the door. He had his hand on the handle when Lady Amaranthe spoke.

"Your Highness?"

Recalled to his surroundings, and his purpose in approaching the pair, Rian turned reluctantly around. Lady Amaranthe was watching him with a politely furrowed brow. He couldn't blame her for wondering what he was doing, chasing through the castle after some...but what was the girl? She wasn't a castle servant, surely. She was dressed more expensively than she had been in the market, but not finely enough to be attending a ball.

"Lady Amaranthe," he said, hearing the stiffness in his voice, and inclining his head politely in an attempt to soften it. "Good evening."

She sank into a bow, her eyes traveling quickly back up to his. "Good evening, Your Highness. I trust you are well?"

Rian paused, searching the noblewoman's face. He'd never had much to do with her family, but he knew she was the only daughter of a minor lord, and that she was perhaps ten years older than him. He had no idea whether to be direct, or to dance around the issue. After only a moment's hesitation, he made up his mind. He'd never had much interest in dancing—behold him hiding behind a row of pillars during a betrothal ball.

"I think perhaps you overheard something I said to my brother just now, My Lady," he said curtly.

She inclined her head graciously, saying nothing.

"I spoke in jest, you understand," he said, keeping his face as unexpressive as he could. "I would not wish you to have the impression that my brother has ever done anything to—"

"Mine is not a wagging tongue, I believe, Your Highness," said Lady Amaranthe calmly. Her face gave nothing away, but Rian realized he had little choice but to accept her assurance, such as it was.

He bowed his head in acknowledgment.

"Who was that girl?" he asked, his eyes straying toward the door.

"We only met tonight," said Lady Amaranthe. "She was in the ballroom by accident, it seems."

Rian frowned, trying to imagine what accident could have brought the very girl he'd been thinking about every day of the last week to the corner of the ballroom where he loitered, dodging the many women trying to catch his eye.

"I need to speak to her," he pressed, when Lady Amaranthe said no more. "She also deserves an explanation of what she heard." Still Lady Amaranthe was silent. "Do you know where I can find her?" Rian said, with a touch of impatience.

The uncertain expression on the noblewoman's face made Rian's heart leap. She knew something more of the girl, he was sure of it.

"Tell me," he said, the words coming out more of a command than he'd intended.

"She told me where she lives," admitted Lady Amaranthe. "But I don't wish to betray her confidence."

"I mean her no harm," Rian said hurriedly. "I swear it."

She considered him for a silent moment, then nodded slowly. "She is the daughter of a local vintner, apparently." Concisely, she described the location of the girl's home.

An unsettling tangle of excitement and nerves roiled inside Rian at the idea of going looking for her. He knew he should be anxious—his careless words could cause real trouble for Ben if heard by the wrong ears. But he couldn't help feeling pleased with himself for unintentionally providing an excuse to approach the girl, when he hadn't expected ever to have an opportunity to find out who she was.

"And her name?" he asked suddenly, as Lady Amaranthe started to move away. "Did you get her name?"

She gave him a smile that he couldn't quite read. "Forgive me, Your Highness, but I think that must be up to the young lady."

"Lady?" Rian repeated, a tiny flash of hope that was illogical in more ways than one shooting through him.

Lady Amaranthe looked slightly startled at his tone. "The young woman, is all I meant," she said carefully.

Rian nodded, already regretting his unguarded question. "Of course. Thank you for your assistance, My Lady."

She swept into a stately curtsy and melted back into the

crowd. Rian turned to find Ben and Azalea a few steps behind him, both staring at him with unabashed astonishment.

"What was all that about?" Ben demanded, just as Azalea also spoke.

"Do you think either of them will make trouble for Ben?"

Rian directed his gaze to Azalea, whose question was easier to answer. "I don't think so."

"Ri?" Ben's insistent tone brought Rian's gaze reluctantly to him. "Who was that girl?"

Rian shrugged helplessly. "No idea." He saw his brother's skepticism and added, "It's true! I recognized her, because I saw her the other day in the market, but I didn't speak to her then, and I didn't speak to her tonight." Well, unless you counted shouting stupidly after her to wait, he added in his head. "Lady Amaranthe said she's the daughter of a local vintner. I'll speak to her, make sure she doesn't intend any trouble."

Bentleigh raised an eyebrow at him.

"What?" Rian asked, nettled.

"She's very pretty," said Ben, much too casually.

Rian shrugged one shoulder. "I suppose so." Goaded by the look on his brother's face, he added, "You're bold, saying such things in front of your betrothed."

"No, I agree," said Azalea, a wicked glint in her eye. "She *is* very pretty."

"Don't be ridiculous," said Rian, abandoning pretense and letting his impatience show. "I don't even know her name." His eyes met Bentleigh's, their expression reproachful. "All I know is that she's the daughter of a local vintner."

Ben's smirk slid away, his own expression becoming serious. He gave Rian an apologetic nod, and Rian knew he'd understood. Bentleigh knew perfectly well that it was neither helpful nor kind to tease Rian about a pretty common girl. No matter how much her arresting green eyes might haunt him with their secrets.

The rest of the ball passed in a blur of impatience. Rian could think of nothing but the girl, and what in the kingdom he was going to say to her. He remembered how her eyes had seemed to flash fire at him in the marketplace, as if she was angry about some previous encounter. But he was certain that had been the first time they'd seen each other. He would have remembered her if they'd met before. And tonight...well, the look on her face when she'd caught sight of him had been even worse.

Fear. He hated the very thought that his presence was enough to create fear in the people of his kingdom. Surely he'd never done anything to warrant such a reaction. Even his father, although inflexible on the issue of magic, was generally a fair ruler. But he was sure he hadn't misread her look. And the idea that this girl—he really must discover her name—was afraid of him, somehow made him feel dirty.

She hadn't shown even a hint of fear when confronting that repulsive man in the market, the one who'd been beating the mongrel, and had clearly been only too ready to turn on his young challenger. But when she locked eyes with Rian, she was so frightened she ran.

To add to his depression, Rian could find nothing to appeal in any of the candidates his mother presented to him throughout the evening. Of course, she didn't say anything about marriage. But he understood perfectly the import of her recommending to him which young ladies he should ask to dance.

Obediently, but without the tiniest shred of enthusiasm, Rian danced with each of them. They were all attractive enough, dressed in the height of fashion, and twinkling with jewels. But there was little to distinguish one from the next. The faces were different, the manner was the same. They all smiled and nodded, agreeing with his every inane utterance, and confining their conversation to admiring compliments to the royal family, the castle, the kingdom itself. Any one of them would make the kind of queen his parents wanted for him—one who wouldn't challenge, wouldn't question.

One whose eyes would never flash fire at a prince, or make a scene in a market because a stray dog was being bullied.

"Shocking about that child with the hidden magic, wasn't it? Terrible business."

Rian's attention flicked to his current partner, his eyebrows lifting in slight surprise. The girl seemed to be clinging to his arm rather more possessively than the dance required, but her eyes were serious enough as they met his.

"You're inclined to think the response was too harsh?" he asked, taking in her grave expression.

Her eyes widened, and she sounded horrified. "Of course not, Your Highness! I meant the deception was terrible, breaking the law in secret for all those years."

"Ah." Rian nodded, hiding his disappointment. It had been too much to hope for a real conversation.

The mention of magic sent his thoughts back to his unguarded words before, and a ripple of unease went through him. He'd been unforgivably careless to banter like that with Bentleigh when others could hear. Who knew what the consequences might be of the girl spreading that tale?

At the end of the dance, Rian thanked his partner politely, then strode across the room to his brother, before the queen could thrust another woman across his path. As soon as he could get away with doing so, he excused himself from the ball altogether.

The next day, he was up with the sun. He was impatient to go looking for the girl, not just out of curiosity, but to right his mistake. But he knew he couldn't knock on the vintner's door at the crack of dawn. He spent an hour sparring in the castle's training yard, but he was so distracted by his thoughts that he gave a poor account of himself.

"Not up to your usual formidable form, Your Highness," said his opponent cheerfully. The knight was an easy-going man with whom Rian often sparred. They were usually fairly well-matched, but the other man had bested him quickly on the day.

"I'm not, am I?" smiled Rian, flexing a bruised arm. He appreciated about this knight that he didn't go easy on the prince simply because of his status. "Clearly I need more practice."

"Well, you know where to find me," the knight said amicably.

Nodding, Rian took a towel offered him by a helpful squire, and wiped the sweat from his face. He turned to put his shirt back on, and heard a muffled giggle. He was too used to the inevitable conspicuousness of his position to give any sign that he'd heard, but he hastened to clothe himself.

He was unsurprised to find a small knot of girls hovering near the entrance to the training yard, recognizable as the daughters of some of his father's court. Rian felt aggrieved. The place was supposed to be a sanctuary. It was unusual for there to be spectators of any kind, especially not giggling girls.

None of that showed on his face, of course, as he nodded calmly in response to their unnecessarily deep curtsies.

"Well fought, Your Highness," said one of them breathlessly, setting off another stifled giggle from one of her companions.

Rian responded with a tight smile, not missing the way the girl's eyes flicked to his now-covered chest. He was going to have to get up even earlier to spar in future. He didn't think he could handle an ogling audience every time he trained.

The incident was the first of several throughout the course of the morning. After the third time of almost stumbling into a small group of eager-faced girls who seemed to have been tailing him, Rian was forced to accept the unpleasant truth. With a sinking heart, he realized that his parents' intention to marry him off as soon as Ben was married had somehow leaked out. Perhaps it would be best to ask them to choose someone straight away, to spare him months of being pursued by every eligible girl in the kingdom.

And yet, somehow he couldn't bring himself to do that. For over twenty years, the knowledge that he would be tied to a wife of his parents' choosing had caused him little concern. Now, when it was about to be a reality, it had suddenly become enormously troubling.

He would once have been able to seek refuge with his brother to avoid being cornered by admirers, but Bentleigh was nowhere to be found. Presumably he was preparing for his departure to Listernia in a few short hours. He'd barely been to the neighboring kingdom since his betrothal was formalized, and he was apparently needed for wedding preparations. It was probably for the best, Rian thought gloomily. He'd better get in the habit of dealing with his problems without his brother's assistance.

In his efforts to evade a pair of determined looking ladies, Rian found himself in the corridor leading to the kitchens. It had been a long time since he'd been in that part of the castle. He couldn't help thinking nostalgically of the days when he and Ben had snuck down there to wheedle sweets from the cook.

Thoughts of his childhood somehow made his steps heavier as he made his way out of the servants' wing. He'd only been four when his parents made the fateful trip to Listernia with a two-year-old Bentleigh. He'd been left in Bant, so he hadn't experienced the magic cast by the Listernian king's embittered enchanter cousin. But he remembered his parents' return. To this day, he didn't think he'd seen his father so angry. But he also remembered another emotion. He'd taken note of it, young as he was, because it was so unusual for his father to show fear.

Rian knew that Bentleigh thought their parents had simply been offended at being subjected to a magical attack, in spite of their exalted position. But Rian was sure there was more to it than that. And little as he might agree with his parents' response, he recognized that it wasn't motivated by selfishness. If they were afraid, it was for their kingdom as much as for themselves. And given Listernia's experience, the fear wasn't without foundation. On one thing Rian was united with his parents—he didn't want to see Bansford come under such a kingdom-wide attack.

But still, there was no denying that his life had been simpler, his childhood more relaxed, before the ban. Lost in his thoughts, Rian didn't spare a glance for the passing steward, until the man's words caught him up short.

"...and remind me to send someone to the vintner's residence. His daughter took off last night without receiving the payment, and I—"

"Did you say the vintner's daughter?" Rian interrupted, coming to an abrupt halt in the middle of the corridor.

The steward's eyes widened as he caught sight of the prince, far from his usual domain. He dropped into a smooth bow.

"Your Highness," he said quickly. "I beg your pardon. I didn't perceive you there. How can I assist you?"

"I don't need anything," said Rian. "I just thought I heard you mention the vintner's residence."

"That's right, Your Highness," said the steward, blinking. "There was a delivery of wine last night for which payment wasn't received. I intend to send someone to—"

"I can take the payment," said Rian abruptly. He saw that not only the steward, but the servant with whom he was talking, was now staring at him in astonishment.

"Y-you, Your Highness?" the steward asked blankly.

"I know the place," Rian said, attempting to speak casually. "And I have business out that way this morning."

"Well, that's very kind of you, Your Highness," said the steward, in the same bewildered voice. "But there's no need for you to trouble yourself with such details."

"I wish to compliment the vintner on the excellence of the wine," said Rian glibly.

The steward seemed to catch from Rian's tone that the decision was made, because he bowed again. "Someone will bring you the payment, and the relevant records, as soon as they have been prepared, Your Highness."

"Excellent," said Rian brightly.

He strode away, an extra bounce in his step. If nothing else, having a different excuse for finding the girl would make it less obvious how concerned he was about what she'd overheard. If she was inclined to make use of the information, it would be better if she didn't know how much power the overheard conversation had given her.

The hope that she might be more likely to receive him favorably if he didn't come empty-handed had nothing whatsoever to do with it, of course.

CHAPTER SIX

Penny

Penny didn't need to open her eyes to know where she was. The colors weren't just brighter here. The air smelled different—sharper, fresher. Even the sounds were clearer, as though she usually heard them through muffling fabric, but now her ears were unhindered. She had been to this place—if these visions really constituted being—many times in the four years since the dragon first approached her in sleep.

She opened her eyes anyway, of course, and was unsurprised to see the purple dragon standing before her.

"Greetings, Mighty Beast," she said cautiously, following the accepted mode of address for humans speaking to dragons.

The dragon tilted her head to one side, considering Penny. She was undoubtedly aware that in spite of her various efforts to engage with the human, this was the first time Penny had initiated conversation.

"Greetings, Enchantress," said the dragon calmly. Its orb-like eyes seemed to bore into her, watching for her reaction.

Penny dipped her head respectfully, meeting the creature's eyes once she straightened again. "My name is Penny, should you wish to use it."

The dragon rocked back on her haunches, regarding Penny still more curiously. "Not only do you speak, but you do not shy away from me when I call you what you are. Penny," she added, as if testing how the name sounded in her lilting voice. "My name is Dannsair, and you may use it if you choose."

Penny swallowed. "Is this real, then? Is this more than just a dream?"

The dragon inclined her head in a stately fashion. "It is indeed real. I am communicating with you through your sleep, when your mind is more malleable. But it is not a true dream."

"Why are you communicating with me?" Penny asked, a little desperately. "Why do you seek me out? And why now? It's been a year at least since my last dream, or vision, or whatever it is."

The dragon looked faintly amused. "Are you in such a hurry that you cannot wait for the answer to one question before posing two more? Our time is not so limited, Penny."

"Yours might not be," said Penny heavily. "But human time is limited."

The dragon's eyes narrowed in concentration, and she snaked her long neck down so that her reptilian head hovered less than a foot from Penny's face.

"What is the source of the grief in your words, Young Enchantress? Why does time feel so short to you?"

Penny's eyes prickled painfully, but she wasn't going to waste this dream time crying. "My father's time has run out," she said dully. "Just as my mother's did years ago."

"You have my sympathy," said the dragon gravely. "I too have lost my parents, and I understand the sorrow of your parting. Take comfort in the fact that you have some hope of rejoining them in time, whereas I will never be reunited with my sires, in any form of existence."

Penny blinked, trying to remember the little she knew of dragon lore. "You...you're immortal?" she asked slowly. "You can choose, can't you? Either to be immortal, or to have offspring?"

The dragon dipped her head again. "In crude terms, yes. And my choice has been made."

Penny looked frankly into the dragon's face. "I don't envy you," she said softly. And it was true. At the moment, the idea of her life continuing indefinitely, with the same fear, the same loneliness, the same restrictions, held no appeal to her.

"Nor do I envy you, Enchantress," smiled the dragon. "At least I had the choice, whereas you do not."

"True," said Penny.

A smile was growing on her face, in spite of herself. She knew the beast before her was fearsome and infinitely more powerful than she was. But she felt comfortable in its presence, for reasons she couldn't explain.

"Now, I shall answer your questions," Dannsair said placidly. "I communicate with you because I wish to. I seek you out because your magic calls to me across the distance between us. It is like a spring in an otherwise barren desert. Not the only spring, certainly, but rare enough to draw my attention. And as for why now...well, the concentration of power around you was strong tonight. It caught my interest."

Penny frowned, trying to remember what the dragon was talking about. Her other life—her real life, she supposed—seemed far away, almost meaningless, when she was in this place. Why would her magic have seemed particularly strong tonight?

Then her fingers tingled with remembered power, and it came rushing back. Covering her face with her hands, she groaned.

"I'm ashamed," she whispered. "I tried to use my power to hurt someone. I've never done that before." Her voice, still muffled, turned bitter. "It's exactly what the royals feared when they outlawed magic. It's because of people like me that there's a ban in place, and so many have suffered from it."

"That," said Dannsair calmly, "is demonstrably false. From what I know of the situation, your role in the ban on magic is thus far entirely nonexistent."

"Thus far?" Penny repeated, lowering her hands from her face to look apprehensively at the dragon. The words sounded ominous to her.

An odd rippling motion passed over Dannsair, from her neck all the way down her back, to the tip of her tail. It took Penny a moment to realize it was a shrug.

"Dragons cannot see the future any more than humans can," the beast said calmly. "But as one of only a few magic-users still to be found in Bansford, it does not seem outside the realm of possibility that you might play a role in the future of magic in the kingdom."

"Magic has no future in this kingdom," said Penny bitterly. "And I don't want to play a role. I don't want any part of it."

The dragon tilted her head to the side, and her tone was curious rather than admonitory. "Is that so? Even if you could influence the situation for the better?"

"Influence is something I don't have," said Penny dryly. "And I never will."

The dragon smiled, the expression a trifle indulgent. "Am I to understand that you *can* see the future, then? Do you have a magical power thus far unprecedented?"

"Of course not," said Penny. "But I don't need to see the future to know that."

Still smiling, the dragon made no response. "I am glad you have chosen to give me your name, Penny, after all these years. I trust we will speak again."

Penny opened her mouth to reply, but the image of the dragon had already disappeared. Penny seemed to be falling upward somehow, the bright colors replaced by thick gray fog.

.   .   .

With a small gasp, Penny awoke, her eyes landing on the familiar ceiling of her own room. Her heart was racing, but it was more with excitement than fear. She'd spoken to a dragon! A real dragon, even if Penny had only seen her in vision form.

She sat up, and the excitement instantly faded as all her real life problems came rushing in on her. Her father was gone, and as if that wasn't enough, she'd attracted the attention of a member of the royal family, in the most dangerous way possible.

She tried to shake off her fear at the memory of the recognition in Prince Rian's eyes. Surely he would dismiss her from his mind. And he hadn't seen her use her magic. Lady Amaranthe had saved her from herself. Along with the rush of gratitude for the noblewoman's intervention came a fresh surge of shame. However consumed she'd been by her grief and her anger, it didn't justify what she'd almost done. She'd been ready to attack not only the two Bansfordian princes, but the Listernian princess as well! Their subsequent conversation had shown that the princess and Prince Bentleigh were both sympathetic to the cause of the enchanters. Even Prince Rian had spoken of magic with surprising levity, teasing his brother about talking to dragons. It wasn't at all what she'd expected of any of them, and the challenge to her long-held perception made her uncomfortable.

Whether she really would have gone through with hurling that urn at them, she would never know. But she was still ashamed of how close she'd come.

Barely noticing what she was doing, Penny dressed and made her way down the stairs. She had overslept—the invariable result of her dragon dream, she had discovered over the years—and the sun had well and truly risen. She was too distracted by her dream, and the alarming events of the evening before, even to remember that she should be donning black.

When she entered the dining room, and saw Sapphira and her stepsisters already seated around the table, she realized her mistake. They were all dressed in somber hues, their expressions matching their attire.

"Completed your mourning already, have you, Penelope?" asked Sapphira, her voice as devoid of emotion as always.

Penny looked down at her own, pale green dress and flushed. "I forgot," she said. She saw her stepmother raise an eyebrow and hurried to clarify. "About the clothes, I mean. Not about...not about..."

"We knew what you meant," said Sophia, standing quickly, and coming over to Penny. "Sit down. You must be tired. When you took so long to come home last night, I was worried you'd run into trouble."

Penny felt vaguely surprised by the solicitude, but she sank gratefully into a chair. Olivia passed her some bread, and a small pat of butter. The breakfast seemed sparse compared to usual, but even Olivia wasn't complaining. Her eyes were on Penny, and for once they showed neither suspicion nor calculation.

"Sophia is right," said Sapphira, as Penny buttered her bread. "You were out late last night. I haven't yet seen the payment for the delivery. Did you leave it with Harry?"

Penny stared at her stepmother. The payment! She'd been so distracted by everything else, it hadn't even occurred to her until now.

"Penelope?" Sapphira pressed, a sharp note entering her voice. "The payment?"

Penny swallowed. "I'm sorry, Stepmother," she said. "I didn't receive the payment. I...I forgot."

Sapphira was silent for a moment, her face so expressionless that a tiny shiver ran over Penny. It wasn't natural, she thought desperately. The woman had watched her husband die the day before. Would it kill her to show a little emotion?

"You seem to be especially forgetful at present," Sapphira

said at last. "Do I need to remind you how much this household needs that payment?"

"No, of course not," said Penny quickly. "I'm sure they won't try to cheat us. The steward I dealt with seemed very honest, and he took notice of me. He'll remember me. I'll go back to the castle, and—"

"Why did he take notice of you?" Sapphira asked, her shrewd eyes on Penny's face.

Debating whether to answer, Penny hesitated. "To be honest, Stepmother," she said, "I believe it was because he was surprised to see a member of the household making the delivery, rather than a servant."

Sophia shifted uncomfortably in her seat, and Penny saw Olivia's eyes flick between her and Sapphira. The latter's silence was ominous.

"Naturally, I have no way of knowing what you said to the man to make him think you'd been ill used," said Sapphira at last. "But it seems you have suffered yet another lapse in memory, and have forgotten the respect due to your family."

Penny started to protest, but her stepmother cut her off. "I see that I cannot trust to your memory, Penelope, so you had best go into the kitchen now, and ask the cook to give you another lesson on cooking eggs."

"What?" Penny asked blankly, completely bewildered. She couldn't even pretend to follow the convoluted reasoning behind this order. "Why does forgetting the payment mean I need a reminder on how to cook eggs?"

"Because it seems we cannot be confident that your memory will serve you tomorrow," said Sapphira calmly.

Penny looked around helplessly at her stepsisters. Sophia uttered a faint sound of protest, but said nothing. To Penny's surprise, it was Olivia who spoke up.

"Mama, her father died yesterday. Don't you think—"

"I'm sure the cook will be delighted to teach *you* to prepare eggs, if that is your preference, Olivia," said Sapphira.

Olivia exchanged a glance with Sophia. They both looked conflicted, but neither spoke again. Penny looked from them to their mother, a crawling sensation moving up her arms.

"With the expense of a funeral on top of everything else," Sapphira said calmly, "we will have to release all but the most essential workers. The cook has been made aware that today is her last day with us."

Another moment passed before comprehension finally came. "You expect *me* to cook for the family?" Penny asked hollowly. "By myself? From tomorrow?"

"Have you not been regularly learning from our cook for several years?" asked Sapphira, as if it was the most obvious solution imaginable. "None of the rest of us have had that benefit, and we would be foolish to waste your skill. Best to get started immediately, perhaps."

Penny put down her uneaten bread, something she couldn't name welling up inside her. She looked dazedly round the table and saw that both her stepsisters had their eyes on their plates, still looking miserable. Their silence made perfect sense to Penny now. They had understood well before she had that whoever stuck their neck out on this occasion was to become the new cook, on a permanent basis. No wonder they hadn't been willing to push harder against their mother's treatment of her. Not that there had ever been any real doubt who would be chosen.

If anything, it was surprising how much defiance they had showed, especially Olivia. The older girl didn't usually betray any discomfort about Sapphira's injustices. When Olivia glanced up, an unreadable expression in her eyes, it suddenly hit Penny that the answer to this mystery was obvious as well.

She knew neither Olivia nor Sophia had bonded much with

their stepfather. At first she'd blamed them for not making more effort, but in hindsight, she had to acknowledge that he'd been courteous, but not warm. And, probably more to the point, the loss of their own father, whom she now knew they had both truly loved, had been so recent when they joined her family. Too recent, probably, for them to be expected to bond with a new father.

And that very experience was surely what had softened even Olivia, at least for this moment. Both of Penny's stepsisters knew what it meant to lose a father. They'd suffered the same grief themselves. Perhaps this day was almost as painful for them as it was for her, as they relived their own loss, and saw their remembered pain reflected in Penny's eyes.

Remembering their early interactions, Penny felt a wave of regret. She should have been more understanding of their lack of warmth. If they'd felt anything like she felt now, it was no wonder they hadn't been in a good state for forming new friendships. In fact, they probably felt worse than she did now, because in addition to losing their father, they'd had to leave their home in Entolia, to escape the war that had just broken out there.

Propelled by her belated sympathy, Penny's only thought was to soften their present discomfort. Without so much as a glance at her stepmother, she rose to her feet and walked into the kitchen.

"What are you doing in here, Miss Penny?" asked the harried-looking cook, who was leaning over a pan of boiling water with eggs bobbing around in it.

"I'm your replacement," said Penny. She tried to inject humor into the words, but didn't quite succeed.

The cook straightened, looking at her with a horror that would have been comical if not for the hollow feeling that seemed to be swallowing Penny's insides.

"You can't be serious, child!"

Penny nodded.

"I won't have it," said the cook stoutly. "I'll stay on without wages. I'll—"

"You can't do that," said Penny quickly. "You need to find a position that will pay you according to what your skills deserve. Don't think I don't know that you've been accepting smaller and smaller wages over the last two years."

"Never mind that," said the cook. "I'll not leave you to fend for yourself without aid."

"Who's fending for themselves without aid?" Harry had just entered the kitchen, and his sharp voice told Penny that he was ready to do battle on her behalf. She appreciated the gesture, but she knew it wouldn't help.

His scowl darkened as the cook explained what Penny had told her. "I won't allow it," he said grimly.

"Enough fussing," said Penny firmly. "Before the week is out, she'll realize I don't have the skills she thinks I do in the kitchen, and she'll find another solution rather than eat burned porridge every morning."

"Even if that were true, it's not how you should be spending this week, Pen," said Harry seriously.

She turned from him, not wanting him to see the tears that started to her eyes at this reminder of her father's death. "It won't kill me," she said quietly.

"What if the mistress lets you go, too?" The cook asked Harry. "Who'll watch out for her then?"

"I'm not a child, you know," said Penny, regaining control of herself and turning back around. "I'll be fine. And I don't think Harry will be let go. He's so delightfully versatile. He could probably run the place all by himself, couldn't you, Harry? In fact," she sent him the ghost of a grin, "maybe you should be the new cook."

"I'll help you in here as best I can," he said seriously, and Penny couldn't help laughing at the image.

"I was joking, Harry."

"Well, I won't be leaving, that's for certain," he said grimly. "And if I was forced to, I'd take you with me, and we'd make a run for it."

Penny couldn't help laughing again at his determined expression. "Where would we go?"

"I don't know," Harry admitted, his face relaxing at her mirth. "We'd figure it out."

"Well, it sounds quite exciting," said Penny, with a hint of wistfulness. "But for the moment, I need to stay in this kitchen and re-learn how to cook eggs."

It was no surprise to Penny to discover, before the morning was out, that running the kitchen was not to be her only new duty. She had no idea how she would manage it all, but she found she didn't have space in her head to worry about that. She was too focused on making it through that day, and a perverse part of her welcomed the extra labor, unjust as it might be. Perhaps if she kept herself unrelentingly busy, she could outrun her grief, if not forever, then at least until its sharp edges had dulled somewhat.

It occurred to her, as she lugged a heavy bucket to the barn late in the morning, that her chores would be much easier with the use of her magic. The thought turned her mind instantly to Lady Amaranthe. Could it really be true that the noblewoman was an enchantress, hiding within the very court of the king? And she had spoken of magic as if it was natural, not something to be feared, in spite of seeing what Penny had been about to do with hers. Would Lady Amaranthe really seek her out? What would she say? Penny found herself eager for more conversation with the older woman. She had never had another enchantress to discuss her magic with. She had so many questions.

So much did the noblewoman occupy Penny's thoughts, that when she heard approaching hooves on her way back to the house, she turned eagerly, sure Lady Amaranthe had come.

What she saw instead almost made her drop her now-empty bucket. Cantering up the carriageway, tawny hair glinting slightly in the noon sun, flanked by two royal guards, was the unmistakable form of Crown Prince Rian.

CHAPTER SEVEN

Penny

Penny's first instinct was to run, to attempt to hide, but she dismissed it immediately as foolishness. Even from a distance, she could see the prince's eyes fixed on her. Clearly, he'd already seen her. Besides, he obviously knew where to find her, so it was only a matter of time. Her heart seemed to stand still in her chest as he drew nearer. Had he seen her use her magic after all? Or—horrible thought—had Lady Amaranthe reported her? And she'd been so eager to get to know the other enchantress.

Sensing her tension, Al pressed himself against Penny's side, whining slightly. She felt other eyes on her from the doorway of the barn, and turned her head to see Harry hovering there, looking between her and the approaching riders with a furrowed brow. When he saw her looking, he gave her a reassuring nod, and she managed a small smile. The knowledge of his presence bolstered her. Consideration for her stepsisters had led her to give in to Sapphira's demands, but she refused to cower in fear before this prince. There was nothing she could do about the power that allowed him and his family to exile and punish people like her, but she could at least refuse to be intimidated by that power.

She'd expected the prince to ride up to the house, perhaps produce a formal order for her arrest. But instead, he reined his horse to a stop right in front of her. Just as Penny looked up, resenting his elevated position, he swung himself down from the saddle.

Thrown by his proximity, Penny just stared at him. He retained his horse's reins in one strong hand, keeping the animal under strict control. He still seemed to tower above her, but up close like this, he didn't look nearly as stiff as he did from a distance. He was standing so near, they must have looked like two friends, stopping for a chat after a chance encounter.

His boots were once again dusty, and his clothes, while clearly expensive, were practical. He wore a signet ring on one hand, but otherwise his person was as free of adornments as it had been in the market. His tawny hair was a little disarranged from the ride, and up close, Penny was surprised to see the barest hint of stubble across his strong, rather square chin.

These details humanized him so much that Penny found herself completely at a loss. As she had so defiantly intended, she felt no intimidation. But she also felt no anger, no fear. The young man before her didn't seem like a personification of the crown she so resented. He seemed like, well, a person. And while crowns were heartless and knew no mercy, humans had emotions of their own.

Except for her stepmother, it seemed.

Her examination of the prince complete, Penny looked up and realized with a jolt that he was examining her with just as much curiosity as she felt regarding him.

"Forgive my intrusion," he said smoothly, when he caught her eye. "But I came to deliver this." He held out a pouch, and Penny stared at it.

"Your...Your Highness?" It didn't look like an order for her arrest, but after all she knew nothing of these things.

"It's the payment for the wine you delivered last night," Prince Rian explained.

Penny was even more bewildered. The crown prince had delivered her forgotten payment himself? That couldn't be the real reason he was here. Surely the castle employed about a hundred servants suitable for such a task. Hand shaking slightly, she reached out and took the pouch.

"Thank you, Your Highness," she said, lowering herself into an inexpert curtsy. "It was foolish of me to forget it."

The prince regarded her in silence for a moment.

"I'm glad to run into you alone," he said abruptly.

Penny stiffened. Her hand searched at her side, reassuring herself of Al's proximity, and her eyes flicked to Harry, still in the doorway of the barn. He'd clearly recognized the crown prince, because his expression was thunderstruck. Even, Penny thought, a little afraid, although she had no idea what would cause Harry to be afraid of the prince.

Prince Rian's eyes followed hers, and he seemed to notice Harry for the first time. In an apparently involuntary movement, he shifted slightly, so that he wasn't standing quite so close to Penny. Evidently taking in the wariness now in her eyes, he hastened to explain.

"I was hoping to speak to you alone because I think you may have heard a private conversation between my brother and myself last night."

Penny wanted to retort that she could hardly be blamed for his carelessness in discussing sensitive topics in a crowded ballroom. But the knowledge that she had not been invited to the ball, that she wasn't supposed to be there at all, held her mouth closed. Plus her conscience squirmed slightly. The truth was, she'd known they thought themselves alone, and she'd eavesdropped anyway.

At her silence, the prince's expression became more serious. "I believe I gave the wrong impression through my words. I felt you were perhaps owed some explanation."

Penny felt her mouth fall open. "You...you came to explain, Your Highness? To me? I'm not to be punished?"

Neither his words nor his tone were at all what she'd expected. She had been sure he'd come here to arrest her. When he'd made no mention of her magic, she'd been relieved, but had quickly assumed that she was to be reprimanded for her eavesdropping instead, or at the very least for pushing her way into the ball uninvited.

"Punished?" the prince repeated, clearly startled. "Of course not." His eyes searched hers with a look that she found highly disconcerting. It felt like he could read her thoughts, and she was painfully aware of her secret crimes. "Are our laws so unreasonable that you see a member of the royal family and assume you're to be punished?"

The prince's voice had dropped slightly on the question, creating the illusion that they really were alone, without Harry lurking nearby, or the two royal guards not far behind the prince.

Yes, Penny wanted to retort, but she held her peace. Even saying that might reveal her as an enchantress in hiding. She lowered her eyes, and the prince went on, his voice a little harder.

"As I said, I believe my words last night gave the wrong impression. I would not wish them to be repeated in a context where they might be misconstrued."

Penny's eyes shot back up, another wave of astonishment washing over her as she understood at last the real reason for the prince's visit. He hadn't come to chastise, or to threaten. He'd come because *he* was worried, because he feared the consequences she might bring about as a result of his unguarded words. It didn't even matter that she had no idea what he'd said at the ball that would make him nervous about her response. The fact was that he was nervous.

The shock of the realization was so strong, Penny actually wobbled slightly on her feet. She had been determined not to give the prince the satisfaction of seeing how aware she was of his power over her. Never in her wildest imaginings could she have predicted that he would instead acknowledge a power she had over him, and would seek her out specifically to ask her not to abuse it.

Not only was it overwhelming to discover that she had any kind of power over a royal, but this admission of vulnerability—to her, who had attended the castle as little better than a servant—was so contrary to what she expected of the royal family, that she found herself questioning everything she'd ever thought of them.

In her discomposure, her hands shook, and the bucket she'd placed at her feet wobbled, without her touching it. She balled her trembling fingers into her gown, clutching at the fabric to try to control the magic clamoring for release. Not only was this the most dangerous moment to let her power slip, but the impulse reminded her of what she'd almost done the night before. Standing face to face with a prince who was not only human, but here to solicit her kindness, made her more ashamed than she could bear of her moment of violence at the ball.

"Do you...do you understand?" the prince asked, looking tense at her prolonged silence.

Pulling herself together, Penny uncurled her fists and found her voice. "I think so, Your Highness," she said quietly.

It wasn't entirely true. She was still searching vainly through her memory for anything in the prince's overheard conversation that would be incriminating. She remembered Lady Amaranthe seeming shocked by something, but Penny couldn't remember what exactly had caused that reaction. None of it had made such a strong impression on her, except perhaps for her surprise at the prince's casual way of speaking about dragons and magic.

It didn't matter. She'd never been one to carry tales. There was one thing she could say with total honesty, and she looked unflinchingly into the prince's eyes as she did so.

"At any rate, you have nothing to fear from me, Your Highness."

Still holding his gaze, Penny poured into the words a silent apology for the injury she'd tried to do him the night before. She vowed to herself that no matter how angry she might be, she would never again even consider using her magic to hurt anyone.

The prince's whole posture relaxed at her words, and his brown eyes—so striking a combination with his light hair—searched hers once again.

"Thank you," he said, and she was amazed to see the hint of a smile curl his lips. It changed his face dramatically, completely erasing the stiffness of his usual look. He seemed suddenly younger, not so different in age from herself.

"To tell you the truth, Your Highness," Penny said frankly, responding almost unconsciously to that softened demeanor, "you needn't have come at all. I did hear you speaking with Their Highnesses, but I don't know what in your words could be supposed to cause trouble if repeated."

The prince gave the ghost of a chuckle. "Is that so?" he mused, almost to himself. He shook his head slightly. "But that's not why I'm here, anyway. I came, of course, to deliver your payment." He gestured to the pouch clutched in Penny's hand.

"Of course," said Penny, hiding a smile of her own. It ought to have been impossible, given the resentment she'd always felt toward the royal family, but he was almost endearing in his transparency. She knew perfectly well now that the payment had been an excuse.

"I remember you," the prince said abruptly, and Penny's eyes once again shot to his, a measure of wariness returning. "From the market that day." A frown marred the prince's face, giving it once again its usual serious cast. "That's a dangerous part of the city for a young woman all alone."

"Nevertheless," said Penny lightly, "it's where I buy my family's food." She reached down to pat Al, who was sitting in a relaxed posture now that her tension had fled. "And I wasn't alone, you know."

The prince's frown didn't lift, but he followed her gaze to the dog. "Hey there, fella," he said quietly, no change to his tone. "I see you take good care of her."

Al's tail thumped against the ground in an acknowledging sort of way. To Penny's astonishment, the prince bent down and scratched behind Al's ear, causing the thud thud of the dog's tail to become a frantic beat.

When the prince straightened, Penny was staring at him. She couldn't help herself.

"You're the vintner's daughter, aren't you?" he asked suddenly.

Penny nodded reluctantly. So the steward had shared that information, had he? Or perhaps Lady Amaranthe.

"What's your name?" The question was disconcertingly soft, like the prince was asking a favor, rather than issuing a royal decree. Still, the idea of not answering didn't even cross Penny's mind.

"Penny," she said, just as softly.

"Penny," he repeated, as if testing it out. "Does your father truly send you to the market alone to buy food for the household?"

There was a moment of painful silence. "My father..." Penny's voice seemed to be swallowed mid-sentence by something hard and tight that was closing in on her throat. She cleared her throat and tried again. "My father passed away yesterday morning."

"Yesterday morning?" The prince started visibly, his eyes latching on to hers in a look of unmistakable horror. "I'm so sorry."

"Penelope!" The voice from the manor made Penny start. She glanced back at the house, relieved that her stepmother was calling her from inside, and hadn't actually emerged to see Penny's visitor.

She dropped a clumsy curtsy. "Thank you, Your Highness, for bringing the payment. I'm very grateful to you." Hesitating, she softened her voice slightly. "And please think no more of the other matter."

He looked like he wanted to say more, but she'd already started toward the house. On a sudden impulse, she turned back.

"Is it true that a child was arrested yesterday?" she asked abruptly.

The prince looked taken aback by the change in topic, but he answered readily enough. "The child was not arrested. The boy's father was. I believe he attacked the guards who came to apprehend the child."

Penny hovered for another moment, troubled by this information. She had no doubt that the man's supposed attack had been defense of his child. She couldn't help thinking of her own father. Would he have gone to such lengths for her? Or would he have stepped back from her, fear replacing the relief that had emanated from him the day she'd lied about her magic?

The disloyal thought brought the clawing feeling back to her throat. Suddenly in a hurry to be away from the prince's searching gaze, Penny bobbed her head again and hastened toward the house. She couldn't quite help glancing back as she reached the door, however. Prince Rian was standing right where she'd left him, watching her retreat with troubled eyes. Catching her gaze, he seemed to come to a decision. With a surprisingly graceful movement given his tall frame, he swung himself up into the saddle, and turned his horse's head toward the capital.

Exchanging her garden boots for slippers, Penny hurried to the sitting room. Her stepmother was seated at a desk in the corner, frowning over a ledger.

"Penelope, you really must work on your tardiness," she said, by way of greeting. "What took you so long?"

Penny hesitated, and Sapphira pushed on. "Never mind, we need to discuss the payment for last night's delivery. You'll need to—"

She broke off as a distinctive clinking sounded from Penny's pockets. Sapphira's gaze traveled down Penny's person, one eyebrow eloquently raised.

"What was that?"

"Oh, it's the payment," said Penny brightly. She pulled the pouch out and held it up. "It was just delivered by the...by the messenger from the castle," she amended. She didn't quite know why she hadn't told her stepmother of the prince's involvement, just that she felt reluctant to do so.

She had the sense that Sapphira had caught the mid-sentence change of words. A crease appeared between the older woman's eyes as they passed from the pouch to Penny's face.

"A messenger delivered it in person? Just now?"

Penny nodded, feeling unaccountably nervous.

Sapphira stood slowly. She was no taller than Penny, but she seemed to tower over her nevertheless. "Is it possible that you had it all along?" she asked, her voice alarmingly quiet. "Is it possible you hoped to keep it for yourself, to pass it off as the castle's mistake?"

"What?" Penny protested. "Of course not!"

"Do you think," Sapphira continued ominously, "that I am lining my own pockets with the proceeds of our last harvest? The household is barely running as it is, and you sought to steal the final payment?"

"I didn't!" Penny cried. "I would never do something like that. It truly was just delivered! Harry saw, ask him if you don't believe me."

Her stepmother's lip curled slightly, and Penny realized with a sinking heart that Sapphira knew as well as she did that Harry would cover for her without hesitation, whether she was telling the truth or not. It was unfortunate that it hadn't been one of the other servants who'd witnessed the interaction. But then, there were hardly any other servants left.

"We will say no more," Sapphira held out her hand, and Penny dropped the pouch into it, "for the present." She sat back down in front of her ledger. "You will be wanting to start on lunch, I imagine."

Torn between hurt and anger, Penny strode from the room. Ignoring her stepmother's last comment, she made her way out of the house again. Al appeared immediately at her side, but she barely noticed his antics. Her thoughts were too full, her emotions too strained from the prince's unexpected visit, his even more unexpected vulnerability, and her stepmother's unjust suspicions.

Heading for the barn, she blundered across the yard, forgetting that she was still wearing her thin slippers. She barely saw Al as he loped beside her, whining slightly at her tension. By the time she reached the haven, her shoes were muddy, and her feet were wet. Ignoring this, she leaned against the inside wall of the barn, inhaling a lungful of hay-scented air.

"What's she done now, Pen?"

Penny's eyes flew open at the calm question. She hadn't even realized that Harry was in the barn, but the sight of his familiar face almost broke her flimsy control.

"Sapphira accused me of hiding the money. She doesn't believe the payment was just delivered, and she thinks I was keeping it for myself."

Harry's face darkened, but he said nothing. His eyes dropped to Penny's fists, trembling at her sides, then back up to her tense, scrunched face.

"Wouldn't it be easier to just let it out, Pen?"

"Releasing my frustration won't achieve anything except scaring the chickens," said Penny darkly. "There's nothing to be gained by shouting about it."

Harry looked faintly amused. "I think the chickens can handle it," he said. "But I wasn't talking about letting out your frustration. I was talking about letting out your magic."

CHAPTER EIGHT

Rian

With a tug on the reins, Rian slowed his horse to a trot as the walls of Bant came into view. He was in no hurry to return to the castle. His encounter with the girl—with Penny—was occupying his mind so completely, he didn't think he'd be able to hide his distraction.

If any part of him had thought that seeing her again, discovering who she was, might strip her of mystery and help him overcome his strange fascination with her, nothing could be further from the truth. The more he saw of her, the more he wanted to know of her life. And the certain knowledge that no good could come of it was doing nothing to stop his mind from dwelling on what she'd said, and how she'd looked at him.

It wasn't just that she was pretty, although she undeniably was. Even dressed much more simply than she had been at the ball, she was eye-catching. Her hair, a fairer gold than his, curled around her face in a way that defied formality, and he couldn't recall ever seeing eyes as striking as her emerald green ones.

Not that he'd gotten any pleasure from their expression when he rode into her yard. His stomach dropped at the memory of her manner toward him. If he wanted proof that he hadn't misread her reaction to him at the ball, she'd given it to him today. She really was afraid of him.

Or at least, she had been. By the end of their conversation, she'd lost the frightened rabbit look that made him want to apologize, for what crime he couldn't say. But she still hadn't been quite natural, and who could blame her? It was hard to believe her father really had died the day before. He was horrified to think of her being forced to undertake an errand as mundane as delivering goods mere hours after losing a parent. How had it come about? Rian pictured the grizzled man who'd hovered in the barnyard while he spoke with Penny. Surely that man had been a servant, one who could have spared her the task at such a moment.

Rian's two guards trailed behind him as he rode up Bant's cobbled main street. Their presence irked him. He would have preferred to have no witnesses to his errand. At least he didn't need to fear the news passing around that far from delivering the payment on his way to another destination, he'd left the capital with the sole purpose of seeking out the vintner's daughter. His guards were well-trained, and they were loyal to him. Well, they were loyal to the position he held. They wouldn't gossip about him, and they wouldn't carry tales.

Navigating a slight bend in the long street, Rian emerged into the city's central square. He drew in a breath at the scene before him. He'd taken a different route when leaving Bant, so it was his first glimpse of the square, and he'd forgotten what he would find there. But the sight of the crowd gathered in the open space instantly reminded him of his father's decree.

Resisting a cowardly impulse to turn away, to avoid the area altogether, Rian steered his horse across the bustling square. It was harder than usual to keep his face impassive as his eyes were drawn irresistibly to the raised platform located at the square's far end.

The look of defiance on the face of the man currently restrained in the stocks was really quite impressive, given he had been there for hours already. Splattered remains around him showed that he'd been pelted with the usual rotting produce, but no one was throwing anything at him right now.

Rian saw someone walk past, pausing to spit at the restrained man, and heard a jeer of "magic-lover" from another onlooker. But a glance around the square showed him that not all the passersby shared this sentiment. He saw many throwing sympathetic looks at the man in the stocks. Rian even surprised one or two throwing a dark glance his own way. When they realized the prince was watching them, they all lowered their gaze, scurrying away rapidly.

The sight sobered him. Bentleigh had talked about the ban causing fractures in the kingdom. But ensconced in the castle, constantly privy to his father's tirades, Rian hadn't fully realized how many of Bant's people still had mixed reactions to the law. It was rattling, but in a strange way, it was also encouraging.

Perhaps it was a recent development. Perhaps the emergence of Listernia from its curse had swung popular opinion back toward magic. Did the king realize that his law wasn't universally popular? Was that why he was pushing so hard with these recent arrests, trying to quell any rising protest? Or was he even more oblivious than Rian had been, surrounded by advisors ready to tell him what he wanted to hear?

Rian's conscience squirmed uncomfortably. As his father's heir, *he* was one of the king's advisors. If he suspected that the others weren't willing to tell King Rhinehart what he needed—but might not want—to hear, he should be the one to speak up.

But it wasn't as though his father was going to listen to him. King Rhinehart might expect his eldest son to faithfully perform all the duties of crown prince, but he'd never sought Rian's opinion on matters of state, never shown much indication that he would value his son's input.

The same craven urge that had made Rian want to dodge the square prompted him to keep his eyes straight, to avoid looking too closely at the man in the stocks. But he suppressed it once again, knowing such cowardice was unworthy of his position. He slowed his horse to a sedate walk, studying the criminal gravely. Perhaps the man felt his gaze, because his eyes flicked up, and locked with Rian's.

There was no remorse there, no shame. Only burning defiance and bitter reproach. Rian could hardly bear to hold the man's gaze, but he forced himself to do so. As his subject, the prisoner deserved at least that small measure of dignity.

The activity in the square had stilled somewhat at the arrival of the prince. Rian was aware of many eyes on him, and he wished he knew what response would be true to both his heart and his position. But he couldn't seem to find anything to say or do that would soothe his conscience without undermining his father's decree.

As Rian hesitated, a swarthy farmer walked past. He cuffed the restrained man over the head with a gesture that was almost idle, although it still contained considerable force, judging by the criminal's involuntary grunt of pain. The blow drew the unfortunate man's eyes from Rian's, but far from feeling released, Rian felt more convicted than ever.

Spurring his horse forward, Rian let out an admonishing cry. He swung himself from the saddle straight onto the slightly elevated dais. The man who had dealt the blow stood frozen, staring at the prince with his mouth hanging open.

"There is no place for violence in this city," Rian said firmly, his voice loud enough to catch the attention of most of the square. "This man is serving his penalty already, and it is no one's place but the king's to impose further punishment."

The man's mouth was wider than ever. Rian could feel his blood thundering in his ears, but with the aid of long practice, his features remained calm and commanding. A steady glance around the square showed mixed reactions to his intervention. He caught his own guards, who had followed close behind him, exchanging looks of surprise. Some in the crowd nodded, but others muttered mutinously.

"What's the point of the stocks if we can't have a little fun with 'em?" muttered someone.

By the time Rian turned his head, it was impossible to distinguish the speaker from the rest of the crowd. If he was honest, he was glad of it. His actions were already risky, and he didn't want to seem to be openly defying his father's punishment of the man in the stocks. Plus, how could he refute what he knew to be true? The purpose of the stocks was to humiliate. It made no real sense to insist that onlookers treat the punished one with respect. Rian didn't want anyone digging too deep into this inconsistency and uncovering the discomfort with his father's decrees that formed the prince's real motivation.

Showing none of his unease, Rian passed his gaze challengingly across the crowd. No one else said a word. Steeling himself, he turned back to the man still contained in the stocks. If he'd expected relief, perhaps even gratitude, he was destined to be disappointed. The criminal glared at him more furiously than ever. Silent as the man was, his expression spoke volumes, seeming to expose Rian's hypocrisy.

What more was there to say? The prince turned away, preparing to mount his horse once again. But the criminal's low voice pulled him up short.

"Where's me son?"

"What?" Rian turned in surprise. "Your son?"

"What've ye done with 'im? If 'e's been 'urt, I'll burn yer castle to the ground, crown or no."

Rian stared into the man's muck-splattered face, and saw fear beneath the anger. The same fear that had the crowd watching in tense silence as he approached the stocks. The same fear that he'd seen on Penny's face when they locked eyes at the ball, when he rode into her yard a mere hour ago. Her words seemed to ring in his ears.

You came to explain? I'm not to be punished?

The surprise, the mistrust in her green eyes flashed before his vision and struck once again at his heart. He hated it. More passionately than he'd ever hated anything in his life, he hated that fear.

"Of course your son won't be harmed," he said, disregarding the man's futile threats of violence. "He's a child. He must leave the kingdom, but he won't be hurt in any way." Rian felt a frown crease his forehead. "Surely you were informed of that."

The man spat on the ground. "I wasn't informed of nothin'," he growled. His face had lightened slightly, however, and Rian took comfort from the fact that the man seemed to believe him, at least.

"Your Highness." One of the guards, still mounted, had approached. His eyes were on the imprisoned man, and Rian could tell from his scowl that he'd heard the man's muttered threats.

"Yes, we must keep moving," Rian said quickly, before the prisoner could incriminate himself further. Without looking again at the man, he swung himself into the saddle and urged his horse toward the castle.

Glancing up at the sun, Rian increased his pace still further. He was expected by the captain of the guard for a routine briefing regarding the protective force stationed on the kingdom's eastern border, over which Rian theoretically had oversight. If he didn't hurry, he'd get caught up in the briefing, and would miss seeing his brother off on his journey to Listernia.

But he needn't have worried. The captain's report was short, and to the point.

"There's been another incursion, Your Highness," said the captain gruffly. "The worst we've seen in some time."

"Another one?" Rian asked, his brows drawing together. "That must be...what? The fourth the last few months?"

"Fifth," grunted the captain. "But this one was the worst, as I said. We lost three men."

"There were casualties?"

Rian felt a flush of anger. For as long as he could remember, there had been occasional skirmishes on the kingdom's eastern border, which ran along the edge of Solstice's unsettled desert region. The area was mostly uninhabited, but it wasn't unheard of for fugitives to seek an isolated existence in the harsh environment. Small groups of roving bandits made periodic attempts to raid Bansford's easternmost settlements, using the desert as a base. It had always been necessary to patrol the eastern border, but for the skirmishes to actually escalate to the point of deaths was almost unheard of.

The captain nodded, his expression grim. "It was a larger group of bandits than we usually see. And..." He hesitated. Rian was sure the captain had been about to say more, but for some reason he stopped himself. "The details will be discussed at the full briefing His Majesty has ordered for an hour's time, Your Highness."

Rian nodded curtly, not sorry to cut the conversation short so that he could find Ben. "I'll be there."

Bowing, the captain turned and strode away, the stiffness of his frame communicating stress. Rian watched him go for a moment, frowning. The increased activity on the border struck him as sinister, although he couldn't immediately put his finger on why it troubled him so deeply.

Shaking the thought off for the moment, he went in search

of his brother. An inquiry of a passing servant sent him toward a small private dining room used by the royal family. But when he entered, no one was inside.

He hovered for a moment, wondering if he'd missed his family, when the familiar voice of his father drifted in from the adjoining room.

"That's right, I received another report last night. A silversmith in the west district. I'm not sure of his name, but some simple inquiries should identify him."

"Yes, Your Majesty," responded another voice Rian knew. It seemed King Rhinehart was speaking with Dreyton, the chief guard in charge of enforcing the ban. "I'll take a squad immediately."

Apparently the guard took his leave, because when King Rhinehart strode into the dining room a moment later, he was alone. He raised an eyebrow at his son, who was still standing frozen, trying to make sense of what he'd heard.

"Rian. Here to see Bentleigh off? I gather your mother wished us to say a private farewell before the delegation departs."

"What were you speaking to Dreyton about, Father?" Rian asked, ignoring the king's words.

King Rhinehart's brow lowered slightly. "Surely you weren't eavesdropping on your king, Rian?"

"I didn't set out to eavesdrop," said Rian, his impatience showing more than was probably wise. The rising discomfort he felt about the fear he evoked in his people had eroded his usual caution. "I was sent here to see Bentleigh the same as you, and I happened to hear you speaking with Dreyton. Who's the silversmith you mentioned? Surely not another concealed enchanter."

The king regarded his son in silence for a moment, then gave a curt nod. "I'm afraid so."

"That's two in two days," Rian protested.

Again his father nodded. "You see I was right that the problem is more rampant than we suspected."

But the high number of hidden enchanters wasn't what was troubling Rian. "You told Dreyton you received another report last night," he pressed. "Who was it from? I thought Dreyton was the one receiving the reports, and passing them to you."

"I don't believe I ever said as much," said King Rhinehart dismissively.

His regal air failed to impress his son. "Father, who is making these reports?" he asked, surprising himself by the challenging edge to his tone. "Who can possibly be identifying enchanters with such accuracy, when they've all managed to stay hidden for so many years?"

"As I told you before, Rian, the reports are made anonymously." The king's patience was clearly wearing thin, but still Rian couldn't restrain his suspicion.

"How anonymous can they be, if they're being made directly to you?" He stared at his father, a horrible realization dawning on him. "It's someone with magic, isn't it? Enchanters and enchantresses can recognize each other as part of their magic, right? You've got one of them working for you, ratting out the others."

King Rhinehart raised one speaking eyebrow. "Ratting out? Identifying concealed lawbreakers is a service to the kingdom, Rian."

Rian's chest swelled, outraged by his father's hypocrisy. "So you are using an ench—"

"Of course I'm not." The king waved him off with an impatient gesture. "No enchanters or enchantresses are welcome in Bansford, you know that. No exceptions."

Rian searched his father's face. King Rhinehart was many

things, but not a liar. Still, he didn't know how else to interpret his father's sudden, unnaturally accurate knowledge.

"An artifact, then?" he muttered, half to himself. "One that can somehow identify enchanters? It has to be some kind of magic."

The king's brows lowered further, anger starting to show through his kingly calm. "I will not tolerate being accused by my own son."

Rian noticed that his father hadn't denied the suggestion. He frowned. His father said he'd received the report the night before. Rian should have watched his parents more closely at the ball—had someone approached them then? Someone in possession of a magic-identifying artifact? That must have been it. They'd all been at the ball until late. It wasn't as though his father had *dreamed* the report.

But before he had decided whether to press the issue, the door to the corridor opened to admit Bentleigh and Azalea.

"Rian," Ben said, smiling at him. "I'm glad you made it. When no one could find you earlier, I was worried you wouldn't be back in time to see us off."

Seeing the searching look thrown at him by his father, Rian hid a grimace. He had hoped no one would notice his absence from the castle that morning.

"I wouldn't let you disappear back to Listernia without saying goodbye," he said, smiling as naturally as he could manage. He offered his arm, and Bentleigh gripped it. Then Rian turned to Azalea, embracing her lightly. "We'll miss you both."

"You must come and visit," his future sister-in-law said brightly. "I'd love to show you Liss."

"I'd like that," said Rian, smiling.

"You're very kind, Princess Azalea, but there will be time enough for visits in the future," King Rhinehart interjected.

Rian noticed that although his father was speaking to Azalea, his gaze was still fixed on Rian. Possibly the talk of ratting out enchanters had made the king wary of sending his heir to magic-friendly Listernia, where he might get dangerous ideas.

Rian saw Ben and Azalea exchange a subtle glance, but he was too used to his father's heavy-handed ways to feel irritation on his own behalf. Restraining an impulse to roll his eyes, he once again addressed Azalea.

"Will we see you in Bansford again before the wedding?"

"I don't think so," said the princess, with a glance toward Rian's father. Clearly Listernia's royals were as wary of their supposed allies as Bansford's monarchs were of Listernia. She probably thought that Bentleigh was escaping a dark fate, fleeing Bansford to live in his bride's kingdom. In all honesty, Rian sometimes suspected that Ben thought so himself.

There was no denying the thought stung. Rian knew Bentleigh had always been frustrated by their parents' rigid ways, but in most ways Bansford was a vibrant and beautiful kingdom. Rian wasn't just bound to the land by his birthright. His heart belonged to Bansford as much as his future did.

At that moment, Queen Eliza entered the room, a lady-in-waiting hovering behind her.

"Bentleigh, Azalea." She inclined her head elegantly toward her younger son and her future daughter-in-law. "I had hoped for more of an opportunity for us all to say goodbye, but I'm afraid the captain of the guard is here to speak to your father."

King Rhinehart grunted. "He's early. I'll see him in my study."

"Is this about the border skirmish, Father?" Rian cut in sharply. "I would like to be present for the briefing."

The king gave him a calculating look, and Rian noticed Ben's eyes passing between his brother and his father.

"What border skirmish?"

"Don't concern yourself, Bentleigh," said King Rhinehart calmly. "Your delegation leaves within the hour."

Ben's forehead creased in a frown, but he didn't argue. As always, his mind was already half in Listernia.

"Come along then, Rian, if you intend to join me," said the king curtly. "I don't wish to keep the captain waiting."

CHAPTER NINE

Penny

Penny stared at Harry, her hands strangely numb as they clutched at the wood of the barn wall behind her. This sensation of the world reeling around her had become so frequent in the last few days, she feared she'd soon lose her bearings altogether.

"Release my...my magic?" she repeated stupidly.

"That's right." Harry leaned on the pitchfork he was holding, looking ridiculously unconcerned. "I don't know much about these things, but you look like it's making you sick, trying to hold it in."

Penny's lips were painfully dry. She moistened them and managed a whisper. "How long have you known?"

Harry shrugged. "A couple of years. I've suspected for longer, but I knew for sure when I saw you in the field one day, pulling up flowers without touching them."

Penny put a hand over her mouth. She remembered that day. It wasn't long after her father had fallen ill. She'd been feeling afraid. The crown prince of Albury had fallen afoul of some kind of curse not long before, and word had just gotten out that in spite of all caution, the curse against the crown princess of

Listernia had been activated, and she'd fallen into an enchanted slumber. Rumor was that Bansford's king and queen had returned from their visit to Listernia in a state of fury, and had become more fierce than ever regarding magic. To Penny's horror, she'd found that the more she tried to hold her magic in, the more it clamored for release. So she'd slipped out of the manor and found a place where she could vent the pressure unobserved.

Or so she'd thought.

"I didn't think anyone could see me," she said hollowly.

Harry looked amused by her shock. "Well it was only me, Pen, so no harm done."

"Why didn't you say anything?" she demanded, feeling aggrieved that she'd carried her burden alone for so long, apparently unnecessarily.

"It didn't seem you wanted anyone to know," said Harry simply. "You or your father. I know how nervous he was about magic, rest his soul. I reckon he trusted me pretty thoroughly, and if he didn't even tell me, I figured he didn't want it talked of at all."

"He didn't know," said Penny, her voice dull in her own ears.

"What?!"

She'd managed to startle Harry out of his relaxed posture at last.

"You're telling me your own father didn't know? But he must have suspected, given your mother's magic."

Penny found herself staring again. "You knew about Mama?"

"Course I did," scoffed Harry. "More'n once she fixed me up for something or other. Mended my broken arm once." His eyes slid out of focus as he remembered. "That was something to behold, that was. Hurt like the blazes of course, but still. Marvelous thing."

"How did she die, Harry?" Penny could hear the painful

eagerness in her voice, but she didn't care. She had to know. "Father would only tell me it was an accident, and it was because of her magic."

Harry's brows drew together. "That's not right," he said stoutly. "To keep you in the dark. If I'd realized you didn't know, I'd have told you years ago."

"Well?" Penny pressed impatiently.

Harry sighed. "It was a family who lived on the other side of the east vineyards. Their daughter, not much older'n you, had fallen down a well, and her leg was broken pretty bad. They were saying that it wouldn't set properly, and she might never be able to walk right again."

"Did they know about Mama's power?" Penny breathed.

Harry shook his head. "No, but word had spread all through the neighborhood that they were looking for an enchanter or enchantress who could fix her up. They were ready to defy the ban, and willing to pay handsomely. Your mother didn't care about the gold, of course. But she wanted to help them. Bless her, she always wanted to help every soul she met. Used to drive your father to distraction with fear for her."

Harry heaved a sigh. Penny was silent, motionless, spellbound by his words.

"She went over there, in the dead of night. Fixed the girl up, and if the time she did my arm was anything to go by, she must have been pretty weak when she was done. The trouble was, we weren't the only ones to hear the rumor of what kind of help the family was looking for."

"The guards," whispered Penny, horrified.

Harry nodded heavily. "A group of them came to investigate. Found the girl all fixed, and the family refusing to say a word about how. Of course they could tell it was magic, and they must have been able to tell that whoever did it had only just left. They spread out, searching. From what I understand, your mother ran for it, trying to reach home. Well, she never made it, did she?"

His voice was suddenly thick, and he stopped, but Penny felt impatient of his emotion. She needed answers, needed the truth.

"Why not? Did they catch her?"

Harry shook his head. "They never knew it was her. But she must've been weak, like I said. And it was dark. I guess she couldn't see where she was going. Fell straight into the well where the girl had gotten hurt. But she wasn't so lucky as just to break a leg. The mercy is they said she died straight away. Hit her head, most likely."

Penny's own legs suddenly gave way, and she slid down the barn wall. Al nosed her face anxiously as she settled herself on the floor and covered her face in her hands. Her mother had died falling into the same well. The irony was painful.

"Her death was never connected to the girl's recovery," Harry went on, perhaps realizing Penny needed time to recover herself. "She was close enough to home that her presence in the area wasn't suspicious. The story we spread around was that she'd been going to visit the girl the next morning, to see how she was getting on, and she fell then."

Penny's hand shook as she lowered it from her face, but her voice was quite steady. "Thank you for telling me, Harry," she said quietly. She buried a hand in Al's fur, taking comfort from his warm, familiar presence.

He nodded, still looking troubled. "Should've never been kept from you," he repeated.

"What happened to the girl?"

Harry blinked, seeming surprised by her question. Shaking his head, he gave a barely perceptible chuckle. "You're very like her, aren't you? The girl recovered, no damage. The family never said a word about who fixed her, but they were still punished for accessing magic. Fined, I think. Suppose they paid it with the same gold they offered to anyone who could save their daughter's leg. They left soon after. I think they were going to settle in Entolia."

"Hopefully they didn't get caught up in the war," said Penny absently. Her thoughts were still on the horrible image of her mother, running from guards in the darkness, unable to see the well looming up before her. Anger bubbled up in Penny, hot and corrosive, and for a moment she was filled with the desire to see them all punished, the guards who had chased her mother, the royals who had ordered it.

But no! She'd learned that lesson at the ball the night before. She was in no position to judge who was really responsible, and she had no right to mete out punishment even if she could. She'd vowed, a mere hour before, when looking into the prince's unexpectedly gentle eyes, that she would never again consider using her magic to hurt someone. Was she going to abandon that vow so quickly, because of something that happened almost fourteen years ago?

She shook her head slightly. Of course she wasn't.

"So what are we going to do?" Harry asked, his tone suddenly serious. "Should we run for it? I could get you over the border before nightfall, I reckon."

Penny stared at him. "Run? Leave Bansford forever?"

"There's little enough left for you to stay for," said Harry gently.

"It's my home, Harry," Penny protested. "And yours." She shook her head. "It might seem foolish to you, but in spite of it all I don't want to leave Bansford." Especially not now she'd met Lady Amaranthe, and had the promise of answers to questions even Harry couldn't possibly understand.

If she was also influenced by the thought that leaving would remove all chance of ever again locking gazes with a certain pair of searching brown eyes set in a serious, square-jawed face, she didn't acknowledge it, even to herself.

"I've kept it from Sapphira and the girls this long," shrugged Penny.

Harry was frowning. "I don't like it, Pen. You've attracted the notice of the royals now. I've no idea how that came about, but it makes your position far too precarious for my liking."

"I don't *think* Prince Rian is a threat to me," said Penny thoughtfully. "I'm not even sure he's against magic, at least not as completely as the king. I overheard him at the ball last night, talking quite casually about dragons and such."

Harry raised two bushy eyebrows. "What do you mean you overheard him at the ball?"

Penny grimaced, but before she could respond, they were both distracted by the sound of approaching hoofbeats.

"He's come back?" Harry muttered anxiously, and Penny's heart did an inexplicable little flop.

She hurried to the door of the barn, but checked on the threshold. The figure now riding smartly up the laneway was certainly not Prince Rian. Tall, elegant, decidedly feminine.

"Lady Amaranthe," gasped Penny, warmth spreading through her chest at the sight of the noblewoman. *Kin*, Lady Amaranthe had called her. That was something Penny could use more of.

Without pausing to explain to Harry, she hurried out into the yard, Al at her heels. Lady Amaranthe reined in at sight of Penny, her lovely face breaking into a smile.

"Penelope! I'm obviously at the right place."

"My Lady." Penny sank into a curtsy that wobbled far too much for dignity. Straightening, she glanced between her second visitor and the manor. "I would like to invite you inside, but..."

"I quite understand," said Lady Amaranthe quickly. "I would

prefer to speak alone, also. Is there somewhere nearby where we can walk, perhaps?"

Penny nodded, eager to be gone before any of her family caught sight of the noblewoman. "I can show you."

Lady Amaranthe gestured for Penny to precede her, and within ten minutes they were strolling in the very field where Harry had seen Penny use her magic. Lady Amaranthe had dismounted, and was leading her horse with one confident hand on the reins, while Al gamboled around them.

"I'm so glad you came," said Penny, a little shy.

"I said I would, didn't I?" smiled Lady Amaranthe.

Penny nodded. "You weren't my first visitor today," she ventured. Lady Amaranthe looked inquiring, and Penny hurried on. "The prince was here not an hour ago. Prince Rian."

Lady Amaranthe's mouth dropped slightly open in her surprise. "My word. He was quick, wasn't he?" Her forehead creased as she mused, and when she turned to Penny, her expression was apologetic. "I had hoped to warn you when I came that I'd told the prince where to find you. I'm sorry you were taken unawares."

Penny shook her head. "You don't need to apologize. You could hardly have said no to a prince."

"You're very gracious," smiled Lady Amaranthe. "He didn't suspect about your magic, did he? I didn't think he saw anything last night, or I'd never have told him where you live."

"No, no," Penny hastened to reassure her. "He brought the payment for the wine—I stupidly forgot it when I ran away last night—but I'm pretty sure that was just an excuse. The real reason he came was to reassure himself that I wasn't going to repeat what he said to his brother."

"Yes," said Lady Amaranthe dryly. "He sought a similar assurance from me last night."

Penny frowned. "I don't understand, though. What did he

say that might cause him trouble? Was it because he was too casual in the way he spoke of magic?"

Lady Amaranthe looked surprised, but the expression quickly melted away. "Of course, it wouldn't have meant much to you," she murmured. "But I confess, I was shocked. It could certainly cause him trouble, or more accurately, his brother. The prince was concerned because we overheard him saying that Prince Bentleigh went to the dragons for help breaking the Listernian princess's curse."

"And that's...dangerous?" Penny asked blankly.

There was an edge to Lady Amaranthe's smile that Penny couldn't quite read. "Very dangerous. I daresay you wouldn't have been taught much about dragons, but as royals, both of the princes would have been. They would know that the peace we humans have with dragons is built upon a mutual agreement that they won't use their magic on humans—either to help or hinder—and we humans," she gestured between the two of them, "won't use *our* magic on dragons."

Penny frowned, still confused. "So if a dragon helped break Listernia's curse, isn't the dragon the one who broke the rules?"

"I wonder if a dragon *did* help break the curse," Lady Amaranthe mused. "The prince only said that Prince Bentleigh asked the dragons. And *that* is the information Prince Rian didn't want repeated. From what I understand, asking the dragons to use their magic to break a human-cast enchantment would be tantamount to breaking the agreement. It could offend the dragons, and perhaps even lead to war." Her voice was once again dry. "And not even our rulers are foolish enough to risk that. I imagine King Rhinehart and Queen Eliza would be livid if they discovered their own son had risked the agreement."

"I must say," objected Penny, "if the risk is so great, I think this dragon lore should be taught to everyone, not just royals, and nobles. What if a commoner like me inadvertently started a war?"

Lady Amaranthe smiled. "You couldn't, because you wouldn't have the opportunity. Dragons are proud creatures. They are, to some small extent, impressed by crowns. But someone like you would never have the chance to speak to a dragon, and even if you did, a request for help from you—which they would certainly ignore—wouldn't be taken to represent the kingdom, or the crown. It wouldn't cause offense in the way a request from a prince might. No offense," she added quickly, when Penny didn't answer.

"I'm not offended," Penny said slowly. And she wasn't. She was silent because she was trying to decide whether to tell Lady Amaranthe that she actually had spoken to a dragon, only the night before. But after all, she didn't really know the other enchantress. It might be wise to be cautious.

"I have so many questions," she said abruptly. "About my magic."

"I'm sure you do," Lady Amaranthe smiled. "You said your mother had magic, but she's no longer with us?"

Penny nodded. "She died when I was a small child, before I even knew I had magic."

"And your father?"

Penny hesitated. "He was so worried about my mother's magic that I never had the heart to tell him I have it too."

Lady Amaranthe stopped walking, turning to face her companion. "*Was?*" she repeated delicately. "*Had?*"

Penny's eyes were on her feet. "He died. Yesterday."

Lady Amaranthe's sharp intake of breath brought Penny's eyes back up. The sympathy in the other woman's eyes almost broke Penny's control, but she was determined not to waste her time with the enchantress crying.

"I'm so sorry, my child," said Lady Amaranthe softly. Her

voice became pained. "How did it come about that you were delivering goods to the castle when your grief was so fresh?"

Penny hadn't planned to bother the noblewoman with her troubles, but somehow it all poured out. Her stepmother's coldness, the competition she so hated between herself and the stepsisters she wished she could claim as friends. Her father's illness and, even before that, his inaction.

Lady Amaranthe listened in silence, her expression not only sympathetic but knowing. "No wonder you were ready to take out your anger on the royals last night," she said quietly, when Penny was finished.

A shudder went over Penny's frame. "It was very wrong of me to consider it. They aren't the cause of my problems."

"Not all of your problems, certainly," said Lady Amaranthe.

Again, Penny hesitated. "Even if they were, I don't want the role of punishing them."

Lady Amaranthe smiled. "Again, you are very gracious, Penelope. If only they could see how good you are, how little you deserve their persecution."

"Do you think there's a chance of that?" Penny asked eagerly, thinking of Prince Rian's unexpected approachability. "Do you think they could be brought to see that magic isn't so dangerous? To embrace it, if enough magic-users showed them kindness instead of anger?"

Lady Amaranthe's smile was a little twisted. "Your belief that it could be so is further sign of your goodness, Penelope," she said heavily. "But I'm afraid the king is too set in his view of magic, at least judging by all I've seen."

Penny deflated. As a member of King Rhinehart's court, Lady Amaranthe knew much better than she did what the true state of the royals' minds must be. Still, the thought lingered. King Rhinehart might be inflexible, but he wasn't the only royal. There was someone else with influence in Bansford's future, someone with brown eyes that were surprisingly warm up close, whose serious voice held a hidden laugh if you were listening for it...

"So what action comes most easily to your magic?" Lady Amaranthe asked abruptly. She started walking again. "What was your mother's magic?"

"My mother could heal injuries," said Penny, hurrying to catch up. Al had wandered off to sniff at a rabbit hole, but a low whistle brought him back to Penny's side.

"Healing?" Lady Amaranthe raised her eyebrows. "That's a special gift."

Penny nodded. "I don't have it, I'm afraid. I can move objects, that's about all I've discovered."

"Move objects?" Lady Amaranthe prompted. "Show me."

Penny stared at her. "Use my magic? Now? Here?"

"Why not?" Lady Amaranthe scanned the area carefully. "There's no one here but us." She gestured to a rock at her feet, the size of Penny's palm. "Can you lift that?"

Penny chuckled. "I imagine so." Disregarding the indicated rock, she studied a row of nearby trees, looking for something more interesting.

Ah, there. A boulder, three times the size of her head, was half-buried in the soil, covered in moss. Penny lifted a hand, palm upward, fingers slightly curled. With a casual roll of her fingers, she raised the boulder from the earth, letting it hover for a moment as chunks of soil fell from it. Then, with a further flick, she brought it zooming through the air toward them, and placed it gently at Lady Amaranthe's feet.

The noblewoman stared at it for so long that Penny wondered if she'd caused offense. Lady Amaranthe's head traveled slowly, her gaze moving from the boulder up to Penny's face.

"How large an item have you tried to lift?" she asked quietly.

Penny shrugged. "Nothing much bigger than that. It's hard to shift large things surreptitiously, isn't it?"

"But that seemed to cost you almost no effort."

Penny shrugged. "Well, it's not like I'm actually lifting it."

Lady Amaranthe was still staring at Penny, and the look in her eyes made Penny uncomfortable.

"I don't think you realize how strong a power you have, Penelope," she said, an unreadable note in her voice. "No incantation, no materials, barely a gesture." She was speaking almost to herself now. "The potential applications of that are almost endless. And such strength, even without training." She shot Penny a look. "You haven't really trained with it, have you?"

Penny shook her head, feeling rattled. "I've never had the opportunity."

"Well," said Lady Amaranthe briskly. "We can change that, at least."

Rian

Rian entered the king's study in his father's wake. The captain, following close behind, glanced between the two royals, and Rian remembered the deputy's hesitation earlier. It struck him that he'd never before been present when his father was receiving a report from the captain. He'd always heard the information separately, in his own briefing.

Did his father trust him so little? Or was it just that the king preferred to operate in total isolation? Either situation was undesirable, and Rian wondered how he'd let things reach such a pass without intervening.

"I was troubled by the scout's report, Captain," the king started, as soon as the door was closed behind the three men. "Was it accurate?"

Rian had no idea what his father was talking about, but the captain clearly did.

"I'm afraid so, Your Majesty. One of the raiders used magic, I saw it with my own eyes."

Rian realized his mouth was open, and he closed it quickly. The bandits were using magic? Were there enchanters among them, then?

The king drew in a breath, showing no surprise at the pronouncement. "Why weren't the casualties higher, then? The scout said it was some kind of wind power, that the sand was swept up with such force that none of our soldiers could see their hands in front of their faces. I'm surprised the raiders weren't able to incapacitate more than three."

The captain hesitated. "I couldn't say for sure, Your Majesty. But my impression was that the use of magic was accidental."

"Accidental?" The king's eyebrow was once again raised.

"Unplanned," the captain corrected himself. "The raider who did it, and his companion, were the ones who felled three of our men. But it didn't seem to me that they were praised for it by the rest of their fellows. I believe it may have been unsanctioned. Like perhaps he lost control, or lost his temper."

The king had picked up a feather quill from his desk, and was passing it through his hand in a tense, methodical way.

"But then..." Rian looked between them. "Are you saying you think they were trying to keep their magic a secret? That the bandits have had enchanters among them all along, and they're intentionally not using their power so as to keep it hidden?"

The captain's gaze passed warily between the king and the prince, and Rian let out a frustrated breath, turning to his father.

"I'm your heir, Father. If you can't speak freely before me, then who?"

King Rhinehart considered him for a moment, then nodded to the captain.

"We have suspected for some time that the so-called bandits are actually enchanters, Your Highness," said the captain.

"What, all of them?" Rian asked, startled.

The captain shrugged. "Who can say?"

Rian resisted the impulse to glance at his father. The king's *anonymous* source probably could say, but Rian wasn't about to raise that matter in front of the captain.

"Some of them at least," the captain went on. "Their movement has increased in recent months, but the raids on nearby settlements have decreased. We believe they're planning something."

Rian turned to his father, unable to keep an accusatory note from his voice. "Why didn't you tell me about this, Father? Isn't the eastern border supposed to be my responsibility?"

"The situation changed when magic became involved," said the king. "Such matters are always to be reported directly to me."

Rian frowned, dissatisfied with this answer. "Did you say that the movement on the border has increased in recent months?" he demanded of the captain.

The man nodded. Still frowning, Rian tried to put the pieces together. Increased border activity, the appearance of magic among the bandits. Suddenly the dots connected in his mind.

"The recent arrests!" he said, his eyes whipping to his father's. "The greater activity on the border coincides with the sudden increase in magic-related arrests over the last few months."

His father's stony expression gave little away, but it was clear that the thought was not a revelation to him.

"You knew that," said Rian. "You knew there was a connection."

"We *know* very little," the king said heavily. "But we suspect a connection, yes."

Rian frowned. "And this most recent border incident comes immediately after a controversial arrest, involving a child." Could that be why the clash had been more deadly than usual? Were the exiled desert enchanters even angrier because of what had happened?

"The clash was too soon after the arrest for it to be related, Your Highness," said the captain.

But Rian's eyes remained fixed on his father, and he could almost read the same thought in the king's mind as was racing through his own. It wasn't too soon for the news to have reached the desert if some magical means of communication was being used. Was this, then, the explanation for his father's sudden determination to weed out every last outlaw who might be concealed in Bant? Did he suspect someone in the capital of conspiring with the desert-dwellers against him?

The understanding that passed between the two royals created a strange mix of emotions in Rian. There was meaning in his father's gaze. It almost felt as though the king was sharing a confidence with Rian, giving him some measure of trust. But while Rian valued that connection, he wasn't at all sure he could share his father's view on the matter.

He shared his father's suspicions, no question. When he thought of the open anger shown by the man in the stocks, it wasn't a stretch to imagine such a person passing news to exiled enchanters. But would Rian really blame him for doing something like that, given what had happened to his family? The killing of the three soldiers Rian didn't condone, not for a moment. But then, Rian wasn't living in an unforgiving desert, exiled for a crime he couldn't control.

"What became of the child with magic?" he asked abruptly.

The king looked faintly surprised at the change in topic, but he had an answer ready. "He and his family left immediately upon discovery. They are being escorted out of the kingdom. They elected to make for Fernedell, and may have crossed the border already."

"Not all his family," said Rian dryly, thinking again of the man in the stocks.

His father didn't pretend to misunderstand him. "I daresay the boy's father will join them once he has served his sentence," he said coldly.

"And how long is that?"

"Only a twelvemonth."

"A twelvemonth?" Rian protested. "He's been given a year of labor for trying to stop his son from being seized?"

King Rhinehart's expression become even icier. The moment of shared understanding was gone, the king's usual impenetrable manner returning. "The report you've heard today should be enough to remind you that a strong response is necessary to address the magic problem, Rian. The man concealed his son's magic for twelve years, then turned a weapon on our guards when they uncovered his crime."

"Were any of them hurt?" Rian demanded.

"Of course not," said his father. "They were members of the royal guard, armed and well-trained."

"Not such a threat, was he, then?" Rian asked dryly.

"If that is all, Rian, I wish to speak to the captain," said King Rhinehart with cold calm.

Rian hesitated, frustrated both with himself and with his father. He wanted to earn his father's trust, to be the most effective crown prince he could be. But his desire to stand against this inflexible law on magic was growing by the day. The two drives seemed incompatible, and he could see no way forward. His fleeting thought of pleading for clemency on behalf of the man in the stocks fled at the look on his father's face. Clearly there would be no point. Inclining his head stiffly, he strode from the room.

The troubling situation occupied his thoughts so fully, he was barely aware of his surroundings as he watched Ben's delegation leave. He made no attempt to tell his brother what he'd learned. For one thing, there was nothing Ben could do about it. He was on his way out of the kingdom. For another...well, Ben was as fixed in his views as their father, in his own way. He would be consumed by his indignation at Rian's suspicion that the king was using magic to identify hidden enchanters, not to mention the disproportionately harsh penalty imposed on the man currently in the stocks. He would never be able to see past those things to even attempt to understand King Rhinehart's valid fears regarding the group in the desert.

But Rian could understand. He thought his father was wrong in his approach to magic, no question. But that didn't mean his father was the unreasonable tyrant the Listernians seemed to think him. The king had his reasons for the approach he'd taken, and therefore he could surely be reasoned with.

That was why the king's stubbornness on the issue was all the more frustrating. Rian believed his father was capable of being more reasonable, and he wished he could convince the king to trust him, to let him in. Then maybe he could influence things for the better. As troubled—even angry—as he felt about the king's hypocrisy in the way he was hunting down magic-users, he mustn't let it show. That would only drive his father further away.

Rian's resolve was sorely tested when the news leaked around, just after dark, that there had been yet another arrest.

A silversmith from the city's west district.

Rian had just left the formal dining hall when he heard the news, and his hand clenched into a fist at his side. Would the new arrest be followed by a fresh skirmish at the border in mere hours? Would he even be informed if that happened?

He was halfway to his room, barely aware of where he was going, when he heard himself hailed. Turning, he saw with surprise that Lady Amaranthe was hurrying after him.

"My Lady." He inclined his head distractedly, his thoughts still on the news of the latest arrest.

"I'm glad for the opportunity to speak with you again, Your Highness," the noblewoman said, dipping into a quick but very graceful curtsy. "I visited our young friend today, and learned that you had been before me. I must confess, I didn't expect you to be so quick."

Rian started, fully distracted from the arrest now. He had almost forgotten that Lady Amaranthe was the one who'd told him where to find Penny.

"I had an unexpected opportunity to speak with her when I discovered that she was yet to receive the payment for the wine she delivered," he said quickly, then wondered why he'd thought an explanation necessary. Pulling himself together, he said, with an attempt at an unconcerned smile, "I'm afraid our conversation was interrupted, so I wasn't able to say all I intended. I didn't speak to Penny about you—I hope she wasn't displeased with you for providing me with her address."

"Penny?" The noblewoman raised one elegant eyebrow. "So she gave you her name, did she?" Her tone turned musing. "Although that's not the name she gave me."

Rian felt his brows drawing together, and a rock seemed to plummet through his stomach. He didn't want to believe that Penny had shown him a false front. For some reason, he couldn't bear the thought.

Lady Amaranthe clearly noticed his expression. "I only meant that she told me her name was Penelope," she clarified, laughing lightly. "She must have formed a good impression of you, Your Highness, to be less formal in spite of your position."

Rian felt a flush rising up his neck, and tried his utmost to suppress it. Struggling also to fight down the smile that wanted to break loose, he attempted a casual reply. "A heartening thought."

Lady Amaranthe's smile was uncomfortably knowing. "She is certainly a special girl," she said softly. Her eyes were searching as they examined his face. "I made plans to see her again," she said, a tiny trace of hesitation in her voice. "Next week, an hour before sunset in a field to the east of her home.

Since you said you weren't able to say all you intended. Good evening, Your Highness."

With another graceful curtsy, she sailed down the corridor and out of sight, leaving Rian staring after her. Had the noblewoman really just invited him to join her in visiting Penny again? Did he dare to accept the invitation? Could he bring himself to refuse it?

Wondering what Penny would think of it all, Rian resumed his interrupted walk toward his suite. He knew it was early to retire. But the three separate groups of giggling girls he passed in the short walk was enough to show him the wisdom of retreating immediately to a private place to wrestle with his thoughts. At least Lady Amaranthe hadn't approached him to flirt with him. He felt a surge of warmth for the noblewoman. It wasn't just girls who were batting their eyelids at him. Some of those angling for his attention were quite as old as Lady Amaranthe. Anyone would have thought they'd have learned more sense. Did they really imagine that his parents would marry him off to whoever giggled most loudly as he passed?

He reached his own suite in minutes, but he made no move to prepare himself for sleep. Instead, he paced the room with agitated strides. Thoughts of Lady Amaranthe's invitation battled with the return of his tension over the latest arrest. Questions whirled through his mind in an endless stream.

Was the newly arrested silversmith being marched out of the kingdom even now? Or would he have to serve time in hard labor first, since he wasn't a child? Would he eventually join the desert outlaws, embittered enough to lash out at the kingdom which had exiled them? How many others were still hiding, hoping to evade notice, afraid they'd be next?

And, perhaps most troubling of all, what was the king's mysterious source of information regarding the fugitives among them?

In all that had happened since, the encounter with Penny by the vineyards that morning should have been the last thing on Rian's mind. Perhaps it was Lady Amaranthe's unexpected words that brought Penny's wary face, with those striking green eyes, popping up before his vision with every turn of the room. She'd been afraid by his presence at first, but she'd softened, hadn't she? Surely it wasn't too late to change the tide of opinion. He'd tried, hadn't he, in the square? To protect the man from further harm?

But that intervention suddenly felt so weak, Rian was ashamed even of that. Yet if he confronted his father on this man's behalf, would he put himself further from the goal of changing his father's mind more completely?

People like the vintner's daughter must think that, as a prince, he had so much power, Rian thought bitterly. Little could she guess how powerless he felt, how caught between duty and conviction.

It was the memory of her final question that decided him. *Is it true that a child was arrested yesterday?* Her voice had been far too heavy and somber for her years, and her expression had clearly showed her feelings on the matter. She'd hurried from him then, as though she couldn't bear to look at him a moment longer. How could she know that he was as troubled by the incident as she was?

Well, he was troubled. His thoughts flew to Princess Azalea's defiant words at the ball the night before, and a foolhardy idea took root in his mind. There was a way to intervene without challenging his father. Even if this girl Penny never knew it, even if no one ever knew, at least Rian would be able to sleep tonight.

He looked at the clock. Still much too early. The hours seemed to pass at a snail's pace, with little to do but watch the embers dim in the grate. Rian allowed a servant to assist him out of his heavy boots and prepare him for sleep. Soft shoes would serve him better tonight anyway. At last, more than an hour past midnight, he decided the castle would be quiet enough.

Donning his darkest cloak, Rian eased out of his window. It had been years since he'd done this, but his feet remembered their way onto the stone ridge that ran along the castle's wall. It was a shame Bentleigh was gone, really. Rian would have liked to have seen the look on his little brother's face when he dropped silently into Ben's neighboring suite in the dead of night.

Not that it was especially silent. The window clearly hadn't been used recently, and it made an alarming noise when Rian eventually pried it open. But there was no occupant to hear it, and more to the point, no guards outside the unoccupied suite to notice a cloaked figure slipping out of the door into the rest of the castle. Soon Rian was padding his way through the empty corridors, taking a circuitous route to avoid the guards stationed at regular intervals.

The castle was so familiar to him, it presented no challenge to reach his destination unseen. He'd given some thought, in the hours of waiting, as to how to achieve the prison break without being seen himself, or bringing consequences down on which-ever guard was on duty. Accordingly, although he descended to the castle's lowest level, he didn't make for the dungeons them-selves. Instead, he slipped into a small storage room one corridor over from where a guard was covering the door that led into the dungeons.

Muscles bulging, he shifted a large cupboard to one side to reveal a small door beyond, half his height. After waiting for a moment to ensure no one had heard his efforts, Rian pulled out the ring of unmarked keys he always kept on his person. Selecting the smallest one, he knelt before the door, inserted the key into the rusty keyhole and pushed with one shoulder. With a grating sound, the door swung inward to reveal a low passage, hung with spiderwebs.

Rian glanced behind him again. He had no way to cover his tracks while he was still in the tunnel. He would need to be quick. Pushing webs aside, he crawled through the space, hoping his sense of direction wouldn't fail him in the enclosing darkness. A fork emerged, and he went left. As he crawled, he remembered with perfect clarity the day when the king had shown this small tunnel network to Rian and Bentleigh. Rian could still hear his father's voice, at its crispest, telling his sons that these tunnels were for the escape of the royal family in direst circumstances, and that the princes were never to use them for play.

The boys knew that voice, and neither of them ever even suggested entering the tunnels. Rian hadn't been in them since then, but he was fairly sure he was going the right way. It was no labyrinth. It was a simple tunnel, with only a few entrances, all on the dungeon level, and a short stretch leading out beyond the castle's wall.

Another solid door met his questing fingers, and he pulled out his keys again. It took a few attempts to find the keyhole in the dark, but eventually he heard the telltale click. Heart hammering, he found the rusted iron ring and tugged, wincing as the door creaked on its journey inward.

Rian emerged into a space just as dark as the one he'd left. But on feeling for the walls around him, he found that he could stand. He did so, resisting the urge to dust himself off. He didn't want to leave any betraying traces of dust or webs. His hands moved through the darkness, discovering what seemed to be shelves on either side of him, stacked with miscellaneous items. The tiniest sliver of light showed ahead, and Rian moved carefully toward what he knew to be a door.

This one opened without need of a key, and thin moonlight

pierced the darkness all around him. Heart lifting, Rian stepped through into the dungeon's central space, from which all the cells opened. He closed the door behind him and turned to survey the scene.

Only one cell was currently occupied, so if the silversmith was being held, it wasn't in the castle. For a moment Rian just stared at the man sleeping uneasily on a hard pallet. Was he doing the right thing? He knew how his father would see this use of the secret tunnel.

But the image of Penny's wistful face, clearly disapproving but either too kind or too frightened to say so, restored his resolve. A day in the stocks, while probably undeserved, hadn't been incentive enough for Rian to intervene. But a year of hard labor, separated from a family that must need him, wasn't something Rian could countenance.

Once again extracting his keys, he unlocked the man's cell as quietly as he could. At such close proximity, however, even this small noise roused the prisoner. He sat up with a gasp that was stifled by Rian's hand over his mouth.

"Don't be afraid," Rian breathed. "I'm here to free you. But you must be silent, or the guard will hear us."

The man stilled. In the dim light, Rian could see the prisoner's eyes searching fruitlessly under Rian's hood, trying to recognize his rescuer. Satisfied the man wasn't going to cry out, Rian removed his hand and stepped back. Scanning the cell, Rian's eyes settled on the small window, above head height. It showed a strip of sky between close-set metal bars.

Rian turned back to his companion. "Give me your tunic." He pulled a small knife from his belt.

"What?"

The man's gasp was too loud for Rian's liking, and he gestured furiously for silence. After an agonized moment of listening, he let out his breath. It seemed the guard hadn't heard.

"Your tunic," Rian growled again, and this time the prisoner complied. Rian felt a fresh surge of discomfort at the sight of the angry red welts now visible on the man's exposed wrists. A day in the stocks had left its mark.

Using his knife, Rian ripped two ragged strips from the garment, then handed it back. Looking perplexed, the man donned it again.

Rian strode to the window, and took a minute to wedge one wad of fabric securely into a jagged gap in the stone, where one of the bars emerged.

"What are you doin'?" muttered the prisoner, closer than Rian had realized.

"I need it to look like you escaped out the window," Rian said, even more quietly.

The man's snort was almost inaudible. "How'm I supposed to have done that?"

Rian shrugged. "Magic."

"I don't have magic!"

Rian shushed the man with a gesture. "So they believed."

The man looked utterly perplexed, but said no more. Rian stepped forward, lifting the other strip of fabric.

"I'm going to blindfold you," he whispered.

The man opened his mouth to speak, but Rian again shushed him. With deft fingers, he tied the fabric around his companion's eyes, checking twice to ensure it was secure. Then, moving as quickly as he dared, he led the prisoner out of the cell —locking the door again behind them—and into the supply cupboard where the secret door was cleverly concealed.

The man gave a hastily stifled exclamation when Rian pushed him to his knees, but at a whispered instruction, he crawled into the tunnel after his guide. This time Rian didn't return to his original point of entry. Instead, he turned at the first fork he came to, and crawled steadily toward what he hoped was north. He knew the dungeons sat close to the castle wall, so he was relieved when, in a fairly short time, his head knocked into a solid, wooden door. He reached behind him, groping until he felt his companion's face, and satisfied himself that the blindfold was still on.

"I've done as I'm told," grunted the prisoner, clearly grasping Rian's purpose.

Rian didn't respond. Fumbling with his keys, he opened the heavy door with many grunts. Dappled moonlight crept into the tunnel, and Rian let out a breath. They'd made it. He carefully pulled back the overgrown branches concealing the door, trying not to damage any of them and leave signs of their passage. At his quiet urging, the prisoner crawled out into the glade, making a soft noise of surprise at feeling bracken beneath his hands. He made to pull the blindfold off, but Rian stopped him.

"Not yet."

Gripping his companion's arm, Rian led him swiftly through the trees, weaving around in an unnecessarily circuitous route in the hope the man would have no idea where the secret door was concealed. Eventually, they reached the edge of the copse, and Rian deemed it safe to remove the fabric from around the prisoner's eyes.

The man blinked in the low light, his eyes searching the peaceful nighttime scene before them. A large farmhouse stood not far away, its field stretching around it. The prisoner turned to Rian, perhaps to thank him. But as that moment, wispy clouds skidded across the sky, exposing the moon, and the man's expression changed. Rian grimaced internally. He hadn't initially expected to be able to hide his identity from the prisoner, but when the man had failed to recognize him, he'd begun to hope he might be able to remain a mystery. No hope of that now.

"You," his companion hissed, features twisted in anger.

Rian did his best to ignore the venom in the man's voice. "Your family has left for Fernedell. They've probably already crossed the border. But my advice would be to make for the nearer border, with Listernia. You won't be pursued if you make it out of the kingdom. You can then make your way to Fernedell by a longer road. I'm afraid I don't have a horse for you."

The man was still staring at Rian with hard eyes. "What did you spring me out for? Is it some sport, to watch me get chased and captured? Or some excuse to execute me for tryin' to escape?"

"Of course not," said Rian impatiently. "Don't be foolish. And don't waste time. You've a long way to go to reach the border on foot, and I can't say how long it will be before your absence is noticed."

Momentarily distracted, the prisoner glanced toward the farmhouse. "I reckon I can get a horse there. Then I'll be over the border before sunrise, with any luck."

Rian's brows drew together as he followed the man's gaze. Seeing his look, his companion rolled his eyes.

"I'm no thief. It's not so far to the border—I'll release the horse once I cross, and I reckon the animal will find its way home easy enough."

Rian wasn't entirely satisfied. Who knew if the man would really set the horse free? But he was in no position to argue. He'd released the prisoner, and he shouldn't have done that if there was no hope of the man retaining his freedom.

"I hope you don't expect me to thank you, Your Highness." The harsh voice pulled Rian's attention back to the man beside him. "If you disagree with the law, that only makes it worse, not better. If you had the gumption to stand up to it, you wouldn't need to be breaking me out in the dead of night."

Rian was silent for a moment. "I don't expect anything from you," he said at last. "But I would be grateful for your silence."

His companion studied him, seeming unsure how to respond. "Well, you've certainly surprised me, I'll give you that," he muttered. And without a further word, he loped off toward the farmhouse.

Rian didn't stay to watch his progress. He made his way swiftly back through the grove, taking a different route so as not to deepen any tracks they might have left. He did his best to rearrange the branches behind him, to make the entrance to the tunnel look undisturbed. To his relief, when he emerged back into the store room where he'd first entered the tunnel, he found no sign that anyone had discovered his passage. Grunting quietly, he pushed the heavy cupboard back into place, and crept out into the corridor.

Two floors above, he was forced to wait a full fifteen minutes for a drawn out guard change to be effected, but eventually he eased himself back into Bentleigh's suite unseen. He felt a surge of wistfulness as he glanced around at the unoccupied rooms. Ben had only left that day, but the suite still had an unlived-in feel. Rian knew why. This castle had ceased to be Ben's true home a long time ago. As foolish as it would be to say it so plainly in front of their parents, Bentleigh was at heart a Listern-ian. He neither owed Bansford the responsibility, nor gave it the devotion, that defined Rian's life. If someone from the next generation was going to care about the impact of the ban on the kingdom's future, it would have to be Rian.

Even if no one stood beside him.

Rian had to admit it to himself as he eased into his own bed several minutes later...the thought was daunting.

CHAPTER ELEVEN

Penny

Penny whistled to herself as she assessed the open sack of lentils before her. Yes, these would do nicely.

A low whine brought her gaze down to Al, whose eyes were fixed on her in bewilderment.

"Sorry, Al," she laughed. "I wasn't whistling for you, just...whistling."

Her fingers twitched as she reached for a jar inside her own sack. The jar flew up an inch, meeting her hand before she'd delved far enough in. She silently chastised herself. Her time with Lady Amaranthe the day before had been one of the most satisfying afternoons of her life, but she needed to get hold of herself. She couldn't afford to slip up in the public market.

"I'll take some lentils," she told the merchant, as she dipped her jar into the sack of lentils. The woman nodded briskly, assessing the quantity with an expert eye. Penny was too distracted even to haggle, but she was familiar to the merchant, and the woman asked a fair price.

Penny wandered toward her favorite produce stall, an extra spring in her step. Another glance down at Al brought her black skirt into view, and she sobered at once. It was almost impossible to believe it had only been two days ago that her father had died. It felt like a lifetime. An eventful lifetime. As guilty as she felt for indulging even a shred of happiness so soon after the loss, she couldn't help but celebrate Lady Amaranthe's entrance into her life. Penny had been amazed at what she'd been capable of in the field the day before. With a bit of training from an experienced enchantress, she'd been able to glimpse a level of finesse that she'd never dreamed of. She'd only ever moved a simple object from one place to another, but already the endless possibilities of more delicate movement were opening before her eyes.

"Good morning," she said, as she reached the stall. Her voice was clearly a little too bright, because the merchant eyed her with a look of sympathetic concern.

"Penelope," he said uncertainly. "I heard a rumor about your father...I'm so sorry."

Penny lowered her eyes, a stab that was half grief, half guilt racing through her. "Thank you," she said quietly.

What must the merchant think of her, whistling as she shopped, when her father was barely in the ground? It wasn't as though she'd forgotten. The dull ache of his loss was still with her, a constant presence in her stomach. But after the simple funeral the day before, she felt like she'd begun to emerge from the fog that had descended at his passing. The funeral had been a quiet affair. Remembering her mother's funeral, Penny wished there could have been more fanfare. But she felt no resentment toward Sapphira for the simplicity of the event. Penny knew the decision had been driven by financial considerations.

"Talking about the rumor, are ya?"

The gleeful voice made both Penny and the merchant look up. An older woman, her eyes alight with gossip, was waiting to buy produce as well.

"Quite the embarrassment for the royals, isn't it?" she cackled.

"What is?" Penny asked, her thoughts flying unbidden to the member of the royal family she'd met just the day before.

"So you haven't heard?" the woman said, looking delighted to be the bearer of the news. "The prisoner, one what was in the stocks yesterday, escaped."

Penny's mouth fell open. "The one whose son was an enchanter?" she asked.

"Not just the son, by the looks," said the woman, with a chuckle. "Seems the father had it, too, but no one realized. Word is he somehow got out through a tiny window, not big enough for a man, without even shifting the bars."

Penny frowned. What kind of magic could do that? "Didn't you say he was in the stocks all day yesterday? If he could escape by magic, why didn't he do it then?"

The woman hesitated, apparently stumped. "Guess he had his reasons," she shrugged eventually.

Penny felt her frown deepen.

"Maybe it was too public a place," suggested the merchant. "Did he get away cleanly from the dungeon, then?"

The woman nodded sagely. "Must've used his magic to get out quickly, mustn't he? Apparently they haven't been able to catch him."

The merchant gave a low whistle, causing Al to once again prick up his ears. Penny, lost in thought, stroked the dog's head absently. Al suddenly stiffened, and let out a sharp bark. Looking down, Penny was just in time to see a small and grimy boy withdraw an arm from her sack, a loaf of bread clutched in his fist. With a terrified glance at her face, the boy fled.

"Oi!" yelled the merchant, but Penny dove toward him, gripping his arm before he could set up the cry of *thief!* that she knew was hovering on his lips.

"Leave it," she said hastily. "It's all right. He's just a child."

The merchant scowled at her. "It isn't," he said forcefully. "It's all well and good to be soft-hearted, but we can't have thieves hanging around our market."

"I know," said Penny earnestly. "And normally I'd agree. But can you let this one go? Just this time?"

The merchant stared at her like she'd lost her mind. But after a tense moment, he let his breath out in a sigh. "He's gone now, anyway," he muttered, turning away with a shrug.

Al gave another bark, as if to disagree. He was rigid with the strain of staying by Penny's side, and his eyes clearly begged her to give him leave to follow the scent of the thief. But she shook her head. "No, Al. Leave the boy alone."

She stared unseeingly at the crowd into which the child had disappeared. Unless she *should* follow him? Could Al really track the boy? Perhaps Penny could help him. Her heart lurched with a combination of nerves and pity. She wasn't as soft-hearted as the merchant thought. Normally she would be ready to defend her property against thieves in the market. But in the brief moment when she'd locked eyes with the child, she'd felt something that shocked her. Something she'd felt recently, when she met Lady Amaranthe. Something she might not have recognized if the noblewoman hadn't opened her eyes to it.

Just how many enchanters were still hiding in Bansford? And how alone and afraid must a child like that feel, knowing the danger he was in? On some level, Penny had been afraid all her life. But she'd never been alone, not in the way that boy was. She still wasn't alone. However unfeeling her stepmother might be, however distant her stepsisters, Penny had a home with them. She had food on her table, and people she could turn to.

And she had something more. She had magic—powerful magic, according to Lady Amaranthe. She could understand the struggle of the hidden magic-users in a way someone without magic never could. Perhaps she could do for others what the noblewoman was doing for her. Penny recalled the words of the dragon, Dannsair, in her dream-vision.

As one of only a few magic-users still to be found in Bansford, it does not seem outside the realm of possibility that you might play a role in the future of magic in the kingdom.

Could that be true? Could Penny influence things for the better? After only one afternoon of training with Lady Amaranthe, she felt empowered in a way she never had before. But it still seemed foolish beyond reason to imagine she would ever have influence over the laws of the kingdom.

"I wondered if I'd see you here again."

Penny jumped, whirling around at the sound of the voice that was somehow already familiar. Prince Rian stood several feet away, but he was definitely speaking to her. His clear brown eyes were fixed unblinkingly on her face, and the hint of a smile softened his severe mouth.

She must have been caught up in her thoughts indeed to have failed to notice the interested hush that once again preceded the prince through the market. Sinking into a clumsy curtsy—she really needed to work on that if the prince was going to keep popping up—she abandoned all thought of pursuing the boy. No matter how pleasantly Prince Rian had surprised her, the last thing she wanted to do was bring the royal's attention to the enchanter child.

"Your Highness," she said, standing upright again. "This is a surprise."

Prince Rian actually smiled this time, although the expression was carefully controlled. "Yes, I'm not usually in this part of the city. But today there are patrols going in all directions, and..."

He trailed off, looking slightly confused, and Penny couldn't help flushing. Was she being vain to imagine that he'd volunteered to join this particular patrol in the hope of seeing her at the market again? He certainly didn't seem interested in joining the other members of his group, who were currently combing the crowd. Penny hoped nervously that the boy from before had made a clean escape.

"Are the patrols looking for the escaped criminal, Your Highness?" the merchant cut in boldly. Prince Rian's gaze flicked to him, his face once again a calm and impenetrable mask.

"That's right."

The old woman, who had been openly goggling at the exchange, shot Penny a meaningful look, as if Penny had doubted her gossip, and was now being proved wrong.

The prince's eyes flicked down to Penny's black gown, then back up, and his expression softened. "I don't feel I adequately expressed my condolences yesterday," he said quietly.

Unable to hold that searching gaze, Penny lowered her eyes to her feet. "You're very kind, Your Highness," she said.

She realized with something of a jolt that it was true. The kindness in his eyes and voice were more uncomfortable than coldness would have been. The upending of her long-held perception of the royal family was almost too unsettling for her to take, on top of her other losses. And yet...she peeked back up to find his eyes still fixed on her face. She couldn't quite bring herself to wish he'd be cold.

"What will happen to the man if he's found?" The merchant's question seemed to startle Prince Rian as much as it did Penny. The prince turned to the other man, looking like it was a struggle to return his thoughts to the topic.

"He will serve his original sentence, with an additional penalty for attempting to escape," said Prince Rian expressionlessly.

"Is that all?" interjected the old woman, sounding faintly disappointed.

Did Penny imagine the wry look that came over the prince's face at this slightly bloodthirsty response?

"He didn't injure anyone in his escape," was all the prince replied aloud. "If he had, I daresay the penalty would be harsher." His eyes slid to the merchant. "Why do you ask? Do you know him?"

The merchant shrugged, looking half wary, half defiant. "Not well, Your Highness. But I supplied produce to the noble family he worked for. I met him and his wife a number of times." He hesitated, then met the prince's eye with obvious determination. "I used to give their boy sweet apples, when I had them in. He seemed like a normal, friendly child to me. I never would've guessed he had magic, because he was as gentle a lad as I ever saw."

Prince Rian listened to this speech gravely, his expression showing neither anger nor offense. Penny, who had been painfully conscious of the curious crowd since the prince first addressed her, noticed that she wasn't the only one listening closely for his response.

"I don't doubt it," the prince said politely. "It is a difficult situation."

"Is it?" Penny retorted, before she could stop herself. Prince Rian's eyes snapped to her, and she felt color rising up her cheeks. But she pushed on. It was too late to stay silent, so she may as well make it worthwhile. "The other kingdoms don't seem to find it so difficult."

"And some of them have suffered for it," said Prince Rian seriously.

Penny met his look unflinchingly. "And are we not suffering for it?"

The prince took a long moment to respond, his eyes not wavering from hers. "I take it you are opposed to the ban, then?"

Penny drew in a slow breath. She was aware of Al, hovering

at her side, alert to her tension. The dog showed no sign of aggression or discomfort himself, like he would if he thought she was in danger.

For her own part, although her heart was hammering, she found that she wasn't afraid. It was almost impossible to believe that little more than a week ago, in this same market, she'd been terrified of attracting the prince's attention, of being exposed to her enemy. She knew in her head that the prince's position still made him a threat to her, with her illicit secret. But somehow, now that he had become human to her, she found it impossible to think of him as her enemy.

"I am, Your Highness," she said boldly, and she heard mutters from the watching crowd. To her surprise, the merchant cleared his throat.

"So am I, Your Highness."

The prince's eyes, more serious than ever, passed between them, his brow furrowed thoughtfully. Before he could respond, however, a guard hailed him.

"Your Highness, no sign of him in the market."

Prince Rian nodded, his eyes still on Penny, although his words were addressed to the guard. "Thank you," he said in a crisp, clear voice. "We'll continue to the south." The guard gave a smart salute and started calling orders to his fellows. Still, the prince made no move to turn away.

"Thank you for sharing your concerns," he said at last, his gaze encompassing both Penny and the merchant. But a moment later, his eyes were once again fixed on Penny's face, and his voice had dropped to a softer pitch. "I'm glad to run into you again, Penny."

Penny once again attempted a curtsy, but this time it was mainly to hide her burning face. The effect of hearing her name in the prince's steady, serious voice was rattling, to say the least. If her heart had been racing before, it was careening wildly toward a cliff edge now. She stayed down until the prince's dusty boots had passed out of her vision, and she deemed it safe to straighten.

"Well," said the merchant, sounding almost as dazed as Penny felt. "He was unexpectedly reasonable."

A grunt from the gossiping old woman suggested disappointment at the prince's tame response to Penny's defiance. No doubt she'd been hoping for a show. "That's how they fool you," she predicted darkly. "Make you think they're listening, but really they're just taking your name down, marking you as a troublemaker."

Penny ignored the dramatic warning, her eyes fixed on the tawny head moving away from her through the crowd, which parted before the prince. She could hardly believe she'd run into the heir to the throne three times in as many days.

"Speaking of taking down names," demanded the old woman, "how in Solstice does the prince know yours?"

Penny brought her gaze to the speaker warily. The woman's eyes were alight with interest, apparently recognizing a new and potentially more promising piece of gossip.

"I met him quite by chance when I delivered goods to the castle once," Penny shrugged, as casually as she could.

"Hmm." The woman looked unconvinced as her gaze traveled over Penny. "You are very pretty, I suppose. But I never heard that the prince was one to make light with merchants' daughters, be they ever so pretty." She gave a cackle. "And I would have heard."

Penny scowled at the nosy old woman, even as she internally acknowledged the truth of the boast. If there was any sordid gossip about the crown prince, this woman would certainly have acquired it.

"I'm not a merchant's daughter," she snapped. "And no one's *making light* with me."

"No need to take offense," grinned the woman. "You know what I mean. I just thought you looked a little too genteel to be a proper servant, but I've been wrong afore. One thing I'm not wrong about, though. You ain't of the upper class that's supposed to mingle with princes and the like. You'd best be glad if the prince's eyes haven't fallen on you, because if they had, it wouldn't be for no honest purpose."

Penny turned away, too filled with indignation to reply. She conducted her shopping with more than usual dignity, barely even heartened by the sympathetic way the merchant rolled his eyes at her. She didn't appreciate the woman's insinuations about her, but for no logical reason she could discern, she was even more offended by the aspersions cast on the crown prince. The very suggestion that he would toy with pretty girls of the lower classes filled Penny with a desire to rise to his defense.

Internally she had to admit, as she trudged from the market with a bulging sack, that she was annoyed with herself as much as with the old woman. Try as she might, she couldn't help wondering again whether the prince had come to the market especially to look for her. She even, to her private embarrassment, found herself wondering whether he, like the gossipy woman, thought Penny was *very pretty*.

She reached home in a somber mood, to find Harry waiting for her. Al bounded up to the grizzled servant, frisking delightedly around his feet.

"All safe and sound, Pen?" Harry asked, his eyes passing over her anxiously.

Penny sent him a look. "Harry, you know I appreciate your concern, but you have to relax. I'm in no more danger now than I was a week ago. Just because I know that you know about my magic, doesn't mean it's any more at risk of discovery by the rest of the kingdom."

Harry blinked, looking confused by her convoluted speech,

and Penny took the opportunity to push past him toward the manor.

"It's all well and good to say your situation hasn't changed," he said darkly, following her into the kitchen, and peering around to make sure it was empty. "But it has. For one thing, you don't have a father to protect you anymore."

Penny paused, her hand still on the sack she'd just hoisted onto the scrubbed wooden table. "Did you think I'd forgotten?" she asked quietly. She turned to her companion, her expression pained. "Harry, you know I loved Father, and I'm devastated to lose him. But you also know as well as I do that he hasn't done much to protect me in a long time. Years, even." She sighed, dropping her voice to a mutter. "I'm inclined to think that the last thing he tried to do was marry Sapphira, to protect me from being unmothered."

Harry leaned on the table, his sleeves rolled up to the elbow, and his hands still caked in dirt from whatever he'd been doing in the yard. "He meant it for the best, Pen," he said gently. "I never thought it was a good idea, but it was for him to decide what was best for you, after all."

She turned beseeching eyes on him, desperate for the answers her father would never be able to give her now. "Why did he think being pinched and poked and criticized would be best for me?"

Harry grunted. "It's like how I'm good with the soil, but can't cook an egg to save my life, Pen. Oftentimes it's that way, that people are skilled in one thing, but hopeless in another. Your father was a confident businessman, but not a confident father. I often observed it. It was what happened to your mother that rattled him."

"Shouldn't that have made him hold me closer, if anything?" Penny demanded.

Harry regarded her in silence for a moment. "Many would

have responded that way," he said. "But you have to understand that your father was always so confident in himself when he was younger. His parents didn't want him to marry your mother, but he was sure of his decision, like he was with everything. I think maybe...maybe later events made him question if he'd been wrong, if his wisdom had failed him."

"He regretted marrying my mother?" Penny asked, unwilling tears pricking her eyes.

"Regret is a big word," said Harry solemnly. "He loved her, I don't doubt it. But she wasn't quite what he expected. She didn't always recognize his wisdom, as it were. She often defied him, not out of a desire to vex him, but out of that big heart of hers. He didn't like her using her magic, even before the ban, but especially after. He thought it was dangerous, and he asked her not to do it. But she couldn't bring herself to ignore the needs around her. She had too big a heart."

"All of that went over my head," said Penny, her voice hushed. "I never knew he was frustrated with her. I suppose I was so young."

"And he never said a word against her after she was gone," Harry pointed out. "Which is to his credit."

Penny nodded slowly. "He said something like this to me," she said suddenly. "Not a week before he died. He said that I was like her in more than looks, and that my mother had also never had enough thought for her safety."

Harry nodded. "We could all tell from an early age that you're much like your mother in temperament, Pen. Bless you, it's something to celebrate. But I could see it made your father anxious. He worried that you would be as stubborn, as determined to help others at your own cost, as your mother was before you. And he knew he didn't have the knack of making you see his type of reason, because he'd never been able to convince your mother." Harry's voice became sad. "Not even when her life was on the line."

There was an ache in Penny's chest that made it hard to breathe. "So he brought Sapphira into our home, in the hope she would break me as he failed to do."

"I don't think he would have seen it quite like that," said Harry dryly, a spark of humor in his gray eyes.

Penny sighed. "I suppose not. Now," she straightened, her voice becoming stern, "enough reminiscing. I have dinner to cook, and you've made the table filthy." With a flick of her head, she sent the cakes of dirt flying from the table onto the floor. A further gesture gathered the dirt neatly by the back door, next to a broom.

"Pen!" gasped Harry, although he looked as much awed as reproving. "What if someone saw?"

Penny shrugged. "Who is there to see? We're just about the only servants left, and when was the last time you saw any of the family in the kitchen?"

Harry frowned at her. "You're not a servant, Pen."

"Whatever," said Penny, with another shrug. "If the shoe fits." For all her talk, Penny looked around carefully to make sure they really were alone before she rolled her fingers. A heavy pot flew from a cupboard under the sink, landing on the table before her with such force that it bounced right off the other side, missing Harry's foot only thanks to his quick reflexes.

"Oops," said Penny, with a grimace. "Sorry, Harry. I'm still in desperate need of practice."

Harry frowned at her, although Penny was fairly sure it wasn't his foot he was worried about. "That's what you were doing with that noblewoman yesterday, isn't it? Practicing your magic."

Penny nodded, casting another glance around the room and dropping her voice. "Can you keep a secret, Harry?"

He grunted. "Stupid question."

"True," acknowledged Penny with a grin. "Lady Amaranthe is an enchantress too, Harry. She's been hidden all these years in the heart of the court! She helped me see that hiding my magic doesn't necessarily mean not using it. Just being smart about how I use it." She brightened, pulling out a knife with her actual hands rather than her magic, to be on the safe side. "Just like my mother."

"Your mother wasn't smart that one night," Harry objected, but without any real heat. He was scrutinizing Penny's glowing face with a thoughtful expression. "I'm not out to spoil your fun, Pen. But that's the other thing that's changed, the other reason I'm more worried about you than I was before. You're rubbing shoulders with royalty now. You can't afford to attract the notice of people like that."

Penny felt her cheeks heating as she remembered the encounter with the prince in the market, and she cursed her expressive reactions. "I'll be careful, Harry, you know I will. But I can't help that the prince now knows my name. And I truly don't think he means me any harm." She thought of the insinuations of the woman in the market, and her cheeks heated all over again as it occurred to her that Harry might be concerned about a different danger altogether.

But Harry's next words set her mind at ease on that point. "That's because he doesn't know about your magic," he grunted.

She sighed, acknowledging the truth of his words. Whatever softness the prince might have shown toward her, it was intended for a thoroughly non-magical Penny, not an enchantress in hiding. But she couldn't do anything about that.

"And there's no reason to think he ever will know," she said, attempting to speak lightly even as the words made her heart sink for some reason. "He's already delivered the payment, anyway," she added. "It's not like he's going to come back to the manor for another visit."

Harry grunted yet again. "If you ask me," he muttered, "the payment wasn't what brought him in the first place."

He said no more, but the suspicious glance he threw in the direction of the distant castle made Penny wonder if his thoughts aligned somewhat with the gossipmonger's after all.

CHAPTER TWELVE

Penny

"Do dragons have specific skills, like human magic-users?" Penny asked, her eyes fixed eagerly on Dannsair's face. "I didn't realize how unusual my power is, but Lady Amaranthe says that most enchanters can't lift things without even an incantation, the way I can."

"That does sound powerful," mused the dragon, eyes alight with interest. "I don't think I've seen that before, even in my part of Solstice, where enchanters are more common. And no, dragons' magic does not work quite like humans'. We do not lift things with our minds, or have specific individual skills. But we do have areas of strength from dragon to dragon."

It sounded like specific skills to Penny, but she refrained from saying so. "What's yours?" she asked. "If it's not impolite to ask," she added hastily.

Dannsair gave an aloof smile, the impossible sunlight sparkling off her purple scales. "I don't know that I can reduce it to words that you would understand," she said calmly. "But this conversation is evidence of it. Not all dragons can see from afar like this." She shifted as she said it, her tail flicking across the ground as if she was uncomfortable.

"What's wrong?" Penny asked.

A rippling motion passed over Dannsair, from her neck down to her tail—the dragon equivalent of a shrug. "Something I do not intend to discuss with you."

Penny made no attempt to press further. "So you can see from afar, then? Is that what this is?"

"In a manner of speaking," replied the dragon placidly. "I cannot see fully. I am drawn to your magic, as I have told you before. It is not really like sight. It is more like an extra sense, one humans do not have. Or at least," she tilted her head thoughtfully to the side, "most humans do not."

"I think I know what you mean," Penny said excitedly, thinking of how she'd been able to recognize Lady Amaranthe's magic and, with a little more practice, that of the boy in the market. "Enchantresses have it, I think."

The dragon nodded slowly, her voice solemn. "It is a mark of magic." She studied Penny's face. "I am glad you are using your magic now, Penny. It is not wise to bottle it up. And it is difficult to use your power for good if you do not use your power at all."

Penny raised her eyes to the vast reptilian head above her. "So you still think I could change things for good somehow?"

The dragon just smiled cryptically, and a mist started descending around Penny.

"Wait!"

The mist continued to descend, but the dragon inclined her head inquiringly at Penny's cry.

"Will..." Penny felt suddenly shy. "Will you come again? Or...see me from afar again, or whatever this is?"

Dannsair was still smiling. "Regularly, if you wish it."

"I do," said Penny earnestly. "I'm grateful for your communication. More than I can say."

The dragon dipped her head regally, her shockingly purple figure already mostly obscured.

.   .   .

Penny woke with a start, staring at the pale sunlight illuminating her room. She'd overslept, of course, and it would set her whole day behind. But she didn't care. She'd meant what she said to the dragon. She *was* grateful for their strange meetings. With Lady Amaranthe's arrival, and the increasingly frequent visions of the dragon, Penny could feel the erosion of that sense of isolation that had set her apart all her life. It was a timely change, since her former supports were almost all gone.

She hurried through her morning chores, still too caught up in the vision-conversation with the dragon to worry about her tardiness. By the time the sun had risen above the vineyards, and she still hadn't begun making breakfast, she was relieved to see that Harry had been ahead of her and had fed the animals in their small barnyard. She should have known he'd have her back.

Her own stomach was growling by the time she reached the kitchen, so she knew her stepmother and stepsisters must be in a similar state. With a quick glance around, she held out a taut hand, lowering the pot of water so that it was right in the flames, the orange tongues licking its sides. In no time at all, the water was bubbling merrily. Smiling in satisfaction, Penny raised her other hand, so that the eggs traveled from their basket into the pot. The focus required to keep the pot suspended the whole time was a stretch for her distracted mind, however, and she failed to notice the sound of approaching footsteps. When the door slammed behind her, she started, losing focus altogether. The pot fell into the fire with a splash followed by a hiss.

Whirling around, Penny let out a sigh that was half relief, half exasperation. "Harry, it's you. You made me drop the eggs! They're probably ruined."

"What happened to being careful, Pen?" growled Harry. "I could've been anyone, couldn't I?"

"I know, and I'm sorry," said Penny distractedly, as she retrieved the pot from the fire with the long-handled fire tongs. She groaned at the sight of two cracked eggs, their contents already forming rubbery clouds through the water. "I'm just running so late this morning."

"Late for what?" grunted Harry. "For Her Majesty's breakfast?"

"It's my breakfast too," Penny reminded him wryly. "And I'm hungry."

Harry strode over to help her, but she waved him away.

"No offense, Harry, but you sort of destroy everything you touch in the kitchen."

He grinned, making no attempt to deny the accusation.

Tipping the mess into a bowl, Penny salvaged what she could before refilling the pot with fresh water. With difficulty she pulled her thoughts from her conversation with Dannsair, and from the visit Lady Amaranthe had promised to make that afternoon. She needed to be ahead in her chores, not behind, if Harry was going to once again successfully cover her absence. Avoiding her magic this time, she set about making a breakfast that would be edible if not exciting.

Apparently this view was shared by Sapphira, who received her eggs without comment but with a speaking glance at her stepdaughter.

Olivia made a grunt of dissatisfaction. She didn't voice her complaint though, so that was something. Since her first uncharacteristic defense of Penny the morning after Penny's father died, Olivia hadn't shown any overt kindness. But she'd been less quick to criticize. Penny didn't have any illusions that the change was permanent. Already it had begun to wear off.

But in the meantime she would take whatever softness she could get.

"Are you aware of the time, Penelope?" asked Sapphira, in the tone Penny most hated, that voice of everlasting patience.

"Yes," said Penny quickly. "And I'm sorry breakfast is ready so late in the morning. I'm afraid I overslept."

Sapphira raised an eyebrow. "Perhaps it would be more efficient for you to sleep in a room next to the kitchen, Penelope. Cook even used to sleep in the kitchen itself in winter, I believe, to ensure the fire stayed lit all night."

"Mother." Sophia's protest caused everyone in the room to blink at her in surprise. "Penny shouldn't have to move out of her room."

There was a beat of silence, then Olivia spoke up, even more unexpectedly. "It seems unnecessary." Her voice was cold, and she didn't look at Penny. Nevertheless, Penny was grateful that the older girl's sympathy apparently hadn't quite run out yet.

Even Sapphira betrayed a hint of emotion, her eyes showing both surprise and irritation as they passed between her daughters. But in face of their united front, she said nothing more.

Penny tried to meet her stepsisters' eyes to express her gratitude, but she found both of them focused on their plates. She held in a sigh. Sapphira's daughters weren't chillingly emotionless like their mother, but that didn't mean they were good with emotion. And perhaps it was no surprise.

"I'll be meeting with the bailiff this afternoon," Sapphira said with her usual calm. "As you would all know, Penelope delivered the final shipment of our wines to the publican yesterday. We have also received the payment for the remaining vineyard."

Penny drew a breath. "The proceeds of that won't keep us going forever," she said softly. "And the land we have won't bring in enough to live on."

"No, it won't," Sapphira agreed. "I have laid by as much as I thought we could spare, so we will manage for a little while. But we will need to find another way to contrive." Her eyes lingered on Sophia as she spoke. Penny noticed that the younger of her stepsisters looked uncomfortable as she fidgeted with her spoon. Penny wasn't entirely sure what Sophia was expected to do, but it was certainly novel to see her stepmother expecting anyone other than Penny to solve their problems.

Dismissing the matter from her mind, Penny allowed her thoughts to return to her magic. Would Lady Amaranthe really come a second time? Penny could scarcely contain her impatience to train with her magic again.

The day passed slowly, filled with more chores than Penny could keep up with. The two servants who still remained, other than Harry, looked so stressed every time Penny crossed paths with them, that she wondered if they would leave by choice even before they were let go. It couldn't be long before that happened, as they must know perfectly well. Penny found herself hoping it would be soon. In a strange paradox, while it would add to her workload, it would make her work easier by removing the primary potential witnesses to her using her magic. Her stepfamily didn't tend to hang around in the kitchen, or the barnyard, or any of the other places Penny spent most of her time now.

When the afternoon finally arrived, Penny was almost bursting with eagerness to reach the field. Harry encountered her on her last trip to the house, carrying more wood in her arms than was safe. Not that it was a danger to her physically. Her arms were in fact bearing very little of the weight. The danger came from the suspicious picture she presented, loaded down with much more than she could carry with her normal strength.

"Pen," scolded Harry, and she grimaced.

"I know, I know," she said. "But I don't have time to do five trips. I'll be late for Lady Amaranthe."

"Do you really think she's coming?" Harry asked skeptically. "Mayhap she's lost interest by now. Fancy folk like her tend to have short attention spans, Pen."

Penny shook her head resolutely. "Lady Amaranthe isn't like that. She said she'll be here, and I'm sure she will."

"Well," said Harry, in his gruff way, "I won't deny that I'm glad you've got someone teaching you how to use your...what you've got."

Penny raised an amused eyebrow. "I thought I was supposed to be careful."

"You are," Harry shot back. "And it's harder to be careful if you don't know how to control it."

Penny couldn't argue with that. "So you'll cover for me if I'm missed?"

"Do you need to ask?" Harry grunted.

"Of course I don't," beamed Penny. "What would I do without you, Harry?"

"Ah, get on with you," scoffed Harry, but Penny noticed that his ears were slightly pink.

Still smiling, she hurried out of the yard, making for the east field. Al appeared from nowhere as she left the manor's property, trotting along at her side with tongue lolling out. For all her assurances to Harry, Penny felt a thrill of relief when she emerged from the row of trees and saw Lady Amaranthe's elegant form waiting for her.

"You came!" she said delightedly.

Lady Amaranthe laughed. "Of course. I said I would, didn't I?"

"I've been practicing," Penny rushed on eagerly. "I'm getting much better with more delicate movements, look."

With a twirl of her fingers, she pulled a decorative comb

from Lady Amaranthe's hair, making it fly into her own palm. When the older woman gave a laughing protest, Penny swept her other hand upward, sending the comb back to its original destination. Screwing up her face in concentration, she caused the comb to sweep its owner's hair back from her brow, before it settled perfectly into place.

"Impressive," grinned her companion. "You could be a common pickpocket, no problem."

Penny laughed. "My ambitions aren't as grand as that, I'm afraid. I'm just glad to have the extra help with all the housework I'm expected to do now. It's like having two additional people helping out."

A frown marred Lady Amaranthe's lovely features. "Your magic is meant for more than helping you become a more docile servant, Penny."

Penny paused, wondering what about the other woman's speech had sounded strange.

Seeing her hesitation, Lady Amaranthe added, "I'm sorry, do you prefer Penelope?"

Ah, that was it. She hadn't given the other enchantress her nickname, and she didn't think Lady Amaranthe had ever used it before. "No, Penny is fine," she assured the older woman quickly. "I'm usually called Penny."

The noblewoman nodded, looking thoughtful for a reason Penny couldn't fathom. "Can you lift your dog?" she asked after a moment.

Penny glanced at Al, chasing a butterfly nearby. The big softie.

"I'm afraid not." She shook her head. "I can't move living creatures."

"Interesting," mused Lady Amaranthe. "But plants you can move?"

Penny nodded. "Look at that sapling." Once the other

woman had followed her gaze, Penny clenched her hand around the air in front of her and yanked. The motion was overly enthusiastic, and the sapling shot all the way out of the ground, roots dangling beneath it.

"Oops," said Penny ruefully. She let her hand drop, so that the tree reinserted itself into the ground. "If only I could get the roots back into position," she muttered. Closing her eyes, she tried to use the extra sense that Dannsair had described, straining to recognize the location of the roots even though she couldn't see them with her physical eyes. "Nothing," she sighed. "Maybe I should come back later with a shovel, and try to replant it the old-fashioned way."

"Forget about the tree," chuckled Lady Amaranthe. "I wonder if we can expand your power with practice, so you could move living creatures. Is it such a stretch from moving plants?"

Penny shrugged, uninterested. "Why would I want to move creatures?" she said. "Surely our time is better spent honing the skill I do have, not trying to acquire another that will probably never come."

Lady Amaranthe shot her a knowing look. "Would it convince you if I told you the skill would be useful for milking your cow or something?"

Penny brightened. "We have two cows actually," she corrected. "And yes, it would help convince me."

Lady Amaranthe laughed yet again. "Your priorities are a mess," she scolded, but there was no true irritation in her eyes.

"You said you'd show me your magic today," Penny reminded her, timidly. "I'd love to see, if I'm not overstepping."

"Oh, of course," said Lady Amaranthe. "Well, I can't move things like you can, at least, not without crafting an enchantment to that effect. And I've never actually tried that, to be honest. The magic that comes most naturally to me is that of appearance."

"Appearance?" Penny repeated blankly. Her eyes scanned Lady Amaranthe's immaculate form.

The noblewoman was laughing again. "Not *my* appearance," she clarified. Her voice turned musing. "Although it could be used for that, of course." She dusted off her hands meaningfully. "Simply put, my magic is well-formed for changing how things look," she explained. She scrutinized Penny carefully. "Hold out your hand."

Penny did as instructed. Lady Amaranthe muttered something she couldn't hear, and at once, a feeling washed over her skin that was reminiscent of the times her mother had healed her. Looking down, Penny let out a gasp of horror at the sight of the deeply wrinkled hand of a much older woman, emerging from her own sleeve.

"What have you done to my hand?" she protested, unable to help herself.

"I haven't done anything," smiled Lady Amaranthe. "I haven't changed its nature at all, just its appearance." She made a graceful flourish with her own hands, murmuring once again, and Penny's skin returned to its normal smooth state.

"Did you have to pick that example?" Penny demanded, rubbing her hand in alarm.

"Perhaps it was a little grim," acknowledged Lady Amaranthe, still sounding amused. "How about this?" She flicked her hand again, and Penny's mud-encrusted garden boots suddenly became elegantly embroidered dancing slippers.

"Ooh," exclaimed Penny, lifting shining eyes to her companion. "I like that much better!"

Lady Amaranthe grinned, but Penny's eyes were already back on her shoes. She realized, when she focused her senses on her feet, that Lady Amaranthe was right. Her eyes saw dainty slippers, but her feet still felt her heavy, unembellished garden boots.

"Fascinating," she muttered.

"Isn't it?" agreed Lady Amaranthe lightly.

Penny glanced at the noblewoman again, taking in her gorgeous gown and the jewels twinkling tastefully at throat and ears. "How much of that is real?" Penny asked suspiciously.

"All of it," Lady Amaranthe assured her in amusement. "I'm not in the habit of prancing around in false finery. The illusions don't last forever, you know. I have to actively maintain them, which is exhausting, and even so they run out after a while."

Penny nodded, taking it all in. "And can you use yours on animals?"

By way of answer, Lady Amaranthe turned her head toward Al, her face suddenly intent and focused. Penny followed her gaze and saw with a jolt that the dog was gone, an unnaturally large tabby cat in its place. Al froze, clearly realizing something was up. But before he could do more than whip around to face Penny, he had resumed his normal form. He gave the human pair a suspicious look, but when Penny turned back to her companion, he returned to sniffing at an anthill, none the worse for wear.

"Animals are harder for me too," smiled Lady Amaranthe. "Usually I would take some time to prepare for enchanting a living creature, build up some stamina, perhaps store magic in an artifact if something suitable is to hand."

She did indeed look more tired than before, but Penny was too fascinated by the other woman's words to take much notice of her appearance.

"You can store magic in artifacts?" she asked, amazed.

"I forget how much you don't know," said Lady Amaranthe, shaking her head. "We must definitely spend some time on artifacts. They could be very useful for you. But not today. Today let's continue practicing with your raw magic."

Penny certainly had no objection. For two solid hours she

worked with the other enchantress, following Lady Amaranthe's instructions and watching in amazement as her familiar power seemed to blossom before her very eyes. She was so absorbed, she forgot even to wonder whether Harry had managed to allay suspicion for such an extended absence. But when the afternoon was well advanced, she saw her companion's eyes flick up to the sun, then to the tree line from which Penny had emerged.

"I've kept you too long," Penny said guiltily, also looking up at the sky.

"Not at all," Lady Amaranthe assured her. "This is time well spent as far as I'm concerned." Her eyes raked over Penny's form, and she shook her head. "You're nowhere near spent, even after all that."

Penny grimaced ruefully. "I feel twice as tired as I did when we started," she admitted.

Lady Amaranthe smiled indulgently. "Which is much less tired than you *should* feel, given the amount of power you've expended."

As she said it Penny realized for the first time just how tired her mentor now looked. The power Lady Amaranthe had used in her various demonstrations for Penny's benefit had clearly taken a toll.

"I'm sorry," Penny said. "I've been selfish, caught up in my own world, not thinking about you."

"Nonsense," said Lady Amaranthe, with a touch of impatience. "I've told you, I'm glad to spend my time and energy this way. That's not the reason we need to stop." She drew a breath. "I have a confession to make, and I hope you'll forgive me for it."

"Of course I will," said Penny without hesitation. "What is it?"

"I spoke to Prince Rian about you," said Lady Amaranthe, "after our last visit."

Penny felt her face pale, then flush, and once again berated herself for her open emotions. "Why?" she asked, a little lamely.

"Even at the ball, I had the impression he was quite struck by you," Lady Amaranthe said. "And when you told me he'd raced out here to meet you the very next morning, it only strengthened that impression."

Penny narrowed her eyes, her suspicion growing that the true confession was still to come. And sure enough...

"So I invited him to join us here, an hour before sunset. Which is why we need to stop practicing our illegal magic, in case he turns up."

"Why?" Penny asked again, aghast. Her heart was beating as erratically as it had when she'd encountered the prince in the market almost a week before. It was an uncomfortable sensation.

"I thought it would be a good idea to further your...connection."

"But why?" Penny said yet again, almost wailing this time. "Why would you think that was a good idea? When you know what I'm hiding? What I am?"

"That," said Lady Amaranthe sternly, "Is exactly why I wanted to give him another chance to see what kind of person you are. He's our future ruler, and he needs to see that enchanters and enchantresses aren't evil masterminds, but regular—and in your case, kind and generous-hearted —people."

"You want me to tell him about my magic?" Penny demanded, disregarding the compliment entirely.

"Of course not!" Lady Amaranthe said, startled. "That's the last thing I want you to do. He's not ready for that, and I wouldn't put you in danger for the world."

"Then what's the point of him getting to know me?" Penny protested.

"The time may come when our magic is exposed," said Lady Amaranthe gently. "We both know it's true—don't tell me you don't live with that fear as surely as I do."

Penny remained silent, unable to deny it.

"When that time comes—*if* that time comes—perhaps one at least of the royal family can be convinced that we are human beings, not dangerous animals. But even if none of that comes to pass," she hurried on, seeing Penny's skeptical expression, "you can have a positive influence without him knowing you're an enchantress, you know. If you're subtle about it, you can champion our cause without him being any the wiser."

Penny pondered this. The enchantress was more right than she knew. Penny's thoughts were drawn inevitably to the confrontation in the market, when she'd told the prince so boldly that she objected to the ban. She hadn't even told Lady Amaranthe about that encounter.

"It still feels like just the kind of dangerous situation I've been avoiding all my life," she said frankly. Her gaze passed around the field, searching for any betraying sign of their magic.

Lady Amaranthe looked remorseful. "I should have asked you first. I'm sorry, Penny. It was a week ago, and I acted on the impulse of the moment. Perhaps it was foolish."

"No, don't apologize," sighed Penny. "You're trying to help the plight of Bansford's magic-users, which is more than I've ever done. It's only right that I do my part."

The words had barely left her mouth when a flash of movement drew their eyes to the tree line. Penny's heart leaped into her throat at the sight of the prince's tall, muscular figure. He must have left his horse nearby, perhaps in the keeping of his guards, because neither were with him.

"He actually came," she murmured, half to herself.

"Of course he came," said Lady Amaranthe, sounding a trifle smug.

Penny wanted to send her a scowl, but she refrained, because the prince was striding toward them, close enough now to see such goings on.

"Your Highness," Lady Amaranthe greeted him, curtsying gracefully. "I'm so glad you could join us."

"Lady Amaranthe." Prince Rian inclined his head, but his eyes flicked only briefly to the noblewoman before returning to Penny. "So am I."

Penny knew she should curtsy, but her legs seemed to have lost all strength for movement. Besides, she would only make a fool of herself. So she dipped her head and cleared her throat. Her voice still came out unnaturally husky.

"Your Highness."

The prince hesitated, clearly sensing her discomfort. "I'm sorry if I intrude," he said uncertainly, glancing between the two women. "Is..." He glanced around. "Is this field part of your estate, then?"

"No," confessed Penny. "It's used as grazing land by a number of neighboring farms, but I believe it actually belongs to the crown." She gave an unconvincing smile. "It's yours, in other words."

"We meet here because Penny's stepmother doesn't treat her very well," said Lady Amaranthe matter-of-factly. "We don't know how she would react to Penny spending time with me."

"Lady Amaranthe!" Penny hissed, her face burning.

"Well, it's true, isn't it?" the noblewoman shrugged. "She's turning you into little better than a servant now your father is dead."

Penny's eyes widened in horror. She tried to protest, but her words seemed to be stuck in her throat.

"I'm sorry," said Prince Rian, after an awkward silence.

Penny could hear the concern in his voice, but she didn't

dare look at his face. Her eyes were on her boots, and her face burned.

"It's not like that," she muttered.

She shot Lady Amaranthe a look, irritated. Penny should have been more careful when venting her frustration to the other woman. She'd never imagined her petty comments would be repeated to the prince, of all people. And it was unjust, after all. Lady Amaranthe knew perfectly well that Penny's new duties weren't the reason they were meeting in secret. It was so that they could use their magic without anyone being the wiser, and that would've been the case regardless of her stepmother's treatment of her.

A bark of greeting drew Penny's attention to Al. She'd lost track of him, but he must have been caught up in activities of his own, because he was now racing across the field toward Prince Rian. For a brief and foolish moment, Penny thought her dog was coming to protect her, but Al clearly had no such thought on his mind. Apparently recognizing a sympathetic presence, he frisked around the prince's feet, wagging his tail and barking excitedly.

"Hello again," chuckled the prince, attempting to scratch Al's ears—no easy feat as the dog continued to dance frantically on the spot.

"Al, down!" Penny cried in alarm, as her supposed protector jumped up and placed his filthy paws on Prince Rian's finely embroidered tunic.

But the prince just laughed. "You're all right, aren't you, fella?"

Al, still up on his hind legs as he attempted to lick the prince's mercifully out-of-reach face, wagged a furious tail.

Penny blinked at the display, so surprised by the prince's response that she almost forgot to apologize on behalf of her dog.

"I'm sorry, Your Highness," she managed at last. "He's usually better trained."

"It's all right," smiled the price, kneeling down to allow Al to reach him at last. "Calm down, boy," he said with a hint of sternness in his voice. "You're carrying on like a pup, and you're much too old for that."

To Penny's further amazement, Al subsided. With one last eager wag of his tail, he sat. His lolling tongue made it look for all the world like he was grinning at the prince, as at an old friend.

"I like dogs," Prince Rian explained to Penny, his lips relaxing into a smile that softened his square jaw. "And they usually like me."

"So I see," said Penny, staring at her dog with a hint of accusation in her eyes. Al laid his ears back and panted happily at her. "Traitor," she muttered, but her lips twitched.

Prince Rian glanced quickly at her, and she suddenly remembered her observation at the ball that he had excellent hearing. Before he could say anything, however, Lady Amaranthe spoke. She had remained silent throughout the exchange regarding Al, and Penny thought she still looked faintly smug.

"Well, I'm sorry to run away just as you arrive, Prince Rian." The noblewoman's regretful tone was entirely unconvincing. "But I'm afraid I've been away from the capital for too long." She curtsied again to Prince Rian, and took Penny's hand. "Thank you for your company, Penny."

Her eyes twinkled slightly in response to the silent daggers Penny was sending her at this blatant piece of scheming. Without another word, Lady Amaranthe turned and strode from the field, not toward the trees, but over a slight rise, in the direction of the capital. She must have walked all the way from Bant. The noblewoman was full of surprises.

Penny drew her eyes reluctantly from Lady Amaranthe's retreating back, trying to control the pounding of her heart. Al's behavior had momentarily driven her discomfort from her mind, but it returned in full force now that she found herself essentially alone with the prince. Her hands shook slightly, and her magic—so delightfully unconfined all afternoon—jostled for release. She took a deep breath, forcing herself to be calm, and looked up into Prince Rian's eyes.

To her surprise, there was humor lurking there.

"That's quite rude of her, isn't it?" he said lightly. "To invite someone else on your behalf, and then abandon you?"

Penny laughed reluctantly, unable to resist the appeal in those clear eyes. "Not at all, Your Highness. You're very welcome."

"I doubt it," said the prince frankly. "But I'll take it. I'm glad for a chance to continue our conversation."

"Continue our...?" Penny started, confused.

"You said you're opposed to the ban," Prince Rian said. "I was wondering if you could tell me why."

CHAPTER THIRTEEN

Rian

With the ease of long practice, Rian held his expression steady, but inside he was cringing. He'd cast around for a presentable excuse for why he'd come here, but clearly he'd erred in settling on their conversation in the market. He shouldn't have led with such a tense topic. Penny's shock was evident in her face, and the wariness had returned to her eyes.

"Tell you...why?" Penny repeated, as if weighing each word carefully.

"We don't have to discuss it if you don't wish to," Rian said evenly. "I'm just interested in your perspective."

"You are?" Penny's face was blank with astonishment, and Rian couldn't help laughing.

"Of course I am. You're a subject of this kingdom, aren't you?"

"Yes," said Penny, still wary, as though she thought he was leading her into a trap.

Rian sighed. "I'm not an ogre, Penny. And I'm not so proud—or so foolish—that I fly into a rage whenever anyone disagrees with me."

"I don't think you're an ogre, Your Highness," said Penny.

Her eyes were on her feet again, her cheeks tinged with a color that made her gentle face much too appealing. Rian swallowed.

"You don't need to say 'Your Highness' every time you speak, you know," he said. "You gave me your name. I have one as well."

"You'd prefer me to call you Prince Rian?" Penny asked, looking bewildered.

The sound of his name in her soft, lilting voice did something strange to Rian's insides. The sensation demonstrated with painful clarity just how much danger lay this way. Ignoring the internal warning, he cleared his throat.

"Yes, I'd prefer that." He'd prefer her to drop the prince altogether, if they were being honest, but he wasn't about to say that. Quite apart from being inappropriate, it would probably alarm her.

"I should really be going home," Penny said, fidgeting with a fold of her gown. "They'll be wondering where I am."

Rian studied her face in silence, trying to master his disappointment at her obvious reluctance to spend time with him. It seemed she hadn't been privy to Lady Amaranthe's plan to invite him to whatever this rendezvous had been.

"Let me at least walk you home," he said, gesturing toward the out of sight manor house he'd visited once before.

Penny hesitated, and for a moment he thought she'd refuse. But then she nodded, moving forward to walk by his side. Her dog, who'd still been sitting on his haunches, bounded up, frisking around them as they walked.

"What's your dog's name?" Rian asked, his eyes on the alaunt.

"Al," said Penny, and for some bizarre reason, there was a definite note of defiance in her voice as she said it.

Al glanced over at the sound of his name, but realizing that nothing was required of him, he returned to chasing a butterfly. Rian watched his antics fondly. He'd seen the way the dog stuck to his mistress in the market. However wary Penny might be of Rian, her dog clearly didn't consider him a threat, and he took comfort from that fact. He hadn't lied when he said he liked dogs, and in his experience, their instincts were rarely wrong. Hopefully Penny would reach the same conclusion, and stop acting like a spooked deer every time she saw him approach.

It took Rian a moment to realize the assumption behind his thoughts—that he would be seeking Penny out again. It was a shame he didn't have one of his own mastiffs with him, he thought ruefully, to look out for *his* interests. Not that he needed a dog to tell him what a danger the girl beside him posed to his rigidly controlled life. Not to mention to his peace of mind.

"Well, Prince Rian," Penny said, breaking what had become a prolonged silence, and bringing his attention back to her. Her cheeks colored again as his name came out, and she didn't quite meet his eye. "What is it you want to know?"

"You said you think Bansford is suffering because of the ban," Rian said promptly, shortening his strides to match her smaller stature. He'd committed to the topic now, so he may as well find out what she actually thought. "Are you talking about the recent arrests?"

Penny let out an audible breath. "That's part of it," she said. "But it's more than that. The other kingdoms have things we don't. Things we used to have."

"How old are you?" Rian asked curiously.

Penny hesitated, and he wondered if it was too personal a question. "I'll be nineteen in a week's time."

"So the ban has been in place your whole life," Rian mused.

She nodded. "It came into place a couple of months before I was born."

"I was four," Rian informed her conversationally. "So I have memories from before the ban, although not many." He tilted his head inquiringly toward her, and she looked up at him. "What is it you feel we've lost?"

"Well, for one example, dragons."

Penny dropped her gaze as soon as she'd said the dangerous word, a golden curl falling loosely over her heated cheeks. It was a distracting sight, if Rian was honest. So much so that he almost missed her next words.

"And I think you know that's a loss. Or at least your brother does."

It took Rian a moment to realize Penny was referring to the comment she'd overheard at the ball. He'd forgotten she already knew about his casual attitude toward the magical creatures. He was grateful she didn't intend to use the information to get him or Bentleigh in trouble—he couldn't blame her for using it to challenge him.

"It is a loss," he said, equally alarmed and exhilarated by how easy it was to be honest with her. "And I'm reasonable enough to admit that there's no safety to counteract that loss. With human enchanters, their absence removes both the benefits and the dangers of their magic. But with the dragons…"

Penny nodded, clearly grasping his point. "No law of ours would stop them attacking us if they wanted to. In fact, it might make them more likely to attack, if they were offended."

"There's no law attempting to prevent the dragons from entering Bansford," said Rian quickly. "They avoid the kingdom by choice. And they don't seem to have taken any undue offense in the nineteen years the ban has been in place."

"You don't consider them avoiding our skies altogether to be an indication of offense?" Penny asked dryly.

Rian felt a grimace cross his face. They'd reached the trees now, and were picking their way through the small copse that separated the field from a vineyard.

"As long as we don't breach the agreement between the dragons and the human crowns, they won't attack us," Rian said at last.

A crease formed between Penny's delicate eyebrows, and it occurred to Rian that she was a commoner. She wouldn't be trained in dragon lore and may not even know what he was talking about. He opened his mouth to explain, but she forestalled him.

"It's not just the dragons." She stopped walking, turning to face him. "It's the human magic-users as well. We lose the benefit of their presence along with the danger. I've heard that in other kingdoms, there are people who can heal life-threatening injuries, clean water that's become foul...in short, help those around them in a myriad of ways."

"I've heard the same," said Rian gravely, his eyes searching Penny's serious face. "And I've also heard there are those who can kill with a gesture, steal the very words from people's mouths. Put princesses into enchanted slumbers, and turn princes into savage beasts."

"Of course you would focus on the threats to the royals," muttered Penny.

Rian couldn't help smiling at her indignation. "Not because others don't matter," he assured her. "But it goes to show the dangerous power of magic, doesn't it? Even the most powerful, the best protected people in the kingdom are at the mercy of the enchanters."

"Those same people make use of magic, though, don't they?" Penny challenged. "Didn't the princess who was cursed at her christening first receive gifts like beauty, and wit? Magical gifts? Is there *no* purpose for which your family would wish to access magic?"

Rian was silent. Discomfort swelled inside him as he remembered his suspicions that his father's source of intelligence was magical. How despicable Penny would find him, and all his family, if she knew of this hypocrisy.

"It's not for me to say," Penny said, when she realized he wasn't going to answer. "I don't mean to be impertinent." She shrugged eloquently, and started walking again. "But you asked what I thought."

"I was sincere in my interest," Rian said. "I want to understand opinions like yours, and the merchant at the market the other day."

Penny cast an anxious look at him. "That merchant is a friend of mine," she said. "He thinks he needs to look out for me, because I'm usually on my own at the market. He was coming to my defense as much as anything, I think. He won't get in trouble for what he said, will he?"

Rian stopped, not quite able to keep his expression even. Penny had a way of getting past his defenses, although he doubted it was done intentionally.

"Of course he won't get in trouble. Penny, I don't go around looking for reasons to punish my people."

She arched one eyebrow. "Can you blame me for thinking that? I might be wrong, but I haven't heard that the child who was just exiled was using his magic to do anyone harm. He was trying to hide it, wasn't he? Someone must have been looking for a reason to punish him."

Rian was again silent, his eyes troubled as they met hers. He longed to tell her that he agreed, that he'd change the ban if he could. Childishly, he craved the approval that would surely leap to her eyes if he told her his real view on the matter. But he owed more to his position—to his father—than that.

Guilty as he felt, it was Penny who dropped her gaze first. "It's not my place, as I said," she muttered, starting to walk again.

But Rian's hand shot out without his permission, closing around her wrist and stopping her. A delicate metal bracelet, cold against the warmth of her skin, pressed into his hand. Penny stared at his fingers, and he dropped his grip quickly.

"It is your place," he said quietly. "Because I asked you. And because a good ruler understands that it matters what his people think."

Penny's eyes were still on her wrist, fixed unseeingly on the bracelet. "I think...I think you'll be a good ruler," she said softly, sounding as though the words surprised even her.

Warmth roared into life inside Rian's chest at the praise, and for once he was completely unable to gather his self-possession. He just stared at her face, which was still directed at the ground, and was heating rapidly.

"Thank you," he managed at last. "I will certainly try to be."

Sensing that she needed a minute, he started to walk again. Al had run ahead, but he bounded back into sight now, and his presence seemed to set Penny at her ease. She caught up to Rian in moments. They were walking through the vineyard now, and Rian knew that Penny's manor would come into sight as soon as they emerged from it.

"I don't mean to be rude, Your High—Prince Rian," Penny said, pausing yet again. "But I think it might be better if I continue alone."

"Don't want your family to know you were speaking with me?" Rian asked shrewdly.

Penny's expression was rueful. "To be honest, I'm not sure they'd believe me. Lady Amaranthe is a stretch, but a royal?" She shook her head.

Rian felt a frown creasing his brow. "Is it true what Lady Amaranthe said? About your stepmother using you as a servant?"

The ready color rushed to Penny's cheeks yet again. "She was exaggerating," she said, clearly hedging. "The truth is we've had to sell the vineyards. We're not vintners anymore." The sadness in her voice made Rian want to grip her arm again, offer some kind of comfort, but he didn't dare. "We've had to let most of the servants go, and we all have to take on roles we had the luxury of not doing before." She gave a crooked smile. "It's been a gradual change over the last couple of years, so it's not so bad. I'm quite used to doing chores now. I'm not the frippery girl I once was."

No, she certainly wasn't a frippery girl. Rian remembered the impression he'd formed of her, the first time he saw her at the market. She'd seemed delicate to the point of being fragile, perhaps because of the wispy paleness of her coloring, or just the fact that she was all alone in a seedy marketplace. The thought had flashed through his mind that a heavy gust of wind might blow her over. In that moment he would have been surprised to learn she was almost nineteen. She looked younger, more vulnerable.

But that had been before he'd seen her wade into battle on behalf of a starved mongrel. Let alone challenge a prince to his face on the kingdom's most unyielding law. And now he'd learned—reading between the lines—that she was carrying the burden of a household on her young shoulders, mere days after the death of her father. He was almost surprised to discover she wasn't older than nineteen.

She wasn't a frippery girl—she was a woman, responsible and strong, but with a softness of heart that was all the more impressive given the losses she'd sustained. She made *him* feel frippery. She'd spoken her mind to him, despite the danger of such defiance, and she'd managed to do so without displaying the anger shown by the man in the stocks. Meanwhile, Rian was the heir to the throne, and he was still too afraid to tell his own father what he really thought.

"Is Lady Amaranthe coming again?" he asked abruptly.

Looking surprised at the change in topic, Penny nodded. "At the same time next week." She swallowed. "You...you're welcome to join, if you wish."

The invitation sent Rian's heart soaring up, above the rows of grapes, into the blue chamber opening over their heads. Lady Amaranthe wasn't pulling the strings this time. Penny wanted him to come. He knew he shouldn't accept. He wasn't so blind to his own emotions that he didn't recognize his attraction to Penny. And he wasn't so lost in that attraction as to forget the danger of pursuing any kind of connection with her. Even if her common status wasn't enough to make her ineligible to his parents, her tolerant attitude toward magic would be.

But somehow, he just couldn't bring himself to be responsible, not this time.

"I would be delighted," he said, inclining his torso in a graceful bow.

For some reason, the gesture made Penny giggle, although she hastily stifled the sound. "I'm not inviting you to a ball," she told him, eyes dancing. "We'll just be standing around in a field."

"Will I disgrace the crown I wear if I tell you that I prefer standing around in a field to attending a ball?" Rian asked, his lips curving responsively.

"Do you really?" Penny sounded amused. "The one I saw looked pleasant enough." Her face darkened. "If I'd been in more of a mood to appreciate it."

"I believe they are pleasant for the guests," Rian agreed lightly. "For the hosts, a little tedious. But don't tell anyone I said that," he hastened to add.

Penny chuckled. "You forget—no one would even believe I've spoken to you."

"So you say," said Rian in some amusement. He swept her

another of the bows she seemed to find so entertaining. "Until next time, then, My Lady."

Penny lowered herself into a curtsy that was endearingly wobbly. "Until next time, Your Highness."

Rian

"And another hit for me, Your Highness."

Rian grimaced as his opponent helped him to his feet. "It seems I'm distracted again this morning. Poor sport for you."

"Not at all," said the knight courteously. "I hope all is well?"

"Oh yes," said Rian, hiding a smile. "My mind is just elsewhere."

It was certainly true. There was a spring in Rian's step as he made his way across the training yard, to where he'd left his tunic. He'd been in a bit of a daze since returning to the castle the evening before, trailed by the bewildered guards who, along with his horse, had kept out of sight in a small copse not far from Penny's manor. He'd taken care to bring different guards from his first visit to the manor, in the hope that no one would connect his latest outing with the pretty daughter of the vintner, to whom he'd delivered the overdue payment. But realistically he knew there was no chance they hadn't seen. He wondered if he'd be able to find some way of ditching guards altogether the next time he went to see Penny. Probably not, but even a prince could dream, couldn't he?

Rian wiped his face, thinking he should probably find Lady Amaranthe and tell her he intended to once again follow her to the field near Penny's manor. He was hesitant to do it, though. Her smile had been a little too knowing at their last meeting.

He was so caught up in his thoughts about the following week, he barely noticed the group of admiring young noblewomen who had once again gathered to watch him train.

"You fight valiantly, Your Highness," said one of them as he passed, sinking into a curtsy that was as graceful as Penny's had been clumsy.

The memory brought the ghost of a smile to Rian's face. The girl in front of him clearly thought the smile was for her. Emboldened, she lowered her chin so she could look up at him through lashes that he had to admit were impressively dark and long.

"It would be an honor for anyone to be protected from danger by you, Your Highness."

"Uh..." Rian blinked, pulling himself back to the present. His usually ordered mind struggled to find a suitable response to the inane compliment. "You are too kind."

"Your Highness?" interrupted a new voice. Rian turned toward the page with relief, nodding for him to continue. "The queen has requested your company in her suite."

"Thank you," said Rian, inclining his head to the girl who had spoken, and who looked slightly sulky at the interruption to an interview she clearly felt had been going well. If she had the slightest inkling of what kind of girl Rian actually found appealing, she would know better than to waste her time.

Only too delighted to have escaped what had threatened to be a tedious encounter, Rian directed his steps toward the wing of the castle which contained the royal suites. He was admitted into his mother's rooms by the guards standing outside it, and he bowed politely to her, and the two ladies-in-waiting with her.

"Ah, Rian, I'm glad to see you," said his mother, an enthusiasm in her eyes that he found slightly disconcerting. She nodded dismissal to the ladies-in-waiting, and they drifted gracefully from the room. "Your father should be here any minute. In the meantime, sit. We might as well be comfortable while we wait."

Rian sank onto a settle, eyeing his mother's bright smile suspiciously. His father was to be part of this conversation? He assumed from the queen's eager expression that he wasn't in trouble, but he still missed his brother's support at the prospect of being called to meet with both of Bansford's monarchs together.

"No need to look so wary," his mother scolded him. "Just because I asked to speak with you."

"Sorry Mother," smiled Rian. "Is everything all right?"

"Of course it is," she said, with dignity. "Better than all right." She eyed him. "You're usually very low when Bentleigh is away, but you look quite happy today. I'm glad to see you adjusting so well."

Rian smiled. "I always miss Ben when he's in Listernia. And I'll miss him more than ever after the wedding. But there's plenty to occupy me right here, after all."

"Well said." The queen nodded approvingly. "Which brings me to—"

But before she could continue, there was a sharp knock at the door leading from her suite into the king's adjoining one.

"Yes, we're in here, Rhinehart," called the queen calmly.

A moment later, Rian's father swept into the room, looking, as always, like he had several other places he needed to be. His grim expression caused Rian's heart to lurch uncomfortably. Had he misread the summons? Was his father here to reprimand him after all? The escape of the prisoner the previous week had so far been interpreted just as Rian had hoped it would. But if his father had become suspicious for some reason, and had thought to search the secret tunnel, Rian couldn't be sure that signs of his passage would go unnoticed.

But the king's face showed no anger, just its usual impatience.

"My dear," he kissed his wife's hand punctiliously, "Rian," with a nod a to his son. "Let's get this over with, my captain is waiting for me."

"Not another skirmish on the desert border?" Rian demanded, alarmed.

The king shook his head. "No, nothing to do with the border," he said. "Some conflict between guilds in the south, I believe. I'll know more once I have the opportunity to receive the report."

He looked pointedly at his wife, and she cleared her throat.

"Yes, Rian. As you may have guessed, we wish to discuss your marriage with you."

Rian's stomach lurched more uncomfortably still. Of course that was the purpose of this meeting. How could he have forgotten his parents' imminent intentions for him?

"What of it?" he asked cautiously.

"Well, as you know, Bentleigh's wedding to Princess Azalea will take place in four months' time. We've discussed the matter, and we would like your wedding to occur first."

Rian barely refrained from rolling his eyes. Of course they would. If his parents had to compete with their neighboring kingdoms, he wished they wouldn't do it with his life.

"As a royal wedding will take some time to plan, that means it is past time for you to choose your bride."

"For me to choose?" Rian repeated, raising an eyebrow.

"Of course," said his mother, with dignity. "The law entitles you to—"

"We can speak plainly with Rian, Eliza," said the king impatiently. "He's sensible, and I somehow doubt he's forgotten his promise to us not to invoke his right to choose a queen of whom we wouldn't approve."

"I'm not sure that's quite how the law phrases my right, Father," said Rian, with a touch of humor. The king gave him a look he knew well, and he raised his hands in surrender. "I haven't forgotten my promise. And you can certainly speak plainly with me."

"Good," said his father briskly. "In that case, your mother has proposed that we hold a ball in order to—"

"Another ball?" Rian protested, unable to hide his dismay.

His father paused, for once not chastising him for the interruption. "My reaction was much along the same lines," he said dryly. "However, your mother feels it's the best way to commemorate—"

"Not just to commemorate the decision," cut in the queen, her voice eager. Her husband looked irritated at once again being interrupted, but he let it pass without comment in face of his wife's enthusiasm. "I want to host a ball in order to *make* the decision."

Rian stared at his mother, remembering his brother's flippant words before the betrothal ball, suggesting that their parents were going to make Rian choose his bride at the event, out of those present.

"How will a ball help make the decision?" Rian asked.

The queen shrugged. "Isn't it obvious? The young ladies we are considering will have an excellent opportunity to display themselves to best advantage at a royal ball."

Rian's mouth fell open in horror. "You want them to parade before me like prize animals at a county fair, and have me select the winner?"

The king cleared his throat, and Rian sighed in concession.

"Have *you* select the winner, then. Either way, it seems an outrageous way to choose Bansford's future queen."

The queen raised an eyebrow at his strong words, and King Rhinehart pierced his son with a look. "We aren't the only ones speaking plainly, I see."

Rian shrugged. "Do you really think a woman's presentation at a ball is the way to judge her worth?"

"Of course not," said his mother. "We have been carefully considering eligible options for some time, as you know. The ball is simply a chance for you to...enter into the spirit of it."

Rian exchanged a look with his father, the two men enjoying a rare moment of shared sentiment. Neither spoke their thoughts aloud, however.

"Do you intend to let me choose from this list you've compiled, then?" Rian asked slowly.

"That's the general idea, yes," said the queen enthusiastically.

Surprise held Rian silent for a moment. "I didn't realize that was your intention," he said at last. "I thought you were just going to tell me who you'd picked."

"Well, we'd assumed that was best," his mother nodded. "But I must confess that seeing how Bentleigh has come alive since his own betrothal has made us—"

The king cleared his throat, and Queen Eliza paused. If Rian didn't know better, he'd think she was trying to stop herself from rolling her eyes.

"Very well, it's made *me* wish to see you happy with your choice of betrothed as well."

"Thank you, Mother," said Rian, taken aback. "That's very... considerate of you."

His mother gave a dignified nod. "It will be for your father to make the final decision, of course. But I would like to see that choice be someone you think well of."

Rian's mind whirled, half-formed possibilities pushing their way into his thoughts.

"Have you thought any more about any of the young women you danced with at your brother's betrothal ball?" his mother asked hopefully.

"No, I haven't," said Rian, with perfect truth.

The queen pursed her lips, looking displeased.

"I'm sorry, Mother," said Rian, half-smiling. "I'm not trying to be contrary, but none of them were particularly memorable, to tell you the truth."

She sighed. "Well, there are others."

"I'm sure there are," said Rian dryly, "but I doubt I'll have much more success forming a reasonable impression of their characters from one encounter at a ball."

"Well, we can make it a series of balls, if you prefer," said the queen, shrugging a shoulder. Her husband grimaced, but made no comment on the additional expense this would entail. It was clear to Rian that the king had agreed to let his wife take the lead on the pomp and ceremony side of Rian's upcoming betrothal. "Three nights in a row," her eyes lit up, "what a gala that would be!"

"How about three balls, but a week between each?" suggested Rian firmly. "That would give me opportunity to pursue any promising acquaintances in between the balls."

"An excellent notion," the queen approved. "I imagine the kitchens would be grateful for a more staggered approach as well."

Rian nodded, trying to keep his voice and manner casual. He was touched by his mother's sentiments, but he wasn't a fool. If his parents had the slightest inkling of his thoughts, they would shut his idea down before he could so much as blink. He had to tread carefully.

"I've noticed some unease in the city," he said, looking at his father. "As you predicted, the arrest involving a child has put some people on edge."

"What unease?" the king asked, a ready frown springing to his brow. "Have you encountered defiance?"

"Nothing to cause concern," Rian said placatingly. "Just some muttering, some discomfort. And news of the border skirmish with the desert raiders has spread as well. It occurs to me that the balls could be a good opportunity to lift the morale of the city, give everyone a reason to think positively of the castle, and the crown."

"Indeed," agreed his mother brightly. "Everyone loves a ball."

"Precisely," said Rian, jumping on the best opening he thought he was likely to get. "*Everyone* loves a ball." His father sent him a disbelieving look, and Rian kept a straight face with difficulty. "What I mean is, it's not just nobles who enjoy such celebrations. If we want to make a grand statement, create some excitement around the announcement of our future queen, shouldn't we invite everyone to be part of it?"

The queen frowned, the expression thoughtful rather than disapproving. "You mean invite commoners to the ball as well? Some well-connected merchants perhaps, or wealthy business people? It's not a bad idea."

Rian shook his head. "Not just the wealthy and well-connected," he explained. "I want to remind the populace that we're their royals as well as the court's. That they have a share in the benefits our rule brings to the kingdom." He raised a humorous eyebrow at his mother. "Can you really tell me that there's a girl in the kingdom who wouldn't be delighted to be invited to a series of royals balls in my honor? They'll all be talking about it for the rest of their lives, feeling like they were somehow part of choosing their crown princess."

The queen looked thoughtful, but King Rhinehart's gaze was a trifle suspicious as it rested on his son and heir.

"But they *won't* be part of choosing their future princess," he reminded Rian. "It's not a popularity contest."

"I know that, Father," said Rian. "It's just about creating a sense of inclusion. Of encouraging them to share our excitement in the upcoming event of my wedding."

"Well," said Queen Eliza, looking delighted to hear Rian acknowledging even a scrap of excitement about his upcoming wedding, "I think it's a wonderful idea. I don't know that we could manage a ball including every girl in the kingdom. But certainly every girl within Bant," Rian held his breath, "and the surrounding area."

Rian nodded, trying not to show his relief at the addition. "I'm sure that would have the same effect."

"Not *every* girl," the king amended, still looking unconvinced. "I won't host serving wenches from the local tavern here in our castle. The court wouldn't stand for it."

"No, no, we're not talking about servants," the queen said soothingly. "Are we, Rian? Just genteel commoners."

Rian nodded sagely, trying to look the picture of filial obedience, and the king nodded his reluctant consent.

"Well, then, it's decided!" Queen Eliza's eyes glowed with excitement. "Three balls, a week between each, and invitations to go to every genteel girl of marriageable age within Bant and its surrounds." She pushed herself to her feet in a rustle of silks. "Goodness, there's a great deal to organize if the first ball is to be held in a fortnight."

"A fortnight?" Rian repeated, startled. "So soon?"

"Of course," said the queen impatiently, already gliding toward the door. "The wedding is only months away, remember?"

She left the room, leaving the two men facing one another.

"I'm surprised by your enthusiasm for more balls than strictly necessary," King Rhinehart said, his eyes fixed shrewdly on his son's face.

Rian smiled. "It will make Mother happy. To be honest," he grimaced, "part of me will be glad to have the matter decided. I'm so hounded by every noblewoman between fifteen and thirty-five, I can barely move through the castle."

His father sighed. "I am sorry about that," he said. "I have gathered before now that our intentions regarding your marriage have leaked out in the way such things always seem to."

Rian shrugged. "Just part of wearing the crown, I suppose."

His father nodded slowly, eyes once again scanning his son. "You said part of you will be glad to have the matter decided. Does the other part not wish to marry?"

Rian took a moment before answering. "I've been happy as I am," he said carefully. "I know I need to marry at some stage, but I can't pretend to be excited about a union with someone I don't know, and may not even like. I daresay you think that attitude is irresponsible."

His father's pause was even longer than his had been. "I understand your feelings," he said at last. "I felt similarly when my parents arranged my marriage to your mother."

Rian couldn't help staring. He could never remember his father speaking so honestly about something so personal.

"But their choice was a sound one," the king continued calmly. "And I never had cause to regret it. Nor will you. The ladies on your mother's list are all eminently suitable."

Rian hesitated. He didn't want to push his luck, and ruin the moment of connection. But who knew when he would get another such chance?

"You didn't invoke your right to choose your own bride, then?"

"I did not," said King Rhinehart steadily. "I wanted what was best for Bansford."

"So do I, Father," said Rian earnestly. He held his father's gaze, trying to put every ounce of his sincerity into his expression. "I truly want what's best for our kingdom. You believe that, don't you?"

His father searched Rian's face carefully before speaking, not as though he was unsure of his answer, but as though he wanted to show that it was genuine, considered.

"I do, Rian," he said at last. "You have always shown yourself to be responsible, and sensible."

A feeling of strength spread through Rian at the rare words of praise. It wasn't like the intoxicating warmth he'd felt when Penny praised him. It was deeper, less pleasant but more stable.

Then he remembered his secret crime in releasing the prisoner from the dungeon, and discomfort pricked at him. He pushed it to one side. His father might not see it the same way, but Rian knew with certainty that his actions had been motivated by his desire to see Bansford prosper, not just right now, but in the future.

"Thank you, Father," he said seriously. "I hope you will believe, then, that this suggestion is intended to serve Bansford's interests."

"What suggestion?" the king asked, instantly suspicious.

Rian barely restrained a sigh at his father's expression. For a moment he considered backing down, saying nothing. But Penny's face flashed before his eyes, wary but determined, as she told him why she disagreed with the ban. And she had clearly feared repercussions for expressing that view. If she could be brave to a prince she hardly knew, surely Rian could be brave to a king who was his father.

"I know that you've recently acquired a source that's been identifying hidden enchanters and enchantresses with great success," he started, gathering his courage. The king's face hardened, and Rian hurried to clarify. "I'm not asking for information regarding that source. I'm just thinking about this idea of engendering goodwill among the common populace as well as the court. With that in mind, I wonder if we would be wise to refrain from further arrests. At least until the balls are over."

King Rhinehart's expression was still hard, but he searched his son's face thoughtfully before responding.

"I don't begrudge you your shrewd observations, Rian," he said. "And I can even appreciate your reasoning. But I cannot agree with your conclusion. It has occurred to me, even if it hasn't to you, that a ball where nobles and commoners alike are invited to infiltrate the castle, would be an ideal opportunity for an embittered enchanter to mount an attack. Weeding out any remaining fugitives is more of a priority than ever."

Or we could stop embittering them! Rian wanted to protest. But he kept his mouth firmly shut, knowing when it was wise to refrain.

"Very well, Father," he said calmly. "Thank you for taking my suggestion seriously."

The king once again searched his face, perhaps looking for any hint of sarcasm. Apparently finding none, he nodded to Rian before sweeping from the room.

Left alone with his thoughts, Rian couldn't help but reflect that although his father had said he was in a hurry, he had taken the time to connect with his son, even to discuss his feelings regarding marriage. It was progress.

Disappointed as he was with the failure of his attempt to slow his father's vendetta against magic-users, Rian was pleased with what he *had* achieved.

He knew that getting Penny—and others like her, of course —invited to his bride-selecting balls was a small step, which by itself would achieve nothing at all. But it still seemed like movement in the right direction. He would have to be clever in how he went about it, though. He would like to believe that his parents were more reasonable than Bentleigh thought them, and that Rian could soften them toward his own way of thinking. But even if he was right, there was no denying it—a fortnight didn't leave him much time to achieve the impossible goal he had set for himself.

CHAPTER FIFTEEN

Penny

Penny chewed her lip in concentration as she pinned the ripped flounce. "There we go," she said cheerfully, and Sophia stepped down off the small stool. "If you get the dress off, I'll have it fixed up in no time."

"Thanks, Penny," said Sophia, not quite meeting her eye.

"I'm sure Penelope doesn't do her chores for thanks," said Sapphira calmly, from the far side of the sitting room. "I'm sure she does her part out of duty, like the rest of us."

Sophia, who from what Penny had observed, had spent the better part of the morning gazing out the sitting room window, at least had the decency to look embarrassed. She mumbled something unintelligible as she hurried from the room.

Penny, untroubled for once by her stepmother's high-handed manner, gathered up the sewing kit.

"Hold on, Penny," said Olivia imperiously. She stepped up onto the stool Sophia had just vacated. "My gown needs letting down. It's a touch too short."

Penny, still on her knees, stared at the hem now swishing before her eyes. "It looks fine to me."

"Don't try to get out of helping," sniffed Olivia. "You're the only one who's good with a needle, Penny. If you shirk your duties, how will we all stay clothed?"

Irritation flared within Penny at these unjust words, but before she could retort, she saw Olivia's eyes flick to Sapphira, their expression almost hopeful.

"Quite right," said the older woman placidly, not lifting her gaze from the ledger before her.

Penny sighed, her annoyance melting away to be replaced by sympathy for her unfortunate oldest stepsister. Olivia's softer attitude—which Penny had always known to be temporary— had disappeared completely in the last week, and life had become less pleasant as a result. But it had served the purpose of reminding Penny that her stepsister felt things more keenly than she let on. Penny was starting to understand that Olivia's desire to please her emotionless—and, in Penny's experience, unpleasable—mother made Olivia's life much more miserable than Penny's busy, productive existence.

"Well, there's not much more to let down, but I'll see what I can do," she said patiently. "You can send the gown to the kitchen with Sophia when she brings hers." Just because she felt sorry for Olivia didn't mean she wanted to spend more time with her than necessary.

"The kitchen?" Olivia protested. "It'll get filthy if you work on it there." She glanced at Penny's hands. "Come to think of it, I hope you're going to wash your hands before you work on my dress. I shouldn't have let you touch it with such grimy fingers. What have you been doing, sorting through the cinders in the fireplace?"

She spoke with such derision in her voice that Penny felt her face burn. A quick glance revealed that Olivia was right, and the fact that Penny hadn't even noticed the state of her hands was a powerful statement of how dramatically her life had changed in recent weeks. Penny didn't answer. What could she say? The truth was that she *had* been sorting through the soot in the cold fireplace, salvaging any wood that still had enough structure to burn in tonight's fire.

Without a word, Penny gathered up her supplies and pushed herself to her feet.

"Be sure you don't trail soot on the carpet," said Sapphira placidly, as Penny made her way out of the room.

When Penny reached the sanctuary of the kitchen, she paused for a moment, closing her eyes as she leaned back against the wall. A low whine brought her attention to the half-open back door, through which Al had managed to push his head.

"What are you doing, Al?" Penny laughed, crossing the room to him. "You know you're not allowed inside." She glanced behind her, then shrugged. "Oh, what does it matter? You're no filthier than I am, apparently." She pushed the door fully open, and Al bounded in, tail wagging.

Penny knelt down and flung her arms around him, pressing her face into his short fur. Apparently sensing her need for comfort, the dog stilled, allowing her to hug him without protest. When she pulled back, he gave her face a hopeful lick.

"Yuck!" Penny said, but she was laughing again. "You're very sweet," she amended, dropping a kiss on top of the dog's head. "And you're quite right," she added, dusting off her hands. "I shouldn't let it get to me." She felt her brows draw together sorrowfully. "It's really Olivia who deserves the sympathy. At least *my* mother was kind."

She shot a stern look at the dog. "That comment is for canine ears only, Alchemist. No tattling."

Al flattened his ears placatingly, tail once again wagging, and Penny couldn't help smiling. It was amazing how much the dog's silent presence bolstered her. She began to pull out ingredients for dinner, and by the time she heard a timid knock on the door, she was whistling cheerfully.

"Come in," she called out, hastily burying her now-clean hands in the dough that had been kneading itself—a tricky skill, which had taken some practice to master.

Sophia's face, framed by her gloriously thick brown hair, poked through the doorway.

"I don't mean to interrupt," she said uncertainly, glancing with surprise at Al, curled up by the hearth.

"Not at all," Penny smiled. "As you see, we're not doing anything important." As she spoke, she followed Sophia's gaze to Al, and grinned as he lifted a back paw to scratch vigorously behind one ear. Penny turned back to Sophia. "Did you bring Olivia's dress as well?"

"Oh, yes," Sophia nodded, tearing her gaze from the dog. She entered the room properly, and deposited the two gowns on a clean bench.

"I'll get to them once I've set the dough to rise," Penny said kindly. "My hands are all floury now." She held them up as evidence, only just remembering in time to stop her magic from continuing the task without their assistance.

Sophia nodded, looking more than usually subdued. Penny had assumed that her stepsister would leave as soon as she'd dropped the dresses off, but she lingered, fidgeting with her sleeve. Restraining her impatience with difficulty, Penny began manually kneading the dough again. Her progress was much slower with Sophia's restrictive presence. She'd forgotten how frustrating it was to only be able to do one task at a time.

"It's kind of you to do the dresses," Sophia said at last. "I know there's no real reason it should be your job." She colored slightly. "I've had opportunities enough to learn to sew better. I just could never get the knack of it."

"I'm not especially good myself, to be honest," said Penny

cheerfully. "But I can fix up a hem or a ripped flounce easily enough." She saw Sophia's continued discomfort, and added quickly, "And I don't mind doing it."

Was this the reason Sophia was lingering? Because her conscience was troubling her regarding Penny's situation, as it did from time to time? The impulse might be good, but Penny wished Sophia would either do something about it, or leave it be. Her habit of hovering in the metaphorical doorway was as frustrating as her literal hovering right now.

"You're always so good, Penny," Sophia burst out suddenly. "I will *try* to be good like you, and not say no." She raised a slightly desperate face to Penny's, and Penny was amazed by the distress in Sophia's warm brown eyes. "But it is hard to do things one doesn't want to do, isn't it?"

"Yes," said Penny, in astonishment. "I think everyone finds that hard."

She waited for Sophia to say more, agog with curiosity to know when the cosseted Sophia had been asked to do anything she hadn't wanted to do. But apparently her stepsister had either said all she wished to, or lost her nerve. Without another word, Sophia turned on her heel and fled from the kitchen.

Penny stared after her, discomfort leaking into her gut to join the curiosity. Sophia had said that Penny was always so good. Penny knew that wasn't true, of course, but the exaggeration wasn't what bothered her. It was the realization that her example had apparently taught Sophia to believe that being good meant never saying no. Penny thought of all the unreasonable demands she'd given in to without even putting up a fight, and her unease grew. Sophia thought her stepsister was kind, but if Penny was honest, she'd been motivated as much by cowardice as by kindness.

Before she could sink too deep into these reflections, the outside door swung open, and Harry tromped in.

Penny made a tutting noise with her tongue, sending the trail of mud back outside with a wave of her hand. The broom sped across the floor for good measure, catching any bits her raw magic had missed.

Harry rolled his eyes. "You've become a tyrant, Pen."

She grinned at him. "My power has gone to my head."

"The ironies of life," Harry muttered, dropping his load of wood next to the fire. "Shall I light her up?"

"Yes, thank you," Penny said absently. "My hands are full over here, and I'm not yet confident enough to mess about with fire using my magic."

"Well, thank goodness for that," said Harry fervently. His eyes were drawn to the dresses dumped on the bench, and he frowned. "Don't tell me they've got you doing the mending as well?"

"Who else is going to do it?" Penny asked, amused. Harry knew as well as she did that he was now officially the only servant left to the manor. "You?"

Harry grunted. "I probably could, if I set my mind to it."

"No need," Penny laughed. "It won't take me long."

"Pen," Harry growled warningly. "Needles aren't much better than fire."

"I'll use my hands," Penny reassured him. "I'm practiced enough that I barely need them for cooking now, but needlework is a little too detailed yet. I'm sure I'll get there with practice, though."

"Pen, you can't spend your life this way," Harry said, sounding a little desperate. "You're meant for something more. You've got to get out."

Penny's hands stilled, and she looked up at him, surprised. "What's gotten you upset?"

"Everything!" Harry burst out. "You have all that power, and yet you're powerless!"

"Spoken like someone who's never peeled a bushel of apples without touching them," said Penny, a little offended at being called powerless.

"I'm serious, Pen," Harry growled. "It's great that you're learning to use your magic and all, but for what? Your mother healed people's hurts, and you're doing...what? Cooking and cleaning and mending for a trio of the most selfish—"

"What do you want me to say, Harry?" Penny demanded, firing up. "I know you think I should stand up to Sapphira more, but I don't honestly know what it would achieve. I'd rather do the work than spend my life being pinched at for refusing."

"Forget all that," said Harry dismissively. "I meant it when I said you should get out. Let's leave tonight. The weather's mild enough we could travel by dark. We could be in Entolia morning after tomorrow."

Penny stared at him. "Where is this coming from, Harry? Why the urgency?"

Harry deflated. "Clearly you haven't heard," he said. "I just had it from one of the vineyard workers next door. "Three more arrests today."

"Three?" Penny echoed, alarmed.

"That's right," Harry nodded. "And all three of them were people who no one suspected, who were just living their lives like ordinary folks." He shook his head, his expression anxious. "Beats me how the guards rumbled them, and I can hardly sleep at night for worrying you'll be next, Pen."

"What's happening to them?" Penny asked, her tone betraying her nerves in spite of her best efforts.

"Dunno," shrugged Harry. "They'll be exiled, of course, but I imagine they'll be punished first. Stocks maybe. A while in the dungeons, or some time of hard labor."

"Well, I could break out of a dungeon, most likely," said

Penny lightly. "And hard labor wouldn't be as hard for me as for most, given my...skill set."

"If you're foolish enough to think," Harry growled, "that it would be no hardship for a pretty slip of a girl like you to be sentenced to labor—"

"I'm not," Penny assured him earnestly. "I was just trying to lighten the mood."

"I don't want the mood lightened," Harry said bluntly. "I want you to take me seriously enough to leave, before whoever's ratting on these enchanters rats on you."

Penny's face set in stubborn lines. "This is my home, Harry. I'm not leaving."

Harry waved an incredulous arm around the kitchen. "In what way is it yours? You're a servant in your own home, Pen."

"I thought you said I wasn't a servant," Penny shot back.

"You're letting yourself be treated as one," Harry insisted. "Surely you'd be better off in Entolia, where your talents would be permitted, maybe even celebrated."

"Maybe you're right," Penny said stubbornly. "But I'm not ready to give up on Bansford."

Harry's eyes narrowed as he searched her face, his expression far too shrewd. "It's that noblewoman, isn't it?" he said slowly. "Don't think I haven't noticed you getting brighter the closer we get to her next visit tomorrow. Whatever it is she's teaching you, it's got you excited enough to risk putting your neck in the noose."

Penny sent him a look. "Even our king doesn't hang people just for having magic," she said.

"You know what I mean," Harry said gruffly.

Penny fell silent. She did know what he meant, and he was more right than he knew. It *was* her session the next day that made her completely unwilling to consider leaving. One thing Harry didn't know, however. He couldn't know, because Penny hadn't even told him about her other visitor. But in truth, it was the promise of seeing Prince Rian again that had Penny's mood lifting, more even than further training with Lady Amaranthe. And despite knowing how incredibly dangerous that situation was—to her heart as well as to her secret—Penny couldn't help the jitters that came over her every time she thought of Prince Rian's warm grip on her wrist, or the way his stern mouth softened when he said her name.

Her heart somersaulted at the memory, and she could only hope Harry didn't notice the sudden burning of her cheeks. She felt guilty for keeping her bizarre acquaintance with the prince a secret from her main supporter. But why tell him, and add to his anxieties? It didn't need Harry's warnings for her to know that she was in great danger from the prince, although not in the way Harry would likely fear. She knew it was beyond foolishness—closer to madness—to run the risk of losing her heart to any prince, let alone the crown prince of the only kingdom in Solstice where her very existence was a crime. But she couldn't help counting the days, for all that.

She found herself hoping, as she fell asleep that night, that she would dream of Dannsair again. But she had no way to communicate with the purple dragon unless Dannsair sought her out, and her sleep was uninterrupted. It was unsurprising, as the dragon had already visited her dreams twice that week. Perhaps it was for the best, Penny thought, as she sat on the edge of her bed the next morning. As desperate as she felt for advice, she couldn't really expect a dragon to counsel her on matters of the heart. Or even on the dangers of the ban. It was just reassuring to have another magical being to talk to, to help ease the sense of isolation created by her secret.

But the day would bring exactly that comfort, Penny reminded herself, as she went about preparing the family's breakfast. Lady Amaranthe was coming in a few short hours, and whatever his doubts, Harry had agreed to once again cover for her. His birthday gift to her, he'd said gruffly, and Penny appreciated it. A lesson in using her magic was just the gift she'd choose.

Penny hummed to herself as she stoked the fire. It had been particularly difficult to start, and more than once she'd considered pulling Harry from his early morning chores in the barn to help her get it going.

"Maybe I *should* sleep in the kitchen," she muttered, rising from the hearth at last, with soot all down her front. "Keep the fire going all night, just so I don't have to start it."

"I think it's an excellent idea."

Penny jumped at the unexpected voice, whirling around to see Olivia framed in the doorway. Trying to calm her frantically racing heart, Penny used her extra sense to feel the air around her. No threads of magic were currently reaching out from her. But she would have to be more careful, like Harry always warned her, if members of the family were going to start showing up in the kitchen unannounced.

"What do you want, Olivia?" she asked wearily, once she'd regained some measure of composure. For the briefest, wildest moment, she wondered if Olivia had come to wish her happy birthday. But the foolish thought fled at the sour look on her stepsister's face. She doubted any of the family had even remembered. She hadn't said anything to remind them.

"I'm here for my dress," said Olivia. "And speaking of dresses..." She frowned down at Penny's form. "The day has barely begun, Penny, and you're already filthy. Take some pride in yourself. You're a vintner's daughter, not some cinder-girl."

Penny scowled. "I have plenty of pride in myself," she said, tossing her curls over her shoulder. "Your dress is there."

As she pointed to the two neatly folded, mended gowns, her conversation with Sophia the day before came rushing back. It was time to show some backbone, if not for herself, for others who were watching her.

"But if you want another gown let down, you'll need to do it yourself," she added. "I'm keeping the household running all by myself, and I don't have time for extra chores. You're just as capable as I am of stitching your own hem."

She expected an explosion of anger from Olivia, but the older girl surprised her. "Decided to push back, have you?" she asked quietly. "A little too late, I think."

Instead of spite, her words contained a strange pain that Penny couldn't begin to understand. She frowned. It was enough of a struggle to unravel Sophia's troubles, let alone Olivia's as well.

"What's got Sophia worked up?" she asked abruptly, her thoughts following this track. "What is it she doesn't want to do?"

"I have no idea," said Olivia, lifting her chin. But Penny was sure she was lying. Fire had leaped into her eyes at Penny's words, and again Penny saw hurt beneath the anger. Her frown deepened. She'd clearly been too caught up in her own affairs— not to mention her ever-growing duties—to pay proper attention to what was going on with what family she had left.

Olivia swept from the room, bearing off her unnecessarily altered dress, and Penny returned to her work. But she couldn't banish her stepsister's pained expression from her thoughts for some time.

When Penny at last traipsed off the estate, Al loping alongside her, she still hadn't quite recaptured her excitement over the afternoon's plans. She was eager to see Lady Amaranthe, but the anticipation was mixed with a measure of guilt at how much she was letting her own priorities rule over Harry's fears, Sophia's troubles, and Olivia's pain.

At the sight of Lady Amaranthe once again waiting for her,

however, Penny let her worries drift away for the time being. She still had so much to learn, and she needed all the practice she could get.

"I hope you haven't been waiting long!" she said, smiling at her mentor.

"Not at all," said Lady Amaranthe, her eyes warm. "Are you well, child?"

Penny nodded. "Better than ever," she said brightly. She felt heat rushing to her cheeks, and tried to suppress it. "I should perhaps tell you," she said self-consciously, "that I invited Prince Rian to join us again an hour before sunset today, if he wished to."

"Did you indeed?" Lady Amaranthe's eyes were twinkling. "Well, well, it seems my attempts to bring you together have been successful."

"Your attempts," said Penny, with a touch of sternness, "have been shameless."

Lady Amaranthe laughed. "And yet, I feel sure you'll forgive me."

"I don't know if I should," Penny said, her voice turning suddenly serious. "If I'm honest, when I look ahead, I can't see any outcome that doesn't end in misery for me."

"Oh, my child." Lady Amaranthe put a hand on Penny's shoulder, her brow creased in concern. "It will all be well in the end. You'll see."

"How can you possibly know that?" Penny asked, half-beseeching, half-laughing. "I have it on good authority that the ability to see the future is unprecedented magic. Not even dragons have it."

Lady Amaranthe's eyes widened. "What authority is that? I didn't realize you had another source of information when it came to magic."

"Oh, well..." Penny hesitated, swallowing. She hadn't

intended to bring Dannsair up, but after all, why hide it from a fellow enchantress? "To tell you the truth, there's a dragon who...who visits me in my dreams sometimes."

Lady Amaranthe stared at her blankly. "You have dreams about dragons?" she repeated, as if rearranging Penny's words would help them make more sense.

Penny shook her head. "Just the one dragon. And they're not true dreams. She uses her magic to connect with me somehow, when my mind is at rest." Penny shrugged. "We talk. About magic, mostly."

"Incredible," breathed Lady Amaranthe. "I never imagined such a thing."

"So no dragon has visited you like that?" Penny asked curiously. "I wondered...she said my magic calls to her across the distance like a spring in the desert."

"No, I've never had any kind of experience with a dragon," said Lady Amaranthe, not quite managing to keep a touch of envy out of her voice. "Perhaps your magic reached this dragon because it's so strong." She shook her head as if flicking off a fly, and her voice became brisk. "It is certainly the strongest I've ever seen. Which brings us to our training."

"Actually," said Penny, fidgeting slightly, "I was wondering if you could teach me something not magic-related, before we start."

"Oh?" Lady Amaranthe raised an inquiring eyebrow.

"I want to learn to curtsy," said Penny, in a rush. "It's not something I ever thought I'd need to know, but I seem to be running into royalty every second day, so..."

Lady Amaranthe was grinning openly by the end of this speech, but to her credit she refrained from teasing. "An excellent notion," she said approvingly.

Half an hour later, Penny was wondering why she'd ever asked to spend such valuable time on such a stupid and frustrating skill. She'd honestly thought it would take a few short minutes to learn to curtsy, but she'd underestimated Lady Amaranthe's desire for perfection in her student.

"That's good," said Lady Amaranthe approvingly. "Much better. We can work on it more next time."

Penny grimaced. "I still feel clumsy."

"But you look much less clumsy," the older woman assured her. "Now, shall we start our other training?"

"Please." Penny could hear the note of pleading in her own voice. Glancing around, she realized Al wasn't in sight, and whistled softly. He came bounding over a slight rise, tail wagging. "There you are," she called, smiling. "As you were, I was just checking in."

He returned to whatever canine pursuit he'd been engaged in, and Penny noticed Lady Amaranthe's eyes following him.

"He's very loyal, isn't he?" the older woman mused. "Must be handy, when you're more or less alone."

"Very handy," Penny agreed.

"What's his name?" Lady Amaranthe asked, her tone light. "I realized when I saw the prince greeting him so warmly that I'd been remiss in not getting to know him. It doesn't pay to be outdone in courtesy."

"Oh, I took no offense, and I'm sure he didn't either," said Penny humorously. "Not everyone warms to dogs. Some people do, and some just don't."

"I didn't say I don't warm to dogs," said Lady Amaranthe, the hint of a snap in her voice.

"Oh, I'm sorry," said Penny, a little taken aback. "I didn't mean to imply anything amiss."

"That's quite all right," said Lady Amaranthe, her good humor restored. "So what's the little fellow's name?"

Penny hid a smile. She'd obviously hit a sore spot, for reasons she didn't know. The enchantress could protest all she liked, but she didn't speak to or about Al like someone who warmed to dogs. It just came naturally to some, like Harry, and Prince Rian. And to others, like Sophia, dogs would always be a slightly alarming and thoroughly unpredictable species.

"It's Al," Penny said aloud.

Lady Amaranthe nodded. "Because he's an alaunt?"

"Actually," a smile grew on Penny's face, "no. I mean, he is an alaunt. But that's not why he's called Al." She glanced around, ensuring that they were, as usual, alone. "I've never told anyone this before, but it's actually short for Alchemist. I call him that when he's in trouble sometimes. Only when no one else is around, of course," she added hastily.

Lady Amaranthe threw back her head and let out a genuine laugh. "A private act of defiance!" she said, her eyes once again sparkling. "I love it. There's that fighting spirit that made you want to throw a man-sized vase at a trio of royals."

Penny grimaced. "Don't remind me of my most shameful moment," she begged. "I regret ever entertaining that impulse. And attacking royalty at a ball can't really be considered a *private* act of defiance."

Lady Amaranthe's smile was indulgent. "True, of course. But you're too hard on yourself, my dear. There was no harm done."

The afternoon passed far too quickly for Penny's eager mind. When Lady Amaranthe called a halt half an hour before the time allotted for Prince Rian's arrival, Penny almost regretted inviting the prince.

Almost.

It was perfectly safe to continue talking, at least. The two enchantresses walked slowly up and down the field as Penny grilled the older woman about artifacts, and how they could be used to store magic, and access it later. She learned that a powerful enough enchantment could even turn an object into a permanent artifact, something which served a specified purpose of its own, and could be used even by someone without magic.

Penny soaked up every word, delighted to at last have someone to answer such questions. When she was immersed in discussion of magic with Lady Amaranthe, everything else lost importance. She forgot about Sophia's strange gloominess, Olivia's spite, Sapphira's cold indifference. She even forgot Harry's anxiety on her behalf. It felt like nothing at all could pull her attention from the whole new world opening before her feet.

Until a tall, tawny-haired figure emerged from the trees. Suddenly, Penny found that there was something that could capture her attention, and her latest question died on her lips as she turned toward the prince.

"I think that's my cue to leave," said Lady Amaranthe, sounding amused.

"No," said Penny quickly. "You don't need to leave. You *shouldn't* leave." She remembered the gossiping woman in the market, and scowled to herself. "Someone might form the wrong impression if they knew the prince had been meeting with me all alone, you know."

Lady Amaranthe sent her a look. "If someone was watching us," she said, her voice lowered as Prince Rian approached across the field, "you being alone with the prince would be the least of our concerns."

Penny grimaced, unable to deny the other woman's point. There was no time to say more. The prince had reached them, once again having managed to shed his usual escort.

"Lady Amaranthe," he said, bowing to her. He turned to Penny, his eyes softening perceptibly. "Penny. Happy birthday. This is for you."

CHAPTER SIXTEEN

Rian

Rian soaked in Penny's amazed expression, enjoying the way her eyes lit up at sight of the small parcel he held out to her.

"Prince Rian," she greeted him, sounding dazed. She sank into a curtsy that was noticeably more graceful than the last time he'd seen her. Rian felt a little stab of regret. He would miss her clumsy attempts. But then again, if she'd been practicing, it meant she'd been thinking of their upcoming meeting, preparing for it. He'd take that as a good sign.

"Penny," said Lady Amaranthe, sounding a little taken aback. "You didn't tell me it was your birthday."

"It didn't seem important," said Penny, her cheeks tinged with pink.

After a lifetime surrounded by the careful masks of the court, Rian couldn't help finding it endearing how often Penny seemed to blush. It didn't hurt that the color made her fair face even more attractive, of course.

She looked up into his eyes. "I can't believe you remembered, Your—Prince Rian."

He smiled. "It's almost the only thing you've told me about

yourself," he said lightly, "so it wasn't difficult to remember." He jiggled his outstretched hand expectantly, and Penny took the gift at last, blushing more furiously than ever.

"I have a feeling I shouldn't accept," she said skeptically, but she pulled the simple string tied around the package nonetheless.

When the brown paper opened to reveal a velvet-covered jewelry box, Rian heard Lady Amaranthe's intake of breath. He sent her a small frown, hoping she wouldn't spoil the gesture. She clearly recognized the box as issuing from the highly overpriced jeweler patronized by the royal family, but Rian was counting on Penny being blissfully ignorant of the value of the trinket.

Lady Amaranthe met his eyes, her own expression hard to read. But she kept her peace, and that was all he cared about for the moment. He returned his gaze to Penny, enjoying her poorly suppressed excitement as she flipped the box open.

She let out a soft "ooh" at the sight of the silver charm nestled in silk. It was delicately wrought, and twinkled with tiny gems.

"Now I'm *sure* I shouldn't accept," she said, but she made no move to return the box.

"Of course you should accept," said Rian quickly. "It's your birthday. And it's not as valuable as it looks."

He could feel Lady Amaranthe's wry gaze, but he kept his eyes on the charm. It was true that the gift wasn't as valuable as it looked, he reasoned with himself. It was considerably *more* valuable, because the jeweler always overcharged, doubly so if the client was royal. But Penny didn't need to know those details.

"It's lovely," Penny whispered. "I shouldn't take it..." She glanced up at him, eyes dancing. "But I really want it."

Rian laughed. "I'm glad." He gestured to her wrist. "I noticed last week that you wear a bracelet. I thought perhaps the charm could be added to it."

Penny touched the bracelet, twisting it around her slim wrist. "It was my mother's," she said softly. "The only jewelry I have of hers, actually."

"Oh, well I wouldn't want to take away from—" Rian began hastily, but Penny shook her head.

"I didn't mean that. I would be glad to add your gift to the bracelet." Her voice was a little huskier than usual, and there was something incredibly raw in her eyes when she looked up at him. His heart responded to it without his head's permission, and he found himself stepping closer.

A small throat-clearing provided an abrupt reminder of their audience. "I should be getting back," said Lady Amaranthe quietly.

Penny whipped her head around. "Nonsense, *My Lady*," she said, a frown marring her gentle features. "Surely you were staying for another hour at least."

"The time's run away with you, Penny," laughed the noblewoman. "It'll be sunset soon enough, and I don't care to walk back to Bant after dark." She nodded to Rian. "Your Highness."

Rian returned the gesture, secretly hoping Penny wouldn't protest further. He knew it would be more chivalrous to offer to escort Lady Amaranthe back to the city, but he had no desire to do so. From the little interaction he'd had with her, he'd gotten a strong sense that she was experienced and capable. He doubted she would have walked all the way from the capital if she wasn't confident to walk home as well. An unusual noblewoman, certainly, but he admired her for it.

He waited until Lady Amaranthe was out of earshot, then turned to Penny with a slightly twisted smile. "Afraid to be alone with me?" he teased.

She blushed yet again, her eyes on the ground. "Perhaps I

should be, but I'm not," she said. She looked up slowly, her expression hesitant. "But it's not really proper, is it? I mean...I wouldn't want anyone to get the wrong impression."

Rian stilled, taking her meaning. She was absolutely right, and it was absurd that he hadn't even thought of it before. He'd been so focused on his parents not discovering his attraction to a common girl, he'd given no thought for what anyone else might think of their connection. Everything about Penny was so innocent, he'd forgotten the sordid light in which this innocuous conversation could be viewed. But of course he knew better. In meeting her clandestinely, he was endangering her reputation as much as his. More, because fair or not, his credit would survive being slandered where hers certainly wouldn't.

"I've been thoughtless," he said penitently. "And the last thing I want to do is make you uncomfortable." He jerked his head toward the trees. "I ditched my guards not far away, but they've certainly followed close enough to spy on us, if it makes you feel any better."

"What?" Penny looked as though this information made her feel decidedly worse. "They've been watching us through the trees? Last week as well?"

"I'm afraid so," said Rian apologetically. "An unfortunate but inevitable side effect of being royal."

"But I didn't see any sign of them when you walked me home last week!" Penny protested.

Rian smiled. "They're well trained. They know how to keep out of sight, especially when I've asked them to wait for me somewhere. It's my polite way of telling them I wish them elsewhere, and keeping out of sight is their polite way of pretending to honor that wish."

Penny still looked unduly alarmed. "How long have they been there? Did they come before you, to make sure it was safe?"

"No," said Rian, raising an eyebrow. "They traveled with me, of course."

Penny nodded, looking slightly less anxious, and Rian's curiosity raged. What exactly were she and Lady Amaranthe doing or saying in that field that had her so nervous at the idea of being spied upon? He tried to suppress the question. It would be very wrong of him to pry. But he couldn't help wondering. He'd assumed, when Penny said that Lady Amaranthe was coming again in a week's time, that the noblewoman had taken a fancy to the good-natured vintner's daughter, and was coming to wish her well on her birthday. But Lady Amaranthe had been unaware of Penny's birthday, so she'd clearly come for a different purpose.

He saw that Penny still looked uncomfortable, and he sighed. He might wish they lived in a world where they could meet like this without fear of repercussions, but they didn't. He wasn't allowed to want to get to know a girl before forming a formal attachment. His parents expected him to pick one of their pre-approved options from a parade of girls in ballgowns, regardless of whether there was any spark of connection.

The thought filled Rian with a sensation that was almost desperation. He was convinced that he knew more of Penny's character from their few genuine encounters than he'd ever learn from a dance with a noblewoman at a ball. He had to find a way to change his parents' minds.

But all of that was his problem, and a problem for later. Right now, what mattered was that Penny wasn't comfortable with the situation he'd put her in, and that was something he needed to make right immediately.

"Can I walk you home again?" he asked softly.

She nodded, and the gratitude in her eyes as she looked up at him made him think she understood the message behind his words. It also made his heart lurch in a way that was uncomfortable, but not exactly unpleasant.

"I've been looking forward to seeing you all week," he said abruptly, as they started across the field.

Penny's mouth fell open in refreshingly transparent surprise. She obviously hadn't expected such frankness.

"Because I have something to tell you," Rian added, softening the stark declaration.

"What is it?" Penny asked, tilting her head to the side in a bird-like gesture.

"Remember last week, when you said the ball at the castle looked...pleasant, I think it was?"

"Yes," said Penny cautiously.

"Well, what would you think of actually attending one?" He smiled. "On purpose?"

Penny stopped walking, turning to face him. They'd just entered the vineyard, and her home wasn't yet in sight. "What do you mean?"

"My parents are holding a series of three balls at the castle," said Rian, trying to speak casually, as if it was nothing unusual to host four balls in a few months. "And remembering what you'd said, I convinced them to invite all the young women in Bant and the surrounding area, not just those from the nobility."

Penny stared at him. "Because...because of what I said?" she repeated. "My comment caused the king and queen to open up the ball to commoners?"

"In a manner of speaking, yes," said Rian, struggling to read the look in Penny's eyes. He swallowed. "It wasn't just because of what you said, though. It was because...well, because I wanted you to be able to come."

Penny's eyes flew to his, then down to the box clutched in her hand. "You didn't say as much to Their Majesties, surely?"

"Heavens no," said Rian fervently. A shudder went over him

at the very idea of what his parents' reaction would have been if he'd made such a statement. He regretted the display a moment later, when he saw a rueful light enter Penny's eyes. "So will you come?" he asked quickly.

Penny started walking again, her cheeks showing a hint of color. "It sounds wonderful," she said, her hand clenching and unclenching slightly over the jewelry box. "But I don't know if I'll be able to."

"Of course you will," said Rian anxiously. All his scheming would be for nothing if she didn't even come. "Everyone's invited. Well," he amended, "except servants. That would have been too much to expect."

Penny's expression was more rueful than ever. "The invitation isn't the issue."

"What is?" Rian pressed.

"It's...oh, lots of things," Penny said helplessly. "We have such limited resources now, and if new dresses are needed, I'll be fourth in line. And Harry won't like it at all. Plus, the manor would suffer if I was away for a whole evening, and—"

"Perhaps I've asked the wrong question," said Rian quietly, his heart sinking. "I should've asked, not *will* you come, but do you *want* to come? Do you?"

Penny glanced up at his face, and her eyes locked on to his. She seemed as unable to pull her gaze away as he was.

"Yes," she said, her voice little more than a whisper. "I want to come."

A smile split Rian's face as he read the honesty in her eyes. "Then you'll find a way to make it work," he said cheerfully. "I have faith in you."

Penny was silent, looking unsure how to respond.

"Who's Harry?" Rian asked in a would-be casual voice.

"Our only remaining servant," said Penny absently. "But he's been with us my whole life, and really he's almost like an uncle."

Rian nodded, relieved. "I think I saw him when I delivered that payment to you. Hovering in the doorway of the barn."

Penny smiled. "That would be him," she confirmed. "He does tend to hover, especially if he thinks I'm in any kind of danger. Not," she added hastily, looking confused, "that I was in danger that day, of course."

"It's all right," Rian reassured her. "It's been brought home to me lately that the presence of royalty does tend to make people uneasy." He frowned to himself. "It's something I intend to change."

Penny glanced up at him, but made no comment. Shaking off the thought, Rian returned to the topic at hand.

"Well, I'm glad you have someone looking out for you," he said, still frowning. He glanced at the dog bounding some way ahead of them. "Al is a good sort, of course, but there's only so much a dog can do."

"Alas, too true," Penny sighed. "I've had no success at all training him to help me with the chores, and not for lack of trying."

Rian laughed. "That I would like to see."

"Well, you can't," said Penny frankly. "I might indulge this bizarre twist in reality enough to meet a prince in a field, perhaps even to attend a ball where I clearly don't belong. But I draw the line at having the heir to the throne in my kitchen."

Rian fell silent, thinking over this speech. Was that what he was to her? A *bizarre twist in reality*? Could he blame her for thinking their interactions made no sense? It was true, after all. What was he doing, giving her jewelry, and convincing his parents to change the whole structure of his betrothal balls just so she could attend? He shouldn't try to draw her into this... whatever it was he was feeling, if there was no hope for him to follow through.

But how could he give her up? An image flashed before his

eyes, of the giggling noble girls watching him spar. He knew enough of the court to see through their coquettish curtsies to the greed for his crown that lay underneath. Forget about Penny entirely, and embrace a loveless marriage to someone like that? Unthinkable.

"When is the first ball?" Penny asked.

"A week and a half away," said Rian. "I believe the invitations will be arriving at any time, but..." he hesitated, "but I wanted to tell you first."

"I'm glad you did," said Penny softly. She came to a stop. They were almost at the edge of the vineyard, and Rian could tell she once again wanted to return home alone.

"Is Lady Amaranthe coming back next week?" Rian asked, stopping beside her. Penny nodded, and he couldn't help sighing. "I wish I could join her again, but I doubt I'll be able to get away. Not so soon before my bet—before the first ball."

He saw Penny's eyes flick curiously to his face at the slip, but she didn't ask what he'd been going to say. "I wouldn't expect it," she said simply. Then she ducked into another curtsy and hurried toward the edge of the vineyard.

"Penny," Rian called, reluctant to let her go. She turned, Al also stopping and cocking an ear. "Happy birthday," Rian said again, with a crooked smile. "I'm glad you were born, here, into my kingdom."

Penny stared at him with unfathomable eyes, not breaking into the smile he expected. "Thank you, Your Highness," she said at last, before she turned and all but fled from him.

CHAPTER SEVENTEEN

Penny

Kneeling over the garden bed, Penny heard the sound of approaching hooves. But since a quick glance showed that the visitor was no one she recognized, she returned to her task. Someone in the house could answer the door. As expected, she heard a booming knock moments after the rider passed from her sight. What she didn't expect was the shrill screech that followed.

Dropping her shovel in alarm, she hurried toward the manor. Surely the messenger hadn't brought bad news? They'd lost her father and all their vineyards already. What more could there be? A sudden thought occurred to her, and she checked her pace, heart racing. Could she have been discovered somehow? Harry said that someone was identifying enchanters, and no one quite knew how.

Forcing her feet to move, she rounded the corner and saw the messenger riding away. Well, he wasn't here to arrest her, at least. Penny pushed through the front door, and was confronted by the sight of both of her stepsisters having near hysterics.

"What's happened?" she asked urgently. "What's wrong?"

But the faces turned to her were shining with excitement,

not fear. "We've been invited to a ball at the castle!" Sophia cried.

"Three balls!" corrected Olivia enthusiastically.

"Look." Sophia shoved the gilded invitation into Penny's hand.

She stared down at it, her mind racing. Of course. She should have connected the messenger with what Prince Rian had told her the day before. There it was, plainly inscribed. Three balls, a week between each, the first to be held in a week's time. In addition to the court, all young ladies of marriageable age were invited to attend.

"Young ladies of marriageable age, that's us!" Sophia declared. She shot an oddly challenging look at her mother. "You can't deny that, at least."

"Of course I don't deny it," said Sapphira, who was watching their impassioned display with a frown.

"I'm sure it doesn't really mean *all* young ladies," Olivia commented, snatching the invitation back from Penny and scanning it again. "Ooh, look, the first one is a masked ball!"

"No," Penny agreed, "it won't include servants." She hardly knew how to feel about the invitation. Prince Rian's words—the look in his eyes when he'd told her the lengths he'd gone to in order for her to be invited—kept running around her head.

Sapphira shot her a look. "Of course servants won't be receiving invitations."

"But we can all go, can't we, Mother?" Sophia asked, her face shining.

Sapphira didn't answer at once, and an ominous feeling stole over Penny.

"I wonder what the purpose of these balls is," said the older woman thoughtfully. "They've just held a ball, for Prince Bentleigh's betrothal. It's very soon to host another one, isn't it?"

Penny frowned. It was a good point, and one she hadn't even thought of when the prince had told her about the balls.

"I wonder..." Sapphira seemed to be speaking to herself. "Girls," her eyes snapped to her daughters, and then to Penny. "I'm going into the capital. Harry can drive me. I expect you to occupy yourselves helpfully while I'm gone."

"But why?" Olivia asked, frowning.

Her mother didn't answer, sweeping from the room without another word. The three girls exchanged bewildered looks. Sophia was the first to shrug.

"Who knows?" she said lightly, leaning over Olivia's shoulder to look again at the invitation. "Three royal balls! Can you even imagine it? The dancing, the food." Her eyes gleamed. "The men."

Penny couldn't help laughing. "I didn't realize you were so eager for romance, Sophia."

To her surprise, Sophia's face dropped at once. "A girl can dream, can't she?" she asked uncomfortably.

Penny stared at her, but before she could ask, Olivia cut in with an observation of her own.

"You don't look very excited about the balls, Penny."

Penny shrugged. "Do you really think we'll be able to manage it? Unless you both have hidden wardrobes I don't know about, none of us have gowns suitable for a royal ball. And we don't have the money for new dresses. Stepmother never approves spending money on luxuries, and I must say I think she's right. We're barely keeping things running as it is."

Sophia's face fell further at this prosaic comment, but Olivia looked thoughtful. The expression was reminiscent of the calculating look in her mother's eye when she'd sailed out of the room shortly before.

"We'll just have to convince her that it's not a luxury," Olivia commented cryptically. She cast a glance at Sophia, and there was a touch of resentment in her eyes. "I don't think it will be so difficult."

To Penny's amazement, Olivia proved to be right. When Sapphira returned from the capital, so far from needing persuading about the ball, she was full of plans for their attendance.

"So we're to go?" Sophia squealed, and her mother nodded.

"What did you find out in Bant, Mama?" Olivia asked shrewdly, over the top of Sophia's raptures.

"It's as I suspected," Sapphira said briskly. "The balls are not for mere frivolity. The rumor is that the king and queen are determined to marry the crown prince off before his brother weds the Listernian princess. The purpose of these balls is to select his bride."

All three girls stilled, staring at her with open mouths. "To choose his...bride?" Penny repeated stupidly. Her mind whirled with questions. And Prince Rian had moved mountains to secure her an invitation. Did that mean...

"Is that why the commoners are invited as well?" breathed Sophia, awe on her face. "Could he choose someone who isn't even noble?"

"I highly doubt it," said Sapphira in a practical spirit. "But if there is any chance that he has such an intention, I intend to make the most of it." Her eyes lingered on Sophia's lusciously curling hair, and her huge, shining eyes.

"And...and there will be others there, besides the prince, won't there?" Sophia said timidly. "From the commoners, it's only the girls who are invited, and I suppose their chaperones. So most of the men attending will be wealthy enough, won't they, Mama?"

Sapphira nodded. "My thoughts precisely. We will hold off on any decisions until after the final ball."

Sophia sagged with relief, as Penny stared from her stepmother to her stepsister in bewilderment.

"But can we afford new gowns, Mama?" Olivia asked, her voice painfully hopeful.

Sapphira sighed. "It is a gamble. It has taken most of my savings, but I've ordered two new dresses to be made. I have some from the old days that will do well enough for a chaperone. I'm afraid you'll have to wear the same dress to each ball. It's not ideal, but it can't be helped. And I purchased these at an excellent price." She held out three masks, simple, but elegantly embroidered.

"Two?" Penny's calm voice cut across the other girls' murmurings, and brought instant silence to the room. "Did you say two dresses, Stepmother?"

Sapphira turned to her, neither sympathy nor spite in her eyes. "I'm afraid that was all we could afford."

The silence was by now so absolute that Penny thought she heard a mouse scuttling somewhere within the walls.

"And who is to wear those two dresses?" she asked quietly.

Sapphira surveyed the three of them. "It's a simple matter of deciding who can least be spared from the manor," she said.

Frustration and bitterness rose up within Penny, nearly as potent as they'd been the night of the other ball, when she'd almost lashed out in violence against the very prince she was now desperate to see.

She knew this game. She knew how it ended, and she couldn't bear to play it. But she also couldn't bear to give in tamely, not this time. Not with everything that was on the line. Not with *Rian* on the line. She knew her stepmother would never let Sophia miss out—it was clear to Penny that she thought the youngest of the three most likely to catch the attention of the available prince. But the very thought of Sophia pursuing Rian made Penny sick to her stomach.

In her head she knew it was foolish to be so upset—the prince was almost certainly going to have to marry a noble, and she didn't believe he'd fall all over himself for Sophia just because she was beautiful. But it didn't matter—her heart still raged against the idea. These people were supposed to be her family. And instead they'd taken her home and turned her into a servant. They weren't taking Rian, too.

Dimly, Penny wondered when she'd dropped the title and started thinking of the prince by his first name, but it didn't matter right now.

"That's not fair," she said quietly. "The fact that I work the hardest, do the most for the household, means that I deserve to go more, not less."

Sapphira raised her eyebrows. "That is a selfish way to think, Penelope. What will happen if you're unable to complete your chores all afternoon, while you get ready, and then you're out late into the night, leaving things to fall apart? How will the animals fare? Is Harry supposed to do everything on his own?"

"Why don't we call Harry in right now?" retorted Penny angrily. "Ask him what he thinks."

"Hardly," said Sapphira, her lip curling. "He is a servant in our household, and it is not for him to decide what is best for this family."

"Is Penny even invited?" cut in Olivia, an edge of desperation to her voice. Clearly, she also knew that Sophia wasn't the one who would miss out if Penny made the cut. "You said yourself, Penny, that servants aren't included, and you're basically—"

"That's enough, Olivia," interjected Sapphira sharply.

Tears pricked Penny's eyes, but she wouldn't let them fall as she glared between her stepmother and her oldest stepsister. She longed to tell them the truth, to shout into their faces that the prince had no interest in either of her stepsisters, that she was the only reason commoners were invited at all. But they probably wouldn't believe a word. And even if they did, she had no desire to give her stepmother information which she would surely find a way to use against her.

Instead, Penny turned on her heel and stormed to the kitchens, where she commenced banging pots and pans with unnecessary force. Al, who had taken that first time as license to set up a permanent home by the hearth, lifted his head and whined in distress.

"I'm sorry," Penny told him, rubbing her hands over her face. She realized too late that they were still filthy from her gardening. She stared into the tiny warped mirror above the mantel, hardly recognizing the dirt-streaked face, framed by a pale tangled mess that resembled a haystack more than ordered curls. "I *have* become a servant," she whispered. "Who am I fooling to think I could attend a royal ball?"

The rest of the day passed slowly, uncomfortable silence reigning any time any of the sisters came across one another's paths. Penny had deplored the competition Sapphira encouraged between them since the moment their families first joined. But this time was so much worse than any that had come before it. The stakes, for Penny at least, were too high to even contemplate. And she knew from bitter experience that she had no real chance of winning the competition.

At dinner that night, they could barely look at each other. Penny could see the same frustration, the same determination that was fueling her, reflected in Olivia's eyes. But Sophia, who must have known as well as they did that her place was secure, had no need of determination. She simply looked miserable, all her earlier excitement having fled. Penny felt her heart go out to her stepsister in spite of herself. She could see no triumph on Sophia's face, and it softened her to the girl who, while spineless, had never been malicious.

After the meal, she sought Sophia out, determined not to vent her anger on someone who didn't deserve it.

"What was Stepmother talking about before?" she asked softly, when they were alone. "When she said she would hold off making a decision until after the balls?"

Sophia hugged herself uncomfortably. "She was talking about choosing me a husband."

"What?" Penny hadn't expected that.

Sophia sighed. "You know we don't have enough money to last long like this, even before Mama spent it on dresses. And we don't have an income source anymore. Mama told me some time ago that our best chance to maintain this lifestyle is for me to marry someone with money. Apparently two men have already approached her, and she said it's my duty to do my part. She said not to be selfish, that she married your father for the sake of our fortunes, and I should do no less."

Sophia's voice was quavering by the end of this speech, and Penny could only stare openmouthed. She'd never suspected any of this.

"But they're both so old, Penny!" Sophia said, in what was almost a sob. "And I don't like them. One is a farmer, with plenty of money, but not very...genteel. And the other is a merchant. Mother says he's even wealthier, but I've seen him around, and he seems...oily, somehow. Do you know what I mean?"

Penny nodded, her heart filling with sympathy. Poor Sophia. She'd thought her own lot was hard, with her stepmother's constant unreasonable expectations of her. She now realized she should have been thankful that Sapphira hadn't chosen an even worse way for Penny to contribute to the family's needs.

Another thought followed close on that one. Sapphira was hoping that Sophia would catch the eye, if not of the prince, at least of some wealthy noble. If Sapphira had any inkling of what had passed between Penny and Prince Rian, she would probably change her tune regarding who was to attend the ball. Penny shivered. She had no intention of enlightening her stepmother. The idea of being pressured to catch the prince, knowing the secret she hid, was worse than not attending the ball. Her stepmother would never understand either her fear or her scruples. Not when even Sophia, the favorite daughter, turned out to be nothing more than a cog in the wheel of the household, expected to turn as required, to make everything run.

Penny spent most of the week trying in vain to come up with a solution that would satisfy everyone, but no inspiration came. She was almost certain that she wanted to go to the ball. Sometimes she felt the cowardly impulse to surrender to Sapphira's game, just for the excuse to avoid the fraught situation. But then she remembered the hope in Prince Rian's voice when he'd asked her if she wanted to go, and she couldn't bear the thought of disappointing him.

When she walked over the fields to meet Lady Amaranthe, the day before the ball, her heart was too heavy even to look forward to a lesson in magic.

"What's wrong, child?" the noblewoman exclaimed, the moment she caught sight of Penny's expression. "You must be the only maiden in the land with a long face."

Penny smiled weakly. "Tomorrow's ball has turned everyone's heads, has it? I've been cooped up at the manor all week, so I haven't heard much about it."

"But you received your invitation, surely?" Lady Amaranthe frowned.

Penny nodded. "I don't know if I'll be able to go, though," she said, trying to speak nonchalantly. "We don't have enough money to provide gowns for all of us, and..."

She trailed off, but the grim look that descended on Lady Amaranthe's face showed that she understood.

"You *must* be at that ball, Penny," she said, with determination. "Do what you must to get hold of one of those gowns."

Penny sighed. It sounded so simple, but Lady Amaranthe didn't know Olivia, or Sapphira.

She was so inattentive to Lady Amaranthe's instructions, that the noblewoman called a halt to their practice well before sunset. Even though he'd said he wouldn't come, Penny couldn't help looking hopefully for Prince Rian's tall figure, and when it failed to appear, she trudged home in considerable gloom.

The morning of the ball brought the arrival of the gowns from a very harried dressmaker, who had clearly been inundated by eager damsels. Sophia, forgetting her melancholy, squealed with delight over the packages.

But Sapphira wouldn't allow her to open them, declaring instead that the matter of who was to attend must still be settled. Already weary, although the day had barely begun, Penny said nothing. She was torn between wanting to refuse to play, and wanting desperately to win, so she could go to the ball and see Rian.

"Penelope," said Sapphira. "You expressed the view that you are somehow more deserving of the outing. But I cannot in good conscience leave the manor untended. If you wish to earn your place, you must show that you can be efficient enough before our departure that your absence won't be felt. I've prepared a list of what needs to be done, in addition to your regular duties."

Penny took the parchment from Sapphira's hand, running an indignant eye down its contents. It would take four days, not one, to complete this list.

Behind her, Olivia sniggered, and the sound tipped Penny over the edge. She squared her shoulders, determination coursing through her.

It would take a *normal* person four days to complete the list.

CHAPTER EIGHTEEN

Penny

"Very well, Stepmother," Penny said, with dignity. "I'd best get started immediately."

"Indeed," Sapphira agreed, inclining her head. Looking gleeful, Olivia followed Penny from the room.

"It's such an awful lot to do," she said in mock sympathy. "If only you had someone to help you." She traipsed past Penny, opening the back door and shouting for Harry across the yard. He entered the kitchen a couple minutes later, looking disgruntled. "Harry," said Olivia, her voice still smug, "we need you to go into Bant to buy ribbons. To go with our ball gowns, you understand."

"You want me to buy ribbons?" Harry asked blankly. "But I don't know the first thing about—"

"No matter," said Olivia airily. "Just get something pretty. Whatever color you think is best."

Utterly perplexed, Harry watched Olivia flit from the room, shooting a malevolent glance at Penny on her way past.

"What in dragon's flame was that about?" he asked.

Penny just grunted. The moment the door had closed behind Olivia, she'd raised her hands with a flourish. A sack of lentils rose from the floor to the table before her, while a pitcher of water raced across the room and emptied itself into the pot hung over the fire. At a further flick, a broom burst from the cupboard, and began to sweep the floor, followed closely by a mop.

"What are you doing?" yelped Harry, leaping out of the way of the mop, which was rapping his hip aggressively with its handle.

"I'm finishing this list before it's time to leave for the ball," grunted Penny, barely able to spare the focus required to form the words. She'd just added shelling peas to the list of tasks her magic was completing, and it was one that required considerable finesse. "So that I can win Sapphira's stupid game, and go to the ball tonight instead of Olivia."

Even in her peripheral vision, she could see Harry's mouth drop open. "But you can't achieve all this! It's impossible."

"For you, maybe," Penny said, poking her head out the door to check the coast was clear. Seeing no one, she sent the broom down the hallway to disappear into a rarely used front room, chased by the dripping mop.

"Pen, look at yourself! Think what you're doing! One of them will see, and then where will you be?"

"Not if I'm careful," argued Penny. "I didn't even realize it, but I've been training for this moment for weeks."

"Pen."

Harry seized her wrist, forcing her to look at him. The pitcher fell with a clunk, and all the peas dropped to the table like so many fat raindrops. She could feel her magic stutter to a halt in the front room as well, and heard the faint clatter of the mop and broom falling to the floor.

"Surely a ball isn't worth this kind of risk," Harry said earnestly. "Surely you don't *want* to go to a ball at the castle! The castle, Pen!"

"You don't understand." To her own frustration, Penny felt her eyes filling with tears. She didn't have time for this. "I *have* to go."

"But why?"

She drew a deep breath. "I haven't just been meeting Lady Amaranthe in that field, Harry," she said, her voice barely above a whisper. "Prince Rian has been coming too. He...he wants me to go. It's because of me that he convinced his parents to open the balls to commoners as well as nobles."

Harry let her wrist drop, horror in his eyes. "Pen," he whispered, and his voice sent a chill down her spine. "What fire have you been playing with? Surely...surely he doesn't *know*?"

"Of course not!" Penny assured him, although she couldn't quite meet his eye.

"Then what future could there be?" Harry demanded. "Pen, let me take you across the border. I watched both your parents die. I won't see you go the same way, not while there's breath in me."

"Stop being dramatic," said Penny irritably. "No one's dying. It's just a ball."

"Tell that to the twenty year old woman who was arrested yesterday afternoon," said Harry grimly. "I heard she was buying a dress for the ball when the guards dragged her away."

Penny stared, horrorstruck. Seeing Harry's grim satisfaction at her reaction, she pulled herself together. "That's not going to happen to me," she said stubbornly.

"Why?" Harry scoffed. "You think your prince will protect you? He's one of the royals, Pen. He'll click the lock on the stocks himself."

"Well, the joke would be on him, because I can move locks with my mind," said Penny flippantly. With a flick of her hand, she started her various tasks up again, turning back to the list. "I don't have time for this, Harry. And you're supposed to be off buying completely unnecessary ribbons with money we don't have to spare."

Muttering darkly, Harry left her to it. Penny suspected she hadn't heard the last of it, and she was right. The moment Harry returned—with a truly hideous pair of ribbons, that a half-blind old dowager *might* consider using to string on a brooch, but that no girl would ever put in her hair—he sought Penny out, and began once again trying to dissuade her. She ignored his every argument as surely as he refused to help with any of her tasks. He insisted he'd rather she failed, and stayed home from what he called a death-trap. He did, however, grudgingly agree to act as lookout, warning her when any of her stepfamily were coming to check on her.

In that way, Penny managed to defy Harry's dire predictions, and reach mid-afternoon without anyone discovering her magic. In fact, she had done more than that. She'd completed almost all of the impossible list Sapphira had set for her, and she was confident of finishing the last few items with enough time to get ready.

"And how are you going to explain that?" demanded Harry, when she cheerfully informed him of her progress.

Before Penny could answer, a tall, elegant figure appeared in the doorway of the barn, where Penny was mucking out two stalls at once, one by use of her actual hands, and one...not.

"Penelope?"

Penny straightened at Sapphira's familiar voice, stilling her magic with a surreptitious gesture so no telltale noises from an apparently empty stall would give her away.

"Yes, Stepmother?"

"How have you progressed with your tasks?"

"Very well," said Penny brightly. "I'm almost finished."

Sapphira raised an eyebrow. "Hand me the list."

Penny did so, and a crease appeared between Sapphira's

brows as she scanned the page, noting everything Penny had crossed off.

"It's a great many tasks to have completed on your own," she said, in a voice laced with suspicion.

Penny wiped an arm across her sweaty forehead. "But clearly you thought it was possible for me to achieve it all in one day," she said sweetly. "Or you wouldn't have assigned it all to me. It seems you were right."

Sapphira regarded her shrewdly, and Penny found great satisfaction in keeping her face as expressionless as her step-mother's usually was.

"I will check your work, of course," said the older woman coldly. And she swept from the barn.

Chuckling to herself, Penny returned to her task.

"It's nothing to laugh about," said Harry darkly. "She's going to know something's up."

"Why should she," Penny shrugged, "when she hasn't figured it out all this time?" She scoffed. "You'd think she would have been suspicious long ago. How does she think I've been doing all the work for the household day in and day out, if I didn't have any help? She doesn't even know what's involved in these tasks, because she's never had to do them."

"If you ask me, she knows more than you give her credit for," predicted Harry.

But when Penny returned to the kitchen shortly after, it wasn't Sapphira who confronted her, but Olivia.

"I heard you've completed your tasks," she said, her eyes narrowed in anger. "But I know you can't have. You cheated, pretended some were done that weren't."

"Ask your mother," shrugged Penny. "She's checked my work. All I need to do is prepare the food for—"

"This food?" Olivia asked innocently. As she spoke, she tipped the sack of lentils over. It hit the bench hard, and its contents spilled across the surface, all over the floor, and into the soot-filled hearth. Olivia's eyes passed triumphantly from the hopeless mess to Penny's horrified face. "Oops."

"Olivia!" cried Penny, frustration and despair mingling in her voice. "Why would you do something so stupid?! I'll have to throw it all out, and you know we can't afford that kind of waste! Do you know how many meals those lentils could have provided?"

"Throw it all out?" The cold voice came from the doorway, and Penny's stomach dropped. Sapphira's tone was more than usually emotionless, and that never boded well. "Of course we won't throw it out. I can hardly believe you'd suggest something so wasteful, Penelope. I thought I'd taught you better economy than that."

She strode over to the hearth, and bent down. Lifting a single lentil between her fingers, she blew on it.

"These can be salvaged," she said calmly. "They'll need to be individually cleaned, of course. But they'll still cook just the same."

Penny stared at her, too stunned to even respond. Sapphira raised an eyebrow. "What's wrong, Penelope? For someone as efficient as you, surely it won't be any great challenge to complete this last task before it's time to go. You could still claim that dress yet."

And with that, she swept from the room, Olivia in her wake. Penny stood motionless where they'd left her, a trembling beginning in her hands. She forced herself to take one, two, three deep breaths. But the trembling was worse, if anything. A hysterical scream threatened to rise within her, but she clamped down on it. Glancing around, to make sure the others really had left, she raised her still-shaking hands.

Screwing up her eyes in concentration, she focused on harnessing the power that was jostling around within her. She could feel its potential, feel the way her unstable emotions wanted to send it raging out, destroying, manipulating, releasing her pent-up frustration. But instead, she called to her mind everything Lady Amaranthe had ever taught her about control. She sculpted the magic, sending it out not in lightning strikes, or in a forceful wave, but in a thousand tiny tendrils, each one minute and gentle.

She didn't even need to open her eyes to feel the lentils lift from the bench, the floor, the hearth. She used her power to probe all the corners, make sure she had every single one. The ones from the bench she sent flying back into the sack, which righted itself at a flick of her chin. The ones from the floor, she caused to shake, and jiggle in the air, until any clinging dirt had fallen off, before sending them to join their fellows. The ones she'd rescued from the hearth, she separated out, so that they formed a mid-air web stretching across most of the kitchen. Holding them in place with focused effort, she sent another burst of power out, this one seeking to latch on to the soot and cinders. She felt her magic connect, felt each speck of dust as she took control of it. With a grunt, she gave a downward flick that sent it all hurtling back into the hearth. The lentils followed the others back to the sack, and she pulled the rope tight with her actual hands.

Feeling half pleased with herself, half frightened by her own abilities, Penny knelt down by the hearth, sifting through the soot for anything she might have missed. There was nothing.

She heard the steady approach of footsteps, and remained where she was, willing her racing heart to calm. The door swung open, and Sapphira's voice cut across the silence.

"Oh, and Penelope, you'll need to—"

Her stepmother's voice cut off, and Penny rose slowly to her feet, dusting off her sooty skirts.

"I think I've gotten them all," she said docilely. "But feel free to check."

"How..." Sapphira trailed off, for once at a loss for words.

"It wasn't as bad as it looked," Penny shrugged. "Most were on the bench. Not many actually went into the hearth."

There was a prolonged moment of silence, then Sapphira strode to the sack, pulling open the tie and sifting through the lentils within. Penny knew she was searching for any sign of soot or dirt, and she felt a grim satisfaction as the silence stretched out. Clearly Sapphira could find nothing to criticize.

"Well," said Sapphira at last, her gaze calculating as she looked Penny over. "It seems things are well enough in hand that you can be spared for a few hours, after all. You'd better come and see your dress."

Heart soaring, hardly able to believe her success, Penny hurried after her stepmother. They ascended the stairs to Sophia's room, where Penny's stepsisters were holding the two new dresses up against themselves, admiring the effect in the mirror. Their hair was beautifully arranged—not, Penny noticed, tied with the garish ribbons of Harry's selection—and they wore simple jewelry around their necks. Penny surreptitiously touched her sleeve, feeling for the single adornment hidden underneath. The bracelet from her mother which now bore Rian's charm. It was all she had, so it would have to be enough.

"What's she doing here?" Olivia demanded uneasily, lowering the gorgeous full-skirted dusky pink dress she held.

"Penelope has completed all the tasks set for her," Sapphira said calmly, "and has earned the right to wear one of the new gowns."

"What?" shrieked Olivia, the color fading from her face. "But that's impossible."

"Only for those lacking sufficient drive, apparently," said Sapphira coldly. "Give her the dress, Olivia."

"But—"

"That dress won't fit me," said Penny suddenly, over the top of Olivia's protest. "It's clearly made for Olivia. It's much too long for me."

"Well, a skilled seamstress like you should have no trouble fixing it up," said Sapphira dismissively.

Frustration boiled up in Penny once again. She didn't know what made her feel worse—the realization that Sapphira had never intended to honor her bargain, or the look of half-hope, half-fear in Olivia's eyes. After all her hard work, after killing herself all day to get everything done, it wasn't going to make any difference. Fixing simple hems was one thing, but she couldn't take in a ballgown.

Determination rose up within her. Couldn't she? Not without magic, but why shouldn't she use her magic? It had gotten her this far. She opened her mouth, ready to declare that she would take the dress, but something made her pause. Harry's warnings rang through her mind—she'd already pushed her stepmother's incredulity to its limit. How could she explain adjusting a full ballgown in a matter of minutes? Defeat washed over her. She'd been so sure she could win Sapphira's game, just once.

But it was the miserable look of defeat on Olivia's face that suddenly woke Penny up to the truth of the situation. There were no winners in Sapphira's games. Even if Penny could succeed, it would be at the expense of her stepsister, and there was no joy in that. Failing to displace Olivia wasn't the true loss. True defeat would be buying into the game at all. Penny had never been willing to do it before. Why would she start now, when things most important to her were at stake? It was all the more reason not to attain her means in such a despicable way.

"You keep the dress, Olivia," she said quietly. "You want it more than I do, I think."

Confusion raced across Olivia's features, but it was quickly replaced by triumph. She clutched the gown to her like it was a precious treasure, and her eyes flicked to her mother before returning to Penny.

"You made the right choice, Penny," she said. "You're in no state to go to a ball."

Penny didn't even need to look down at herself to know Olivia was right. She was filthy from head to booted foot, her hair matted, dirt crusted under her nails. She could see Sophia's discomfort, but as usual the other girl said nothing. Sapphira, on the other hand, looked disappointed, as though Penny had shown signs of promise, but was now letting her down. The reaction only confirmed Penny in her choice.

Feeling richer in spite of the loss of the dress, Penny walked from the room with steady strides. Still, it was all she could do to hold her head high, a short time later, when the three women prepared to depart. To her credit, Sapphira hadn't been lying about her own gown. It wasn't in the latest style, and it looked almost shabby beside the girls' new dresses. But she wore it with her usual quiet elegance. Olivia looked very pretty compared to normal, the mask giving her an air of mystery, and her mousy hair piled becomingly on top of her head. The pink dress fanned majestically around her. Penny knew the color would have been even better on her, and the thought cost her a bitter pang.

Sophia, of course, was the jewel of the display. Even under her mask, Penny could see that the other girl's cheeks were prettily flushed. Her even features were framed by deliciously curled tresses, and those brown eyes of hers seemed larger and softer than Penny had ever seen them. The tightly fitted bodice of her deep green dress hugged her slim form, tastefully cut, but still showing off her figure to admiration. And the skirt was so full, she could barely get out the door. She looked a vision. Surely there would be some man at the ball ready to lose himself in those sparkling eyes and save the family from the poverty that loomed.

Just as long as it wasn't Prince Rian.

It was only after she heard the hired carriage pull away that Penny allowed herself to collapse onto a seat in the kitchen and bury her face in her hands. Al, who had wandered over from the hearth, nuzzled her tentatively with his nose. Receiving no response, he laid his snout on her lap, and whined in a sympathetic sort of way.

Penny had thought she was in control of herself, but this sign of affection from the dog undid her. Tears welled up, turning quickly to sobs so loud they brought Harry looking for her.

"Don't cry, Pen," he said, kneeling down so that his lined face was just below hers. "It'll be all right. It's all for the best, you'll see."

"He'll be looking for me," Penny sobbed, not very coherently. "He'll be looking for me, and I'll disappoint him. And Sophia's so beautiful. What if he falls in love with her instead?"

Harry scratched his grizzled head, looking bewildered and wrong-footed. Clearly this situation was beyond his area of expertise, and mercifully he knew better than to try to fix it with empty words.

It took Penny a few minutes to hiccup herself into silence, but she felt better for her tears. "It was an impossible dream, anyway," she sighed, running her thumb over the charm Prince Rian had given her. "And I suspect he knows it as much as I do."

She pushed herself to her feet, looking reluctantly in the small mirror. As expected, she was a mess. The tear tracks made her face even grimier, and her hair looked like a bird had made its nest there.

"I may not be going to the ball," she said wearily, "but I'd still best clean myself up." She brightened slightly. "I have hours to myself, and all the work is done. Maybe I'll heat some water, have a proper bath. It's been a while."

"That's the spirit," said Harry encouragingly.

Penny gave him a dull smile. There was no use expecting Harry to understand something like a royal ball. She closed her eyes, letting her fingers rest while she instead sent her magic threading up into her own hair, untangling it strand by strand. This task took a considerable time, and Penny was just stoking the fire to heat some water when a smart rap at the kitchen door made her, Harry, and Al all turn.

"Who could that be?" Harry asked, sounding nervous.

"Penny, I know you're in there," called a voice Penny knew. "Now open the door!"

Penny flew across the room, astonishment stopping her tongue. She could hardly believe the evidence of her eyes when the door swung wide to reveal a resplendent Lady Amaranthe, in a ballgown of deep purple, a mask dangling from one hand, and jewels twinkling from her throat.

"What are you doing here?" Penny gasped, forgetting politeness in her stupor.

"That," said Lady Amaranthe in irritation, "is what I should be asking you. What happened? I thought you were going to get that gown."

Penny sighed. "I couldn't, Lady Amaranthe. I mean, I *could* have, but I couldn't bring myself to do it."

The noblewoman clucked her tongue disapprovingly. "It's time you started sticking up for yourself, Penelope, but we can talk about that later. Right now we have a ball to get to, and my coachman won't like keeping the horses standing." She cast an appraising eye over Penny. "My dear, you're a mess."

"I know," Penny sighed. "And I can't go to the ball, because I don't have a gown to wear. It seems like such a foolish reason to miss out, but I can't exactly go in this old thing, can I?" She gestured down at her worn and filthy work dress.

"Actually," said Lady Amaranthe curtly, "that's exactly what you'll do. Have you forgotten who you're talking to?"

Penny's eyes widened as she grasped the other woman's meaning. "I can't let you do that," she croaked. "It'll be too much for you!"

"I'll be the judge of what's too much for me," Lady Amaranthe said, unimpressed. She turned a calm eye on Harry. "Is this the one you've told me about? The one who's in your confidence? Harry, is it?"

"Yes, My Lady," said Harry, bowing stiffly, his wide eyes never leaving the gorgeously arrayed noblewoman. "I'm Harry, right enough."

"And yes, he knows about my magic," Penny chipped in.

Harry looked nervously between them, but said nothing.

"Good," said Lady Amaranthe. "That makes things considerably easier." She turned back to Penny. "Wash yourself off, child, no need to waste magic covering up dirt that can be removed the old-fashioned way."

Penny hastened to comply, not even flinching at the freezing water from the pitcher. She was fervently glad that she'd untangled her hair, just so that Lady Amaranthe didn't see how knotted it had become.

"Now, I brought this," said Lady Amaranthe, handing her a topaz-colored mask. "Much easier to acquire than a dress, since one size basically fits everyone." She frowned at Penny's skirt. "Shall we make the gown match?"

"If...if you like," said Penny nervously. "If you're sure it won't be too much for you to—"

"Oh, enough of that," scolded Lady Amaranthe. "I've been

afraid of something like this, so I've been storing my magic all week."

She screwed her eyes up in concentration, muttering under her breath. Penny felt the rather unyielding tug of the other woman's magic worrying at her clothes. Harry's gasp of shock brought Penny's eyes flicking down to her dress. She cried out in delight, half spinning this way and that, to admire the folds of topaz silk now rippling around her.

"It's beautiful," she breathed.

"No, it just *looks* beautiful," Lady Amaranthe reminded her, but she was smiling. "Now, fetch your best slippers."

Penny raced upstairs, hurrying down with a faded pair of embroidered dancing slippers. "They're not great," she said apologetically. "But they're the best I have."

"They'll do just fine," said Lady Amaranthe reassuringly. "Put them on." Once Penny had done so, she once again began to murmur. As she spoke, she twirled her fingers in a strained, slow motion wave that sent power washing over Penny's feet. Then she rocked back on her heels, looking satisfied.

Penny looked down eagerly. Her embroidered slippers had disappeared, replaced with elegant, high-heeled shoes made of what appeared to be glass.

"They're stunning, but how will I walk in them?" she laughed. "I've never worn shoes anything like this. I don't think anyone has."

Lady Amaranthe chuckled. "A royal ball is the time for making a statement. And you'll walk in them like you always do. They're your same slippers underneath, remember?"

Penny tried it out, and found that the other enchantress was right. The shoes, while they looked as incredibly impractical as they were elegant, were as comfortable as flat slippers to walk in. Yet somehow, when she moved, the effect to watching eyes was of walking in elevated heels.

A glance in the mirror showed her that her hair now bore the appearance of being pulled back into an elegant bun, her curls falling loosely around her face. She thought that, with a little focus, she could probably make the strands actually travel into those positions, and stay there.

"That's amazing magic," she marveled. She squinted at Lady Amaranthe. "And you don't look too tired."

"Thank you, Penny, most complimentary," said the older woman dryly.

Penny laughed. "Sorry. You look absolutely divine. But you know what I mean."

Lady Amaranthe nodded. "I won't be able to hold it all night. But for a few hours, I think. Until midnight should be safe."

"That's when the unmasking is, isn't it?" Penny asked. She felt almost giddy with excitement, hardly able to believe she was going to the ball after all, and in a gown more beautiful than the one she'd relinquished to Olivia. She turned to Harry. "I wish you could come too."

He guffawed. "Not likely."

Penny chuckled. It was a little hard to picture the grizzled old servant at a royal ball. Al nuzzled her dress, looking bewildered, and she leaned down to pull one of his ears gently through her fingers. "I don't think dogs are allowed at balls, sorry Al." She glanced up at Lady Amaranthe, humor in her eyes. "How much magic do you have left? Does your carriage need an extra horse?"

The enchantress made a sound that in a lesser person would be a snort. "You are *not* bringing your dog, Penny, not as a horse, or anything else. Now let's go before all the good food is gone."

Penny had no arguments. She paused on her way to the door, her eyes searching Harry's face, which was lined with worry. "I know you think it's dangerous Harry, but I'll be all right. Lady Amaranthe will take care of me."

"I do feel better knowing she's with you," he admitted gruffly. "But I still don't like it, Pen."

"Don't worry, you old sour puss," smiled Penny, dropping a light kiss on his forehead. "You heard her. I'll be back by midnight."

A minute later, she was seated in Lady Amaranthe's elegant carriage, waving to a barking Al as the horses pulled them out of her dusty barnyard, and toward the lights and music of the distant castle.

CHAPTER NINETEEN

Rian

Rian watched the arrivals anxiously, resisting the urge to check the elaborate timepiece mounted on the wall of the ballroom. The long space was packed full of people, the swish of skirts in every color imaginable adding a constant background murmur to the efforts of the musicians seated in one corner.

Candles glinted in chandeliers hung from the ceiling, and the glass doors that ran down one long side of the room were flung open, to reveal lanterns burning in the gardens beyond. Tables covered in food lined the other wall, with an enormous bowl of punch gracing the middle such surface.

None of this held the smallest interest for Rian. He scanned the attendees, trying to mentally remove the masks that covered everyone's faces. He would surely recognize her even under a mask, wouldn't he? Was it possible she'd already come, and he'd missed her arrival? The herald announcing everyone's names had definitely slowed. Most guests were here.

So where was Penny?

Deftly dodging around a hopeful-looking woman who had to be at least ten years his senior, Rian moved closer to the door.

Perhaps there was a hold up with one of the carriages, and the latest arrivals had been delayed in reaching the door.

"Rian, where are you going so purposefully?"

Rian jumped at the sound of his mother's voice. "Nowhere, Mother," he said, in what he hoped was a stately tone. "I'm just enjoying the display."

"I'm glad to hear you say so," his mother smiled. "Display is certainly the word for it." She inclined her head toward a girl in a blue gown cut daringly low across the bosom, the better to display an elaborate necklace of sapphires. "Lady Britta is an excellently connected option, for example. And not at all unpleasant to look at." She frowned slightly. "Even if her taste is a little dashing."

"Mother," Rian said, pained. "I meant I was admiring the room, and the..." he waved his hand vaguely, "general activity."

"If you say so," smiled his mother. "Be that as it may, she would be an excellent choice to open the dancing with." Her tone made it clear that *choice* was not at all the word she really meant.

Rian sighed, resigned to the inevitable, but still feeling that he should put up at least a token resistance. "I thought we agreed that I should dance with some of the commoners as well as the nobles, Mother. Otherwise what's the point of inviting them and trying to make them feel included?"

"Of course you can dance with all manner of young ladies," said his mother, with dignity. "But," she abandoned her pretense of suggestion, "you will *open* the dancing with Lady Britta."

"Yes, Mother," said Rian wearily.

Truth be told, he didn't care who he danced with, if Penny wasn't there. One stranger was as good as the next. Not that Lady Britta was precisely a stranger. She was several years younger than him, so she'd only recently come out. But he'd spoken with her enough times to recognize her, even through her mask. He'd always found her a little overwhelming. He wasn't surprised his mother had selected her, however. Lady Britta's father was a duke, from one of Bansford's oldest and most influential families. They'd traveled halfway across the kingdom to attend these balls.

As if on cue—probably exactly on cue, judging by the pointed way the queen was looking into their corner—the musicians struck up a stately tune. Accepting his fate, Rian approached Lady Britta and solicited her hand for the dance.

She threw him a confident smile, and placed her hand on his offered arm with alacrity. Rian cringed internally as her slender fingers wrapped possessively around his arm. He wondered whether she didn't realize she was being singled out because of her father's status, or just didn't care.

He half expected her to pull herself flush against him when he swept her into the dance, as more than one bold young damsel had done at Bentleigh's betrothal ball. But Lady Britta held herself at an elegant distance as the rest of the attendees watched them move through the steps of the dance. After a few bars, the music changed slightly, and other couples mercifully took their cue and joined the dance. Rian was struggling to find anything to say, but his companion saved him the necessity.

"Rumor is that you're choosing your bride at these balls, Prince Rian."

"Is it?" he asked, noncommittally. "I try not to listen to rumors, My Lady."

"Ooh, what a shame," she said, grinning. "Such fun you miss out on."

Rian gave a reluctant laugh. "If you say so."

"Oh, I do," she assured him. She glanced around, then nodded at a couple dancing nearby. "You'd hardly believe the rumors about that viscount's daughter, for example."

Rian kept his face blank and unresponsive, disgusted by this transparent attempt to discredit her competition. He knew that the girl in question was one of the candidates his mother had selected, and Lady Britta must have guessed it.

"Do you like my gown, Your Highness?" his companion asked innocently, when he made no response. "I've heard that blue is your favorite color, which is convenient, since I adore sapphires."

Reflexively, Rian glanced down at her dress, then wished he hadn't. Its low cut was even more striking up close, and he suddenly realized why she was holding herself at a distance. He wouldn't be able to admire the effect nearly as well from a closer angle. He was suddenly uncomfortably aware of her waist under his hand, and the unnecessary firmness of her grip on him.

"It's lovely," he said stiffly, fixing his gaze on a spot above her left shoulder.

Far from being offended, Lady Britta seemed delighted to have discomposed him. "I'm so glad you think so," she grinned. Her eyes settled on something behind him, and her voice turned thoughtful. "I heard it was your idea to invite some commoners as well as the nobility. That was very forward-thinking of you."

Rian hesitated, unsure whether she was complimenting him or complaining.

"I have ideas of my own, you know," she said abruptly. "About the way the court operates. I think we could use some change."

"You do?" Rian asked, bringing his eyes back to hers. "What ideas?" Was it possible there was someone within the court actually willing to speak out about the ban?

Lady Britta nodded. "I think we're far too formal. The older generation is so set in its ways, but I can't see any reason why we can't have a little more fun in the upper circles, a little less standing on ceremony."

Rian raised an eyebrow, suspecting that her version of fun

wouldn't be acceptable to most of the "upper circles". "When you started talking about change, I thought you were going to comment on the magic ban," he said daringly.

The look Lady Britta cast at him suggested he was mad. "Of course not! Let the curse-muttering rabble back in? I don't think so."

Rian felt a surge of irritation, disproportionate to her petty comment. This was the type of woman his parents wanted him to marry? Someone who spurned those who needed her help, but thought she was forward-thinking because she wanted to be free of the restrictions that came with her elevated position? Granted, his parents likely had no concept of just how lax Lady Britta was in her manners when with those of her own generation, but still. Rian would never consent to marry someone so self-focused.

Then he remembered that he had promised to relinquish his right to consent to his parents' choice, and his heart plummeted. Hopefully all of his approved candidates weren't like Lady Britta.

The song mercifully drew to a close, and Rian cast around for someone, anyone else to ask to dance, so as to avoid further time with Lady Britta. Movement at the entrance to the long ballroom drew his eyes, and he paused at the sight of a new figure entering the room. The woman, clad in deep purple, looked familiar, although he couldn't immediately identify her.

Then another figure followed her through, and Rian's heart did a somersault. It was her. She was here.

Abandoning his partner without a word, he strode across the ballroom, past couples bowing and curtsying to one another to mark the end of the song. The musicians struck up another tune immediately, and the herald's announcement of the newcomers' names was lost in the chaos. Not that Rian needed it. He'd know Penny anywhere, and he realized now that her companion must be Lady Amaranthe. Bless her for whatever part she'd played in Penny being there! He was sure, given their lateness, that there must be a story to tell. But none of that mattered right now.

"Rian."

He checked his pace in irritation, wondering where his mother had acquired her unerring talent for popping up at the least convenient moments.

"Where are you going? You've only taken part in one dance."

"I danced with Lady Britta, as instructed," said Rian impatiently.

Penny had moved fully into the room now, and she was glorious. An orangey-bronze silk rustled around her slim form, and golden curls danced around her face, which was predictably flushed. The mask did little to disguise her beauty, and he could see other men eyeing her off. If he didn't hurry, she'd be claimed for the next dance by someone else. And he wasn't having that.

"Now I think I should dance with a commoner, as we discussed," he continued, tilting his head in Penny's direction. "I'm pretty confident that girl who's just arrived isn't part of the court."

The queen followed his gaze, frowning in concentration as her eyes raked over Penny's figure. "I believe you're right," she said, nodding. "I don't recognize her." She stepped back. "Very well."

"Mother," Rian said, daring to delay for valuable seconds. "This ball is supposed to be a relaxed celebration, leading up to the formal announcement. Can we take a step back? It's hard for me to mingle and show interest in our guests if you're chasing me across the room every time I move."

Queen Eliza's lips pursed disapprovingly at this description of her activities, but after a moment's consideration, she gave him a curt nod. "Very well." And she retreated, trailed as usual by two ladies-in-waiting.

Rian rushed forward, with a little more speed than dignity, just as a masked young man bowed over Penny's hand.

The royals were not wearing masks, so there was no doubt of Rian's identity as he cleared his throat. The man bowed deeply, although his disappointed expression showed that he already knew he was about to be outranked.

"May I cut in?" Rian asked anyway, for form's sake.

"Of course, Your Highness," the man said, bowing once again.

Rian turned at once to Penny, his voice softening. "May I have this dance?"

Her eyes were full of unnameable emotion as they locked on his, and her hand trembled as she took his arm.

"Of course." Her voice was little more than a whisper, but as Rian swept her out among the other couples, she spoke up again. "I'm afraid I'm not very practiced at dancing," she admitted, a touch of humor in her lilting voice. "It's years since I had lessons, and I don't remember all of it."

"Given many of tonight's guests aren't practiced in dancing, they're keeping to the simplest songs," Rian reassured her. He smiled down at her, wishing she wasn't wearing a mask, so he could better read her expression. "And I won't let you stumble," he promised, tightening his grip on her waist.

He felt no discomfort this time, even as he pulled her considerably closer than he'd held Lady Britta. Unlike Penny, he'd attended many balls, danced with countless partners. But holding Penny in his arms like this was an entirely new experience. Strange jitters were running out from her warm touch, and it was hard to marshal his thoughts.

Focusing on the dance to clear his head, he tried to steer her more forcefully than he normally would. Hopefully that would make the movement of the dance predictable, and help cover her uncertainty.

"I was afraid you weren't coming."

"I almost didn't," Penny said ruefully. "It's a long story. But I'm glad I'm here." She looked around, her eyes widening as she took in the decadent array. "It's even more impressive from the middle of the room."

Rian laughed loudly enough to draw a look from a couple passing nearby. "Instead of from the side, skulking between pillars because you're not supposed to be here?"

She grinned. "Something like that. Although I seem to remember that *you* were skulking between pillars, Your Highness, and I can only assume that you were supposed to be here."

Rian chuckled. "Yes, well, balls have always felt like more of a punishment than a celebration." He held her gaze unblinkingly. "Until now, that is."

As he'd hoped, color rushed delightfully across Penny's partially covered face.

"I heard," she said, swallowing audibly, "that the purpose of these balls is to celebrate your upcoming marriage."

Rian's grip on her tightened convulsively, even as he continued to mechanically steer her through the steps of the dance.

"Is that more of a punishment than a celebration as well?" Penny continued, her voice so quiet he had to incline his head toward hers to hear it.

Rian hesitated before responding, recognizing that the musicians were winding down toward the end of the song. "Will you walk outside with me?" he asked, nodding to an open double door nearby. "So we can talk? Or will your chaperone object?"

Penny took his arm again willingly enough. "To be honest, my stepfamily don't know I'm here," she said. She glanced toward a refreshment table. "That's them over there." Her words tumbled out with a strange energy. "The stunningly beautiful one is my stepsister Sophia."

Rian blinked at the trio. For the life of him he couldn't tell which of the many nameless girls was supposed to be "the stunningly beautiful one".

"In the deep green gown," Penny prompted, and he nodded vaguely. "With the brown hair."

"Ah." He wasn't sure why he was supposed to care, but he didn't say so. "Why don't they know you're here?"

"I came with Lady Amaranthe," Penny said, in what he considered a very inadequate explanation. Her voice turned rueful. "And I think we both know that she has no scruples about leaving me alone with you."

Rian grinned. "For which I must thank her sometime."

"You're shameless," Penny scolded, but she was smiling as he led her down the few shallow stone steps that led from ballroom to garden. A flash in the moonlight drew his eye to her feet as they poked out from beneath the huge skirt of her gown, and he raised his eyebrows.

"Are your shoes made of glass?"

"Pretty unusual, isn't it?" she smiled. "More comfortable than they look though."

"I still say better you than me," said Rian fervently, and Penny chuckled.

The evening was fine, and there were a number of couples strolling through the gardens. Lanterns had been lit at regular intervals, turning the familiar grounds into a multi-colored fairyland. A few more daring guests had removed their masks, but it didn't make Rian stand out any less. He was, as always, depressingly visible.

"Have you ever been into a hedge maze?" he asked brightly, an idea seizing him.

"No," said Penny. "Although one of our vineyards was pretty maze-like. It wasn't planted straight."

"Tell me about it," said Rian, smiling down at her. "About the life of a vintner."

And she did. She told him all about her father's business, about how, motherless as she was, she ran a little wild, turning the vineyards into her kingdom. He could picture the child Penny, barefoot and laughing as she helped crush the grapes, until discovered by her father and forced to soak her feet in a solution that never succeeded in washing all the purple away. It was a happy image, and seemed a far cry from the sense he'd gotten about her current life.

"How did your mother die?" he asked gently.

Penny stiffened slightly, and it was a long moment before she answered. "An accident," she said colorlessly. "I'd rather not talk about it."

"I'm sorry," said Rian, regretting the insensitive question.

"It's..." There was intense emotion in Penny's voice, and it took her a moment to pull herself together enough to finish. "It's not your fault." Her voice dropped, so that she seemed almost to be talking to herself. "It's really not."

Rian hesitated, unsure what to say. He had the sense she was holding back tears, and he longed to take her in his arms, to comfort her. But he didn't dare do it.

"Where are we?" Penny asked suddenly, with a return to her normal manner. She glanced around, seeming to realize for the first time that they'd left the lantern-lit gardens behind and were in a part of the grounds illuminated only by moonlight. "Have you brought me to the hedge maze?"

"That's right," nodded Rian. He dropped his voice to a theatrical whisper. "Do you dare to go in?"

"I'm not sure I do," laughed Penny. "I'll get lost."

"Not with me," Rian assured her confidently. "I know this maze like the back of my hand." He seized her hand as he spoke, dragging her into the maze behind him. He wondered if she felt it, too, the spark that seemed to leap from the point where their hands connected.

"It is pretty amazing," Penny acknowledged, gazing up at the tall hedges on either side. "But can you afford to wander through a maze? Won't you be missed?"

Rian sighed, coming to a stop and looking wistfully toward the distant heart of the maze. "Yes, I suppose I will." He frowned. "You're much too responsible."

Penny laughed. "When a crown prince tells you you're too responsible, you know it's time to lighten up."

In the moonlight, Rian couldn't see the green of Penny's eyes as she smiled up at him, but he could call it perfectly to mind. He took her hand in his, turning it over and smiling at the sight of his charm on her delicate silver bracelet. He hadn't noticed before now that it was her only adornment, but the simple elegance of the look suited her perfectly.

"The truth is," he said in a rush, "I wanted to talk to you somewhere private. Because your question in the ballroom deserves an answer."

Penny's face became serious, but she didn't interrupt, just watched him expectantly.

"These balls *are* supposed to mark my betrothal," he said. "You were right."

Penny's intake of breath was audible in the stillness of the night. "So you're betrothed?" She started to draw her hand away.

"No," said Rian hastily, gripping it more tightly. "Of course not. If I was, I wouldn't have..." He trailed off. Wouldn't have what? Led her on? But that was still what he was doing, if it came down to it. He had to be honest with her.

"I'm not betrothed," he said. "But my parents wish me to be. The identity of my..." his lips stumbled over the words, "my future wife, isn't yet decided. But they'll choose her, over the course of these balls."

This time, Penny succeeded in drawing her hand away. "And they certainly don't want to choose someone like me," she said, with too much conviction for Rian's liking.

He stepped closer, touching her chin with featherlight fingers until she tilted her face up to his.

"I want to convince them that they should choose someone exactly like you," he said, his voice coming out a rough whisper. He couldn't see Penny's blush in the silvery light, but he could feel the heat radiating out from her face. "Can I take your mask off?" he asked, and she nodded breathlessly.

Rian reached out both hands and slid his fingers into her hair, finding where the ties met within the glorious riot of golden curls. Carefully, so as not to disarrange the elegant style, he untied the strings, and pulled the mask gently away. A beautiful face was revealed to him, with features he'd come to regard as perfect, and huge, speaking eyes that met his with the tiniest hint of shyness.

"Am I who you expected?" Penny asked, a humorous tilt to her lips.

Rian smiled, holding her mask loosely in one hand as he brought the other back up to touch her cheek. "Not at all who I expected," he said. "But maybe exactly who I need."

Penny's breath caught, and Rian could feel his own senses spinning away from him, taking his logic with them. Clinging on with an effort, he reminded himself of what he'd come here to say. He needed to tell her the truth, not dig them both in deeper.

"Penny," he started, his voice husky. Clearing his throat, he tried again. "I want to convince my parents to abandon their current thinking, but...I can't deny to you that I have no reason to think I'll be successful." His eyes pleaded with her to understand, to forgive his weakness in embroiling her when there was so little hope. "If it was just a matter of my own determination, I'd have no doubts. But..."

"It's all right, Rian," Penny whispered, and he thrilled to hear his name without the title. Involuntarily, he moved even closer. "I never really thought it could be different. Trust me when I say that your parents would never approve of me."

"You can't know that," Rian said, his eyes searching hers. "There might not be much hope, but there's some. If they just knew you…"

Penny gave a harsh little laugh which didn't suit her at all. "If they knew me, they'd—" She cut herself off, and shook her head so that her curls danced distractingly. "Even you can't stop the tide, Rian." Her voice softened again. "But I have no doubt you'll be a good king."

Rian dropped her mask into the grass, recklessly twining his free hand loosely around her waist. Her silky dress didn't feel like he expected—it was almost rough to the touch. But he had no thought to spare for her fashion. "I'll be a much better king if I have the right queen by my side."

"Rian," Penny whispered, shaking her head.

"Please, Penny," he said, his voice pained. "Won't you let me at least fight for you, even if there's little hope of victory?"

Penny hesitated, but even while her words refused to form, her hand had found its way up to rest on Rian's chest.

Losing his head completely, Rian pulled her close and lowered his lips to hers. Penny's soft gasp was cut off as she leaned up into him, returning the embrace with the same desperation he felt. They both knew the kiss was a stolen one, but it lost none of its fire for being bittersweet.

Penny was the one to pull back, breathing hard. Rian felt winded himself, his mind in a daze.

"The ball," Penny gasped. "What time is it? I need to find Lady Amaranthe."

"Lady Amaranthe?" Rian repeated stupidly. The rest of the world had ceased to exist while he held Penny in his arms, and it was something of a surprise to discover that it was still there. Shaking his head like a dog ridding itself of water, he forced his thoughts back into order. "I should return as well," he said reluctantly. "I'm sure my absence has been noticed, and there's supposed to be an announcement before the unmasking."

"The unmasking is at midnight, isn't it?" Penny asked, alarmed. "I can't stay that late. I need to go home."

"What?" Rian said, confused. "Why?"

Penny ignored his question, leaning down to retrieve her mask from the grass. She tied it on with shaking fingers, not quite meeting Rian's eyes. "Will you take me back, please?"

"Of course," he said, pulling himself together and offering her his arm. "I'm...I'm sorry if I—"

"Don't apologize," she said quickly, squeezing his arms with fingers that were still not quite steady. "I don't regret...I could never..."

Rian placed his hand over her trembling one, telling her without words that he understood. He hardly knew whether his heart was soaring or breaking as he led her back through the gardens, toward the noise and light of the ballroom. His mind kept replaying their kiss, the softness of her lips, the warmth of her in his arms, the pressure of her hand on his chest. He didn't think he could bear to give her up, to enter a marriage as bloodless as his parents'.

It seemed that there was still some time to go before his father would address the guests, because the dance was in full swing. Rian walked Penny slowly through the well-lit garden paths, neither speaking. He hoped that mingling with the other strolling couples for a while would make their reentry to the ballroom less conspicuous.

But all too soon, he saw his father through the doors, stepping onto a slightly raised dais at one end of the long ballroom.

"I'm needed," he said apologetically, as others around them began to move back into the ballroom as well. "Shall we—?"

But Penny shook her head, removing her hand from his arm. "You go ahead."

Regretfully, he turned from her, mounting the shallow steps and emerging back into the crowd.

CHAPTER TWENTY

Penny

Penny hovered silently in the semi-darkness of the gardens, thinking she'd better wait for her cheeks to cool before reentering the ballroom.

Then again...she might be waiting forever.

Had the crown prince really just kissed her? Just told her he wanted to convince his parents to let him choose her for his bride?

Forget the crown—had *Rian* just kissed her? The warm-eyed, stern-mouthed man whose serious voice hid the hint of a laugh for those who were listening? The man who could still an entire market with his presence, but who chatted to her dog like he was an old friend? Who worried about her safety when she wandered the city alone, even when they were strangers? Who, unlike her own supposed family, remembered her birthday, and brought her a gift?

Her cheeks burned all over again at the memory of his touch, of the intoxicating freedom she'd felt when he lowered her mask, looked full into her face, and told her she was the one he needed.

She covered her face in her hands, trying to get hold of

herself. As was always the case when in the grip of strong emotion, she could feel her magic clamoring for release. But she had to be controlled, she had to be careful. She was truly in the den of the beast now, no matter how tousle-haired and gentle-hearted that beast had turned out to be.

And *he* felt guilty for leading *her* on! She had recognized the danger to her own heart in her growing attraction to Rian, but she realized how selfish she'd been in disregarding the danger to his heart. He had no idea how utterly hopeless their cause really was. She shuddered at the thought of what his parents would say if they knew the truth. The memory of Rian's lips on hers surged up once again without warning, taking possession of her mind. And with it came a longing to be genuine with him, to tell him the truth of who she was.

But that thought was the greatest foolishness of all, even in this night of foolish decisions. She needed to go home. She needed to leave before her beautiful gown returned to a soot-stained work dress, and she was exposed not only as little better than a servant, but as a magic-user.

She hurried up the steps and into the ballroom, scanning the room for Lady Amaranthe. The point where she entered wasn't far from the front, where King Rhinehart was addressing his guests. But Penny had no attention for the king's welcoming platitudes. She needed to find the other enchantress and get out. If only the room wasn't so crowded!

Closing her eyes, Penny tried to draw on her other sense, the one the rest of the room didn't have. She felt the tug of power, and opened her eyes, expecting to see Lady Amaranthe. But it wasn't the noblewoman. The magic—gathering now into a crescendo—seemed to be coming from a masked man some distance in front of her. He was shifting through the crowd with movements that were a little too casual, toward the dais where the king stood with his wife on one side, and his son on the other. Perhaps the man was one of the musicians, because he was carrying several long wooden sticks that Penny had seen used to beat time on a drum.

An unnamed dread rose up within Penny, and she stumbled forward, her hand extended across the distance toward Rian. Before she could cry out a warning, however, a firm grip closed around her other arm.

"Penny, no!"

"But—" Penny turned at the hissed warning, her eyes wide as they latched on to Lady Amaranthe's face. "Don't you feel the—?"

"Of course I do, and we both know why we can feel it. If you call out, you'll expose yourself."

"But what's he doing?" Penny protested. "It's like he's gathering his strength for—"

The sentence remained unfinished, cut off by Penny's gasp as the man leaped onto the dais. He pulled both hands up, brandishing the sticks like knives.

"You'll pay for what you've done!" he shouted, and before Penny's horrified eyes, the wooden sticks turned into sharpened metal, which the man brought plunging toward his sovereign.

The king's guards raced forward, but someone else was ahead of them. Before Penny could blink, Rian had thrown himself in front of his father, arm upraised.

"*Rian!*" Penny's scream was lost in the general uproar as chaos broke loose. She couldn't even see what had become of the prince, as a dozen guards swarmed over the dais, seizing the attacker, and shielding the royals from view, and from further harm.

"Time to go," said Lady Amaranthe grimly.

"But Rian!" Penny protested, still shaking with horror. "I have to see if—"

"No, you have to get home, before you're arrested as an accomplice," snapped Lady Amaranthe.

"An accomplice?" Penny gasped. "What do you—?" Following her companion's gaze, she drew in a sharp breath at the sight of a worn slipper poking out from her voluminous skirts.

"I can't hold it anymore," muttered Lady Amaranthe through gritted teeth. "So unless you think this is a good moment to be exposed as an enchantress, I suggest we get to the carriage."

Terrified, Penny made no further arguments. Lady Amaranthe had already shepherded her halfway to the door. A few others were fleeing, but most were milling around, watching with wide eyes as the attacker was dragged away, still screaming abuse at his king.

"The fool," Lady Amaranthe spat, angrier than Penny had ever seen her. "The utter fool. Whoever he is, he's made things ten times harder. Does he think that's the way to bring about change?"

"He tried to murder the king," Penny said, shaken. "He used magic to try to kill his sovereign."

Lady Amaranthe shot her a sharp look, but said no more. In a remarkably short time, she'd gotten her carriage pulled around, and bustled Penny into it. As soon as they were alone, Lady Amaranthe's shoulders slumped, and Penny felt the magic leak off her clothing. The topaz silk faded, and the glint of glass on her feet disappeared.

"I'm sorry," she said, her lips bloodless. "I lingered too long, and it took too big a toll on you."

"Where were you?" Lady Amaranthe asked, worry creasing her brow. "I looked everywhere, and couldn't see any sign of you."

Penny's eyes were on her lap, and she was fidgeting with her bracelet. "The prince took me walking in the gardens. He said…"

She shook her head, swallowing. "I don't think you'd believe me if I told you."

Lady Amaranthe took a moment to answer, and when she did, her voice was softer. "I think I would. And do you believe him?"

Penny made a fatalistic gesture. "It's not a matter of believing," she said. "It's a hopeless situation, even he admits it." Her lips twisted slightly as she remembered his words. *There might not be much hope, but there's some.* "Well, he mostly admits it," she whispered.

Evidently sensing her need for space, Lady Amaranthe said no more. The rattling of the carriage over the cobblestones made Penny's head ache, and she longed for the relative peace of her kitchen. When the horses pulled up in the familiar barnyard, Lady Amaranthe rallied enough to re-activate the magic, so that the coachman saw Penny descend in the same dress she'd alighted in.

"I'll see you at our usual time," Lady Amaranthe said, having walked Penny to the kitchen door. "Don't do or say anything foolish to give yourself away."

Penny managed a shaky nod, and Lady Amaranthe hurried back to her carriage, looking as weary as Penny felt. For all the enchantress's talk of not prancing around in false finery, Penny thought she saw a particularly elaborate flounce on the purple dress flicker out of existence and back again as Lady Amaranthe climbed the step.

Penny pushed the kitchen door open, making a small sound of relief as Al bounded over to her.

"Back in one piece, Pen," said Harry, standing quickly from where he sat by the fire. "I can't deny that's a relief to me. Did you have a good time?"

Penny sank onto the chair he'd vacated, shaking her head to

indicate her inability to speak. It was all too much, and she didn't know where she could begin.

"Is everything all right?" Harry asked, concerned.

Penny made a hopeless gesture. "I hardly know," she said, her voice faint. She ran her hands through her hair, releasing those parts she'd managed to style with her own magic. She wanted to look like her usual self—albeit cleaner—when her stepfamily arrived.

It felt like an age before they did, but Penny was deaf to all Harry's attempts to send her to bed. She couldn't even think through the events of the night. Random images kept flashing before her eyes. Rian leaping in front of his father. The multi-colored light of the garden lanterns, turning the night into a surreal dream. Rian taking her hands with strong fingers, his touch the most surreal dream of all. Rian almost running from the gorgeous bejeweled young lady he'd been dancing with when he saw her arrive.

But she couldn't make sense of any of it. Everything was just so much meaningless buzzing in her ears until she knew what had happened to Rian.

At long last, the sound of carriage wheels sent her flying to the front entrance. Remembering Lady Amaranthe's warning, she made a heroic effort to school her features, and present a calm front.

"Oh, Penny!" Sophia cried, erupting through the door in an almighty flounce of green fabric. "That must have been the most exciting ball in the history of balls!"

"It was certainly eventful," Olivia agreed dryly, following her sister. Sapphira floated behind them, looking unshaken by the night's events.

"What happened?" asked Penny, clenching her hands at her sides to keep them from shaking.

"An enchanter tried to kill the king!" Sophia said, eyes wide.

"You should've seen it, Penny! I've never seen magic before—it was terrifying!"

"And impressive," Olivia cut in.

"Olivia," reprimanded Sapphira, and the older girl shrugged.

"I know it's bad, but that doesn't mean it isn't impressive. The man turned wood into metal with the touch of his hand."

"And the king?" Penny asked faintly.

"He wasn't injured," Sophia rushed on, relishing her story. "Prince Rian jumped in front of him! It was so heroic! He really is the most handsome—"

"Yes, but is he all right?" Penny demanded impatiently. "Did the prince get stabbed by the metal?"

Sophia nodded solemnly. "He did, but it was just in his arm. He was so very brave."

Penny let out a shaky breath, feeling suddenly numb with relief. Something close to hysteria rose up within her, and it was all she could do to keep it inside.

"He can't have been too badly hurt," Olivia scoffed. "Since he carried on with the ball."

"The ball kept going?" Penny demanded. "After someone tried to kill the king, and stabbed the prince instead?"

Sophia nodded. "The prince disappeared and got bandaged up, then came back and kept dancing!"

"Is he out of his mind?" Penny said, with a surge of irritation. Here she'd been sitting up, wondering if he was dead, and he was dancing the night away!

"I wondered the same thing," chuckled Olivia. "I guess you don't get to take a break from being royalty."

"I guess not," said Penny heavily.

"Well, I'm glad he stayed," said Sophia frankly. "Or I'd never have gotten to dance with him. I don't think I even saw him before the king's announcement. He must have been called away or something."

"You danced with him?" Penny asked quickly. She knew the flash of jealousy was unreasonable, but she couldn't help it.

Sophia nodded eagerly. "He was really friendly! He asked all about me, about our family, and the vineyards. He wasn't at all stiff and serious, like I thought he'd be."

Penny stared at her stepsister, picturing Rian's encouraging smile as he weaseled information about her out of Sophia. All with a bandaged arm from where a crazed attacker had stabbed him mere minutes before! Suddenly the humor of it all overcame her, and she put a hand over her mouth, once more trying to hold in a hysterical outburst.

"Penny?" Sophia asked, uncertainly. "Are you all right?"

"I'm exhausted," Penny said frankly, lowering her hand. "I'm going to bed."

CHAPTER TWENTY-ONE

Rian

"Hold still, Your Highness!"

Rian sighed at the physician's scolding, but stopped fidgeting. Wincing, he felt the man poking around in his injured arm, tutting distractedly.

"Well, I'm far from an expert, but I see no sign of lingering magic," the bespectacled retainer said. "It's a clean wound from what I can tell. And not too deep."

"It's nothing," said Rian impatiently, as the physician wound a fresh bandage around the multiple small stab wounds on his arm. "It's really not worth all this fuss."

"Not worth all this fuss?" his mother repeated, aghast. "Rian, you've been stabbed by an enchanter!"

"Yes, thank you, Mother," said Rian wearily. The physician stepped back, and the prince flexed his arm carefully before giving a nod. "I'd noticed."

"It's outrageous, is what it is," the king said furiously. "I knew this idea of inviting commoners was dangerous, and now you see what comes of it."

"That's hardly fair, Father," protested Rian. "All the other commoners did nothing to deserve censure. Should they bear the blame for one man's actions?"

"I'm not talking about blame," snapped King Rhinehart. "I'm talking about access. You heard the captain's report. The man was only present because he was escorting his daughter, one of the commoners *you* invited. It was a mistake to give such ready access to the public. The next ball will be restricted to the court only."

"You can't do that!" Rian cried, and both of his parents raised their eyebrows. Moderating his tone with difficulty, he waited until the physician had bowed himself out of the prince's suite. "I think it would be a mistake, Father. It would undo the message we were trying to send, that we value everyone in our kingdom. I truly believe it would do more harm than good."

For a long moment, King Rhinehart glared at his son from under lowered brows. "You are my heir, Rian," he said at last. His scowl softened slightly. "And my son. You protected me last night. Allow me the right to do the same for you."

Rian hesitated, taken aback by the appeal. "I'm grateful for your concern, Father. But I really am all right." He held his arm for his father to see. "You heard the physician yourself. And there's no reason to think I'm in further danger. I mean," he grimaced slightly, "I wasn't the target, was I?"

King Rhinehart began to pace the room. "So you're determined to go ahead as planned, are you?" His gaze encompassed his wife as well as his son.

Queen Eliza lifted one elegant shoulder. "It's for you to decide, Rhinehart. But I agree with Rian that it won't be taken well if we take back our invitation."

"We could cancel the other balls altogether," the king commented.

"Certainly not," said Rian's mother, sounding scandalized. "All the arrangements are made! And we're yet to announce

Rian's bride!" She turned to her son, frowning slightly. "You disappeared into the garden for a long time last night, Rian. Who were you with? Was it one of the candidates I mentioned?"

Rian gave her a look. "I thought you were going to step back."

"I didn't follow you out there, did I?" she asked dryly. "And you didn't answer my question."

Rian sighed. He'd been hoping she wouldn't notice that. "No, I wasn't with one of your candidates. I escorted one of the common girls I danced with out there, and there were a number of others milling around."

The queen's expression told him she wasn't convinced by this incomplete answer, but her husband, who didn't seem to have been listening, cut her off.

"Well, perhaps you are right," he said, earning him identical stares of surprise from his wife and son. He gave them a disgruntled look. "Perhaps it is unreasonable to blame the other commoners for the actions of that enchanter." His eyes rested on his son. "I had inquiries made before the ball. You were right—inviting common girls to attend has had an excellent effect on general morale. Of course, that's probably because popular rumor suggests you're considering selecting one of those common girls for your bride."

It took all Rian's years of practice to keep his expression steady.

"But that's neither here nor there," the king went on. "No one official has made any such pronouncement, so there can be no cause for complaint when your bride is chosen from among the nobility. In the meantime, goodwill toward the crown has never been higher. It would perhaps be a step backward to destroy it by uninviting the commoners to the other balls."

"I agree," said Rian, heartened by this evidence both of his king's general reasonableness, and his father's willingness to listen to his counsel. "Have you thought more about my other suggestion also? That we suspend any further arrests until the balls are over?"

"Certainly not."

The frown was back on King Rhinehart's brow, and Rian felt his heart sink. It was almost as though a veil was lowered over his father's face, cutting off the moment of connection, and leaving Rian once more without access to chip away at his father's fear-fueled obstinacy.

"The attack at the ball further proves how out of hand the enchanter situation is," the king went on. "Stopping the arrests is the last thing I intend to do. On the contrary, it's time to take more drastic steps."

"What drastic steps?" Rian asked, alarmed.

"Hang on," objected his mother. "In case you've both forgotten, there's a more pressing matter requiring a decision!" Both men stared at her blankly, and she lifted her hands skyward in a silent appeal. "Choosing Rian's wife!"

"Oh," said the king. "That." He turned to his son. "Choose from the list your mother has drawn up. How hard can it be?"

Rian resisted the urge to rub his aching temples. He hadn't made it to his bed until hours after midnight, and even then, there'd been more tossing and turning than actual sleeping. He was eager to be gone from the castle, too, to seek Penny out. But this was a conversation that couldn't be rushed.

"Actually, I want to speak with you both about that," he said, trying to keep his voice casual. "About the list."

"What of it?" His mother's voice was ominous.

"Well, I wondered if it could be expanded," Rian said.

"Expanded to include whom?" the king asked, his tone no more encouraging than his wife's.

Rian sent a look of appeal between his parents. "Well, we all agreed that it was worthwhile to invite commoners to the balls, didn't we? That it would help show that we have their interests in mind as well as the higher classes'? Is it such a mad idea to include some of the common girls who came last night, when we consider who I should marry?"

"Yes," said his father shortly. "It is absolutely a mad idea."

"Rian, you can't marry a common girl," said his mother impatiently. "That's not what I meant when I said I want to see you choose someone you're happy with. I'm sure whoever you danced with was very pretty—I seem to remember a rather stunning girl in green—but that's not enough when you're choosing a future queen. You need to marry someone who will bring strength to the crown."

"What, someone like Lady Britta?" scoffed Rian. "Who thinks that the only problem with our court is that we need more frivolity and fewer rules?"

"She said that?" demanded the queen. Her voice dropped to a mutter. "Well, she's coming off the list, I don't care who her father is."

"Thank goodness for that," Rian said tartly. He looked to his father. "Can't you see that a united kingdom is a strong one? That someone whose presence in the castle made the common people feel heard and seen *would* bring strength to the crown?"

King Rhinehart sighed. "I understand your point, Rian," he said, more calmly than Rian expected. "But I'm afraid it's just not what's best for our kingdom. You need someone well-connected, who understands what the royal life requires."

"Someone who won't rock the boat, you mean," Rian said, unable to keep the bitterness from his voice. He was disappointed they weren't agreeing, but if he was honest with himself, they were taking the suggestion better than he'd expected. No one was shouting, or refusing to hear him out.

"There's no way this is all theoretical, Rian," said the queen, inconveniently shrewd. "Who is it you wish to add to the list? Is there something you need to tell us?"

"Actually," said Rian, drawing a breath. His parents were in as good a mood as he could hope for. Maybe they were just softened by his injury, but he'd take what he could get. And if his father was talking about drastic steps, the matter was becoming more urgent. "Actually, there is something I need to tell you. But not about the list."

He looked his father in the eye. "Father, you think I was brave last night, when I acted on instinct and jumped in front of you. But the truth is you'd be ashamed if you knew how much of a coward I've been, and for how long. It's time for me to change that."

"What are you talking about, Rian?"

"I've been too afraid to tell you what I really think, and what could be more cowardly than that? I'm your heir, Father, and you deserve my honest counsel. I'm sorry I've failed to provide it."

The king was silent for a moment. "I never wanted you to be afraid of me, Rian. And I do value your counsel, as long as you understand that I won't always take it."

"Of course I do," said Rian. "And I'm glad to hear you say you value it, because if I'm honest, I've never felt that you invited it."

The king was frowning slightly now, but his voice was still level when he spoke. "What is it that you haven't given honest counsel on, Rian?"

"The ban," said Rian plainly. "I don't agree with it, Father. I don't think it's good for our people, or our kingdom."

This declaration was met by ringing silence. There was no explosion of anger, but Rian again saw that veil descend over his father's eyes. Well, he'd come this far. He may as well say all he needed to, while his father's stormy silence gave him opportunity.

"I've been paying attention these last few months, since

Listernia's curse was lifted. And if you've been making inquiries on the general mood of our people, I think you must know this as well. The situation has changed, and our people's attitude has changed too. There are no more tales of thorns and enchanted slumber creeping over the border. Instead everyone's hearing about the role magic played in saving Listernia. Not to mention all the good things enchanters can do, all the healings, and useful artifacts, and services to the crown."

"Who have you been listening to?" growled his father.

"No single person," Rian responded calmly. "I've just been listening to the chatter that's on the wind. All these arrests aren't helping, either—simply put, the ban is becoming unpopular."

"If I made all my decisions based purely on what's popular in the moment—" King Rhinehart started tartly, but Rian wasn't finished.

"Of course that's not what I'm suggesting. It's not just about what the people want. It's about what's best for the kingdom, and I don't think the ban is good for our future. We're the only kingdom who doesn't embrace magic, and the cost is too great for the dubious benefit of thinking we're safe from magical attack." He gestured at his arm. "Which we're not."

"We will be once we weed out the rest of the enchanters," snapped his father, definitely angry now. "If there weren't so many criminals still hiding in our midst—"

"It's a sign of how much they love Bansford, Father, that they're still here," Rian protested. "It would be much easier for them to flee to a different kingdom, but this is their home. Surely those are the people we want within our borders."

"I don't know who's been addling your mind with this talk of magic," King Rhinehart growled, "but it's clear to me that you're not as ready for a crown as you think you are. I can see you've been mingling too freely with the commoners you love. They always have big ideas, Rian, but they don't understand the pressures of ruling, the things that are at stake."

He glared between his wife and son. "We will not be adding any commoners to the list of eligible candidates for princess. I'll hear no more of it. We'll announce your bride—one of the young ladies your mother has already selected—at the ball next week. Then—"

"Next week?" Rian interrupted, alarmed. "Surely you mean the week after. There are still two more balls."

"The last is a celebration, Rian, a true betrothal ball," his mother cut in. "The plan was always to make the announcement at the second ball, out of one of the guests present. Ideally, you should have spoken to her before the event, of course."

Rian stared at her, breathing hard, his disappointment over his father's reaction to his advice temporarily driven from his mind. He *had* already spoken to her, and he'd thought he had two more weeks to win his parents over, not one.

"What if I don't want to marry any of them?" he asked bluntly.

His father raised an eyebrow, his voice still biting and hard. "Then you'd best leave it to us to choose one, as you agreed to do."

"No," said Rian quickly. "It hasn't come to that, not yet."

His mother sighed. "You're being very dramatic, Rian. Are you sure your arm isn't hurting you?"

Rian didn't even bother to respond. With a nod to his mother and a stiff bow to his still-scowling father, he swept out of his own suite, heading for the stables. They all needed some space, and he needed to find Penny.

Within minutes, he was mounted and riding for the city gates, in defiance of medical advice. But his arm was the least of his concerns. He was disappointed by his father's abrupt change from reasonable and accessible to completely unwilling to listen to Rian's point of view. He supposed he should have known better than to push on after he practically watched the king close his mind.

What was it about magic that made him so unyielding? Rian had always thought of his father as inflexible, and uninterested in his son's opinions. But he realized now that at least as much blame for his limited influence with his father lay with himself, not with the king. Rian had always been too afraid to put himself forward. But now that he'd begun to do so, it hadn't taken much persistence for his father to listen to his views, and show himself unexpectedly open to Rian's suggestions.

Except when it came to the ban on magic. In that, the king seemed not only unwilling, but unable to listen to reason.

Temporarily abandoning a problem for which he had no solution, Rian turned his mind to the other matter consuming his thoughts. He needed to know why Penny had disappeared the night before, and whether she was angry with him for declaring himself when he wasn't free to follow through, for kissing her when he couldn't offer her all she deserved.

The guards trailing behind him had to spur their horses to a gallop to keep up with him on the dusty road leading to the vineyards. Rian wished with all his heart that he could outrun them, but he knew they were too well-trained for that.

When the manor house nestled among the vineyards came into view, Rian reined in to a trot. He wanted to speak to Penny alone, without falling afoul of the friendly but vapid brunette whom he'd danced with, but whose name he'd already forgotten, or the sour-looking taller girl. Or the formidable woman whom he knew must be Penny's stepmother. His thoughts turned dark as he remembered how much willpower it had taken the night before not to give her a piece of his mind. Even the cheerful chatter of the sister he'd danced with had told him how overworked and under-appreciated Penny was, little as the girl had realized she was communicating that information.

Rian stayed on the road, spurring his horse right past the manor before doubling back. There was no sign of activity in the yard, and the front door was firmly shut. A large barn stood at a short distance from the house, and he regarded it thoughtfully. From comments Penny had let drop, he gathered that she did a fair bit of work there. There was always the risk that he'd run into the grizzled old servant first, but that was better than getting drawn into the house for petty conversation with the other ladies of the family.

"I'm going into that barn," he told his guards curtly. "Please stay out here, out of sight."

They blinked at him, and one cleared his throat. "Your Highness, I'm afraid—"

"Check it for hazards if it will make you feel better," said Rian impatiently. "I think you'll find it's an ordinary barn."

With a glance at his companion, the guard who'd spoken slipped from his horse and marched into the barn. He returned a minute later, nodding curtly to his prince.

Rian slid to the ground, handing the reins of his horse over to the mounted guard, who drew back behind the barn. Rian let himself into the structure, looking around him. It was, as he'd predicted, an ordinary barn. A horse nickered softly at him, and he strode over to stroke the animal's nose. A stirring drew his attention to a pile of hay in the corner, and he grinned at the sight of the sleepy occupant.

"Sleeping on the job, Al?" he protested. "Surely not."

The dog leaped to his feet with a joyful bark of greeting, and Rian shushed him in alarm. "Don't get everyone's attention," he scolded. "I only want to speak to one person."

Wagging his tail furiously and disregarding the chastisement, Al barked again. He raced over to Rian's side and leaped up, placing his paws on Rian's clean tunic in a perfunctory salute, then dropping to all fours again and dashing out the door. Rian stared after him, bewildered. "That dog has too much energy," he muttered to himself, returning his attention to the horse.

But he had to admit Al had his uses a few minutes later, when the dog returned, dragging with him a half-laughing, half-irritated—and fully confused—Penny.

"Al, what in the world are you—*Rian!*" Penny's gasp brought a grin to Rian's face, but it quickly faded at the sight of her pale countenance and shaking hands.

"Penny," he started, moving toward her. "I'm sorry to ambush you like this, but I needed to speak to you, and I didn't know how to—"

"Your arm," she interrupted, her voice hushed. She stepped forward, laying a gentle hand on his elbow, below the bandage. "Does it hurt terribly?"

"No, it's fine," said Rian, closing his hand over hers.

She looked up at him, those striking green eyes searching his. "You were so brave last night, Rian. When I saw you jump in front of those knives..." She drew a shaky breath. "You must be so angry someone tried to kill your father. And succeeded in injuring you!"

"My arm is nothing," said Rian dismissively. "And I don't want to talk about the attack right now. Penny, where did you go last night? Why did you run away like that?"

Penny stared up at him, not seeming to hear his words. "I was so afraid for you. I couldn't see what happened, and I thought you'd..." She swallowed, pulling herself together. "I'm sorry I had to leave without saying goodbye. It's difficult to explain." She let go of his elbow, and a dry note entered her voice. "But I gather from Sophia that you recovered quickly enough to rejoin the celebrations."

"Sophia!" said Rian, a triumphant laugh in his voice. "I couldn't for the life of me remember her name."

Penny looked like she was trying to stop herself from grinning, and not quite managing it. "Why are you here, Prince Rian?"

"No, no," protested Rian, frowning at her. "We're not going back to titles, not when we've come so far."

"I'm serious," said Penny. "Why did you come?"

"Why do you think?" Rian asked, reaching out with his good arm to tuck a curl behind Penny's ear. "I wanted to see you. To make sure you're all right."

"I don't know what I am," said Penny distractedly.

"I think I know what you mean," Rian said, with sympathy.

"I doubt it," Penny muttered.

"I spoke to my parents this morning," said Rian, looking at the ground. "About the idea—in a general sense—of a commoner being considered for my choice."

"And?" Penny asked, but her dry tone told Rian she already knew the answer.

He sighed. "It didn't go very well. Better than I expected. But...still not very well."

"Rian," started Penny, and he grimaced.

"I know," he said, anguished. "I shouldn't be putting you through this. I shouldn't be here." His eyes searched hers. "I shouldn't have kissed you last night. But...I can't bring myself to regret it."

"Neither can I," Penny whispered, her lips quivering slightly from withheld emotion.

Rian's eyes were drawn irresistibly to those lips, and they were suddenly all he could think about. Perhaps sensing the drift of his thoughts, Penny shifted closer. His nose was filled with the scent of hay, and his eyes drank Penny in. He dipped his head, wanting nothing more than to feel her lips against his again.

"No." He pulled back, running a hand through his hair. "I can't put us both through this. I shouldn't kiss you if I can't give you my heart."

Penny's eyes were on the ground now, her hands shaking so violently, he wondered what was wrong with them. He saw her ball them into fists, clutching at the fabric of her skirt.

"Penny," he whispered, desperate to make her understand the things he didn't know how to put words to. "If my heart was mine to give away, it would be yours without question."

She kept her eyes lowered, but he heard her breathing hitch. "But it isn't yours to give, is it?"

Rian swallowed, a reckless honesty taking hold of him. "It is by law," he said, and Penny's eyes snapped up to his.

"What do you mean?"

"The law protects my right to choose my own bride," he said, the words painful as they came out.

"So...so..." Penny seemed to be struggling to find words. "So where does that leave you?"

Rian sighed. "I promised my parents that I wouldn't exercise that right. I traded it in exchange for them dropping their opposition to my brother's betrothal."

Penny frowned in confusion. "Didn't they orchestrate your brother's betrothal, when he was a small child?"

"They did," Rian grimaced, "but things got a little complicated."

"Because of Listernia's curse," said Penny darkly. "And your parents' hatred of magic."

"Hatred is a strong word," Rian pleaded. Penny gave him a disbelieving look, and he cringed. "All right. But that's beside the point." Ignoring Penny's rueful expression, he pushed on. "I don't regret the promise I made to my parents, Penny. I wouldn't change it if I could."

Penny blinked, her expression hard to read. Before she could answer, however, a faint cry reached them from the direction of the house.

"That's my stepmother," said Penny, looking almost frightened. "I have to go." She turned to leave, but Rian grabbed her arm.

"Penny, wait! Will you come to the next ball?"

Penny stared at him. "Are they still holding it?"

"Of course," said Rian. "Will you come?"

"I—is there any point?" Penny hedged.

"Please," said Rian, his eyes pleading with hers. "Please come. I need you to come." He swallowed. "My parents are determined to announce my bride at the next ball, from among the guests present. I'm not ready to give up—I still have almost a week to try to convince them. But if you're not there..."

Penny bit her lip, conflict raging in her eyes.

"Say you'll come," Rian begged.

He saw the moment she gave in. "Yes," she said, "I'll come. But now I need to go."

Rian released her, his heart soaring. She'd said yes. He had a week. There was still hope.

Penny had said she needed to leave, but she lingered, her eyes fixed on his exuberant face. Suddenly, without warning, she leaned up on her toes and pressed her lips to his. Heat shot through Rian, and he reached for her, but she was already gone.

"I know I don't have any right," she said, as she fled through the door. "But I couldn't resist."

Closing his eyes, Rian took a deep steadying breath. He would give her that right, if it was the last thing he did.

CHAPTER TWENTY-TWO

Rian

To his frustration, Rian found it almost impossible to make progress on his resolution to convince his parents over the next few days. At first, he thought his best approach was to appeal to the unexpected softness his mother had shown. But while she enthusiastically agreed that he should choose a woman for whom he felt warmth, she gave no encouragement to any suggestion that a commoner could be that woman. If he made any hint to this effect, she just reminded him that the final decision rested with his father, and his father had made his view clear. As these attempts invariably turned into exhaustive discussions of details of Rian's upcoming betrothal that held no interest for him, he soon stopped approaching her.

Clearly it was his father he needed to convince. Unfortunately, the king seemed to be avoiding his son. In their brief interactions, Rian could tell his father was still angry about his declaration against the ban. But he got the sense it was more than that. The king was often to be seen talking seriously with Dreyton, and any time Rian approached, the chief guard would bow and depart. Rian even had to push in order to be included in the report by the captain regarding their protective border force, where all was apparently quiet. He remembered his high hopes, a short time before, about convincing his father to trust him and his counsel, and his heart sank. He seemed to have made quite a mess of things.

A few mornings before the second ball, Rian had still made no progress, and he was beginning to feel desperate. Perhaps it was time to throw caution to the winds, and confess to his father that he had a particular girl in mind. Maybe if the king and queen met Penny, they'd understand why Rian had lost his heart to her. Maybe with an actual person before them, he'd be able to convince them how good a change would be for the kingdom. It wasn't as though this matter had anything to do with magic or the ban. Based on his recent experience, his father would surely be reasonable enough to at least hear him out.

Gathering his courage, he approached his father's study, nodding to the guards stationed outside before rapping on the paneled wood.

"Enter," called an imperial voice.

Pushing the door open, Rian was surprised to discover his father wasn't alone. Dreyton was with him, although he rose and bowed at sight of the prince.

"No need to leave on my account, Dreyton," said Rian lightly.

"We were just finishing, actually," said the king. With a nod, he dismissed the guard, who strode curtly from the room. "I have a great deal to do, Rian, so if—"

"No, Father," Rian cut him off firmly. "I need to speak with you. It can't wait."

The king sighed, lowering his quill and regarding his son through hard eyes. "Very well. Sit."

Rian did so, although he was so full of nervous energy he'd have preferred to stand. His eyes were drawn to a large glass paperweight sitting on his father's desk. He didn't remember ever seeing it before. It looked like a slightly flattened sphere, with something purple and wave-like suspended inside it.

"That's eye-catching," he commented, reaching a hand toward it. "Is it new?"

"Don't touch it," said King Rhinehart, a snap in his voice. He fixed his son with an eagle stare as Rian withdrew his hand. "Well? What's so important?"

Rian resisted the urge to fidget, finding it hard to know where to begin in face of such an unpromising invitation. "What have you and Dreyton been discussing so frequently, Father?" he asked instead. "Have there been more arrests since that young woman last week?" Internally he cringed, even as the words came out. Bringing up the topic of magic was the last thing he should have done to open this conversation.

"No, there haven't," said the king, with satisfaction. "Perhaps we've finally succeeded in getting rid of the last holdouts." He gave a grim smile. "We needn't fear any attending the ball tomorrow night, at least."

"Oh?" Rian asked. "How can you be so sure?"

"Because of this." The king made as if to pat the paperweight, but at the last minute seemed to decide not to touch it, and just gestured awkwardly instead. "Dreyton has just delivered it to me. He sent one of his most trusted guards to Fernedell after the last ball, and the man's just returned."

"What is it?" Rian asked, a sense of foreboding growing within him.

"It was your idea, actually," said the king casually. "You were the one who accused me—unjustly, at the time—of possessing an artifact that could identify enchanters. It got me wondering whether such an item could exist, and now I have the answer. I have it on the best of authority that it will reveal any magic to its holder."

Rian's mouth fell open, horrified. "This is an artifact?" he demanded, staring at the paperweight. "You're breaking your own law!"

The king raised a cold eyebrow. "Drastic steps must be taken in face of drastic threats, Rian. I should have done this years ago, then the recent arrests would never have been necessary. I see now that my own fastidious adherence to the rule against magic has been foolish in light of how many of my subjects have flouted it. Everyone will be checked on arrival at the ball, and we can rest easy in the knowledge that no hidden attackers will be among us."

Rian found himself on his feet. "Thus revealing our hypocrisy to all the kingdom," he said, breathing hard.

His father stood as well, his eyes blazing. "How dare you say such a thing to me?" he shouted, all trace of openness gone from his face. "You will show some respect. Have you forgotten that at the last ball, one of your precious commoners attempted regicide?"

"I haven't forgotten, Father," said Rian, trying to master his emotion. Getting angry wouldn't help bring his father back to that reasonable frame of mind he knew the king was capable of. "And you know I have no sympathy with such violence. You know I'm ready to protect you with my life. But I cannot support this. If you're acknowledging that magic has uses you're willing to embrace, then surely you must see that the ban is not a viable solution!"

Something twitched in the king's face, and for a moment Rian thought his father would acknowledge the truth of his observation. But after a wrestle that looked genuinely painful, the king sat back down.

"I see no such thing." King Rhinehart's dismissive tone sounded forced to Rian. "I've yet to see magic used for good in a way that would outweigh its potential for destruction."

"What if you could see such a thing?" Rian pressed. "Perhaps you could visit Bentleigh in Listernia, see how they approach it there. You could discover what—"

"You're holding Listernia up as an example?" scoffed the king. "After what your mother and I experienced there?" His eyes grew hard. "We didn't just witness a magical attack, Rian, we were among its victims. And I don't want to hear any nonsense about the role magic played in breaking the curse. Counteracting a curse isn't magic that's likely to win me over. It wouldn't have been necessary if the curse had never been cast. If I'd ever seen magic that was genuinely used for good, for the kingdom, not for personal gain, perhaps I'd feel differently. But I haven't. And I never will."

"Because you've banished everyone who could show you that!" Rian protested.

But he knew there was no use. The veil was once again lowered, and his father's face was hard. "Enough, Rian. Do you think I relish the need to use an artifact? But it's the only way to ensure that we remove those who have an unnatural advantage over the rest of us. Then we will be secure, and there will be no more need for such measures."

Rian could find nothing further to say. It would clearly be fruitless to try to convince the king, and worse than fruitless to choose this moment to raise his hopes regarding Penny. With a stiff bow, he strode from the room.

He spent the rest of the morning pacing the castle, grunting at anyone who greeted him, and wrestling with his thoughts. It occurred to him belatedly that if his father hadn't thought of acquiring an artifact until Rian mentioned it, then he must have had some other source of information for all the arrests after all. But it was too late to go back and ask for an explanation of that.

What should he do? His father was justified in his anger— Rian could still feel the sting of the enchanter's knives in his arm. But the hypocrisy of it was still more than he could take.

Should he try to prevent his father from using the artifact, from exposing his own inconsistency to all his people? What would everyone think? What would *Penny* think?

The thought of her sent Rian striding to the stables before he'd even reasoned it through. She always seemed willing to speak her mind, and had the knack of doing it without disrespect. And she was no stranger to complex family relationships. Perhaps she could advise him on what to do.

It was only as he rode out of Bant that he realized what day it was. It was still hours until sunset, but would Penny and Lady Amaranthe already be in the field? It was clear they usually met some time before he joined them. There had been no discussion of him coming this week, but surely Penny wouldn't mind.

He decided it was worth checking the field first, in the hope Penny would be there, and he wouldn't have to run the risk of being required to visit with her family. When he reached the vineyard, he dismounted, handing his reins to one of the guards with him so they could make the usual pretense of waiting there.

He half ran through the copse of trees, his heart hammering with eagerness to see Penny. He didn't really know what he expected her to do, just that her presence was sure to be a balm to his troubled soul. The sound of laughter met his ears before he reached the edge of the trees, and his heart lifted. She was there.

"That was excellent!" Lady Amaranthe's voice declared brightly. "Can you do it again?"

Curious, Rian peered through the branches, and his heart seemed to stop. Penny was visible now, in her worn old work gown, with her golden hair pulled messily back from her eyes. Her face was screwed up in concentration, and her hands were held out before her in a strange gesture that made her look almost unearthly. Foreboding washed over Rian even before his gaze followed hers, and he saw what she was looking at.

Flowers, suspended impossibly in the air, were weaving themselves into a flower crown the way he'd seen small girls do. Except no one was touching them. He saw that Penny was wearing just such a crown, and as he watched, she swept one hand through the air, sending the newly finished construction soaring lightly toward Lady Amaranthe, so that it nestled onto her gleaming locks.

"Your Royal Highness, Princess Amaranthe," Penny said, curtsying with mock solemnity. "What about you, noble Prince Alchemist?" she asked, grinning at her dog, who was lying on his back nearby, limbs splayed in utter relaxation. "Do you want a crown, too?"

The sight of the animal brought Rian back to his senses. Al—was the dog's name really Alchemist?—would soon smell him even if the others couldn't see him. Stumbling backward, he turned in time to intercept one of his guards, who was moving surreptitiously into the copse.

"Time to go," said Rian curtly. He couldn't process what he'd seen yet. His only thought was to prevent anyone else from seeing it.

One glance at the prince's face seemed to be enough to convince the guard not to ask questions. Together, the two men made their way to the edge of the small grove, where the other guard waited with the horses. The three of them mounted up, and within moments were thundering down the road back toward Bant.

Rian's head was spinning, and he clutched at his reins like a lifeline. What had he just seen?

But he knew what he'd just seen. He'd seen Penny—*his Penny*, his heart added—practicing illegal magic. Calling her dog Alchemist, as if he'd needed further proof of her clandestine abilities. She'd been laughing, sending her power through the air like it was nothing, like she did it every day.

She probably did.

His heart squeezed painfully. He'd been so blind, so stupid. So many things made sense to him now. Her willingness to champion the cause of magic. Her fear of him when they first met, and her alarm at the idea that his unseen guards had been watching her in the field. What had she said at the ball, just before he kissed her?

Trust me when I say that your parents would never approve of me.

Well, she was certainly right about that. Despair welled up inside him at the realization of how impossible it truly was that his parents would ever consent to him marrying Penny.

Trust me, she'd said. But how could he ever trust her again? This secret was too big, too dangerous to be forgiven.

But how could she have told you? whispered the part of him that was still desperate for her nearness. *How could she be expected to admit to it, knowing what would happen if she did?*

And what *would* happen? The question swirled through his mind as he galloped for home. Was he going to turn her in, see her arrested? He didn't have to think about it for more than a moment to know the answer. He could never do it. Penny wasn't a child, who would be exiled to another kingdom. She would be punished. Locked in the dungeon, maybe even sent for hard labor. Rian pictured the shutter that seemed to close over the king's eyes every time magic came up. And the king was angrier than ever since the attack at the last ball—might he even consider execution? Rian's heart clenched at the very idea. He would never let that happen.

But he couldn't protect her by keeping her close, that much was certain. The more distance between her secrets and the royal family, the better. He could hardly believe that only hours ago, he'd been planning to tell his parents about her, ask them to meet her. How thankful he was now that his father's revelation had driven the idea from his mind.

His father's revelation! Rian yanked convulsively on the reins, causing his poor horse to falter in its stride. The artifact that could identify magic! It would expose Penny and bring the guards down on her in a trice. And last time they'd spoken, Rian had begged her to come to the ball! He remembered her reluctance to agree, and how he'd pressed until she gave him her yes. No wonder she was hesitant. What had he done? He'd lured her into a trap.

His thoughts turned to Lady Amaranthe, bitterness creeping in. She knew of Penny's magic, and she'd never told him. He'd never even heard her express doubts about the ban, but she'd been laughing as lightly as Penny while the younger woman worked her power. A thought fell through Rian's jumbled mind like a lightning strike. Was Lady Amaranthe an enchantress as well? Was that what had drawn the unlikely pair together? Just how many were hiding among them? And how could the crown be so blind?

A horrible thought occurred to him as he remembered the game they'd been playing in the field. Pretend crowns, false titles. Was that what all this was about? Was Lady Amaranthe coaching Penny on how to win him, how to sneak a magic-user onto the throne at his side? Was none of it real?

A sense of bitter betrayal welled up in Rian, and for the first time in a long time, he wondered if his father was right about the ban. But then he pictured Penny's face as she smiled shyly up at him, her mask removed and her heart in her eyes. Surely that wasn't fake. It wasn't as though she'd ever pushed him for a declaration. Quite the reverse.

Had she really done anything wrong? She'd let their hearts become entangled when she must know there was no hope for a future together, but that was precisely his own crime as well, so he could hardly blame her for that.

Yes, her magic broke the law. But Rian had been convinced before he even met her that the law was wrong, that enchanters and enchantresses had been poorly used. Penny had cause enough for bitterness, but she'd still been willing to give him a chance. His heart lurched as he remembered her reaction to his question about her mother's death. Had her mother had magic as well? Had she paid for it with her life in some way? She wouldn't be the first.

Penny was the most generous-hearted person he knew. By rights she should have hated him on sight, and instead she'd let him into her heart. He couldn't believe she was scheming against him. It wasn't in her nature.

His mind was made up before he reached the castle. He knew he couldn't have her at his side, but he was determined to shield her nonetheless. He would warn her, make sure she didn't walk into the trap being laid for her kind.

He hurried to his suite, pulling parchment toward him with hands that weren't quite steady. But once he'd dipped his quill in the inkwell, he stared at the blank page for so long, he had to dip it again before he commenced. Best to keep it simple, perhaps.

Penny

I came to talk to you today, and I saw you in the field.

He lifted his hand. He hardly knew how to put any of his thoughts or emotions into words. At last, he dipped the quill yet again, and continued.

*I understand a great many things now.
I'm not writing to reproach you, but to
warn you. My father has acquired an
artifact that can identify magic. If you
come to the next ball, you'll be exposed.
I know I begged you to come, but now
I'm begging you to stay away, where
you're safe.
As for everything else...*

His breath caught in his throat, and he rubbed a shaking hand across his eyes before adding more.

*I told you there wasn't much hope, but
some. I think we both know now that
there isn't any. But I still wanted you
to know that I love you. Even though
it changes nothing.
Ever yours, if only in heart,
R*

Rian could hardly bear to read back over the message, before he folded it swiftly, and poured hot wax from the stand on his desk. When he pressed his signet ring into it, the gesture felt so final that a lump rose to his throat. But he wouldn't think about that.

Much to his frustration, his mother accosted him as he left his suite, and it was hours before she released him from yet another painfully detailed discussion about the upcoming ball. An event which now made Rian feel nothing but dread. Wasting no more time, he hurried to the training yard in search of one of the guards he most trusted, who had accompanied him to the vintner's house more than once.

He finally ran the man to ground outside a small audience chamber, where he was evidently standing guard over the king. Rian didn't even know what matter was being discussed within, but it was clearly a public audience, given the members of court drifting into the room.

He pulled the guard slightly aside, slipping the sealed note into his hand. "I want you to deliver this to the vintner's daughter at your earliest opportunity," he muttered.

The guard, a middle-aged man, looked startled. "The vintner's daughter, Your Highness?"

Rian made a shushing gesture, and the guard dropped his voice, looking apologetic. "Certainly, Your Highness. I'll be released from duty in an hour, and I'll take it then."

Rian nodded reluctantly. An extra hour shouldn't make any great difference, he supposed. "Thank you. You know what she looks like—give it into her hands, and no one else's, understand?"

The guard nodded curtly, then slid the parchment into an inner pocket before stepping back to his station. Rian turned, and froze at the sight of Lady Amaranthe, paused in the act of entering the audience chamber.

"Your Highness," she said pleasantly, dipping into a curtsy. "Well met."

Rian stared at her for a prolonged moment, various emotions wrestling within him. It was more than he was capable of to speak with the noblewoman as if everything was normal. But, aware of some curious witnesses, he inclined his head in a passably courteous acknowledgment, before turning on his heel and striding away.

His guard pulled him aside as he left the dining hall after dinner.

"Well?" Rian demanded, and the guard nodded reassuringly.

"Put it into her hand myself, Your Highness," he said. "And I didn't have to alert the rest of the household to do it. I was fortunate to find her walking up the road. Looked like she'd been picking mushrooms nearby."

"Thank you," said Rian. "You've done well." He turned away, his carefully blank face displaying none of what he felt inside.

It was over.

CHAPTER TWENTY-THREE

Penny

Penny kneaded the dough absently, her gaze fixed unseeingly on the tiny specks of flour that drifted through the air, illuminated by the slanting evening light. And she wasn't even dwelling on her session with Lady Amaranthe in the field the day before. It was bizarre to think that such a short time ago, the opportunity to practice her magic had been the most exciting, the most significant feature of her world.

Now, all she could think about was Rian. He'd been on her mind far too often for weeks, but since they'd kissed at the ball, he seemed to occupy every waking moment. She could hardly believe her boldness in stealing that kiss from him in her barn. Not that he'd seemed to mind.

And he'd begged her to come to the next ball, where his bride was to be announced. She knew it was playing with fire, as Harry would say. And not just because of her hidden magic. Even Rian acknowledged there was little chance of him convincing his parents to accept her as his choice, so attending the ball was most likely to end in devastating heartbreak for both of them. She wondered if Rian really understood what he was asking, when he pressed her to come. In all probability, he was asking her to watch him become betrothed to someone else while she melted into the crowd.

But he'd begged, and she'd promised, so there was nothing more to it. She had to get to that ball. And maybe, just maybe, Rian would find a way to talk his parents around. Would he contact her before the ball if that happened? Would she have warning of what was to come?

She frowned to herself. She wasn't at all sure what to make of him saying he didn't regret his promise to let his parents choose his bride. Did he just mean it was worth it for his brother's sake? Or did he mean the kingdom had to come first, above her, above his own heart. Both answers were reasonable, she had to admit. But she also couldn't deny they both stung a little.

"Pen!"

The cry, and the crash as the door banged open, caused Al to leap up in alarm.

"Harry!" Penny scolded, lowering her hand from her throat. "You scared us half to death!"

"Pen, we're in trouble!" Harry gasped, entering the room with less than his usual self-possession. "It's time to be gone. You mustn't go to that next ball."

"What do you mean?" Penny asked, dropping the dough onto the table with a thunk. "Of course I'm going."

Harry shook his head frantically. "I've just been chatting with one of the vineyard workers, and he told me the rumor circulating around Bant."

"I don't want to hear about more arrests, Harry," said Penny wearily.

But he was still shaking his head. "It's not arrests, or at least, not yet. Word is the king has gotten hold of an artifact that can identify magic! He's going to use it to check all the guests coming to the ball, make sure no enchanters can get in and repeat what happened last time!"

Penny's heart lurched, her mouth falling open. "But that can't be true! The king hates magic more than anyone! He wouldn't use an artifact! How could he get away with such hypocrisy?"

Harry snorted. "He's the king. He can get away with whatever he wants. I'm telling you, Pen, you can't go. It's not safe."

Penny chewed her lip. "But we don't know if it's true," she said. "How often are rumors really accurate?"

"Pen!" Harry gasped. "You can't gamble your safety on that!"

Penny winced. "But I promised I'd go, Harry."

"Things have changed," said Harry grimly. "You've got to understand that."

"I need to talk to Lady Amaranthe," said Penny. "I wonder if she knows."

"Aye, we'd best warn her, too," said Harry. He frowned at Penny. "But you're not going anywhere near the castle. I'll go find her tomorrow, and tell her the rumor, if she hasn't heard it already." When Penny didn't say anything, he let out a growl. "At least promise me you'll sleep on it."

Penny nodded slowly, an idea forming in her mind. It had been several days since her last communication with Dannsair. Would tonight bring a vision of the dragon? "I'll certainly sleep on it," she promised.

But when she lay down on her bed, several hours later, sleep proved elusive. Her desperation to reach the dream state made it near impossible to silence her mind enough for repose. She had no way to tell the time, but it seemed like hours before she at last felt herself beginning to drift.

"Penny. I am pleased to see you."

Penny's eyes flew open, and she gasped with delight at the over-whelming colors surrounding her.

"Not as glad as I am to see you!" she assured the purple dragon. "I was hoping you'd come tonight. There's something I need to ask you about."

"Very well," said Dannsair, looking taken aback. "Ask."

"There's a rumor," Penny said, the words tumbling over each other in her haste. She never knew how long the vision would last, it was so variable. "They're saying that the king has acquired an artifact that can identify magic, so he'll be able to tell if any enchanters or enchantresses try to come to the next ball."

The dragon let out a breath that smelled faintly of smoke. "Precisely the type of outrageous hypocrisy I would expect from a human," she said darkly. "The rest of the colony will not be pleased to hear of this."

"Hang on," said Penny, alarmed. "Please don't report this to the other dragons. I'm not trying to bring down trouble on Bansford. I don't even know if the rumor is true. I was wondering if you could tell me whether such artifacts even exist, and whether one's entered Bansford lately."

The dragon shook her vast head slowly. "An artifact with that power is certainly possible. But I couldn't tell you whether one has entered Bansford lately. There are thousands of artifacts in Solstice. We do not track them."

"But you said my magic calls to you from across the distance," Penny said desperately. "Like a spring in the desert. Could the artifact call to you if you looked for it?"

Irritatingly, Dannsair looked amused. "I said your *magic calls to me, Penny. Because it is incredibly strong, and it is a constant burning within you. An artifact, even a powerful one, has nowhere near the potency of a living enchantress."*

Penny deflated. "So Harry's right," she whispered. "I can't go to the ball like I promised. It's too dangerous."

"You promised?" Dannsair asked sharply. "Promises are a serious matter, Penny. Especially from those with magic. They can have power bound up in them that you do not even realize is there. They ought not to be broken."

"I know," said Penny, lifting her arms helplessly. "But if I'll be exposed as an enchantress on arrival, I won't even make it into the ball. What can I do?"

The dragon regarded her shrewdly. "To whom did you make this promise?"

Penny felt her face burn as she looked down at the dragon's clawed front feet. She hadn't told Dannsair anything about Rian. "To Prince Rian," she whispered. "He...he asked me to come."

"The prince?" Dannsair said, her voice alight with interest. "The heir to Bansford's throne personally desires you, an enchantress, to come to his ball?"

"He doesn't know I'm an enchantress," Penny muttered.

The dragon disregarded this detail. Throwing her reptilian head back, she began to make an unfamiliar gurgling sound. For a moment, Penny was terrified, until she recognized it as laughter.

"This is delightful," Dannsair said, when the alarming noise at last subsided. "I see I was right when I predicted that you would play a role in the future of magic in your kingdom. Although I will acknowledge that I never expected it to be quite such a significant role."

Penny shook her head miserably. "Trust me, I've achieved nothing," she said.

"I doubt that," responded the dragon, smiling. "If the prince himself is pursuing you, I daresay you've achieved more than you realize." She let out a musing breath, and Penny noted with relief that the smell of smoke was gone. "But let's return to the question of how to help you keep your promise. It would be a simple matter if we could connect face to face."

"Would it?" Penny demanded. "How?"

"I could use my magic on you," said the dragon simply. She bent her long neck so that her face was level with Penny's. "I could come to you. If you were willing to take the risk."

"Come here?" Penny stared. "To Bansford? But no dragon has done that in nineteen years!"

"Haven't they?" Dannsair asked, the tiniest edge of darkness to her voice. She regarded Penny for a moment, and then her reptilian lips curved upward into a smile. "Am I not in Bansford now, in a manner of speaking? Through our communication, I have entered your kingdom. I am willing to do so corporeally as well."

"You'd do that for me?" Penny asked, awed.

The dragon did her strange rippling shrug. "It is not just for you, Penny. I believe bigger purposes might be achieved. But I do wish to help you, yes. And the risk would not be so great, I think. Perhaps you do not know that dragons can fly so quickly as to be almost invisible to human eyes?"

"I didn't know," said Penny, awed.

Dannsair nodded. "If I fly by night..." she mused, then gave another decisive nod. "Yes. Meet me in that field you talk about, two hours after midnight tomorrow night. That is the night before your ball, yes?"

Penny nodded. "How will you find the field?"

Dannsair smiled. "I will follow my desert spring, of course. Now, what shall I pour my magic into? Something you can carry with you to the castle, without it being conspicuous."

"A purse?" Penny suggested.

The dragon frowned. "Too easy to drop it, or lose it. It should be something that will definitely stay with you."

"Perhaps an item of clothing would be best," said Penny. "A dress, if I knew which one I was going to wear. I know!" she said suddenly. "My dancing slippers! I only have one decent pair, so I'll have to wear them. Lady Amaranthe will presumably enchant them to look *different again, but she said that doesn't change the substance, so it shouldn't matter, should it?"*

"I'd love to learn more of this magic of hers," commented Dannsair, sounding fascinated. "It seems not dissimilar from the concealment magic that we dragons favor. And no, I don't think it will matter. If anything, it might enhance my magic."

The dragon nodded. "It is decided, then. We will meet in the field. Bring your slippers."

Penny spent all the next day in a daze. She refused to tell Harry what was happening, only that she had a plan that might remove the danger. He was far from satisfied, but he took a break from his dire warnings to travel into Bant, in an attempt to find and warn Lady Amaranthe of the looming danger. He returned unsuccessful, having been unable to locate her.

Penny couldn't help but be nervous, worried that Lady Amaranthe would run into trouble before she could be warned. But if all went to plan, the noblewoman would come to collect Penny again as they'd discussed, and Penny could tell her then.

Having successfully avoided her stepfamily for most of the day—a fact they probably attributed to her jealousy, as they spent most of their time discussing the upcoming ball—Penny retired early. But she didn't dare sleep, afraid she'd miss the deadline. When it was an hour past midnight, she rose from her bed, slipped her dancing shoes into a pocket of her warmest cloak, and let herself silently out of the house.

She reached the field without incident, the only moment of alarm being when Al bounded over to meet her as she hurried past the barn. For once, the dog paid heed to her shushing gestures, and trotted silently along beside her. When they'd passed safely through the copse, Penny let out a sigh of relief and gazed upward at the star-strewn sky.

It felt like an eternity of waiting, but although she had no way of knowing the hour, she didn't doubt the dragon arrived right on schedule.

Not all her nighttime visions could prepare Penny for the sight of the enormous dark shape descending from the sky, blotting out the stars with its outstretched wings. And the sight was only part of the effect. The magic she'd learned to recognize in Lady Amaranthe was nothing to the power that rolled off Dannsair in suffocating waves. It made Penny's senses swim. This creature carried a raw magic that Penny had never before encountered.

All said, Dannsair was more imposing in real life than in dreams, and Penny could only imagine that daylight would make her even more so. As it was, she had to swallow several times before she could find her voice.

"You came," she said, with relief.

"Greetings, Penny," said Dannsair placidly. She lowered her head almost to ground level to sniff Al, who was quivering with fright. "What an interesting creature."

"He's my dog," said Penny distractedly. "Alchemist. Do you think anyone saw you?"

"I don't believe so," said the dragon, raising her head again. Her musical voice reverberated inside Penny's chest in a way no dream could capture. "But I will not linger. Neither your kind nor mine would be pleased by my presence here. Did you bring the slippers?"

Penny pulled them hastily from her pocket and held them out. "What will you do with them?" she breathed. "Are you going to turn them into an artifact?"

"I suppose that is what you would call it," said the dragon, examining the slippers in the dim moonlight. "Do you remember I mentioned that dragons are particularly adept at concealment magic?"

Penny nodded.

"We can easily hide things from humans should we wish to do so, including our home, as you probably know. I have begun to suspect," she added, that darkness once again creeping into her voice, "that we can hide things from other dragons more easily than I once supposed." She shook her bearded temples slightly. "But never mind that. I intend to craft a concealment magic on your shoes that will prevent their wearer from being identified by the type of magic you have mentioned. In simple terms, while you are wearing them, no artifact will be able to recognize your magic. Even another enchanter or enchantress should not be able to do so. It will be hidden, so that you appear to be just another human."

"That's perfect," Penny breathed. She frowned as a sudden thought occurred. "I should have brought another pair so that you could have done the same for Lady Amaranthe."

"I would not have done so," Dannsair said, a touch of sternness in her voice. "Dragon magic is powerful, and we do not give it lightly. Truth be told, I ought not to be helping a human to avoid a human-made enchantment. I would not do it for someone I do not know, and I hope you will not divulge that I have done it for you."

"I won't," Penny promised, chastened.

She'd forgotten what Lady Amaranthe had told her about the agreement that dictated dragon-human relations. She wondered why Dannsair was willing to breach the rule for her. But she didn't dare to ask, afraid the dragon would change her mind. At least—going by what Lady Amaranthe had said—as a commoner, Penny couldn't be held to represent the crown, and therefore Bansford wouldn't be held to account if the other dragons found out.

Without another word, Dannsair opened wide her jaws. Involuntarily, Penny flinched, but no flames issued forth.

Instead the shoes were engulfed by a warm gush of air that tingled with a power which made the magic in Penny's blood hum in response.

"That should do it, I think," said Dannsair. "Be warned, the magic is designed specifically to conceal yours. So don't lose the shoes. If they are separated from you, not only will they cease to hide your magic, but they will be recognizable as an artifact."

Penny nodded, only half listening. She wasn't likely to lose a shoe she was actually wearing. Turning the familiar slippers over in her hand, she marveled at the power that now emanated out from them.

"Until next we meet, Penny," Dannsair said. "I will check in with you again after the ball." And with that, she snapped out her wings and shot into the air, creating a gust of wind so powerful that Penny was knocked from her feet.

"Goodness," she said to Al, who cowered at her side. "They're abrupt creatures, aren't they?"

CHAPTER TWENTY-FOUR

Penny

When Sapphira and the girls finally left for the second ball, Penny felt nothing but relief. Her struggle to conceal the various fears and excitements coursing through her had made it impossible to act naturally, and she knew they were all wondering what had gotten into her. Sapphira, especially, gave Penny a long and suspicious look before climbing into the hired carriage.

Once they were out of sight, Penny re-entered the house, leaning back against the closed door. She knew tonight would bring many consequences, one of them being that her stepfamily would discover her presence at the ball. No one was to be masked this time, and it was too much to hope they wouldn't notice when Rian approached her, as he surely would.

She wasn't sure they'd accept the explanation she planned to give. But she found she didn't much care. All her plans, all her hopes, had been centered on tonight's ball, and the announcement to be made. She couldn't think beyond it. She'd have to wait until afterward to sift through whatever wreckage of her life remained.

Trudging to the kitchen, Penny set about making hot tea for herself and Harry. The old servant joined her by the fire, saying nothing, but watching her face tensely. Penny just shrugged at him. She was pinning all her hopes on Lady Amaranthe coming. Since she hadn't heard anything to the contrary, she had to assume the noblewoman intended to honor their arranged meeting.

And sure enough, not long after Sapphira and the girls had left, Penny heard carriage wheels on the drive. She flew to the door and flung it open, watching with eager eyes as Lady Amaranthe descended. It was apparent before the newcomer said a word that she'd heard the rumor of the king's artifact. Lady Amaranthe was dressed with her usual elegance, but even Penny's inexperienced eyes could see that her raiment wasn't suitable for a ball.

"Once we're inside," said Lady Amaranthe, as Penny opened her mouth.

Penny ushered her into the homey kitchen, and Harry leaped out of the chair closest to the fire. With an appreciative nod, Lady Amaranthe sank into it.

"You're not going to the ball," said Penny quietly.

Lady Amaranthe's eyes flew to hers. "Don't tell me you haven't heard?" she demanded. "The rumor is all over Bant, I thought for sure you would know. The king has acquired an artifact that—"

"Yes, we've heard," said Penny quickly. "Harry even went to the capital to warn you, but it seems you had no need of him."

"That was kind," said Lady Amaranthe, looking at Harry with surprise. Her eyes passed back to Penny. "It's outrageous, isn't it? The greatest hypocrisy. I only hope my absence won't be considered suspicious." She sighed. "I thought we may as well sit together, child. Plus, I wanted to be sure you knew, and this was the only time I could be certain your family wouldn't overhear."

"I'm glad you came," said Penny, nerves rushing over her. "Because I need your help if I'm going to make it to that ball."

Lady Amaranthe stared at her. "Penny, you can't possibly be considering going!"

"That's what I said," Harry interjected gruffly.

Penny looked between them, steeling herself. "I am considering it. Thanks to these." She pulled the slippers out of her pocket. She'd kept them on her all day, just to be sure they were safe.

Both Harry and Lady Amaranthe looked utterly bewildered.

"Your slippers?" the noblewoman asked skeptically.

Penny nodded. "I can't tell you how, because I promised not to expose the one who helped me. But they've been turned into an artifact—an extremely powerful artifact. They carry an enchantment of concealment that will prevent my magic from being identified."

Harry spluttered, as a deep crease appeared on Lady Amaranthe's brow.

"Penny," she said slowly. "How can you be sure?"

"I'm absolutely certain," said Penny confidently. "It was *powerful* magic. I wish you could have felt it." She held out the slippers, and Lady Amaranthe took them.

"I can feel the magic," the noblewoman commented, sounding surprised. "I don't recognize it, but it feels strong."

"It is," said Penny confidently. "Try, and you'll see." She took the slippers back. Kicking off her work shoes, she slid her feet into them and looked up at the other enchantress. "Well?"

Lady Amaranthe's eyes were wide. "I can't feel your magic." She screwed her eyes shut, a look of concentration on her face. After a prolonged moment, she opened them again, staring at

Penny in amazement. "No, nothing. It's like your power is just...gone."

"It's not, though," Penny assured her. With a flick of her finger, she caused Harry's tea cup to rise into the air and perform a pirouette, causing the old servant to protest as it splashed its contents onto the floor. "It's just hidden."

"Extraordinary," breathed the noblewoman. "Powerful magic indeed." She studied Penny's face. "I'm amazed you found someone who's powerful enough to create something like this, but still willing to help you."

Penny nodded. "She wanted to help me keep my promise to Rian, that I'd attend the ball. But she said she thought a bigger purpose might be served as well."

"She was right," said Lady Amaranthe, standing abruptly. There was an eager light in her eyes that reminded Penny of the first time Lady Amaranthe had seen her properly use her magic. "And if you made a promise, we must get you to that ball."

Harry began to protest afresh, but the noblewoman pushed briskly on over the top of him.

"Lilac this time, I think, Penny." A wave of her hand, a muttered incantation, and Penny's worn old gown disappeared. In its place was wave upon wave of soft purple tulle. Penny's eyes shone as she twirled, watching the firelight play on the delicate fabric.

"Let me do my hair this time," she said quickly. "I've been practicing." With a minute of focused effort, she pulled her curls back into a style similar to what she'd worn at the first ball, albeit not quite as neat.

"Very nice," said Lady Amaranthe approvingly. "Now," her eyes gleamed again, "the slippers."

Penny held out her slippered feet. A moment later, she was looking at them through clear, glinting glass.

"Stunning," she whispered.

"Come, come," said Lady Amaranthe, clapping her hands. "No time to lose."

With a distracted word of reassurance to Harry, Penny followed her mentor to the carriage. She waited until they were trundling down the road toward Bant before turning to Lady Amaranthe.

"Did you know that Prince Rian's bride is to be announced at tonight's ball?"

Lady Amaranthe's eyes were shrewd. "I've heard that rumor, yes."

Penny nodded slowly. "He said that he suggested to his parents that they should consider choosing a commoner." She stole a glance at her companion's face. "Apparently they didn't take to the idea. But," she added, her eyes turning to the window, picturing the glow of the castle beyond, "that was days ago, and he did make me promise to come. I wonder if..."

"What would you do with your magic if he chose you?" Lady Amaranthe asked frankly.

Penny twisted her hands uncomfortably in the invisible fabric of her simple, rough skirt. "I don't know. I'm not sure I could hide it forever."

"Is that what you would want?" Lady Amaranthe's voice was sharp.

Penny shook her head. "Of course not. I'm only just learning to use it. I don't want to go back to pretending it doesn't exist."

The older woman relaxed, and Penny glanced up at her.

"What do you think I should do? Tell him the whole truth?"

Lady Amaranthe hesitated. "I think if you told him the truth, he'd never be able to marry you. But if you told him afterward...well, it would be too late for his parents to deny their consent, wouldn't it? I don't think they'd arrest their son's wife."

Penny frowned. "That seems so dishonest."

Lady Amaranthe shrugged. "I suppose so. But I can't see any other way for you to be with the prince. And if you love him..."

Penny's face burned, and she said no more for several minutes.

"What will you do at the ball?" she asked quickly. "The shoes won't cover you."

"I won't be coming into the ballroom," said Lady Amaranthe. "But I'll need to be close enough for the enchantments on your clothes to continue to hold."

"That sounds dangerous for you," said Penny anxiously.

"Nonsense." Lady Amaranthe was dismissive. "I'm in the castle constantly. It won't be a problem as long as I keep away from the ballroom." She frowned down at the floor of the carriage. "I think I need to reconstruct my enchantment on your slippers, Penny. They must have resumed their original shape, because I can't feel any magic going out to them."

But when Penny held out one foot, a delicate glass shoe winked at her in the moonlight.

"Incredible," breathed Lady Amaranthe, leaning down to examine it. "It seems that the magic of your mysterious benefactress has melded with mine, strengthening my enchantment and making it permanent. The change has happened, and I no longer need to maintain it."

Penny stared. "You're right," she said slowly, testing her feet. "It actually feels like glass now." She grimaced. "I'm probably going to break an ankle."

But when they arrived at the castle, Penny managed to alight from the carriage and ascend the steps without falling. She was alone—Lady Amaranthe had stayed in the carriage until she could enter the castle less conspicuously. Penny's heart was racing at triple its usual speed, her hands shaking with the effort of keeping her magic inside. She wasn't as late as the time before, and other guests were still arriving. The guards stationed on either side of the castle's doors looked everyone over carefully, but no one challenged her, and she could neither see nor feel any sign of an artifact.

When she reached the entrance to the great ballroom, however, she could feel a slight tug of power reaching out through the doors. Swallowing, she joined the short line of people awaiting entry. Once she reached the door, she was rattled to see the king and queen themselves standing just inside the room, greeting the guests as they arrived. Surely they hadn't done that last time.

Following the trail of the power with her mind, Penny realized it was emanating from King Rhinehart. He must have the artifact on his person. Hardly daring to breathe, she stepped over the threshold into the light-filled, buzzing ballroom. At once, she felt power rush over her, from her feet to her head. She held her breath, knowing her very life might depend on Dannsair's work, then felt the power pass on, reaching for the next guest.

Letting out a long, shaky breath of air, she curtsied to the king and queen as best she could, avoiding meeting their eyes. She felt crushed by the weight of her own absurdity in indulging a moment's hope that these austere, untouchable royals would ever countenance her marriage to their son and heir.

"Penelope of Vin Manor," she told the herald, her voice so quiet she had to repeat herself to be heard. He shouted her name to the room, and with a sinking heart, Penny saw a familiar head of mousy hair whip toward her.

Refusing to lock eyes with her stepfamily, she searched the room for the one she'd really come to see.

There. The dancing hadn't yet begun, so Rian was standing to one side of the room. He had a drink in his hand, and he was speaking with an imposing looking man who wore a richly embroidered tunic, and had a thin blade strapped to his side.

At the announcement of her name, however, Rian's head snapped up, and his eyes latched on to hers across the space between them. For the briefest of moments, Penny saw light spring into them as he took her in. But almost immediately, the expression was replaced by a look of absolute horror.

Faltering, Penny almost tripped in her impractical glass shoes, and a nearby gentleman steadied her chivalrously.

"Are you all right, Miss?" he asked, and she tried to smile.

"Yes, thank you." But was she? Rian was still staring at her like she was the last person in the world he wanted to see, and all her careful planning and impossible hoping was crashing down around her.

"Where did you get that dress?"

The hiss in her ear made Penny turn. Olivia's eyes were full of malice, but it was Sapphira's looming figure that made Penny's insides turn to ice.

"I...I borrowed it," she said, her voice trembling. "From a—"

"Lies," fumed Olivia. "You used magic somehow, I know you did. I've been suspecting it for ages. There's no way you could—"

"Silence, Olivia." Sapphira's voice cut across her daughter's words like a shard of ice. "Do you want to be arrested by extension?" Her gaze passed to Penny. "What have you done? Accessed an artifact? Paid for an enchantment? What?"

Before Penny could respond, an altogether different voice interrupted the family argument. A voice that was serious, but with a light edge that belied the grave mouth from which it issued.

"May I have this dance?"

Penny hadn't even noticed the musicians striking up, but she saw that all eyes were on the prince, waiting for him to open the dancing. She looked up into his face, searching for some sign of the warmth she'd come to expect, but something was definitely off. Still, she placed her hand in his and allowed him to lead her onto the floor.

As soon as they were swirling, as alone as they could be in the vast ballroom, Rian spoke, his voice tense and urgent.

"You came."

Penny smiled hesitantly. "I promised I would, didn't I?"

Rian let out a soft groan. "But I released you from that promise. I begged you not to come."

Penny stared at him. "What are you—?"

But Rian cut her off. "You shouldn't be here, Penny!" Seeming to have worked himself into an almost frantic state, he led her through the dance with such urgency she kept stumbling over her foolishly clad feet.

"You need to leave," he muttered. "I can't think what possessed you to—" He paused, frowning. "Come to think of it, how *are* you here?"

But Penny was beginning to lose her temper. "If you knew what it's taken for me to be here, Rian," she started. Swallowing, she tried to keep control of herself. "I came because you said there was some hope, even if only a tiny bit. But I take it your efforts haven't been successful."

"My efforts?" Rian stared at her. "Do you think I've still been trying to—I told you, Penny, there's no hope! I wish there were, but—"

"You've said enough," said Penny, her voice choked with tears she refused to release. She tried to pull away, but his grip was like iron.

"Be careful, Penny," he said urgently. "Leave unobtrusively. The last thing I want you to do is make a scene."

The movement of the dance had brought them to the edge of the open space, near a crowd of onlookers. Before Penny could retort, Olivia's voice rang out with disastrous volume.

"I hope she managed to scrub all the cinder soot from her

hands before coming here. It's a little far, inviting a servant to a royal ball."

"She's a servant?" Even from amidst the dancers, Penny could hear the mutters.

"The prince opened the dancing with a servant?"

"The girl dancing with Prince Rian is a common servant!"

Penny was too caught up in her devastation over Rian's words to even care about the gossip now spreading through the ballroom like unchecked flames. But to her further mortification, she felt Rian's whole frame stiffen, and saw his eyes flick toward his parents as he let out a groan.

"This is exactly the kind of attention I was hoping to avoid," he ground out between clenched teeth. "I was supposed to open the dancing with the daughter of a viscount. My parents will be furious. There goes any hope of them not noticing that you're here. Penny, you should never have come!"

"That much is painfully clear," said Penny, pulling away from him again. This time he released her, his hands falling limply to his sides. She could hear muttering in the crowd, even some jeers. Every eye in the room seemed to be on her, and not one of them was kind.

"I wish I'd never come," she choked. "I wish I'd never set eyes on you."

A look of anguish passed over Rian's face, before he schooled his features into the serious mask Penny had once thought his true self. Perhaps she'd been more right than she knew.

"Let me spare you further humiliation," she gasped, barely holding herself together. Turning her back on him, she lifted her skirts and fled.

Even still, she half expected Rian to call out, to reach for her. But he didn't. No one tried to stop her. The crowd parted before her, some looking angry at the audacity of the so-called servant, and some openly laughing at her disgrace. Penny ran awkwardly, hampered by the foolish shoes, thinking of nothing but reaching the door, escaping from this nightmare. How had the ball she'd so longed to attend, taken such risks to reach, become such a hideous disaster?

The king and queen scowled at her as she passed, but she didn't dare give them more than a glance. She'd just made it through the double doors and to the top of the shallow staircase when she lost her footing, and one of her shoes fell off with a clink.

She'd already stumbled down several more stairs, and she made no attempt to go back for it. Dimly, she remembered Dannsair warning her not to lose her shoes, but what did it matter now? She was running away from the ballroom, not toward it, so the king would have no opportunity to use his artifact on her. Pulling off the other slipper, she clutched it to her chest and ran, barefoot, across the courtyard and out to the cobbled streets beyond.

Almost an hour later, she threw herself through the kitchen door of her own manor. She'd obviously passed the range of Lady Amaranthe's magic long ago, because her dress was worn and tattered. But her solitary slipper was still made of glass.

"Pen!"

Harry was there as she collapsed to the floor, sobbing brokenly.

"What happened? Didn't it work? Are they coming after you? Talk to me, Pen!"

She shook her head, hiccuping too violently for proper speech. "No one's...coming...after...he...didn't...want me...not enough to...to fight for...he was ashamed of..." She drew a shuddering breath, trying to master herself. "I'm ready, Harry," she sobbed. "There's nothing to stay for. Take me somewhere else, anywhere else!"

"At last," said Harry grimly. "We'll leave at once. I've been ready for weeks, Pen, you don't need to grab a thing." He glared at the glass slipper still clutched in her hand. "But put some proper shoes on, will you?"

As Penny stumbled obediently from the room, she heard Harry give a sharp whistle. "Come on, Al, look lively. You can sleep when we're safe across the border to Listernia."

CHAPTER TWENTY-FIVE

Rian

Rian stood rooted to the spot, his world crashing down around him as Penny's words repeated over and over in his mind.

I wish I'd never set eyes on you.

Everything in Rian longed to chase after her, to tell her she didn't mean that, to tell her he didn't care if she had magic.

But he forced himself to stay in place, and not just because he was desperate to avoid drawing more attention to her suspicious behavior. He couldn't blame her for feeling that way. He knew that if he had any sense, he'd even share the sentiment. But he couldn't bring himself to wish they'd never met. Couldn't bring himself to regret losing his heart to her, being challenged by her bravery and kindness...feeling her lips on his.

Why had she come? Why had she put herself in danger, and put them both through the agony of that encounter? A horrible thought stirred in the fog of his awareness. Was it possible she hadn't gotten his letter? But no. He trusted that guard completely, and the man had told him he'd put it into her hand.

With an effort, Rian pulled his mind back to the chaos of the room before him. Because chaos it was. The musicians had stopped, and the muttering had grown to a frenzy since Penny's departure. Rian realized he wasn't helping matters by standing frozen in the middle of the ballroom, staring at the door through which Penny had disappeared forever.

Gathering what dignity he had left to him, he walked to the edge of the space, aiming for the table where he'd placed his goblet when he caught sight of Penny. Whispers followed him.

"Who was she?"

"A dalliance with a servant?"

"Is *that* why the commoners were invited?"

"Did you see the way he almost ran to her when she arrived?"

Rian's ears burned, but he kept his expression impassive. It wasn't hard. He'd had twenty-three years to practice. He was good at burying his reactions. Now he just needed to learn to bury his heart as well. He wondered idly who his parents were going to choose to be his wife. He didn't even seem to care.

"Rian." His mother's voice was calm on the surface, but Rian knew at once that he was in trouble. "You're needed on an urgent matter."

In a state of numbness, Rian followed her from the room, hardly aware of where he was going. When they came to a stop, he found himself in a small antechamber with both his parents, the door watched by their cumulative personal guards.

"Who was that?" His father made the words three separate sentences, each laden with a world of meaning.

"It doesn't matter," said Rian tonelessly. "She's left now."

"You opened the dancing with a servant?" his mother hissed. "A servant, Rian!"

He shook his head wearily. "She's not a servant. But she's a commoner. I met her in the markets once. She's why I wanted you to expand the list."

"You know you can't marry that common girl, don't you,

Rian?" The words were unyielding, but his father's voice was unexpectedly calm, almost gentle.

"Yes, Father," Rian said dully, too drained to truly feel anything. "I know that."

"If you know that," his mother asked crisply, "then why did you make a scene and humiliate the lady you'd already asked to dance? Why did you make yourself the gossip of every wagging tongue in the city? Everyone could see how smitten you were with that serving girl."

"She's not a—" Rian started, but his mother cut him off.

"What does it matter?" She raised her hands helplessly. "We can't announce a betrothal now. Any eligible girl would be insulted to be named your bride after you've just made a display of yourself with some common—"

"Insulted?" Rian's laugh was bitter and harsh. "To be named future queen? I don't think you can have met the lovely ladies vying for my hand."

"Don't speak to your mother that way," said the king sternly. "You've made things difficult for everyone, and set our plans back."

"I'm just thankful we hadn't officially declared our intention of announcing a betrothal tonight," said the queen tartly. "We'll have to announce it at the last ball, after all."

"As you like," shrugged Rian.

His mother glowered suspiciously at him, but he showed no spark of defiance. He didn't have any left. After another bitter reproach, he was released back into the ballroom, to pass the most unrelentingly miserable evening of his life. It all felt like a nightmare from which he couldn't wake. Perhaps the worst thing of all was the realization that his father hadn't been nearly as angry as his mother. The queen was annoyed that Rian's actions had set back her plans for the much-anticipated event of his betrothal. But the king hadn't shown the fury Rian had expected him to show on learning that Rian had allowed a commoner to catch his eye. Perhaps Rian's efforts to soften his father's mind had achieved more than he'd realized. It was agonizing to think that if, as Rian had at first supposed, the only obstacle had been Penny's common status, there might have been hope of success.

But her status wasn't the only obstacle. There was an infinitely larger one, and Rian knew there was no hope. Picturing the swift change that always came over his father's face at the mention of magic, he could only shudder at the thought of what the king would say if he knew Penny was an enchantress in hiding. Rian had no illusions that he'd succeeded in changing his father's mind in this area.

When at last the guests began to depart, he felt like a wrung out rag, longing for nothing but the oblivion of sleep.

He was making his way out of the ballroom, when a cry from a footman caught his attention.

"My Lady! You dropped this!"

A voice Rian didn't recognize answered, tinged with laughter. "That's not mine. I have both of my shoes, see? Who wears slippers of glass?"

Slippers of glass? Rian turned his head sharply, hurrying to the top of the shallow staircase that led out of the castle. A bewildered footman was holding up a glinting object, turning it to catch the light of the lanterns.

"Can I see that?" Rian demanded, reaching for it. The footman handed it over willingly enough. "Where did you find this?"

"It was on the steps, Your Highness," the footman said. "I saw it when I was coming back from the carriages. A guest must have dropped it when leaving, but it beats me how you can fail to notice losing a shoe."

Rian stared down at the slipper in his hand. He had no difficulty recognizing the unusual item, and he knew exactly what state its owner had been in to leave her shoe and flee.

"What's that?" His father's sharp voice made him turn. The king was staring at the slipper, his brow creased in anger. "Whose is it?"

"No idea, Your Majesty," said the footman. "One of the guests dropped it when leaving."

"It has magic," the king snapped.

"What?" Rian demanded, eyes widening.

The king patted a pocket, where Rian assumed the paperweight must be hidden. "It drew me out here."

Rian stared at the slipper, relieved beyond words that he hadn't blurted out its origin. Why had Penny been wearing enchanted shoes? What had been their purpose? "But how did it get past your check when the guest entered?" he asked blankly.

"An excellent question," said the king, his voice grim. "Give it to me."

Reluctantly, Rian handed it over, feeling foolishly like he was losing the last piece of Penny he had. It was only after his father had disappeared back into the castle, and the footman had moved on, that a quiet voice drew his attention to the shadow of a pillar at the bottom of the stairs.

"I think we both recognize that slipper, Your Highness."

Rian stared at Lady Amaranthe, too weary to feel anything at her sudden appearance.

"I heard the rumors, of a servant girl who had a dalliance with the prince, and humiliated herself by turning up to the ball as if she was a real contender for his hand."

Rian winced.

"She ran away, didn't she?" the noblewoman said. "She ran, and you didn't even try to stop her." She turned away, so her face was hidden in shadow. "I don't think even a heart as warm as Penny's could forgive that."

Her words cut through Rian like a knife. She was right, but he made no reply. He already knew, without her telling him, that he'd lost Penny forever.

Rian was surprised, upon waking, to discover that he'd slept after all. It had seemed an impossible feat. His thoughts flew instantly to Penny. Where was she now? What must she be feeling? She probably hated him for his failure to find a way for them to be together.

A flash of anger passed through his grief and guilt. She had to bear some of the blame for this mess. How could she have been foolish enough to come, knowing she would be exposed as an enchantress?

Frowning, he sat up on the edge of his bed, resting his elbows on his knees. But she hadn't been exposed as an enchantress, had she? She'd been mocked for being a servant, but there had been no mention of magic. At least, not until his father had recognized magic on her abandoned slipper. Had she found a way to evade his father's artifact somehow?

Terrible, wonderful thought...had he somehow misunderstood what he'd seen in the field? Terrible because if she didn't have magic, his betrayal of her last night had been unforgivable. Wonderful because if she didn't have magic, perhaps there was still hope of convincing his parents of her eligibility...

No. There was no hope down that path. Even if Penny could be brought to forgive him, even if his parents forgave her for the scene she'd made, she'd used magic somehow, with those ridiculous slippers. They'd find out, and they'd exile her, at the very least.

Besides, how could he have misunderstood what he saw in the field?

No, it was best to forget Penny altogether, and accept whoever his parents would choose at the third ball.

An impossible task.

Lacking even the heart to train, Rian rose only when it was time for breakfast. The royal family usually ate in a small private dining parlor. This morning it was empty but for the servants standing ready to provide for Rian's needs. Was it his imagination that the serving girls were watching him with wider eyes than usual, and the serving men were stifling laughter at his expense? He couldn't even bring himself to care that he'd been a spectacle the night before. It was the least of his concerns.

Rian ate slowly, in no hurry to face whatever dull misery the day would bring. He wondered if his parents were still sleeping, after the late night. It was hard to imagine the king lying idly in bed. Rian had never known him to do so before.

His eyes dwelt on his brother's empty place. Longing rose up within him for Bentleigh's familiar presence, and the words of support his brother would surely offer if he was here. Ben would be on his side, no doubt.

Or would he?

Ben would certainly support Rian in his defiance of the ban, and he wouldn't have any objection to Rian's interest in Penny. But that very fact might make his brother disapprove of Rian's choices. Would Ben have done the same, in Rian's shoes, and cut ties with Penny in order to protect her? Or would he have stood by her, ready to defend not only her, but the existence of her magic against the repercussions that would surely come?

Rian pushed himself up from the chair, unable to bear being alone with his thoughts any longer. Desperate for something to occupy his mind, he was glad to be approached a short time later by the captain of the guard.

"Do you have a report for me?" Rian asked, trying not to sound too eager. "On the eastern border?"

"Yes, Your Highness," said the captain. "Although the report is that there's nothing to report. No further skirmishes, no sign of any movement."

Rian frowned. "Do you find that suspicious, Captain? After the increased activity of recent weeks?"

The captain hesitated, then gave a curt nod. "I do, Your Highness. But perhaps I'm just easily alarmed."

Rian gave the stalwart man a look as near to amusement as he could manage in his current state. "You've never given me that impression, Captain."

The captain gave a humorless smile, and Rian dismissed him.

Deep in thought, Rian made his way out the castle's front entrance, heading for the stables. A ride might clear his head. He was surprised, on passing through the doors, to see quite a crowd gathered in the courtyard. The sight was unusual in the absence of a market, or some public announcement. The moment he appeared, many eyes flicked to him, and an excited muttering swept across the assembled group.

Frowning, Rian scanned the area, and his eyes alighted on a temporary pedestal that had been placed at the bottom of the steps. It was flanked by two royal guards, and on top of it sat a velvet cushion. Rian's heart lurched horribly when he realized what was perched on the cushion.

A single glass slipper, catching the morning sun and throwing sparkles of light across the stone courtyard.

Forcing himself to walk with stately strides, he descended the steps until he was level with the pedestal. He was about to ask the guards what the slipper was doing there, when he saw a notice affixed below the cushion. Recognizing the dramatic script of the castle's head scribe, Rian scanned the words with dawning horror.

This slipper was left at the second ball by a

guest of Their Majesties. Whoever can

claim it will be named at the third ball

as the bride of Crown Prince Rian.

Waves of shock and fear washed over Rian as he stood motionless, using every ounce of his willpower to keep his reaction from showing. What madness was this? Turning slowly, he saw the crowd watching him with eager expectation, as though they thought he would make a speech.

He didn't. Moving as if in a trance, Rian walked straight back up the castle steps, not daring to breathe freely until he was inside, away from so many prying eyes. Then he lost no time in seeking out his father. He had to know what was happening.

The king was in his study, as demonstrated by the presence of four guards outside the door. Rian pushed his way in without knocking, his jaw set and his eyes hard.

"What's the meaning of that display in the courtyard?" he demanded without preamble.

Mercifully, the king was alone. He lowered the quill he was holding, meeting his son's eyes unblinkingly. Rian's heart sank at sight of that unyielding mask, so different from the look on his father's face when they discussed anything but magic. The king was not going to be reasonable.

"Isn't it obvious? I must know who got past our defenses, and what was their intent. It is imperative that I identify the woman who wore that slipper."

"So you laid a trap?" Rian was breathing hard, his hands balling into fists. "With me as the bait?"

"Relax, Rian," said the king, returning his gaze to the ledger before him. "You're not going to actually be expected to marry the criminal. But since no attack was mounted, it seems a fair guess that the woman who wore the shoe was present at your betrothal ball for the purpose of pursuing you. It's even possible she employed some magic to attempt to ensnare you, and will see our announcement as evidence of her success. Although," he added, "I admit that's a bit of a leap."

He squinted at Rian's furious face, and a frown creased his brow. "Although your sudden tolerance toward magic did appear after the first ball. You don't think you might have been enchanted, do you?"

"Of course not!" Rian protested. For a moment doubt niggled at his mind. It wasn't possible, was it? But no, he refused to believe that of Penny. "My hesitation about the ban started long before any of these balls, Father," he said, with perfect truth.

"Well," said the king, looking as though he wasn't sure whether to be glad or sorry that his son's defiance hadn't been caused by an enchantment, "it may still be that the lure of a crown is enough to bring this girl out of hiding. Or, if she was actually planning some kind of attack for the final ball, the knowledge that we're aware of her will hopefully be enough to make her think better of it."

"Father," said Rian, his voice shaking with anger, "I strongly object to this plan. For you to do it without consulting me—without even *informing* me!"

"I'm the king, Rian, not you!" said his father, suddenly pushing himself to his feet. "You don't understand the pressures that rest on my shoulders."

"You don't think I understand about pressure?" There was no

humor in Rian's laugh. "You don't think I know what it means to be crushed by it?"

"I won't be questioned!" the king roared, such anger in his eyes that Rian actually took a step back.

He stared at his father, sure for a moment that he saw fear beneath the fury. The same fear that had made such an impression on his four-year-old self when his parents had returned from that ill-fated trip to Listernia. But before he could figure out how to reach his father, the king's mask again descended.

"You're dismissed," he told his son. "I have more important matters requiring my attention."

Rian's fists were still clenched at his side. He knew there was no point reasoning with his father when it came to magic, but he couldn't just walk away. "So you won't take down the notice?"

"I certainly will not."

"And what will you do if you catch this girl, whoever she is?"

"That depends," said King Rhinehart testily. "If her dangerous folly extended only so far as to use an artifact in order to gain entrance to our ball, she will be punished as someone committing that crime normally would be."

A shudder went over Rian as he pictured Penny in the stocks, perhaps even in the dungeons.

"But if I discover that an enchantress infiltrated our very castle..." That glint that was half-anger, half-fear was back in the king's eyes. "Well, the incident at the first ball shows that I have been too lenient. A more permanent response is required."

The world seemed to tilt around Rian as he grasped his father's meaning. "You can't be serious!" he protested, aghast. "You would execute a young girl for coming to a ball?"

"No," said the king darkly. "I would execute an enchantress for breaking the law. And who says she's young? She must be cunning to get around my defenses. If her plan was to attack us rather than to win you, she might be older than I am, for all

I know. Now, as I've said, Rian, I have other matters to attend to."

Rian turned without a word, trying to think through the buzzing in his ears. He'd known for some time that his father's fears regarding magic had made him unreasonable in that area. But this absurd trap went beyond everything. In all Rian's darkest fears since discovering Penny's secret, he'd never once imagined that she could actually be executed for her magic. He didn't know if his father would really go through with it, especially once he discovered that the culprit was a nineteen-year-old girl, and one whom Rian happened to be in love with.

But Rian had no desire to find out. His father had shown himself implacable on this topic, and Rian had no reason to think his influence would mean anything. He had to warn Penny.

Leaving by a side entrance to avoid the gawking crowd, Rian took a longer route to the royal stables. He left the city by a small gate, and was soon thundering down the road toward Penny's manor. No time to wait around in barns now. Even now the rumor of the king's announcement might have reached her, and she might be considering revealing herself. Rian would have to face her family.

Sending his guard to knock at the door, Rian hung back, hoping desperately that luck would be with him, and the grizzled servant would answer.

Luck was not with him. The middle-aged woman who answered the door could only be Penny's stepmother.

Her eyes widened only the tiniest amount at the sight of the crown prince in her yard, and she swept a graceful curtsy.

"Your Highness."

"Good morning," said Rian curtly. It was an effort to force even a semblance of politeness into his voice. "My apologies for the intrusion, but I wish to speak with your daughter."

"No apology necessary, Your Highness," she said, lowering herself once again. "You are most welcome. Do..." she looked at a loss for a moment, "do you wish someone to take your horses into the—"

"No need," Rian assured her. "My guards will remain here. I can spare only a few minutes, I'm afraid."

"Of course, Your Highness," said the stately woman, as Rian swung down from his mount. She moved aside, allowing Rian to enter the manor.

Looking around for any sign of Penny, or even of Al, Rian noted that the house was tastefully appointed but sparse. Clearly the manor had seen more prosperous times.

Before his hostess could say a word, a petulant voice issued from the corridor, and he felt the woman beside him stiffen.

"I don't know why *I* have to do it! How am I supposed to know how to cook an—"

The rather tall young woman who had just entered the room broke off at sight of the prince, her eyes widening in horror. A gasp of shock issued from the dainty brunette who had followed in her wake.

"Olivia, Sophia," said the older woman with a fair assumption of calm. "His Highness has honored us with a visit."

The two girls stared at their mother, then lowered themselves into curtsies that were considerably less graceful than hers had been.

"Now, Your Highness," said Penny's stepmother. "With which of my daughters did you wish to speak?"

"Don't you have a third daughter?" Rian asked, looking hopefully over the other girls' heads. "I thought I saw you at the ball with another girl."

The stepmother looked politely bewildered. "I'm afraid not, Your Highness. These are my two daughters. I have no other."

There was fear in the girls' eyes as they looked from their

mother to Rian, and he frowned. Was there more to this situation than he knew? He strained his ears, hoping to hear a telltale clatter of pans, or the pattering of paws as Al approached, once more dragging Penny with him.

But there was total silence in the manor.

"I must have misunderstood," he said stiffly, with a half-bow to the older woman. "My apologies for wasting your time."

With three swift strides, he reached the door, deaf to whatever protest his hostess was making. He mounted his horse in a moment, and thundered out of the yard. If Penny was in that house, he wouldn't find her with her stepfamily hovering nearby. Perhaps it was worth checking the field.

But that proved futile. No figures appeared among the waving grass, except for the cows grazing at a distance. Rian was riding back past the manor, disheartened and anxious, when his horse gave a whinny of alarm, and pranced to one side of the road. Looking down, Rian saw that someone had jumped out from beside a bush, just past the manor's gate.

Reining in his mount, he recognized Penny's brown-haired stepsister. Sophia, if he remembered correctly.

"Please, Your Highness," she said, sounding breathless. "Are you looking for Penny?"

"Yes," he said eagerly, pulling his horse to a standstill. "Is she here?"

The girl shook her head. "We all saw you with her at the ball. Are you...are you in love with Penny, Your Highness?"

Rian's heart clenched, but he ignored the awed question. "Do you know where she is?" he asked urgently. "I must speak with her."

"I'm sorry," said Sophia, raising her hands helplessly. "She's gone."

"Gone?" Rian stared at her. "What do you mean?"

"When we got back from the ball, there was no sign of her.

She'd run away, and it looks like our last servant went with her. And her dog," Sophia added as an afterthought.

Rian was silent, his mind whirling. Where had she fled to? Across the border? Was she truly gone forever, then?

"To be honest," said Sophia ruefully, "she's left us in a bit of trouble. She...well, Penny used to do everything. And none of us know how to fill her shoes."

"I daresay it won't kill you," snapped Rian. At the chastened look on the girl's face, he softened slightly. "Thank you for telling me," he said, then spurred his horse back toward the capital.

He hardly knew whether to be anxious or glad. He took comfort from knowing that the loyal old servant was with her, not to mention Al. And if Penny had left the kingdom, she wouldn't be at risk of falling into his father's trap. But had she left the kingdom? Rian bit his lip. He could think of only one more step he could take in his attempt to protect her.

His father had accused him—when it became clear that news of the king's magic-identifying talisman had leaked out—of spreading the rumor after setting eyes on the enchanted paperweight. Rian had considered the chastisement most unjust. He'd never been one to spread information, and—although of course he didn't tell his father this—the only person he'd confided in was Penny, in his letter. He hadn't thought she'd spread it around, but perhaps he'd been wrong. Or perhaps she'd told Lady Amaranthe. If he was correct in his guess about the noblewoman, Penny would want to warn her, too. Lady Amaranthe might have spread the rumor—he knew all too well that it only took one person for news to spread like flames across the whole city.

Well, that tawdry reality would work in his favor this time. If he couldn't warn Penny directly, he'd throw the truth of his father's proclamation to the four winds, and let them carry it to whatever hiding place she'd found. It wouldn't be difficult. A whisper here, a meaningful comment there, and the thing was done.

And, he thought with a pang, Penny would be smart enough to know that she could never come back to him.

CHAPTER TWENTY-SIX

Penny

"Penny, I've found you. I had difficulty locating your signature. I don't know why. I never have before."

Penny blinked stupidly at the dragon in front of her. The brightness of the colors around her, the light sparkling from the dragon's purple scales, made her head hurt. All she wanted was to sink back into the oblivion of slumber. Why did Dannsair have to wake her mind before her body was forced to rise?

"I imagine it was because I'm not at home," she said dully. "I'm not even in Bansford. Harry, Al, and I crossed the border into Listernia about an hour before dawn."

"You've only just fallen asleep, then," said Dannsair, eyeing her critically. "That must be why you look such a mess."

Penny didn't answer.

"With the superior senses of my kind," the dragon's expression was deadpan, "I deduce that the ball did not go well."

Penny gave a mirthless laugh. "You could say that."

"I did say it," the dragon reminded her calmly. She cocked her head to one side. "But why have you fled across the border, when you refused to do so all this time? Was your magic exposed?"

"Not my magic," said Penny bitterly. "Just my inadequacy. Even *without my magic in the equation, I wasn't good enough for the prince."*

The pain of it swirled through her. She knew it wasn't entirely reasonable—knew she'd never blamed Rian for the fact that they couldn't be together. But knowing he wanted to be with her, and was prevented by their stations, was one thing. Having him publicly reject her and openly show his horror when she was exposed to all the court as little better than a servant, was something else entirely. Even if they couldn't marry, she had expected him to stand by her, to demonstrate by his presence that he wasn't ashamed to acknowledge their acquaintance. Instead, he'd told her she shouldn't have come, and had bemoaned the fact that she'd caused a scene, and brought his parents' anger down on his head. Clearly, as the moment for his betrothal approached, his sense had won over his heart.

And Penny, her own heart silencing her sense completely, had been the one made to look a fool.

The dragon leaned back, pulling her head away from Penny. "The bitterness emanating from you is so potent it makes proximity to you unpleasant."

"I'm sorry," said Penny, a choke in her voice. "I don't want to be bitter. But I've lost everything."

"Demonstrably false," said the dragon evenly. "You have loyal companions, do you not? You have your life. And you have your magic. Now that you are not in Bansford, you can even use it without fear."

"Yes, I suppose so," said Penny, the words coming out dull. "But all I want is to sleep."

"Very well, then," said Dannsair, her voice more gentle. "Sleep." And at once, the mist began to descend...

Penny woke slowly, feeling amazingly well rested. The canopy of trees over her head reminded her instantly of her situation, and she sat up with a grunt. She hadn't expected the forest floor where she and Harry had finally collapsed to be comfortable enough for proper sleep, but judging by the strength of the light, she'd been out for several hours at least.

"Glad to have you rejoin the living," grunted a voice nearby, and she turned to see Harry sitting by a small fire. "Got some food for you."

"Oh Harry, you're a marvel," said Penny, scratching Al's ears as he stirred beside her. "Did you sleep at all?"

"I'm all right," said Harry gruffly.

"Which means no," Penny sighed.

"I'm just glad you slept so long. It's mid-afternoon, I reckon. Wasn't expecting you to get much rest to be honest."

"Neither was I." Penny stretched her arms above her head. "But I do feel the better for it." She rifled through the small satchel she'd brought, looking for a comb. The glass slipper was turfed onto the forest floor, along with sundry other items.

"Course you do," said Harry. His voice darkened. "I still don't understand why you had to bring that thing."

Penny followed his gaze to the slipper, and sighed. "Sentiment, I suppose."

Before Harry could respond, a rush of wind swept around the clearing, sending embers from the fire drifting out and into the bracken. With a cry, Penny jumped up to help Harry stamp them out. It wasn't until they'd successfully contained the fire again that she turned and realized what had caused the wind.

"Dannsair!" she shrieked, jumping so violently that her booted foot almost went into the fire. She stepped quickly away, staring up at the dragon in awe. She'd been right. Dannsair was much more imposing in daylight. Even here, in the realm of men, the dragon's scales were so bright they hurt Penny's eyes, and she towered above the humans, her neck bent to avoid the branches of the tall pines. A flash of yellow drew Penny's eyes to something behind Dannsair, and she squeaked at the sight of a second dragon.

"Greetings, Penny," said Dannsair, inclining her head. "I have brought a companion, since there are two of you. This is Rekavidur."

The yellow dragon, whose scales were edged with purple, inclined his head also. "Greetings, Penny, and Penny's companion."

Penny glanced at Harry. He was staring, mouth and eyes wide open, not even aware that the sausage he'd been roasting had fallen into the fire. Turning back to the dragons, Penny curtsied low.

"Greetings, Rekavidur," she stumbled over the unfamiliar name, "this is Harry. And this," she gestured at her dog, who was hiding behind Harry, "is Al."

"Ah, I made no provision for that creature," said Dannsair thoughtfully. "Do you think you could carry him, Penny? If you wish him to come with you, that is."

"C-carry him?" Penny repeated. "Come with me where?"

"I could see you were in no state for extended travel when we spoke," said Dannsair. "We're here to take you to your destination."

"That's very kind," said Penny, a little stunned. "But we don't have a destination. Our only object was to escape Bansford."

"Ah, the hastiness of humans," commented Rekavidur, in a gravelly voice. "They never fail to rush into things." He paused, considering. "Or out of them, in this case."

Blinking at the dragon, Penny noticed that he was about the same size as Dannsair, and his scales were equally bright. Clearly they were of a similar age, and young for dragonkind. Still many decades older than her, most likely.

"Well, if you have no destination in mind, allow me to suggest one," Dannsair said calmly. "If you are with us, you will be assured a welcome in the castle of any kingdom in Solstice, bar the one you just left."

"We don't need to go to a castle," Penny said quickly.

Dannsair did her rippling shrug. "You need someone's help," she said. "And if I am to solicit kindness on your behalf, it will be with royals." She looked north west, toward Listernia's capital. "In the castle at Liss, perhaps?"

"No," said Penny quickly. "No, thank you," she amended. She had no desire to seek sanctuary at the castle which Rian's brother all but called home.

"Well, I myself am fond of Entolia," said Dannsair. "The capital is by the sea, which I think you will find pleasant. The king and queen are caught up with their silly little war, but the prince and all those princesses are friendly. More than once I've spoken with them, when sunning myself on the rocks that protrude from the ocean near their castle."

For a moment Penny said nothing, rather stunned by this image. "But..." she started at last, "I thought you weren't supposed to help humans."

Dannsair shook her vast head. "We are not supposed to help humans with matters arising from human magic. And we are not supposed to use our magic on humans. But carrying you to Entolia will not breach that agreement."

"But..." Penny started again. "But you..." Her eyes passed to Rekavidur, and she trailed off.

"You are thinking that I used my magic on you when I enchanted your slippers," said Dannsair calmly. "You're right, and you may speak freely in front of Reka. It is his example which has emboldened me to break the rule when it comes to enchantments that we do not believe are truly..." She exchanged a glance with the yellow dragon. "Let us just say, when it comes to enchantments that we believe should be exceptions to the rule. Reka has already played a part in breaking two such enchantments. Compared to his actions, the magic I put into your slippers was of little moment."

"True," agreed Rekavidur calmly. "We are, I suppose you could say, the rebels among our kind."

He spoke with such a straight expression that it took Penny a moment to recognize Dannsair's gurgling response as laughter.

"You speak, as always, in such dramatic terms," said Dannsair, shaking her head at the other dragon. "You have spent too much time with humans, my friend."

Rekavidur's lips curved in a reptilian smile. "You are fast catching up, it seems."

Reminded of Penny's presence, Dannsair turned back to her. "So, will you accept our escort to the castle of the Entolians?"

"I..." Penny looked at Harry hopelessly. He was still staring at the dragons open-mouthed, looking as though he'd been turned to stone. "I don't know why we would refuse."

"Very good," nodded Dannsair curtly. "Take firm hold of your dog. If you drop him, he will perish."

Eyes wide with alarm, Penny hurried over to the cowering Al. Harry was still catatonic with shock, so it fell to Penny to stamp out the fire, and gather their things. Then she prodded Harry gently into the open space beyond the grove, and gathered a quivering Al in her arms. She was worried the dog would squirm, but he huddled into her, clearly seeking reassurance.

She'd barely steadied her bundle when Dannsair leaned down toward her, and she felt talons close around her shoulders. Wincing with the expectation of pain that didn't come, Penny had no warning before she shot into the air, suspended by her shoulders, her legs dangling terrifyingly beneath her. They soared up so quickly, that in a second they were high above the trees. It was all she could do to keep hold of Al, who mercifully pressed himself as close to her as possible rather than trying to wrestle free.

The sensation of flying, at breakneck speed, many feet above the ground, was both the most terrifying and the most exhilarating thing Penny had ever experienced. The flight—skirting around the mountainous border between Bansford and Listernia, then crossing the entirety of Fernedell, and most of Entolia—took less than an hour. Even so, by the time Dannsair alighted in the courtyard of a quaint coastal castle, Penny was barely keeping hold of Al's weight. The moment they touched solid ground, the dog squirmed from her grip, abasing himself on the flagstones, eyes wide with terror.

"Poor Alchemist," Penny said, half-laughing, half-penitent. "I left my stomach behind as well."

"Alchemist?" said an inquisitive voice. "That's an unusual name for a dog."

Penny's head snapped up, and she flushed at the sight of a gorgeously dressed girl, a few years younger than herself, standing in the courtyard and regarding the dragons with untroubled interest. The guards hovering not far behind her told Penny that this must be one of Entolia's numerous princesses. There were twelve, last time she'd heard.

"Greetings, Dannsair, Rekavidur," the girl said, curtsying elegantly. "I thought I heard that telltale rush of wind. We haven't seen you for a while."

"Greetings, Princess Zinnia," said Dannsair regally, inclining her enormous head. "We've brought you visitors who are in dire need of assistance. The girl is Penny. Her heart has become entangled with that of Bansford's crown prince, but she has fled the kingdom because she is secretly an enchantress of incredible power, and therefore not only their love, but her presence in the kingdom, is forbidden."

Long before the end of this matter-of-fact speech, Princess Zinnia's mouth had fallen open in undignified astonishment, and Harry—whom Rekavidur had set down beside Penny—had let out a strangled squeak.

"Dannsair!" gasped Penny, eyes wide with horror as heat rushed across her face.

"Why do you look at me so?" Dannsair asked, bewildered. "Was I mistaken in any of my particulars?"

"Well..." Penny swallowed. "Well, no, but..."

"Perhaps you are unnerved to hear your secret spoken so openly," said Dannsair kindly. "But you are in Bansford no longer, Penny. You need not hide your magic here."

"Very true," said Princess Zinnia, collecting herself. "You are welcome here, Penny. My name is Zinnia, and I will be happy to provide you with any assistance I can." She inclined her head to the dragons. "Thank you for bringing them."

Dannsair and Rekavidur acknowledged the words, then the purple dragon turned to Penny. "We will speak soon," she promised. Then she and Rekavidur unfurled their wings, and with a rush of wind, took once more to the sky. In moments, they were small specks in the vast blue, and in moments more, they were gone.

Penny turned, swallowing nervously, to Princess Zinnia. "Your Highness," she said awkwardly. "Thank you for...for—"

"No need to stand on ceremony," said Princess Zinnia cheerfully. "You've been vouched for by the dragons, so you're basically royalty now. You don't need to call me 'Your Highness'."

Penny said nothing. She'd heard that before. The wound in her heart flared, and she drew a sharp breath as she attempted to master her emotions.

"I can help you get cleaned up, and we'd be delighted to host you here for as long as you like," said Zinnia cheerfully. She shepherded Penny, along with a very stunned looking Harry, who was now carrying Al, into the castle. "But when it comes to Prince Rian..."

She shook her head. "I don't know how much use I can be. I don't know him much. I'll ask Basil. He and Prince Rian have had much more communication, one crown prince to another, you know."

Blinking in the face of this steady flow of words, Penny found herself ushered into a luxurious guest suite. Harry and Al had disappeared along the way, and she could only hope they were being looked after as well. She'd been so overwhelmed by the opulence of her surroundings, she'd failed to even say goodbye to them.

In a remarkably short space of time, Princess Zinnia had coordinated a whole team of maids, who ushered Penny into a bath, pressed her with refreshments, and prepared a gloriously soft bed for her to rest in.

"I know it's not even dinnertime," said Princess Zinnia kindly, "but I get the sense you would welcome the chance to sleep."

Penny nodded fervently. "I would."

The princess nodded. "Rest, then, Penny. Tomorrow we can talk." Her eyes sparkled. "After Dannsair's introduction, I'm dying to hear your story."

And with those portentous words, she danced from the room in a swirl of silk, leaving Penny to her dubious peace.

When Penny awoke, it took her much longer to get her bearings than it had in the forest. The room in which she was lying wasn't overwhelmingly decadent—it was tastefully arranged, but still far more luxurious than anywhere she'd ever slept.

She pushed herself up, only to gasp in surprise at the realization that she wasn't alone.

"Sorry to alarm you, Miss." The maid who was tending the

fire had a cheerful voice. "You've slept right through until morning, and I'm sure it's done you the world of good."

She stood up, dusting off her hands. "I'm Elizabeth, and I asked to wait on you particularly. Normally I wait on Princess Zinnia, you see, so she told me all about you."

Penny ran a hand through her tangled curls, struggling to keep up. "That's...that's very kind of you," she said vaguely. "And of the princess." She couldn't figure out why any maid who had attained the high position of waiting on a princess, would wish to jeopardize it by serving an untitled stranger instead.

"You see, I'm from Bansford, too," Elizabeth said brightly. "And when I heard you come from Bant, I—"

"Just outside Bant," Penny corrected her, hiding a yawn. "To the west of the city."

"What do you know?" beamed Elizabeth. "That's where my family lived. Near some beautiful vineyards. I don't remember much, because I was so young when we left. But I know I used to play in them."

Penny stared at her. "My father owned those vineyards," she said. "I spent half my childhood running wild through them."

"We probably played together!" exclaimed Elizabeth, delighted. "We just wouldn't remember." Her face dropped. "I always look out for fellow Bansfordians when they come through. Entolia's been my home almost as long as I can remember, but my parents often talk about what they miss from Bansford. About what a wonderful kingdom it used to be."

"It still is," said Penny, her throat tight. "In...in many ways."

"Well, if you can say that, as one of the magic folk who've been driven out, then that's something to hold on to, isn't it?" said Elizabeth cheerfully.

She gestured for Penny to stand, and lifted a dress from where it lay across a nearby chair. "Here you go, Miss," she said. "The princess has sent one of her own gowns."

"I can't wear this," Penny protested.

Elizabeth laughed off her objection. "It's her simplest dress, believe it or not."

Penny gazed down at the pale green fabric, beautifully embroidered, and opening at the front to show an under-layer of crisp white, trimmed with lace. "I'm not sure I can believe it," she said dryly.

Still chuckling, Elizabeth helped Penny into an underdress.

"The thing is," she chatted on, "I owe a debt to Bansford's magic-users, and even though I can't repay it, I try to look out for anyone who flees this way, give them a friendly word, that kind of thing. When Her Highness said you was an enchantress who'd had to flee across the border, I knew I had to meet you, give you a bit of encouragement."

"What debt?" Penny asked, seized by a sudden premonition.

Elizabeth's face grew grave as she helped Penny into the gown. "I was injured as a small child. Really badly. I'd fallen into a well, and they didn't know if I'd ever walk again. Magic had already been outlawed by then, but an enchantress risked her safety to come and heal me. That was her gift, you see. My parents said she wouldn't even take the payment they'd offered. But the guards found out, and she ran, and..." Elizabeth trailed off, her voice heavy with emotion even after so many years.

"And she fell into the same well, and died," whispered Penny.

Elizabeth's eyes sprang to hers, full of shock. "How did you know that?" she whispered.

Penny's own eyes were filling, tears beginning to run down her cheeks. "That was my mother."

For one more moment, Elizabeth stood frozen, then she burst into tears as well. Before Penny knew what was happening, the two girls were embracing, both weeping openly.

"I'm so sorry," Elizabeth wailed, but Penny shook her head.

"Don't apologize. It wasn't your fault. And I'm sure she wouldn't regret it. Well," she pulled back, wiping her eyes, "she would probably regret not watching where she was going afterward."

The girls stared at each other, some bond that wasn't magic, but which nevertheless transcended logic, stretching between them.

"Is it true you're in love with the prince?" Elizabeth demanded abruptly.

With an exhilarating feeling of having nothing left to hide, Penny nodded.

"And that he's in love with you?"

Penny shrugged, tears once again threatening to fall. "I thought so. But if he loves me, it's not enough to fight for me."

Elizabeth frowned, but before she could speak, there was a muffled knock. Hurrying through the internal door into the suite's receiving room, Elizabeth answered it, and Penny heard Princess Zinnia's voice drifting through.

"Is she decent, Beth? Basil's here, and I thought we could all have a chat."

Penny hurried after the maid, and found herself face to face with yet another royal. Her life had certainly become more exciting in the last few months.

Prince Basil inclined his head to her in a friendly way, although his face looked too serious for his years. Penny was almost sure he was younger than her. Perhaps that grave expression was an accessory of being heir, she thought wistfully, remembering the stern cast of Rian's square jaw. Except when he smiled at her, and then his mouth softened, and he—but she'd be wiser not to think about it.

"We're very glad to welcome a friend of dragons," said Basil, once introductions had been made, and they were all seated. Elizabeth hovered excitedly. "But I'm afraid my sister may have created false expectations. We cannot interfere in the concerns of Bansford's royal family. I'm sure they would resent it, as we would resent such interference from them." The prince spoke courteously enough, but his tone was frank, and his gaze direct.

"Basil, don't be such a dampener," frowned Princess Zinnia.

But Penny shook her head. "I understand, Your Highness, and I promise I have no such expectation. I'm just grateful for the sanctuary, and if you can assist me to find gainful work, I won't trespass long on your hospitality."

"Work won't be an issue, not if you're an enchantress," said Princess Zinnia. "Your skills will be highly valued here. But I'm not ready to give up on this whole forbidden love situation just yet."

"Zinnia." Prince Basil's voice was pained. He looked at Penny. "I must apologize for my sister. My father is unwell." He paused, perhaps realizing that Penny must have heard of the legendary ill health of Entolia's king. "More unwell even than normal," he added dryly. "And we have all been castle-bound while we await his recovery. It is making some of us," he threw a dark look at his sister, "more eager for excitement than is helpful."

Penny felt a surge of sympathy for the serious young prince. She hoped the king would pull through, if only to give Prince Basil longer before the crushing weight of the crown would fall to him. It would be daunting to become king of any kingdom at his age, let alone a kingdom at war.

But Princess Zinnia just rolled her eyes at her brother. "This has nothing to do with Father's health. Dannsair said herself that Penny and Prince Rian's hearts are entangled."

"It's kind of you to wish to help," said Penny in a constricted voice. "But there's nothing to be done. Prince Rian has made his choice, and it's not me."

"Are you sure about that?" cut in a breathless voice. Everyone turned to look at Elizabeth, who hurried into Penny's sleeping quarters and back. "Forgive my snooping, Miss Penny, but I was unpacking your satchel last night, and I saw this."

She held up the glass slipper, and to Penny's bewilderment, Princess Zinnia gasped. Even Prince Basil looked taken aback.

"What about it?" Penny asked.

"An express arrived this morning from Bansford," said Princess Zinnia, her eyes shining. "I listened at the door when Basil received the report."

"Zinnia," protested Basil, but she waved him off. "King Rhinehart has placed a slipper—a *glass* slipper—in the castle courtyard. He's made a proclamation that says a guest at his son's second ball left it behind, and whoever can claim it will be announced as the prince's bride at the third ball!"

For a long moment there was silence, as Penny stared blankly at the excited princess. Could it be true? Had Rian changed his mind, and decided to fight for her? Had he convinced his parents after all?

It seemed unlikely. She remembered the anger on the monarchs' faces as she fled the ballroom, having exposed their son and heir to the gossip of the court. But why else would such a proclamation be made?

She suddenly realized why else, and a shot of icy dread dropped into her stomach. The slipper was an artifact now. Belatedly, the full details of Dannsair's warning came back to her. Separated from her, it would no longer serve its function to shield her magic. It would just be exposed as a magical item itself. The king must know that someone had gotten past his artifact. And he'd laid a trap to catch them. Did he know it was her? Or was he just gambling on the probability that any woman who'd attended the ball would be eager to marry Rian?

A further wave of dread washed over Penny as she realized the king was right. Surely there must be a line of dozens of girls even at this moment, ready to claim the slipper was theirs, and become a princess.

Would one of them find a way to convince the king she was the owner? And then be arrested as an enchantress for her pains?

In the end, it didn't matter whether the declaration was real, or a trap. Penny's path was the same.

"So, Penny?" Princess Zinnia asked, still looking unduly excited. "What are you going to do about it?"

Penny turned her eyes to the princess, her voice full of grim determination. "I'm going back to claim that slipper."

CHAPTER TWENTY-SEVEN

Rian

Rian stared out at the ballroom, seeing none of the decadence before him. The merciful numbness that had shrouded his senses all week still surrounded him, and he welcomed it. He had no desire to feel anything.

"Well, that was a close thing, but it looks like we made it before any excitement started."

Rian jumped at the sound of the familiar voice, turning in astonishment to see his brother's grinning face.

"Ben! What are you doing here?" His brother's presence sent a stab of emotion slashing through his numbness, and suddenly he could feel the agony threatening to press in on him. With an effort, he clutched mentally at the unfeeling, uncaring shroud he needed to protect himself.

"Princess Azalea," he said formally, nodding to the princess hovering behind her betrothed. Like Ben, she bore the signs of having changed into ball attire in a hurry. Several guards stood behind them, wearing Listernian royal crests and disgruntled expressions. "I didn't expect to see you."

"No one did, to be honest," said Ben. "But we couldn't miss

your betrothal ball, old fellow." He frowned. "Although I'll admit Mother's letter confused me a little. Who's the lucky lady?"

Rian shrugged. "Not sure." At that moment, Queen Eliza bustled up, full of exclamations at the sight of her younger son and his betrothed. "Mother," said Rian tonelessly. "Whom have you selected?"

She frowned at him. "Are you sure you don't wish to choose from the list, Rian? This is your last opportunity."

He shook his head. "No, I don't care. Choose who you like."

"Ri." It was Ben who spoke, but Rian refused to meet his eye. "Can we talk privately?"

"There's no need to sulk, Rian," said Queen Eliza. As in every conversation they'd had in recent days, she looked deeply disappointed by the evaporation of all Rian's interest in choosing his own bride. "It was your own conduct that led you to be humiliated by the imposture of that servant girl."

"Not that it matters," Rian cut in, "but Penny isn't a servant." If Ben's presence had slashed a hole in Rian's defenses, Penny's name ripped them into shreds. The pain of what he'd lost bore down on him with such force, he wondered he was still on his feet. "And she didn't impose on anyone," he said, his voice unsteady. "She's the least assuming, the most selfless person I know. And I love her."

All three royals were now staring at Rian in blank astonishment. The silence stretched out, everyone apparently too stunned to respond. Rian saw something stir in his mother's eyes, something akin to sympathy, but he didn't let her speak. He couldn't bear to witness her softening toward the idea of him marrying a commoner, not now the commoner he wanted to marry was so irrevocably beyond his reach.

"But I know I can't marry her," he added, more calmly. "So it really doesn't matter to me who you choose. Pick whichever one is best connected."

"Rian, a word," said Ben, speaking forcefully this time. He gripped Rian's elbow, and began to steer him toward the closest double door, leading into the gardens. Rian heard his mother's protest, but it was quickly drowned out by Azalea's cheerful voice, launching into discussion of her upcoming wedding.

Reflecting that they were quite the team, Rian gave no resistance, and soon found himself on the lawns. He and Penny had walked here at the first ball. It felt like a lifetime ago.

"Talk," said Ben, the moment they were clear of the ballroom.

Rian shrugged. "What is there to say? After twenty-three years of being sensible, I decided to lose my heart to someone completely ineligible mere weeks before the announcement of my political marriage."

"And you're not even going to fight for this girl, whoever she is?" Ben demanded.

Rian turned at last, glaring at his brother. "You think I don't want to fight for her? I was ready to die on that hill, believe me. But then I found out..." He paused, shaking his head. "I found out something else about her that...that made me see how impossible it was."

"What?" Ben pressed. Rian shook his head, and Ben's voice became a growl. "I'm your brother, Rian. If you can't tell me the truth, who can you—"

"She's an enchantress," hissed Rian, feeling a strange release as the words came out. "She's been hiding her magic all these years. She never breathed a word, but I saw her at it before the second ball." In a sudden gesture, he put one hand over his face. "I begged her not to come, but she did anyway. I don't know what she expected...what else could I do but send her away?"

Ben was silent for so long that Rian lowered his hand, watching his brother in trepidation.

"That is quite a barrier to overcome," the younger prince admitted at last.

Rian snorted at the understatement. He gazed out at the few guests who'd already sought the peace of the gardens, trying not to catch anyone's eye. Then he saw it...a flash of golden curls. He stiffened, and Ben—still gripping his elbow—followed his gaze.

"What is it?"

"Penny?" Rian whispered.

"That's her?" demanded Ben.

Rian didn't answer. He stared, stunned, at the figure now beckoning to him. Surely she hadn't been foolish enough to return! But there was no mistaking that slim figure, those striking eyes. He could even see her bracelet, glinting as it caught the light of the lanterns. As he watched, Penny cast a frightened look around her, then turned, disappearing into the darkness.

"What are you waiting for?" Ben demanded. "Go after her!"

Not needing to be told twice, Rian hurried toward the place where Penny had disappeared. He heard Bentleigh engage an approaching nobleman in cheerful conversation, and blessed his brother for once again being present to cover for him.

He thought Penny would be waiting for him just beyond the lantern light, but he could see no sign of her. Turning wildly, he caught a flash of pink skirts, and hurried after them.

"Penny!" he called, the words a hiss. "Wait!"

He remembered how she'd hurried away the very first time he'd laid eyes on her, at the market. And she'd run from him in earnest at Bentleigh's betrothal ball. He felt like he'd been chasing her since the moment they met, until the last ball, when she fled in humiliation and he didn't follow her. His heart clenched. He wasn't going to make the same mistake again.

He rounded the corner of a darkened hedge, and saw her disappearing up ahead. With a flash of understanding, he realized she was running toward the hedge maze. Where they'd kissed. Heat rushed into him at the memory, driving away the last of the numbness. He picked up his pace.

When he entered the maze, he paused. It was darker in here, and his eyes took a moment to adjust. He couldn't see Penny, but something glinted on the ground in front of him.

A single glass slipper.

The pair of the one that had, until removed in preparation for the ball, sat unclaimed on the cushion before the palace. Thanks to Rian's rumor-mongering, no hopeful girls had falsely claimed the dangerous prize.

Until now. Had its true owner heard the proclamation but not the rumor? Had Penny run back to him, into danger this time? Bending down, he picked up the slipper. But something was wrong. It felt cool, like he expected, but instead of being hard, it was soft, and squishy. And...wet?

"Urgh!" He dropped the squirming toad in disgust, falling back a step. A musical laugh made him squint into the darkness ahead, confusion seizing him. "Penny?"

She stepped out of the gloom, as beautiful as ever, but with an expression on her face Rian had never seen before. A savage grin twisted her delicate features, and there was a feverish light in her eyes.

"Beautiful things aren't always what they seem, Your Highness," she crooned, stepping forward again.

And as she moved, she changed. Rian watched in horror as the familiar face twisted and warped, until another face, beautiful in its own way, but infinitely less dear, took its place.

"Lady Amaranthe?" he whispered, horrified.

She gave another laugh, this one decidedly less musical. "Not what you were expecting, Your Highness? Or should I just call you Rian?" She lifted her wrist, to show Penny's bracelet on her arm. As she touched the charm he'd given Penny, the jewelry changed, reverting to a solid gold band that bore no resemblance to Penny's delicate silver bracelet.

He recoiled from her, his mind reeling. "So you are an enchantress," he said. "I should have turned you in the moment I suspected."

"Ah, but you didn't, did you?" Lady Amaranthe smiled indulgently. "Softened to magic by a pair of..." her face twisted in concentration, once more assuming the features he knew so well, "...such *striking* green eyes."

Those very eyes blinked innocently up at him, and Rian let out a snarl. "Stop that!"

Lady Amaranthe's face returned to its normal state, creased in laughter. "It's quite a useful trick, isn't it? A shame it takes such an incredible amount of power to maintain it, or I'd use it much more often. It served me well when I needed to intercept your little love note, however."

Rian stared in growing horror. "It was you the guard gave it to," he whispered. "She never saw it."

"No," sighed Lady Amaranthe. "It was an unfortunate upset to our plans, that you found out about her magic too soon. I wasn't sure if she would be willing to go through with her role if she knew what danger she was in. You see," Lady Amaranthe strolled forward, to where Rian stood, frozen to the spot, "she wanted to bring down this hypocritical despotic monarchy as much as I did. But naturally she preferred not to give her life in the attempt."

"You're lying," said Rian, his lips numb. "Penny has no part in your plans."

Lady Amaranthe threw back her head, laughing riotously. "Of course not, not sweet, innocent Penny." She circled behind him, and Rian watched her warily. "She's far too kind, far too gentle. Those big eyes, and those..." she reached out, touching an insolent finger to Rian's lips, "soft lips."

"Stop it!" growled Rian, batting her hand away. His pulse was racing, and panic was clawing at him. It wasn't true. It couldn't be true. Not Penny.

"She has incredible power, Penny," mused Lady Amaranthe. "I would kill for magic as strong as hers. When I first saw her, at your brother's ball, consumed with bitterness, moments from using her magic to strike you and the happy couple, I saw at once that she had great promise for my cause. But then," her eyes gleamed hungrily, "I saw the look on your face when you caught sight of her, and I knew she had an even more valuable power than her magic."

The noblewoman gave an unladylike chuckle. "To hold the heart of a prince in your hands, now that's power. Add forbidden magic to that, and..." She gave a contented sigh. "It was better than I could have dreamed. I'd considered trying such a thing myself, of course." She ran a hand over her thick hair. "I've been told I'm not unattractive. But I've been studying you, Your Highness, and I could see it wouldn't do."

She leaned close again, so her breath tickled his ear as she whispered. "There are some who might prefer a more experienced woman."

Her hand trailed across his chest as she spoke, and Rian was as much repulsed with himself as with her at the heat that raced out from her unwelcome touch.

"But you're too rigid, too honorable to be seduced by that type of power," Lady Amaranthe continued regretfully. She stepped back, holding his gaze with malicious eyes. "I saw in a heartbeat that Penny would be much more successful at drawing you in. So innocent." Her eyes glinted as she reached toward him again. "So fresh."

"Enough," Rian snarled, grabbing at her arm. "Don't touch me." But before he could seize her, a knife suddenly flashed into existence in Lady Amaranthe's hand. With a cry, Rian reached for his own sword. His hand had barely found the hilt when flames erupted around his feet, and he leaped backward with another shout. He attempted to stamp them out, but they only grew, licking at his boots, curling up his legs.

Before he knew what was happening, Lady Amaranthe had seized his sword and flung it across the garden. Wondering why she didn't use her knife, Rian realized with confusion that it was gone. In its place was a deadly snake, coiling and writhing around the enchantress's arm. As Rian stared in shock, the noblewoman threw the snake, and it landed, hissing, on his chest.

Struggling with its coils, Rian didn't even see the noblewoman approach. But he certainly felt the blow to the head she dealt him. Dazed, he dropped to his knees. He saw Lady Amaranthe seize the snake and begin to bind his hands. Except it wasn't a snake any longer. It was an ordinary length of rope. And there was no sign of the fire that should by now have consumed Rian's clothes.

"Things are not as they seem," Lady Amaranthe reminded him sweetly, seeing his confusion.

Still disoriented from the blow, Rian started to struggle, but his hands were bound tightly. He managed to push himself to his knees, but a searing pain in his injured arm sent him crashing back down.

"Now, now, Your Highness," said Lady Amaranthe, pressing her long-nailed fingers into his still-healing wound. "Don't be difficult." Deftly, she bound his legs as well, chatting amicably as she did so. "It wasn't hard to throw you and Penny together. The fool girl is too meek to do a thing for herself, but it does make her easy to manipulate. And you...you're the easiest to manipulate of all. A hint here about how misused she is, a flattering suggestion that she's taken with you, and you fancy yourself in love."

She made a bitter noise in her throat. "I wish I'd managed to see you married to her, and *then* exposed her as an enchantress. What a triumph that would have been, when it was Bansford's own queen who burned the kingdom to the ground."

"Princess," corrected Rian feebly, his head spinning so that it was hard to think.

"Oh no," said Lady Amaranthe, bending down so that her face was once again offensively close to his. "That's the other part of the plan. I would have dealt with your parents at your wedding feast had things gone as they ought, but no matter. Your betrothal ball will have to do."

Fear flared in Rian as her words sank in. He flailed, but he was fully bound by now, and utterly helpless. He remembered the sick dread he'd felt when he saw that enchanter lunge for his father, knives splayed. The horror of Penny being involved in a plot to kill the king and queen—to kill Rian's parents—was almost too much for him to take in.

"Wait," he said, his sluggish mind catching up with Lady Amaranthe's taunts. "Is Penny meek and manipulable, or a mastermind of violence and murder?"

A look of annoyance flashed across Lady Amaranthe's face. But she quickly smoothed it away. "Can't someone be both?"

"Maybe someone can," retorted Rian. "But not Penny. She's not either. She can't be meek and easy to manipulate, or she'd be here doing your bidding, not safe across the border. And she can't be murderous, because she simply doesn't have that kind of darkness inside her." Certainty rose within him, buoying him up in spite of his bindings. "Not my Penny."

"You're as big a fool as her," spat Lady Amaranthe, her face an inch from his. "Just like your father, too full of his own importance to see what's right before his nose. From within the court, I've had access to every enchanter he's ever exiled. Not to mention their families—I'm not so shortsighted as to think that only those with magic can make formidable enemies." She frowned to herself. "That child's father had promise. It's a shame he got free before I had the chance to recruit him."

She shook her head, looking back at Rian with a grim smile. "No matter. I have enough. You think those desert fighters are a group of ragtag bandits? They're my own force, with all kinds of magic you've never seen. And they've been preparing for tonight for years. They'll be here soon enough. I hope you don't mind that I invited them to your ball."

Rian was still staring, horrified, as she produced a length of fabric from her sleeve. "And what's your plan?" he spat out, as she twisted the fabric in preparation. "Once you rip down the monarchy, what will take its place?"

"You think I care about that?" scoffed Lady Amaranthe, pausing. "I don't care what happens next—I just want to see the kingdom burn."

"But why?" Rian asked helplessly.

She glared at him. "You can ask that? You, who fell in love with an enchantress? You can't pretend you don't know better than to support this ban." Her expression twisted in fury. "I was fifteen when the ban was imposed, but I'd been living under a ban all my life. My father was ashamed of my power, ashamed of what I was. He was horrified that his father's magic had passed to his children, and he forced me to hide it, to pretend to be just like my unremarkable peers. I longed for the day when I reached adulthood and left my father's house. I dreamed every night of what I would do when I was free to unleash my magic at last. And then," her face darkened still further, "before I ever got the chance, your precious father decided to turn my incredible gift into a crime. If you'd spent your whole life in a cage of others' making, you wouldn't be asking me why."

Giving him no chance to reply, she shoved the fabric into his mouth, tying it painfully tightly. Silent and powerless, Rian raged at himself for falling for her tricks and allowing her to subdue him so easily.

"You stay here nice and safe," she murmured into his ear. "I'm keeping you as security, in case I need to get Penny back on board. The untapped potential of her power still keeps me up at night. I'm glad you rejected and humiliated her at the ball, and sent her running. She's strong enough to ruin everything, if she got in the way."

She leaned insolently close and pressed a quick kiss to his cheek. "Such a valiant prince," she mocked, as Rian jerked his face away from her. "So helpful of you to solve that problem for me. You let Penny go because you were too weak to fight for her. So it's you I have to thank for the success of my plans. Because she's far away, and neither her magic nor your crown has the power to stop me now."

CHAPTER TWENTY-EIGHT

Penny

Penny pushed the kitchen door open, falling through with a rush of mingled exhaustion and relief. It was incredibly surreal to be back in her familiar domain after all that had passed. The kitchen wasn't as tidy as she usually left it, and it showed clear signs of inexpert use. The barn had also looked neglected, but at least her stepfamily had managed to keep the horse alive. She could imagine their astonishment when they saw the two gorgeous steeds, with the Entolian royal crest on their saddles, now peacefully munching hay alongside their lesser fellow.

"It's quiet," she said, turning her worried frown on Harry, who'd loped into the kitchen behind her. "Do you think they've already left for the ball? It can't have started too long ago, can it?"

It would be too heartbreaking to have traveled hard for days only to arrive too late for the ball by mere hours. It would have been nice to travel by dragon again, but there had been no way to contact Dannsair. Apparently even royalty couldn't summon dragons at a whim.

"Good thing if it's over, if you ask me," grunted Harry. "I still don't understand why we made it safely all the way out of here, only to turn around and come right back into danger."

"Yes you do," said Penny impatiently. "If there's the slimmest chance Rian is waiting for me, I have to get to him. And if the king set a trap for me, I have to make sure no one else has walked into it." She grimaced. "I do wish I knew which it was, because if I have to spring someone from the dungeons, I'm going to regret wearing a ballgown."

"Not likely," snorted Harry. "I've seen the way you look at that dress."

"Oh hush," said Penny, the ready color flooding her cheeks. It seemed Harry had noticed her surreptitiously admiring the dress during their journey from Entolia. "When an actual princess gives you her own ballgown, it's the least you can do to make sure it's traveling safely."

Harry gave her a look, and she abandoned the attempt to save her dignity.

"It's time for me to get into it, anyway," she said. "It's not going to be easy without help."

"I'd best check on the horses again," said Harry, a definite note of alarm in his voice. Penny let him go, chuckling. Nothing would prevail upon her to ask Harry to help her with her gown, but it was a little entertaining to see his terror nevertheless.

"I don't suppose you can help me, Al?" Penny asked, smiling down at the dog. He wagged a weary tail. "That's what I thought."

Carrying the overlarge traveling bag that had been strapped onto her saddle, Penny moved out of the kitchen and into the main house. She'd been so sure the others had already left for the ball, she almost screamed at the sight of a tall figure moving toward her.

"Penny?" Olivia looked even more stunned to see Penny.

"What are you doing here?" Penny asked stupidly. "Why aren't you at the ball?"

Olivia made a derisive noise in her throat. "You know why. When you left, who did you imagine would be the new family servant? Not Sophia. She's too pretty for that. Her job is to marry well and provide us with money." She looked Penny over, jealousy clear in her eyes. "I suppose you're pretty enough for that too, if Mama would only admit it. But she'd already invested so much effort in making you the worker of the family, you can hardly blame her for being reluctant to throw it away by sending you out into the world. She's good at economy, is Mama. And you're so very efficient—you do the work of half a dozen servants, with none of the cost."

Penny was silent, at a loss for how to respond to this bitter tirade.

"Do you have magic?" Olivia demanded abruptly.

"Yes," said Penny, her voice calm, even as her pulse thundered in her ears. "I inherited it from my mother."

Olivia's eyes were wide. "What's it like?" she whispered, a definite note of longing in her voice.

"The magic is incredible," said Penny frankly. "The crippling fear of exposure not so much."

"How do you do it?" Olivia asked, her voice almost desperate.

"I don't know," shrugged Penny. "I just...can."

"No." Olivia shook her head. "Not the magic. How do you take everything that's thrown at you without lashing out? You could have punished us if you chose, and instead you used your magic to do our housework. Why?"

Penny took a moment to answer, thrown by the intensity of her stepsister's expression. "I suppose," she said slowly, "I'd rather suffer unkindness than become unkind myself."

Olivia's face was hard to read. "Where did you learn to be like that? Not from Mama, I know. She doesn't understand kindness. Or unkindness. Sometimes I wonder if she even feels emotion."

"I've wondered the same thing," admitted Penny. "Why is she so hard?"

Olivia shrugged. "She's always been that way. I don't think her parents showed her much kindness, but I can't be sure. She doesn't talk about her childhood." She eyed Penny. "She doesn't hate you, you know. She just doesn't love you either. She's calculating, and she thinks not about how people feel, but about how to make best use of every asset she's given."

Olivia's voice caught a little. "Father wasn't like that, and she was a little better when he was alive. I think she cared about him as much as she knows how to care about anyone."

Penny bit her lip, no words coming in response to these disclosures.

"Your father didn't teach you to be this way," said Olivia, apparently not finished. "He wasn't unkind, but he didn't have the kindness you have. I'm not trying to be offensive," she shrugged, "but it's true."

"I don't take any offense," said Penny. "I loved Father, and he loved me. But I understand what you mean, and you're right. He was more worried about safety than kindness, I think." She raised her eyes to Olivia's. "I guess I just need to be grateful that I can remember my mother."

"I wish I could."

The whispered words were so quiet, Penny thought she must have misheard. "What do you mean?"

Olivia swallowed. "Mama is the only mother I've ever known, but she's not the one who gave birth to me. My first mother died when I was an infant, and my father married Mama not long afterward." She gave a twisted smile. "I'm nothing but a stepdaughter, like you."

Penny stared, rocked by this information. How had no one

told her? How had she never guessed? The difference in the sisters' features...Olivia's constant painful attempts to win Sapphira's approval...even the very fact that Sophia was named for her mother, while her older sister wasn't.

"That doesn't mean you're not a true daughter," she said quietly. "I think you're most like her of any of us."

Without warning, Olivia buried her face in her hands and burst into tears. "I know I am," she sobbed. "And I don't want to be."

"You don't have to be," said Penny earnestly. "And I want to help you, Olivia, I really do. I've never been able to see Sapphira as a mother, but I've always wished to have you and Sophia as real sisters. But I'm afraid I just don't have time for an emotional reconciliation right now!"

Olivia lifted her hands, a choke that was half-sob, half-laughter escaping her. "Why ever not?"

"Because I have to get to the ball and claim that slipper, before someone else does!"

Olivia stared. "So the slipper *was* yours!" she gasped. She seized Penny's wrist. "But you can't claim it! It's a trap! Everyone knows. It's an artifact, and the king is trying to find its owner. If she's a regular person who acquired an artifact, she'll be locked up, but if she's an enchantress, he's going to execute her!"

Penny stomach lurched horribly, and her hand jerked convulsively in her stepsister's grip. "Do you know that for sure?"

Olivia shook her head. "It's the rumor, that's all I know."

Penny bit her lip, determined. "I've still got to see him," she muttered. "And make sure no one paid the price for my clumsiness in losing a stupid shoe." She looked up at Olivia with determination. "Will you help me get into my dress?"

Olivia looked at her like she was mad. "If you want to go to the ball, why did you come back? And what happened to the other dress?"

Penny frowned. "Come back? What other dress?"

Olivia made an incredulous noise. "Am I losing my mind, or are you? You arrived an hour ago, gave a big speech to Mama, somehow fit into my dress, and left in the carriage with her and Sophia. I thought you'd be at the ball by now."

"What?" Penny gasped, trying to make sense of it all. "But I've only just arrived from Entolia! Who could impersonate me so successfully as to fool my own family?"

But with a wave of true horror—worse even than what she'd felt when the crowd mocked her at the second ball—she realized who was capable of such an impersonation. The same person who'd made her worn old work dress look like a ballgown, and turned Al into a tabby cat. But what legitimate reason could Lady Amaranthe have for impersonating her at the last ball?

None, was the clear answer.

"I don't know what's going on," said Penny, "but I do know I need to get to that ball. Will you help me?"

Olivia nodded. "Get your dress. I'll drive you in the cart. How hard can it be?"

Apparently, quite hard. In her new spirit of cooperation, Olivia had insisted on driving and letting Penny sit in the back, but by the time she'd been rattled over five minutes of road, Penny regretted allowing it. With her most delicate touch, she used her magic to direct the reins, from below the point where Olivia's hands gripped them, and the journey was much smoother after that.

"I think I'm getting the hang of this," said Olivia brightly, when they reached the castle courtyard.

"Mm," said Penny noncommittally. She tumbled onto the

road, followed by Al—given he'd flown with a dragon and perched on a horse with her, she felt he had the right to drive to the ball at her side.

"I'm sorry, Olivia, but I don't think they'll let you in."

"Don't worry about me," said her stepsister, with one last, slightly envious, glance at Penny's dress. "Just get in there. Here Al." She gave an imperious whistle and, to Penny's great surprise, Al leaped up and sat beside her. With an inexpert flick, Olivia sent the cart trundling on.

Pulling in a shaky breath, Penny climbed the steps. As nervous as she felt, she couldn't help drawing some confidence from Princess Zinnia's dress. It truly was fit for royalty. Layer upon layer of pale blue fabric floated around her, as soft to the touch as feathers. The bodice was embroidered with lacy leaves that came down her shoulders and torso, and stretched toward the full, flowing skirt. Best of all, this dress was real. It wouldn't fade away at midnight, and it didn't depend on Lady Amaranthe, whose motives Penny no longer trusted.

She'd had no time to tie up her hair, but her curls fell around her shoulders in decent order, and Olivia—insisting that if she was trying to catch a prince, she needed to look like a princess—had woven her a simple flower crown to place on top. The length of the dress covered Penny's worn work boots, and her only jewelry was her mother's bracelet, and a simple necklace that belonged to Olivia.

Clutched in her hand was her single glass slipper, with a blue scarf of Olivia's draped over it. She didn't have a purse large enough to hold it. Penny buried the whole bundle nervously in the folds of her skirt as she approached the castle's entrance. It was a risk to bring it, but she needed it to get past the king's artifact. Hopefully her understanding of Dannsair's explanation was correct, and it would work while she was holding it just as well as if she was wearing it.

She paused at the entrance to the ballroom, suddenly remembering the first ball she'd seen, the one she wasn't supposed to attend. That night felt like a lifetime ago, and the Penny who had wallowed in bitterness and grief felt like a stranger she'd long since outgrown. Bracing herself, she stepped through the doors.

She was once again late, and mercifully the king and queen were no longer supervising the entrance. Guards looked her over carefully as she passed in, and the herald called her name to the throng. But this time the dancing was in full swing, and the announcement created no particular reaction. Penny breathed a sigh of relief. The first hurdle was over.

She scanned the crowd for Rian, but saw no sign of him. She also saw no sign of herself, which was both reassuring and alarming. Where was Lady Amaranthe, and what was she up to? The monarchs were positioned near the door, and when they glanced Penny's way, she turned quickly, eager to avoid being recognized as the humiliated servant who'd fled from the previous ball. A gentle wave of power washed over her. No doubt the king was keeping an eye on all arrivals with the use of his artifact, but his eyes moved right past her, so it seemed the slipper was doing its work.

A quick circuit of the room was enough to confirm that neither Rian nor Lady Amaranthe was present. The prince's absence was conspicuous. Penny could see others glancing around, brows creased as they muttered to each other. Her heart clenched. Where was he? Thinking she'd better check the garden, She stepped through the closest pair of glass doors.

"Penny?"

She whirled, her hand flying to her mouth as she recognized the last person she would expect to hail her. Rian's brother, Prince Bentleigh, who was supposed to be in Listernia.

"Your Highness," she said, dipping into a curtsy. Her dress

fanned majestically with the gesture, and she realized irrelevantly that practice wasn't the only thing that made fine ladies curtsy more elegantly.

"It is Penny, isn't it?" the prince asked. He was frowning slightly, but not as though he was annoyed with her. He looked as confused as she felt at being addressed by him.

"It is," she said nervously, struggling to breathe under his intent gaze. His dark hair gave such a different effect from Rian's tawny crop that it was a surprise to see that they shared the same serious brown eyes. "But I don't believe we've met before, Your Highness."

"No, but I know who you are," he said quickly. His eyes settled on her gown, and his frown deepened. "Where's Rian?"

"That's what I'm trying to discover," she said, and Prince Bentleigh raised an eyebrow.

"But you were with him, only a few minutes ago."

Penny gasped, forgetting herself entirely and clutching at his arm. "Where? Where did she take him?"

The prince stared, alarm crossing his features. "She?"

"It wasn't me," Penny said impatiently. "It's too hard to explain. Where did he go?"

"He followed...well, you," said Prince Bentleigh, perplexed. He raised an arm, pointing toward the darkened garden beyond the lantern light. "I'm supposed to be keeping watch to give you a chance to talk."

"He's in danger," said Penny breathlessly, hitching up her skirts. "I have to find them."

"Whoa." Prince Bentleigh put out a hand. "If Rian's in trouble, I'm coming."

"And if *you're* going, I'm coming," cut in a new voice. Penny turned, her feet tapping with impatience, to see Princess Azalea approaching from the open doors behind them. Prince

Bentleigh scowled at his betrothed, who raised a challenging eyebrow.

"I don't have time for an argument about who's more determined to protect whom, Your Highnesses," said Penny, with as much respect as she could muster. "I need you to show me where Rian went."

Exchanging a look, the two royals moved toward the edge of the lantern light.

"I don't know where exactly they went," said Prince Bentleigh. "They disappeared about here."

Penny drew in a breath as she realized the direction they were headed. "The hedge maze," she muttered.

"Well, I can take you there," the prince said, sounding more confident. The three of them hurried through the darkness, Penny's heart in her throat. "So," the prince said conversationally, as they turned a corner, "you're an enchantress."

Penny stopped dead, panic rising within her as Princess Azalea spluttered in surprise.

"Who...who told you that?" she whispered. "I mean, why would you think..."

"Rian told me, of course," said Prince Bentleigh, raising an eyebrow. "And I thought we were in a hurry."

Eyes wide, Penny stumbled forward, her thoughts whirling. "But...but Rian doesn't know."

"Of course he does," said the prince calmly. "That's why he didn't want you to come to the last ball. That's why he told you to leave. He was afraid of what would happen if you were exposed."

Penny was so shocked, she could hardly keep putting one foot in front of the other. Was it true? Had Rian known all along? His behavior at the ball took on a whole new light, and she could have cursed her own foolishness. But why didn't he tell her he knew?

All such questions fled when the hedge maze suddenly loomed up before them in the darkness. Penny stumbled in front of the other two, and a quiet voice wafted to her from out of the maze.

"She's strong enough to ruin everything, if she got in the way."

Penny felt her insides freeze. She both knew and didn't know that voice, for she'd never heard Lady Amaranthe speak like that before. As she stared into the maze, her eyes adjusting to the darkness, she saw that the other enchantress was leaning over a bound figure. With rising fury, Penny watched her mentor lean down and place a kiss on *her* Rian's cheek. She threw out an arm to stop her companions from racing past, needing to hear what was happening.

"Such a valiant prince," purred the musical voice. "So helpful of you to solve that problem for me. You let Penny go because you were too weak to fight for her. So it's you I have to thank for the success of my plans. Because she's far away, and neither her magic nor your crown has the power to stop me now."

"I wouldn't count on it," Penny said, dropping the slipper and bringing her hands up before her.

Lady Amaranthe turned with a gasp, and Penny saw a light spring into Rian's eyes. It bolstered her, sending a surge of something more powerful than magic through her veins.

Planting her feet firmly, she sent a wave of power toward the other enchantress, trying to lift her from her feet. Of course it was futile.

Lady Amaranthe's face twisted in a vicious laugh. "So sweet little Penny sees the appeal of being able to control living creatures with her power now, does she? Too bad you were too noble to try moving people. You should have let me train you."

"There are other ways," said Penny, fury washing over her at the realization of how deeply this woman had exploited her trust. With a twitch of her fingers, she tugged on the elaborate necklace Lady Amaranthe wore, causing the woman to choke and gag as it dragged her away from Rian and toward the trio.

Gesturing frantically, Lady Amaranthe caused fire to spring up all around them. Penny heard Prince Bentleigh cry out, but she kept her eyes on the enchantress.

"It's not real!" she shouted. "She can't actually change things, just change how they look."

"More's the pity," choked out Lady Amaranthe. "Oh how *tedious* it was, leading you with such a gentle hand, pretending to admire your meek, hen-hearted ways. I tried my best to change you, to bring out the potential I knew was in you. But you were too set in your weakness."

"If by potential you mean bitterness," Penny retorted. Her mind was only half on the conversation, the purpose of which was to keep Lady Amaranthe distracted. While she tugged at Lady Amaranthe, her power was also reaching toward Rian, wrapping around his bindings with finesse rather than force, causing the ropes to gently untie.

Suddenly, the prince sprang to his feet, and before Lady Amaranthe could turn, he'd lunged forward and landed such a blow to the back of her head that she crumpled to the ground.

Disregarding the prone woman, Penny stumbled forward and into Rian's arms.

CHAPTER TWENTY-NINE

Rian

Rian's mind reeled from this latest turn of events. Penny's hands were pressed against his chest, and his arms were around her, but he felt something rip the gag from his mouth. A shiver went over him at the evidence of Penny's magic. It was powerful, and it was such a part of her. The idea of it being on his side was intoxicating.

But not as intoxicating as the feel of her slim form pressed against him.

"Rian!" she cried breathlessly. "Are you all right?"

"Of course I am." Rian leaned his forehead against hers, drawing in a deep breath. "Penny, you shouldn't be here. I'm afraid for you." But he made no move to let her go.

She pressed her face into his chest, her voice catching on a sob. "Rian, I'm so sorry I didn't tell you. I wanted to, but I was afraid of what would happen. I wanted so desperately to be with you, but it was always an impossible dream."

He tightened his arms around her, his heart soaring at her declaration. "Penny, there's nothing I want more. And I've tried to be brave like you. But all my efforts have failed. My father is more set against magic than ever. If he finds out that slipper is yours, and that you have magic, he'll execute you."

"Hold on." Ben's exasperated voice broke into their moment. "Let's not be dramatic. There's no way Father will execute Penny."

Rian turned to his brother, desperate to make him understand. "You didn't hear him, Ben. He said—"

"Ri," his brother cut him off. "I don't care what he said. Is there any way, under any circumstances, that you would let Father *kill* Penny?"

Rian stared at him. "No," he said, his arms holding Penny firmly in place against him. A laugh welled up in him at the beautiful simplicity of this truth. "Of course not. Over my dead body would that happen."

"Well then," said Ben, with a touch of humor, "since I think we can be fairly confident Father wouldn't kill *you* under any circumstances, we can stop with any dramatics about Penny being executed."

Azalea gave a stifled choke of laughter, and leaned against Ben's side.

Rian unwound one arm from Penny's waist and lifted it, running his fingers along her cheek. She stared silently up at him, emotion overflowing from those speaking green eyes.

"It's a long jump from not executing you to consenting to me marrying you, though," Rian whispered.

"Yes," Ben sighed. "That will be a bit harder to resolve."

But Rian ignored him, his gaze still locked on Penny's. "I'm sorry for what happened at the last ball," he said. "I wanted to follow you, I wanted to tell everyone how I felt. But I was terrified you'd be exposed. I'd sent a letter, telling you that I knew of your magic, and begging you not to come for fear you'd be caught. But Lady Amaranthe intercepted it. She made herself look like you, so my guard thought you'd received it."

Penny's eyes were wide, and her fist clenched on the fabric of his tunic. "So that was why..." she whispered. She shook her head. "It doesn't matter now. As long as you're safe, and you know I had no part in whatever Lady Amaranthe was trying to do."

He laid his hand on her cheek, and she closed her eyes under his touch. She looked so vulnerable, so fragile in the moonlight, but he knew the incredible strength that lay within her. Strength that wasn't just from her magic.

"I knew," he said. "Even before you came, I knew. You could never have been part of what she was doing. I'll admit that for a moment I was afraid it was true, when she said you'd tried to attack me at Ben and Azalea's ball, and that you'd been plotting to lure me in."

Penny's eyes flew open, and her voice was anguished as she interrupted him. "That part is true."

Rian stilled, dismay coursing through him, and she hastened to clarify.

"Not any rubbish about plotting or luring you in. But I did try to attack you at that betrothal ball." She glanced at Ben and Azalea who were watching silently. "All of you." Penny's voice was little more than a whisper now. "I tried to throw a vase at you, and Lady Amaranthe stopped me. She was drawn by my power. I'm so sorry, and so ashamed. I didn't plan it. I just got swept up in my bitterness. My father had just died, and my step-mother was forcing me to deliver goods like it was any other day. I didn't want to come to the castle—I was afraid of being there, because of my secret, and there you all were, laughing and dancing and drinking wine..."

She tried to pull away, but Rian held her close. "Penny, I know your heart. I would never judge you by your lowest point. You didn't hurt any of us, and you've certainly had opportunities enough to hurt me if that was your wish."

"It's the last thing I wish," she whispered, laying her head on his chest again. But Rian wasn't having that. He wanted to see her face, her real face, not the pale imitation created by Lady Amaranthe, who could never capture Penny's true spirit, no matter how she mimicked her shell. He put his hand under her chin, silently asking her to look up at him.

She raised her gaze slowly to his, and he somehow knew without words that, like him, she was remembering the last time they'd come to the hedge maze.

"I'll fight for you, Penny," Rian whispered, barely aware of deciding to speak. "I'll do whatever it takes."

"I would defy a kingdom for you, Rian," Penny said, her heart in her eyes.

Slowly, as if he was savoring every second, Rian lowered his face to hers. She reached for him, twining her hand around his neck and pulling him closer, until their lips connected. For a glorious, timeless moment she kissed him, and he allowed himself to be lost in the feel of her.

Then Ben cleared his throat pointedly, and the two of them broke apart.

"Don't you have somewhere else to be?" Rian muttered irritably.

"Yes, actually," said Ben, laughing. "And so do you. Your betrothal ball, remember?"

Rian gasped, falling away from Penny as if he'd been doused in cold water. "The ball!" How could he have forgotten? "The desert bandits are actually a group of embittered enchanters, and Lady Amaranthe has rallied them to attack! She said they were coming to the ball tonight!"

Penny started forward in horror. "What? We can't let that happen! We can't let their bitterness lead them to confirm every fear your parents have about us!"

"Surely they won't act without Lady Amaranthe to lead

them," said Princess Azalea. She sent a swift kick toward the noblewoman, still lying prone at her feet, then gasped as her slipper sailed right through Lady Amaranthe's shoulder.

Penny dropped to her knees, her hands scrabbling at the unconscious form. She stared up at Rian, her eyes wide and terrified. "It feels like a log," she said. "She's not here."

The four of them were frozen for the briefest of moments, then they all began to sprint back toward the castle. They knew before they reached the lantern light that something was wrong. Instead of music, they could hear screams issuing from the ballroom, punctuated by a general crashing of destruction.

As they ran up the shallow steps, a crack of splintering glass sounded, as a guard was thrown bodily through a long window. Rian saw Azalea kneel down next to the man, who was stirring feebly, but he didn't pause. He had to reach the ballroom, and his parents.

They entered to a scene of total chaos. Guests in ball attire were fleeing in all directions, while men and women wrapped in the pale garbs favored in the desert seemed to be bent on causing the maximum destruction. Many had their hands raised like Penny had when she faced off against Lady Amaranthe. At their direction, wind swept around the room, and ice shot up from the ground. Others were apparently not enchanters, as they broke things the old-fashioned way, upending tables, and throwing glasses at fleeing guests.

Scanning the space desperately, Rian saw a protective ring of guards at the far end of the room, presumably shielding his parents. He tried to run toward them, Penny at his side, but flames sprang up in their path. Rian reached a hand toward the fire, and pulled it back, crying out in pain.

"It's real!" he shouted, and Penny closed her eyes in concentration.

"It's no use!" she said. "I can't move the fire. It has to be something solid."

The flames were spreading, licking at tapestries, and consuming furniture. The screams intensified as everyone scrambled for the doors, and embers drifted lazily through the air. With a thrill of horror, Rian remembered Lady Amaranthe's words.

I don't care what happens next—I just want to see the kingdom burn.

Suddenly, he spotted her, directing a group of enchanters against the guards who were protecting their sovereigns.

"There!" he cried.

Grabbing Penny's hand, he raced along the room, traveling most of its length before he found a place where he could get past the fire. Coughing, they sprinted toward Lady Amaranthe, and Penny raised a hand.

At once, an entire table rose from where it lay on the floor, and flew through the air toward the other enchantress. Lady Amaranthe turned just in time, ducking as the table flew over her head. Spinning, she locked her gaze on the two of them, and her eyes narrowed.

Rian expected her to mount an attack of the mind, but instead she smiled. "It's not too late, Penny. Do you think they'll forgive you for what you are? We need you on our side. You may as well join with those who'll celebrate all you can do, instead of make you ashamed of it."

Penny's stride faltered, and Rian gasped as he felt her hand slide from his. Before he could say a word, she raised her hands, holding them steady in the air.

"I'm not ashamed of it," she said calmly. "Any more than I'm ashamed of choosing to help even those who hurt me. It's not about them—it's about who I want to be."

Penny fell silent, and Rian held his breath. He could see that she was wrestling with something, reaching some realization. Whatever it was, she didn't speak it aloud.

"All I'm ashamed of," she said, her gaze still locked on Lady Amaranthe's, "is letting you into my mind. I could never be part of this."

And she closed her eyes.

Lady Amaranthe, her features twisted with fury, dove toward her. Rian opened his mouth to shout a warning, but before he could do so, Penny flipped her hands palm up, and jerked them upward with a grunt of effort. Cries rang across the room as every one of the desert fighters was lifted in the air, dragged by an invisible hand to slam into the ceiling. For a moment Rian was confused, wondering if Penny had realized how to move people, in spite of what Lady Amaranthe had said in the hedge maze. But then the truth hit him, and he almost laughed at the simplicity of Penny's tactic. She was moving their clothes, controlling them with an iron hand, and in doing so, turning their wearers into little better than puppets. They all lay there, backs against the ceiling, flailing wildly but unable to fight the tug of Penny's magic.

The only exception was Lady Amaranthe, whom Penny had pressed to the ground, right at her feet. The noblewoman snarled and thrashed ferociously, but she couldn't break free of Penny's hold on her dusky pink ballgown.

Some of the enchanters on the ceiling were still sending out their magic, but the guards were better able to fight its effects without the physical attacks as well.

Other guards, freed from their battles, began to beat frantically at the fire. Eyes still closed, still containing all the fighters, Penny threw one hand to the side. With a crunching snap, several enormous basins detached themselves from their plinths in the gardens. Flying into the ballroom, they emptied their water over the fire, then returned to the fountain again and again, aiding in the guards' efforts. Only when the flames had been extinguished did Penny's eyes flutter open.

Rian could only stare, stunned and overwhelmed at the evidence of Penny's strength. He could see why Lady Amaranthe had been intoxicated by the younger woman's potential. He had never suspected his gentle-hearted Penny hid such an unstoppable power. It wasn't hard to imagine how easily it could be turned to destruction. And yet she was using it to fight for the very monarchs who had hunted her all her life. His heart swelled with pride.

But as their gazes locked, Rian could tell something was wrong. Sweat was pouring down Penny's face, and her eyes were unfocused.

"Penny!" he cried.

Lady Amaranthe grinned savagely. "Even Penny doesn't have unlimited strength. She can't hold it forever, and then we'll end this."

Penny's eyes fixed on Rian, and she grimaced apologetically. "She's right," she gasped, and even as she said the words, she fell to her knees.

"Then let it go!" Rian shouted, dropping down beside her. "Don't kill yourself trying to fight everyone at once!"

He couldn't feel magic, but he could see the moment her power snapped. She dropped her hands in defeat, and he marveled at both the control and the heart that allowed her to lower her enemies gently to the ground instead of letting them drop.

"I'm sorry," she panted. "It was too many all at once."

"Don't apologize," Rian said fiercely, clutching her limp form to him. "You were amazing, and the fire is out now."

But Penny had no time to respond. Lady Amaranthe had leaped forward and seized the younger enchantress by the hair. With a cry, Penny was dragged up onto her feet. Rian lunged forward with a shout of rage, but he couldn't get to them. Wind swept from nowhere, buffeting him back so forcefully that all his efforts did no more than keep him in place.

The same wind swept over the ring of guards, sending them all toppling to the ground and revealing the king and queen, whose eyes widened at the level of chaos before them.

"That's right, little Penny," Lady Amaranthe screamed, sounding quite mad. "Don't try to fight with the grown ups. Stick to what you know. You may have the raw power for great deeds, but you don't have the drive. You'd rather use your magic to cook and clean for a family who don't even want you."

"Oi!"

Rian was still battling uselessly against the wind, but the shout drew his attention to the ballroom's main entrance. The taller of Penny's stepsisters stood there, framed in the doorway, a glower on her face.

"Don't talk about my family that way!" As she spoke, she threw a sturdy wooden shoe, which flew through the air and missed Lady Amaranthe by several inches. With a rustle of skirts, Sophia, once again clad in deep green, ran to her sister's side.

"Yeah!" she shouted, seizing a vase from a nearby table and hurling it at Lady Amaranthe. It fell far short, but shattered with satisfying intensity. "Her magic is way stronger than yours, so shut your mouth!"

At the same moment, something large and furry launched itself at the struggling pair of enchantresses. Lady Amaranthe screamed in pain as Al's teeth latched on to her elbow.

"I always hated you, stupid mutt!" she shouted at the dog.

But still, she didn't let go. Rian's eyes were on Penny, fear in his heart as he saw how limp she still was. But at the insult to her dog, Penny's eyes flew open at last.

"Alchemist is *not* a mutt!" she cried. She raised her hands again at last, and several doors on the inside wall of the ball-room flew open. Staring in confusion, Rian realized they were cleaning cupboards.

"And you're right," Penny continued. "I don't have the drive for great deeds. My magic *is* better suited to the simple domestics of life."

She flourished her hands dramatically, and the air was suddenly thick with dozens of brooms and mops. They flew through the air, whacking enchanters on the head with cracking force, causing them all to raise their arms to protect themselves, so that their magic died down, at least temporarily. Rian saw the enchanter who was controlling the wind being lashed repeatedly in the face by the stiff head of a broom, crying out as he attempted to flee, chased around the room by the airborne weapon.

The wind dropped at last, and Rian staggered forward, sprinting toward Penny and her captor. Lady Amaranthe, glaring in fury at her once-again routed forces, didn't see the mop zooming toward her until it smacked her right in the face. Her howl of rage became a gurgle as dirty water filled her mouth, and she dropped her grip on Penny at last.

Springing to her feet, Penny flourished her hands once again, and all the desert fighters suddenly found their weapons ripped from their grip and thrown forcefully through the windows, where they fell with a clatter into a fountain.

Rian reached Penny's side in time to catch her as she once again faltered.

"Don't push yourself too far!" he shouted over the melee.

She grimaced. "Then tell your guards to hurry up and subdue the fighters! Most of them can't move things the way I can. Regular rope should work!"

Nodding, Rian raced to the nearest guard. He was staring at the rather comical sight of all the attackers shrieking as they tried to outrun dusters and buckets, but at Rian's orders he pulled himself together. Rounding up his fellows, the man charged toward the beleaguered desert fighters, none of whom now had weapons.

Within minutes, the fighting had ceased. Even Lady Amaranthe, who seemed almost as spent as Penny, had been bound. Rian saw Ben and Azalea, fighting back to back, lower their swords, and turn to check that the other remained uninjured. There was a sudden lull in the room, and Rian saw Penny swaying on her feet. He'd taken only one step back toward her, however, when the commanding voice of the king rang through the obliterated ballroom.

"Seize the last enchantress."

Before Rian could give voice to his horrified protest, several guards had run forward and grabbed Penny. Too weak to offer any resistance, she crumpled to her knees, head bowed, before the king.

CHAPTER THIRTY

Penny

Penny didn't even have the energy to feel surprised as a guard grabbed her under each arm and dragged her up to face King Rhinehart. She blinked wearily into the face of her sovereign, noting with relief that he seemed to be unharmed.

"What is your name, Enchantress?" asked the king, in a voice Penny found impossible to read.

"Penelope," she said, her own voice coming out faint.

The king nodded to a page. The boy hurried to his side and produced something Penny had to squint to see, given the way her vision was spinning. Her glass slipper.

"Does this belong to you?"

Penny nodded. "Yes, Your Majesty."

"Father, enough!" Rian's angry voice cut across the conversation, and he suddenly appeared at Penny's side. "What are you doing? Did you not just see her save all of us?"

The king ignored his son, his gaze still on Penny. "Is it an artifact?"

"Yes, Your Majesty."

"What is its purpose?" demanded King Rhinehart.

Penny swallowed. "To conceal my magic, so that I could enter the ballroom without detection."

"And why," the king's voice was chillingly quiet, "did you wish to do that?"

Penny's eyes slid to Rian, her mind still fuzzy, and her arms beginning to ache from the guards' grip.

Curiously, she felt no fear. Her mind was still full of the realization that had washed over her when Lady Amaranthe appealed to her to join the attacking enchanters. Penny had meant what she'd said—she wasn't ashamed of her magic. Her father had wanted to change her, just like he wanted to change her mother. He hadn't wanted either of them to risk their own safety for others. He'd meant well, on some level. But instead of ridding his daughter of a dangerously generous heart, all he'd done was leave her at the mercy of someone ready to exploit it.

If he'd been present, her father would have told her not to use her magic in that moment, for fear she would end up in precisely the situation she was now in. It was what he'd begged of her mother, after all. But having met Elizabeth, Penny didn't blame her mother for her generosity. It had not been wasted.

And Lady Amaranthe had tried to change her too. But Penny took courage from the fact that, like with her magic, the noblewoman hadn't been able to change Penny's true nature. All she'd done was change the way others saw her, and even that was stripped away now.

Even Rian, with nothing but love for her, had wanted Penny to run, to hide her magic from those who would disapprove of it.

But just as Penny was done being exploited, and done letting others try to change her heart, she was done hiding her magic. She knew who she was, and she knew that her magic was meant to be used for good.

There was no more reason to hide anything—either her magic, or her heart.

"Because I love Rian," she said, answering the king's question at last. "And even though I knew there was little hope of being chosen, I wished to be present at the ball where his bride was to be selected."

The king looked between the two of them, his forehead creased. "And how does it come about that a servant girl, who also happens to be an enchantress, has fallen in love with the crown prince?"

Penny sighed, directing a slightly hazy smile toward Rian. "It's just everything about him, Your Majesty. He's impossible not to love."

Rian's eyes held hers for an endless moment, no sign of sternness on his earnest face. Then his gaze slid to his father's.

"I love Penny, Father. She's not a servant, but she is a commoner. She's the reason I requested you to invite commoners to the ball. She's the reason I tried to convince you to let me marry a commoner."

A sudden whisper spread through the room, and Penny felt her cheeks burn. She saw the queen shift beside her husband, her eyes flying between her son and Penny, and an unexpectedly soft expression on her face.

The king was a different matter.

"She—is—an—enchantress," he hissed, his voice quivering with tension.

"Yes, but she couldn't help that," said Rian matter-of-factly. "She was so afraid of her power being discovered, not even her parents knew of her magic. They've both passed away, and she's been all but alone, with no one to counsel her on what to do."

A sudden movement drew Penny's attention to one side of the room, and she saw that Olivia and Sophia stood there together, both looking stricken at the prince's words. Olivia was restraining Al with a hand on his collar, as he strained to get to Penny. Sapphira was nowhere to be seen.

"She has broken the law," the king insisted, bringing Penny's focus back to him.

"The law gave her no choice," Rian said calmly. "You know my views on this matter."

He stepped closer to his father, and lowered his voice. Penny could only just hear him, and she knew the rest of the room wouldn't be able to. The queen drew close to her husband's side, and Prince Bentleigh and his betrothed sidled up behind Rian, where they could also hear. But no one else was bold enough to inch in on the royals' hushed conversation.

"Father," Rian said, "I believe you are a good king. You care about your people, and your kingdom. And you're willing to listen, to learn, and to be challenged. I've seen this, and I've been honored by the times you've taken my counsel."

He drew a breath, and Penny felt her own tension rise in sympathy, even though she didn't know what was coming.

"The exception," Rian continued, "is magic. In that area, you've allowed fear to creep in on your reason, preventing you from making sound decisions. That fear has blinded you to the fact that the magic-users of Bansford are your people too. Some might think you unreasonable," Rian spoke no names, but Penny saw Prince Bentleigh shift uncomfortably, "but I don't think so. Since you've started letting me into your decisions, it's been clear to me that you have reasoned arguments for all you do. And even when you don't agree with my suggestions, you've listened to them. With one exception. The anger you've shown over my opposition to the ban isn't like you. I believe you react so defensively because this is one area where your decision is not well-reasoned, not based on sound logic, or what's truly best for the kingdom."

Rian turned, surveying the room grimly, before turning to Penny. A smile again softened his face, and he faced his father once more.

"Tonight's events have shown us the destructive potential of magic. But Penny has showed us its power for good, for protection. You told me once that if you saw magic used genuinely for good, and for the kingdom instead of for personal gain, it might change your mind. Father, you already know that the rumor of the slipper's true purpose has spread throughout the city. Penny knew she was under a death sentence, but she still raced to your aid. Surely she's shown the purity of her heart."

The queen laid a hand on her husband's arm, and he glanced down into her face. Penny could read nothing of what passed between them, but Rian seemed bolstered by the exchange. When he spoke again, his voice was louder.

"And if you're thinking with logic, Father, you can't deny that she's shown why it's worth having magic as powerful as hers on our side. She's strong—she held off all the attackers on her own."

Penny made a noise of protest, but Rian glared her down.

"It's true, Penny, don't try to deny it." Rian once again lowered his voice, stepping up to meet his father. Penny had to strain to hear his next words.

"Father, I know you realize our need for magic on our side. Otherwise you wouldn't have acquired an artifact to fight magic with magic." He swept an arm out in a general wave. "Magic is spread all across Solstice. We cannot keep it out. All we can do is ensure that our rule strengthens those who would use it for good, and protects against those who would use it for harm."

"Well said." Prince Bentleigh appeared suddenly at his brother's side. "I agree with all that Rian has said." Princess Azalea stepped up beside him, nodding.

Penny didn't know the king well enough to read his reaction to Rian's words, but she took it as a good sign that he had allowed his son to speak freely.

"I've said what I needed to." Rian's voice returned to a

normal volume. He stood straight-backed, holding his father's gaze. "You know I've promised to honor your choice of bride for me." His eyes flicked to Penny's for a moment. "I told Penny once that I didn't regret that promise, and it's true. I have no desire to marry against your wishes, because I want you—I need you—to embrace the wife I take. But that doesn't mean I plan to tamely accept whoever you've chosen. I'm determined to persist, for as long as it takes, until I convince you that the woman who's won my heart also deserves to share my crown."

Penny held her breath. Her heart swelled with pride at Rian's courage, and she appreciated all he was saying. But at the same time, she couldn't help feeling nervous that he was putting their future together in the hands of the king who had just had her arrested after she saved his life.

"Well." Shifting forward beside her husband, Queen Eliza spoke up for the first time. "I for one can see the benefit of you marrying someone with that kind of power, Rian." Her eyes scanned the chaos of the room before settling on Penny. There was unexpected softness in them. "And I see that you have already achieved what I had begun to hope for, Rian."

"Thank you, Mother," said Rian. His eyes passed back to his father. "But I do not believe we can accept an enchantress into the royal family while still maintaining a ban on others of her kind."

"That is certainly true," King Rhinehart said dryly. His piercing gaze searched Penny's face. "I don't even know your family."

A cleared throat made them all turn, and Penny blinked in surprise at a face she'd seen before. It took her a moment to place the man standing just below the dais as the steward who had shown her kindness on her first visit to the castle.

"She is known to me, Your Majesty," he said, inclining his

head respectfully. "I can confirm that she is the daughter of Your Majesty's preferred vintner, of Vin Manor."

"The one who recently passed away?" the king asked.

He sounded startled, but not as startled as Penny was to discover that the monarch had heard of her family. She felt a moment of pride in the quality of her father's work, that it had been impressive enough to catch the attention of a king.

King Rhinehart's gaze passed back to Penny, and he considered her thoughtfully. He waved a casual hand, and the guards holding Penny released her, although they remained standing on either side.

"As a princess," the king began, and Penny's heart lurched, "Prince Rian's bride would be required to take an oath swearing to serve Bansford's interests and to promise lifelong loyalty to the kingdom and the crown."

"That is an oath I would gladly take, Your Majesty," said Penny quietly. "I love Bansford. I always have. It's my home."

The king nodded slowly. His eyes traveled to his eldest son, and his voice was very quiet. "You have showed more wisdom in recent weeks than I have acknowledged, Rian. And while I haven't acceded to your requests, that does not mean I haven't been pondering them." He let out a breath. "I don't think there can be any doubt that you're correct when you say we cannot keep magic out altogether. And that being so," his eyes passed back to Penny, and her heart flopped nervously, "allying ourselves with the strongest type of magic certainly seems wise."

Penny barely dared to hope, but the light in Rian's eyes suggested he believed the battle won. He hurried forward, and for a moment Penny thought he would embrace his father. But instead, he took the glass slipper from the king's hand, and whirled around to face Penny.

"Didn't you say this was yours?"

She nodded, bewildered.

Rian turned to the page who had brought the slipper. "The other one is lying just inside the hedge maze. Retrieve it."

The page streaked from the room, and Rian looked at his father.

The king gave a slow nod, then cleared his throat. When he spoke, his voice rang out across the room. "As everyone present must be aware, the purpose of this ball is to announce my son's choice of bride. And it has been proclaimed that whoever could claim this slipper would be so named."

"Well then," said Rian, turning to Penny with a smile that made her already weakened legs feel wobbly.

She tried to come toward him, but the exertions of the recent battle were catching up with her, and her steps were unsteady. Rian started forward in concern, but she waved him away.

"I've got it." With a flick of her hand, she brought a chair zooming across the room, and sank gratefully into it.

"Penelope of Vin Manor," said Rian, kneeling before her chair and raising the slipper before her. "Should this slipper be yours to claim, you claim my hand with it." He lowered his voice. "My heart is yours already."

Penny didn't know whether to laugh or cry as Rian lifted her foot. She grimaced as her worn old work boots were revealed, but Rian just grinned up at her. He slipped one off, and slid her glass slipper on, so that it nestled perfectly into place.

"Well," Penny whispered, her eyes shining with happiness, "that seems decisive."

At that moment, the puffing page boy raced up, handing Rian the other shoe. The prince slid that onto Penny's other foot, then pulled her to her feet.

"Music!" he declared. Half the musicians seemed to have fled, and those who remained stared at the prince in stupefaction. "This is my betrothal ball, and my choice of bride has just been announced," Rian told them, as if it was obvious. "I want to dance with her!"

Shrugging at each other, the musicians started up a simple tune. People laughed and cheered as Rian swept Penny into motion. She found herself laughing too, wondering if the eager man who held her close as they danced across a debris-strewn floor could really be the severe-mouthed prince she'd seen in the markets that day, scanning the crowd with such serious eyes.

In Rian's arms, Penny's exhaustion was forgotten. Her slippers crunched over the general detritus, and with a flick of her head, she revived several of the fallen brooms, setting them to clearing up the mess. Mops followed behind, and broken glass raised itself from the dance floor to settle in neat piles in the corners of the room.

"Handy," Rian commented over the general gasps and exclamations, his eyes shining.

Penny grinned. "It really is. You know, I'm not very practiced at dancing," she warned him, her eyes laughing up into his. "And it turns out these shoes *are* quite uncomfortable."

His face split in an answering grin. "I can't help you with the shoes, but I can help you with the dancing." He pulled her close, his hand warm on her waist, and leaned down so that his breath tickled her ear and sent a delightful thrill through her. "I won't let you stumble."

Throwing caution to the winds, Penny pushed up onto the toes of her foolish glass slippers and pressed her lips to his. Rian's arm swept all the way around her waist as he returned the embrace. The cheers of the crowd melted away, and there was nothing but Rian, Rian and the thrill of his touch. A thrill made all the more potent by the knowledge that this kiss held the promise of forever.

Penny

"Salt, Azalea?"

"Oh, yes thanks," said the Listernian princess, reaching out to receive the cellar.

But Penny didn't pick it up with her hand, instead sending it flying across the table to sprinkle the other girl's eggs. Azalea laughed so delightedly, Penny repeated the performance with Bentleigh's breakfast. But when King Rhinehart and Queen Eliza strode into the room, she hastily set the salt cellar down, sending the hint of a grimace to Rian. She knew they weren't ready for such a flippant use of magic to be flaunted under their noses at the breakfast table.

Rian smiled reassuringly before greeting his parents. Penny, while perfectly comfortable now with both Bentleigh and Azalea, was still struggling to be natural around the king and queen. They were just so imposing. But she knew she'd get there. Being moved into one of the castle's guest suites had definitely helped. The frequent exposure to Their Majesties was gradually lessening the shock of realizing they would soon be her parents-in-law.

Still, she smiled to herself at the thought of what the king and queen would say if they knew she'd spoken with an actual dragon in her dreams last night. And that said dragon had promised to visit her in person after the wedding, to bring a bride gift which would presumably consist of a powerful magical artifact.

"What of the prisoners, Father?" Rian asked, as the king settled himself at the table.

King Rhinehart sighed. "The process is still ongoing. It will take time. But the enchanters sent by Listernia," he inclined his head toward Azalea, "are helping enormously. Identifying the prisoners' powers is making it much easier to devise appropriate —and safe—penalties for their crimes."

"What of Lady Amaranthe?" Penny's voice sounded small in her own ears, and Rian squeezed her hand under the table. She was still struggling to come to terms with the other enchantress's duplicity, especially since she'd heard exactly what lie the older woman had tried to sell Rian in the hedge maze.

"She is to be exiled," said King Rhinehart, in a hard voice. "And it's only out of respect for her family that her life has been spared. Apparently Fernedell has a magically reinforced prison for the detention of those who have proven themselves ready to use their powers for violence. She will be sent there."

Penny nodded, grieved by the fate Lady Amaranthe's bitterness had driven her to. The lifting of the ban had made the imposition of penalties much more complex, as the crown had all but acknowledged its own role in driving the embittered enchanters to such lengths. Rian had told her that reparations were being offered to those who had been exiled. At least, those who had been exiled and had not attempted regicide as retaliation.

"The question of the desert fighters' travel still troubles me," mused King Rhinehart, his thoughts clearly going in a different direction. "I don't like the uncertainty."

Penny frowned down at her plate. Again, Rian had told her of this report. The border patrol had seen the so-called bandits in the desert on the afternoon of the last ball. No one could understand how they had traveled so quickly from the desert to the capital, and done it without detection. It seemed that none of the powers of those now in the dungeons could explain the occurrence.

Penny knew of a way to travel vast distances in the blink of an eye, because she'd experienced it herself, when Dannsair carried her across three kingdoms. And dragons could move quickly enough to avoid detection, if they wished. But she hadn't said as much. It was utterly unthinkable to imagine dragons transporting the attackers in that way. Why would they? Certainly, they might carry some offense over the magic ban, but if they wanted to destroy Bansford's monarchy, they could do so without the help of a few angry enchanters. And for dragons to provide that kind of assistance to an attack by magic-using humans on other humans would surely breach the agreement Dannsair had talked about.

No, it was best that she keep her reflections to herself. She wasn't eager to explain to her future father-in-law the role dragons had played in her own adventures. And, she thought, with a hint of defiance, she could keep her secrets if the king was going to keep his. Rian had told her about his suspicion that King Rhinehart had dabbled in magic well before he acquired his artifact. Penny agreed with Rian's conclusion that the source of information which led to all those arrests must have been magical in nature. And apparently the king still refused to tell his son who or what that source had been.

"I received a letter from Prince Basil," Rian commented, when the conversation dipped. He glanced at Penny. "He congratulated me on successfully resolving my heart entanglement, whatever that means."

Penny laughed, although her expression was pained. "That's my fault," she said. "I'll tell you all about it sometime. How is Prince Basil?"

"Reading between the lines, he's trying to hold his kingdom together," said Rian frankly. "He said his father seems to have pulled through this latest round of illness, so that's something."

"Poor King Thorn," commented Queen Eliza, making a tutting noise in her throat. "Terrible to be injured in battle like that, and suffer for it for so many years afterward."

Penny said nothing, but privately she couldn't help feeling even more sorry for Prince Basil. Knowing that he was likely to come into the crown far too young, constantly wondering if this would be the winter where he became king, and had to deal with the mess his father had left when he entered into a war with his neighbors. She was glad, at least, to hear that Prince Basil was to be spared that burden for another year.

They waved Bentleigh and Azalea off shortly after breakfast, and Penny was sorry to see them go. She had the sense that life in the castle in Liss was a little less formal than in Bant. Not that she was repining. She was more than satisfied with her own castle, and her own prince.

A week later, she and Rian found themselves again farewelling a group of travelers, although this time the king and queen did not join them.

"You don't have to go with her, you know," Penny said, her eyes passing between the two stepsisters whom she finally felt she could claim as family. "I'm concerned about you both. We all know she won't really be looking out for your interests."

"She won't be required to look out for anyone's interests," Sophia reminded Penny. "To tell you the truth, I'm looking forward to being in Entolia again. And I'm looking forward to seeing our friends."

"Ah yes," Penny nodded. "Your friend whose family has invited you all to stay with them for the time being."

Sophia nodded. "We were very close with their family before Father died, and the war broke out, and we had to leave."

"With one member of their family, at least," said Olivia dryly.

Penny frowned. "It still feels wrong to be sending you to strangers. Especially since you haven't told me anything about this friend, Sophia. What's she like?"

"Actually," Sophia's eyes were on her feet, "I don't really know what he's like anymore. It's been more than four years, and we're not fourteen now."

"He?" Penny repeated, raising an eyebrow. To her amazement, Sophia was blushing. Suddenly her sister's eagerness to accept the unexpected invitation to stay with their Entolian friends made sense.

"The point is, we'll be in someone else's household," Olivia cut in, taking pity on her sister's embarrassment. "Thanks to your generosity," she inclined her head to Rian, "we'll be able to pay board, and won't be dependent on them. But neither will we be dependent on Mama. We're both adults now, and it won't be for her to decide our future."

She gave Penny a look that held a promise, and Penny nodded. Olivia had been like a new person since she'd confessed her insecurities to Penny. Not only was she trying to break the habits built by a lifetime of Sapphira's competition, but she seemed to instead be channeling her considerable determination into protecting her younger sister from their mother's control. She would look after Sophia. The risk was that the passive younger girl might simply let herself be led by a new—if hopefully more benevolent—guiding hand. Penny hoped Sophia would show a little more resolution when in a new circle, with new influences. But that wasn't Penny's problem to solve, and she recognized that she couldn't take responsibility for the choices her sisters would make.

"We were happy in Entolia before," Sophia nodded, agreeing with Olivia. "We'll be happy there again. It sounds like the war hasn't proved to be as disruptive as we feared when we left." Her eyes flicked to Rian, a hint of alarm springing to her face. "Not that I don't like Bansford. It's a wonderful—"

"It's all right," Rian chuckled. "I'm not so easily offended."

"Of course, Your Highness," mumbled Sophia.

"You're going to be family," Penny reminded her. "You'll have to drop all this Your Highness business." She turned to Olivia, and the older girl gave her a slightly strained smile.

"Besides, I think I do have to go with Mama, you know," Olivia said, jerking her head toward the carriage where Sapphira already sat. "There are things I need to say, and things we need to work through. And I think that will be easier to do away from," she gestured vaguely at the castle behind Penny, "all this."

Penny nodded. "I understand."

She followed the other girl's gaze toward the woman in the carriage. Sapphira's goodbye to her soon-to-be-royal stepdaughter had been predictably emotionless. She had shown no dismay over the failure of her long-held plan to secure in Penny a constant source of household work. But neither did she show any joy in the prospect of her stepdaughter's upcoming wedding to royalty.

Penny had half expected her to try to capitalize on Penny's impending status and wealth. But Sapphira had clearly been intelligent enough to know that she could neither control Penny now, nor expect warmth from either her or her betrothed. Rian had never told Penny that Sapphira had denied she had another daughter when he'd gone looking for her. Perhaps he'd wanted to shield her feelings. But Olivia had told Penny the whole story, and it went some way to explaining why Sapphira wasn't trying harder to claim the benefits of a relationship now. Of course, Rian's blatant frostiness during his short interactions with the older woman had probably also informed her restraint. Sapphira had, of course, accepted the offered assistance that would enable her and her two other daughters to relocate to Entolia. But her expression of gratitude, while perfectly respectful, failed entirely to convey any emotion whatsoever.

Penny found that she didn't feel anything either, except perhaps sorrow for how much of life her stepmother was missing by locking her emotions away. Perhaps there would be someone in Sapphira's new circle who could help her work through whatever pain had caused her withdrawal. Perhaps Olivia would even succeed in doing so. But again, Penny knew it wasn't her problem to solve, and she was profoundly grateful for it.

"But," Olivia continued, her eyes on her feet, "once that's all...done, I wouldn't mind coming back. Not to live in the castle," she hastened to add. "But to Bansford."

"You will always be welcome," Rian said courteously, and Penny beamed at him.

"Are you sad to watch them go?" he asked Penny a short while later, as the carriage trundled away.

She rested her head against him, relishing in his solid steadiness. "To be perfectly honest, no," she said. "I'm glad it's not goodbye forever. But with Harry moving to the castle," a sharp bark made her look down, laughing, "and you of course, Al, I have enough of home to feel comfortable." Her eyes returned to the carriage, which was growing smaller. "I feel relieved more than anything. I've been wrestling with so many things for so long. I need some space to just be...me."

Rian pressed a kiss to the top of her head. "I'll give you all the space you need," he promised.

Penny laughed, turning in his arm to fully face him. "That's rubbish," she informed him. She nodded her head at the four guards standing nearby. "You can't fool me. Royals get no space whatsoever."

He grimaced. "Too true."

Penny's eyes softened. "And I only just won you, Your Highness, so I don't want space from you."

"Well, thank goodness for that," grinned Rian, wrapping both arms around her waist and lifting her so that her feet dangled in the air.

"Hey!" she protested. She tried to whack him playfully, but her hands were trapped at an awkward angle. Flicking her head, she seized hold of a small stone nearby, and brought it zooming through the air to wallop his arm, so that he let go.

"Not fair!" Rian said, outraged.

Penny grinned. "I will promise you many things, Prince Rian," she leaned up to drop a light kiss on his nose, "but I don't promise to fight fair."

"As long as we're fighting on the same side, Miss Penny," Rian chuckled, "I'm not afraid of anything."

NOTE FROM THE AUTHOR

Thank you for reading *Kingdom of Cinders*. I hope you enjoyed returning to the continent of Solstice! I would be so grateful if you would consider leaving a review on Amazon—it would really make a difference!

If the mention of Prince Basil's dilemma caught your interest, check out *Kingdom of Feathers*, the next installment of the series. As always, more adventure, fantasy, mystery, and romance await.

Join up to my mailing list at deborahgracewhite.com to be kept up to date on new releases, specials, and giveaways, such as bonus chapters. You will also receive *Dragon's Sight*, an 8,000 word prequel to my first series *The Kyona Chronicles*, told from the perspective of the dragon Elddreki (who just happens to be Rekavidur's father).

Again, thanks for entering the world of *The Kingdom Tales*! I hope to see you back again.

ALSO BY DEBORAH GRACE WHITE

The Kyona Chronicles

Heir of the Curse

Captives of the Curse

Captive's Return (novella)
Legacy of the Curse
Downfall of the Curse
Downfall's Echo

The Kingdom Tales

Kingdom of Beauty: A Retelling of Beauty and the Beast
Kingdom of Slumber: A Retelling of Sleeping Beauty
Kingdom of Cinders: A Retelling of Cinderella
Kingdom of Feathers: A Retelling of The Wild Swans (coming 2021)

ACKNOWLEDGMENTS

Cinderella is such a classic fairy tale, it was both extra exciting, and extra intimidating, to give it my own spin. Once I made the discovery that Penny was an enchantress hidden within the magic-hating Bansford, however, the rest quickly fell into place.

So many people are owed a huge thank you for making this book happen, especially since it ended up being a very short turnaround. As always, Ray is first, my listener, and my cheer squad.

My betas, who dug deep and read it in an amazingly short time: Adrian, Tamara, Mel W, Mum, and Steph. You guys are amazing.

Massive thanks to Dad for developmental and copy editing at record speed!

To Karri for persevering with me to achieve this fabulous cover, and to Becca, for the beautifully drawn map.

To you, the reader, thank you for giving me the privilege of being an author.

And most importantly, to God, who recognizes worth where no one else sees it.

ABOUT THE AUTHOR

I've been a reader since I can remember, growing up on a wide range of books, from classic literature to light-hearted romps. The love of reading has traveled with me unchanged across multiple continents, and carried me from my own childhood all the way to having children of my own.

But if reading is like looking through a window into a magical and beautiful world, beginning to write my own stories was like discovering that I could open that window and climb right out into fantasyland.

I cannot believe how privileged I am to actually be living that childhood dream and publishing my own novels. I do so from my hometown of Adelaide, Australia, where I live with my husband and our three little ones.

I've never outgrown my love of young adult stories, so the genre of young adult fantasy was always going to be my niche. If you enjoy *The Kingdom Tales*, don't miss my finished YA fantasy series *The Kyona Chronicles*.

Feel free to email me at deborah@deborahgracewhite.com and introduce yourself! Or subscribe to my mailing list at deborahgracewhite.com for free giveaways, sales, and updates.

www.ingramcontent.com/pod-product-compliance
Lightning Source LLC
Chambersburg PA
CBHW060729190726
48285CB00001B/126